T0348952

'Featuring a crisp storyline, a strong female lead, mild suspense and some loving descriptions of the Australian countryside, Janu's many fans will greatly enjoy this latest escapade.'

—*Canberra Weekly* on *Shelter from the Storm*

'A rural story that has it all ... simmering romance, international intrigue, a complex heroine and a swoon-worthy hero. What's not to love?'

—Karly Lane, bestselling Australian author, on
Clouds on the Horizon

'When reading a Janu novel, one expects several things: a feisty heroine, gorgeous rural settings, and a passionate, captivating romance. She delivers all that here, in spades.'

—*Better Reading* on *Clouds on the Horizon*

'Encapsulates everything I love about the romance genre and so much more. A go-to author for rural romance for the head as well as the heart ...'

—Joanna Nell, bestselling Australian author

'Endearingly quirky and utterly charming. Funny and sweet and wonderful.'

—Amy Andrews, *USA Today* bestselling author,
on *On the Same Page*

'Penelope Janu's fresh, bright, funny new twist on rural romance is an absolute delight. Her wit is as sharp as a knife. She is one of my absolute must-read authors.'

—Victoria Purman, bestselling author of
The Nurses' War, on *Up on Horseshoe Hill*

'Intriguing characters and a colourful setting: if you like romance and a little mystery, get ready to enjoy this novel.'

—Tricia Stringer, author of *Keeping Up Appearances,* on
On the Right Track

'Take a break from the news and spend time in Horseshoe Hill. Well written, interesting and filled with heart, *Starting from Scratch* is the perfect weekend read.'

—*Better Reading*

'Oh, how I do love reading a novel by Penelope Janu, it's always an absolute pleasure and I find them hard to put down. *Up on Horseshoe Hill* is no exception, I read until the early hours of the morning and picked it up again as soon as I was awake.'

—*Claire's Reads and Reviews*

'*Up on Horseshoe Hill* is a novel that I would recommend for animal lovers, for rural romance lovers and for those seeking an engaging read.'

—*Great Reads and Tea Leaves*

'Penelope Janu succeeds in delivering fans old and new an engrossing tale. *Up on Horseshoe Hill* is a novel that awakens our sense of hope that love can prevail, even when life deals you with a series of devastating setbacks to overcome.'

—*Mrs B's Book Reviews*

'*On the Right Track* by author Penelope Janu is on my unputdownable fave reads category. There was humour, tension, chemistry amongst a backdrop of family drama that just keeps the pages turning.'

—*Talking Books Blog*

ABOUT THE AUTHOR

Penelope Janu lives on the coast in northern Sydney with a distracting husband, a very large dog and, now they're fully grown, six delightful children who come and go. Penelope has a passion for creating stories that explore social and environmental issues, but her novels are fundamentally a celebration of Australian characters and communities. Her first novel, *In at the Deep End*, came out in 2017, followed by *On the Right Track*, *On the Same Page*, *Up on Horseshoe Hill*, *Starting from Scratch, Clouds on the Horizon* and *Shelter from the Storm*, as well as a novella, *The Six Rules of Christmas*. Penelope enjoys riding horses, exploring the Australian countryside and dreaming up challenging hiking adventures. Nothing makes her happier as a writer than readers falling in love with her clever, complex and adventurous heroines and heroes. She loves to hear from readers, and can be contacted at www.penelopejanu.com.

Also by Penelope Janu

In at the Deep End

PENELOPE JANU

FICTION
HQ

First Published 2017
Second Australian Paperback Edition 2023
ISBN 9781867256052

IN AT THE DEEP END
© 2017 by Penelope Janu
Australian Copyright 2017
New Zealand Copyright 2017

Published by
HQ Fiction
An imprint of Harlequin Enterprises (Australia) Pty Ltd.
Level 19, 201 Elizabeth St
SYDNEY NSW 2000
AUSTRALIA

Cataloguing-in-Publication details are available from the National Library of Australia www.librariesaustralia.nla.gov.au

Printed and bound in Australia by McPhersons Printing Group

MIX
Paper | Supporting
responsible forestry
FSC® C001695

To Peter

CHAPTER

1

He vanishes in the sea spray of the stormy Southern Ocean, and then he reappears.

He's hanging from the cargo net on the port side of *The Watch*. I'm on the bridge ten metres above him. When he lifts his hood our gazes lock. I'm stiff with fear and sick with nausea and I don't want to leave my ship. But there's something in the intensity of his stare that tells me he'll come up and get me if I don't go down. He gestures over his shoulder and I see an inflatable boat, battling to stay upright in the waves and gale-force winds.

I climb through the railing and feel for the net. It swings back and forth as I climb, airborne one minute, whacking against the ship's side the next. I'm exhausted and trembling, numb with cold, but finally I reach the second last rung. I link my boot through it and steady myself. The man is hanging next to me. His dry suit outlines the shape of his body; he's tall and lean, athletically built.

His hood is back in place so I can't see his face but I'm sure that he can see mine. The whiteness of my lips, the terror in my eyes.

He unclips a harness attached to a belt on his hip, and reaches for me.

'No!' I push his hand away. 'If we fall, I'll take you down with me.'

He extends his hand again.

I shove it away. 'No! I can't swim.'

There's a moment's hesitation. '*Jesus,*' he says.

He moves behind me and presses his body hard up against mine, so his front is against my back. One of his arms wraps around my chest in an immovable grip, and the other one grasps my waist. I'm pinned to the net between him and the ship. Out of the corner of my eye I see the inflatable, closer to the ship than it was before. There's someone on board, operating the console in the middle of the boat.

The Watch shudders on the crest of another wave, and then she heels to one side. I scream when the net suspends us over the ocean but the sound is lost on the wind. A chunk of ice, white and luminous, drifts below us on the swell. Then the inflatable reappears, impossibly small in the angry grey sea.

The man releases his hold on my body. 'Let go!' he yells. 'Now!'

He throws me into the storm. Silence. I think I black out. And then I crash, legs and arms flailing, into the inflatable. The cacophony of sound returns—the thunderous winds and waves, the creaks and groans of the ship, my gasps as I suck in mouthfuls of air. Someone grabs my jacket and wrenches me onto my side. It's a woman. She pulls back the hood of her jacket and leans over me. She's young. Her voice is low pitched.

'Harriet? You okay?'

I'm retching but nothing's coming up. Migraine lights flash in front of my eyes. My lips move but no words come out.

'Harry,' she says. 'You with me, or not?'

My head jerks, and I nod.

'Right, then. Better go back for the commander.'

I drag myself on my hands and knees to the row of seats on one side of the boat. Then I pull myself into one, grasping rubber handholds to keep myself upright. My shoulder hurts, so does my knee. I can't look at the ocean or I'll retch again. My head feels like it's going to explode. But I can't lose consciousness now. So I swallow down my panic and focus on the woman. She's back at the console. The insignia of the Royal Australian Navy is embossed on the front of her jacket. She raises a hand as if to warn me, and then she spins the boat around. I follow the line of her finger when she points.

We're about twenty metres away from *The Watch*. She's creaking as she lolls, awkwardly and drunkenly, in the water. The cargo net is still hanging from her side but there's no sign of the man. I was wrong when I thought my anxiety had peaked. I'm shaking with guilt and fear and dread.

The woman manoeuvres the inflatable between two waves. We're so close to *The Watch* that the ship blocks out the sky. There's a lull in the wind. The woman's words are clear.

'Lost his grip when he chucked you,' she says. 'Guess we'd better go fish.'

She gives a long shrill whistle when she sees him. I turn in my seat and follow her gaze. The man is a sleek black shadow in the ocean, and then he disappears in the churning waves and white-wash. When we see him again he's on the top of a wave. The inflatable is rising on the swell.

He dives out of the ocean and twists in the air. Then he lands on his feet on the floor of the inflatable. He gets his balance, turns to the woman and nods. She salutes him and laughs. As we plunge down the face of another wave she grasps the wheel with both hands. He pivots and crashes onto the seat next to me.

His arm and leg are pressed up against mine so I'm pinned between him and the bow. He's wearing a balaclava under his hood. It covers his hair and the bottom half of his face. I think he's older than me, but not by much. Thirty? Early thirties? All I can see clearly are his eyes. They're angry eyes, narrowed and gunmetal grey. They share the colours of the ocean, black troughs and white caps that seethe around the boat.

He's shouting, but I can barely hear his words over the roar of the wind and sea.

'What did you mean when you said you couldn't swim?' he says.

'I can't swim.'

'*Jesus.*'

He shoves me sideways so I'm wedged even tighter into my seat, and when I try to push him away he swings one long leg over both of mine, trapping them. Then he pulls a life jacket from under his seat and thrusts it at me. My shoulder won't move like it should but I manage to put the jacket on, struggling to secure the straps because my hands are numb and stiff. He watches me fumble, and then he shoves my hands out of the way and reaches for the straps himself, tugging them even tighter than they are already.

I'm doing my best to hold in my panic but the ocean is too close and the spray is too real. The light show in my head gets brighter and brighter and I want to be sick again. If he's aware of how frightened I am he doesn't seem to care. He shoves his gloved hand under my jacket and feels the inner layers of my clothes. They're almost as sodden as the outer ones.

'What are you wearing?'

I don't answer.

'You really can't swim?'

'No.'

We're moving further and further away from *The Watch*. She's sitting even lower in the water now. Waves crash over her decks as she rolls slowly onto her side. The bridge and stern are inundated. Water cascades into the hold and cabins. Her bow tilts towards the clouds and all I can do is stare, transfixed, until tears obscure my vision. There's a single explosion, and then a series of explosions. It'll be the watertight compartments, and the bulkhead, collapsing under the pressure. I wipe an arm across my face and turn to him.

'Are the rest of the crew all right?'

'You know they are. You were the last one off.'

The sleet whips my face with icy shards. The salt of the sea spray stings my eyes. The woman whistles again and points. *HMAS Torrens*, the navy patrol ship, is in the distance and we're slowly heading towards her. The storm is abating but there's ice to contend with. And there are bergs. No one speaks until we're close to the navy boat.

'You shouldn't have done it,' I say.

When the man takes my shoulders in his hands I flinch.

'Shouldn't have done what?' he says, drawing me closer.

'Come for me.'

He puts his mouth to my ear. I feel the warmth of his breath on my neck.

'Harriet Hillary Amelia Scott,' he says. '*I'll make you wish I never did.*'

I wrench myself out of his grip but I'm still anchored to the seat by his leg. He turns side on and barks instructions to the woman. There are people lining the bridge of the *Torrens*. The woman talks into her headgear about hoisting the boat up onto the deck.

The man knows all of my names. Yet I'm certain we've never met. My thoughts are muddled. I'm light-headed, nauseous, disoriented.

It must be the migraine. Or shock. Hypothermia? I have to move around, to warm up. When I push at his leg he turns and glares, but then the woman asks him something. He removes his leg as he answers.

And then a wave crashes over the bow. It hits me square in the face. There's water in my nose, my mouth, my eyes, my ears. I jump to my feet and twist to escape it but there's something solid against my thigh that's blocking my path. So I dive over it. And then I kick out, more and more frantically, against the vice around my ankle. At last I'm free. But then I'm tumbling, falling.

My head goes beneath the waves as the ocean sucks me in. Water clogs my throat. The cold is paralysing. I'm blind. But then I see Mum and Dad. The three of us are driving along a narrow road in the mountains of Brazil. The trees, and the vines that cling to them, rise up from either side of the road and form a dense green canopy over the car. It's twelve years ago and I've just turned fourteen. I'm flat-chested and leggy. Mum has tied my hair into braids; the plaited ends hang over my shoulders like two flaxen ropes. We're singing *Waltzing Matilda* at the tops of our voices as the car approaches a bend.

*   *   *

'About bloody time.'

The woman from the inflatable boat is gazing down at me and grinning. I didn't get a close look at her before but I remember her gravelly voice. My vision is blurred but I can see that she's young, just like I thought. She has short-cropped bright red hair and a madly freckled face.

When I smile it hurts my lips. My voice is barely a croak. 'Hey.'

I'm aware that I'm lying on a bed and covered by blankets. But the medical paraphernalia in the room, and my hand when I hold it in front of my face, is out of focus. I blink a couple of times. Am

I drugged? Didn't I fall into the Southern Ocean? Shouldn't I be dead?

The woman must see the confusion on my face. She puts a hand on my arm and squeezes.

'You're on board the *Torrens*, Harry. And you'll live. Only just though.' She looks over her shoulder. 'Isn't that right, sir?'

The next time I wake up, the red-haired woman and the man with grey eyes are on either side of the bed, leaning over me. They're rubbing the top half of my body. Forearms, upper arms, across my collarbones, down my sternum, over my breasts, and then my stomach and hips. They're arguing, but I'm too sleepy to stick up for myself, and I have a horrible feeling I'm naked, so I close my eyes again.

'No body fat to keep her warm,' the man says. 'Look at her. Pathetic.'

'She's got breasts, that's body fat,' the woman says. 'And the rest of her is just … lean. Anyway, she'd been on the bridge for hours getting everyone out, so it's no wonder she was frozen.'

'Diving into the sea wouldn't have helped.'

'She didn't know what she was doing.'

'No life jacket until I gave her one. And the ocean terrified her. *Jesus.*'

'She said she couldn't swim.'

'It was more than that. I'm sure of it.'

Someone is wrapping my feet up. They're tingling.

'Easy with the heat packs,' the man says. 'Leave the extremities until her core temperature is up.'

'Yeah, yeah, I know. Do her mouth again. Poor thing.'

He lightly touches my mouth, smoothing something over the bottom lip, and then the top one. At first it stings, but after a while all I'm aware of is the rhythmic slide of his fingertip. I open my mouth a little, and he presses gently into the creases at the sides. I feel his thumb on my chin as his finger returns to my bottom lip. It's tingling now.

The woman is close again. 'Her mouth's not skinny. Look at it. Wish I had lips like that.'

'She's a fraud, Kat,' the man says, as his finger leaves my lip. 'Get over her.'

I turn my face towards him because I like the tingling feeling and I don't want him to stop. But a moment later I feel his hands running up and down my arm again.

'Can't,' says the woman. 'She's only a year older than me, and it's like we grew up together. She was in all those documentaries her parents made, and she's done some great stuff since.'

'Assuming she actually did it. If she can't swim, maybe she can't ride, cycle or climb?'

'You're just pissed because she messed up your schedule.'

'Schedule? She fucked up my project. Put me back a year at least.'

'She's hardly responsible for the iceberg *The Watch* collided with. Or the storm.'

'No. But she is responsible for being stupid enough to be caught in a situation like that. She's a schoolteacher, not a sailor. That ship was under resourced, ill prepared—'

The woman laughs. 'Harsh! Let's turn her again and do her back. Then I need another break. I don't know how you've kept going, it's so bloody hot in here.'

'Watch her shoulder.'

He puts his hands around my waist and eases his arms up my back like he's hugging me. Then he lifts me into a sitting position. *Please* don't let me be naked.

I open my eyes and look straight into his eyes. They're grey and hard like bitumen. He has chiselled features, a firm mouth, and short black hair with a widow's peak. A six-centimetre scar follows the curve of his cheekbone.

Why couldn't a crusty old salt, or a plucky galley cook, have rescued me?

'We're turning you over to warm your other side,' he says. 'This will hurt.'

CHAPTER

2

'Better lying on your stomach or your back?' Kat says.

I've been on *HMAS Torrens* for five days. My shoulder aches when I'm lying on my back because of the torn tendons. It hurts less when I'm on my front, but then my knee's uncomfortable, and I can't eat or drink. I'm thirsty all the time. Kat found me a straw because my lips bleed whenever I sip from a cup. My swollen hands are awkward and clumsy.

'Better when I'm unconscious. Want to flip me over again?'

She grimaces. 'Sorry about the other night. I didn't support your shoulder properly. The commander tore strips off me when you passed out.'

'The first time or the second time?'

'Every bloody time. You slipped in and out of consciousness with the hypothermia, too. We almost lost you a couple of times.'

'But that wasn't your fault.'

She smiles, and fills my cup with juice again. 'Course it wasn't. It was Per's fault, he said it himself, for not strapping you down in the inflatable.'

'Pear? Is that his first name?'

'Yeah. Nordic. It's spelt P-e-r, but it sounds like "pear".'

'But why was he the one looking after me?'

'He is a doctor, you know, but the other kind. PhD.'

'Why didn't I get a proper doctor? A ship this size must have medics.'

She laughs. 'The ship's doc gave you the once over, strapped your shoulder and knee, and then left us to do the nursing. Admitted Per knew more about the treatment of hypothermia than he did anyway. You complaining?'

'Of course not. It's only that you rescued me. You're obviously … I don't know how to put it. Active sailors?'

'Active sailors?' Kat laughs until she's so flushed I can barely see her freckles. 'Yeah, well, we were too "active" for the captain's liking. Per took things into his own hands, coming to get you. The captain said we were so keen to pick you up, we could have the job of keeping you alive afterwards.'

* * *

Kat is doing her best to untangle my hair when the door opens and the captain of the *Torrens* walks in.

'Can I have another word, Harry?'

This is the third time he's interviewed me. He's upfront about his investigation into the sinking of *The Watch*, and I'm grateful for the way he's caring for the crew. Not that I've seen any of them yet—the captain has to guard against collusion, so I'm on my own until he's finished with his questions.

'Sure. Let's get this over with.'

'Lieutenant,' he says to Kat, gesturing skywards, 'Commander Amundsen is flying to the mainland later this morning, then heading back to Bergen. I understand he wants a word.'

Kat gives the captain a sloppy salute. He smiles and tells her she'd better sharpen up, because her sidekick won't be around to stick up for her for a while.

'Sidekick?' I ask, as soon as Kat has gone. 'What's up with those two? And why is he going to Bergen?'

'Because,' the captain says, taking a notebook and pen out of his pocket, and sitting in the chair near my bed, 'that's where he's based. He's on secondment with us from the Norwegian Navy. A Special Ops man. We're lucky enough to have him for a year.'

'He doesn't have much of an accent.'

'He's bilingual.'

'You know he has something against me? He said I'd regret being rescued. What's his problem?'

The captain raises his hand. 'Enough, Harry. Surely Commander Amundsen is the least of your concerns?'

'What do you mean?'

'You had responsibility for communications and safety equipment on *The Watch*. There were significant failures with both. My questions are just the beginning. There's sure to be a maritime inquiry. You'll be up to your neck in it. So will the Scott Foundation as the owner of *The Watch*. And so will Drew McLeish because he was responsible for preparing the ship.'

Drew. The captain is right. Per Amundsen is the least of my concerns. Protecting Drew and his reputation is what's really important.

★ ★ ★

Drew McLeish and my father sailed skiffs in Pittwater when they were boys. In adolescence they took holidays together, crewing on ocean racing yachts. Then they went their separate ways—Drew left school when he was fifteen and joined the merchant navy; Dad finished school and went to university.

By the time Mum and Dad raised the money to finance *The Watch*, well before I was born, they were well-known environmental scientists with a string of documentaries to their names. Even so, it took time to convince Drew to join them as Dad's second in command. This was partly because Drew has never pretended to be anything that he isn't—an honest, modest, largely self-educated man, who cares about his planet. He always called Dad a 'bloody greenie'. He must have thought the same of Mum, but he'd never have sworn at her.

After Mum was killed and Dad badly injured in a car accident in Brazil, Drew took over as captain of *The Watch*. He's a founding member of the Scott Foundation as well. The foundation was set up not long before Dad died. He put most of his assets into it, and gave it ownership and control of his ship.

My students had exams in December so I wasn't supposed to be on the Antarctica voyage. But then I got a voicemail message from Drew.

'Little health problem, Harry,' he said. 'Doc needs to do more tests. I can't go to Antarctica after all, and the foundation wants you to replace me. It's a great crew, and *The Watch* has never been in better shape. Tom Finlay will captain the ship, but we need you to take over my other duties. And you can do the front of camera work. The ship will be leaving on Friday. Want me to call your headmaster and explain the situation?'

Drew had seen the doctor because he'd had problems with his balance. His brain scans showed signs of dementia, even though he'd seemed to be as sharp and organised as ever. I told him I'd go to Antarctica for him, and we'd get a second opinion when I got back.

The night before *The Watch* was due to leave, I called him at eleven and woke him up.

'So the computer upgrade's happened?' I said. 'We had all sorts of trouble with the readings when we went to Guatemala.'

'All fixed, Harry. Weeks ago.'

'Valves all good? Have the watertight checks been done?'

'More than once.'

'And the navigation and other equipment, in case we lose the satellite?'

'You'll find everything you'll ever need on the bridge.'

'Lifeboats okay? Jackets, storm gear, flares?'

'Just go to bed, will you?' Drew said. 'It's all shipshape and ready to go.'

It was only a few days ago that I realised how much Drew's short-term memory had deteriorated. And how the rest of the crew and I had relied far too much on what he'd told us. But by then it was too late. *The Watch* was at sea, hopelessly off course, battling dangerous seas and winds. And that was *before* we hit the iceberg.

When the captain of the *Torrens* clears his throat I adjust my position on the bed, gingerly moving my shoulder into a more comfortable position.

'We don't have to do this now,' he says.

'I'm fine,' I say. 'Really. Ask whatever questions you like and I'll do my best to answer them. I'm not sure what went wrong. Drew did everything he could to make this voyage a successful one …'

CHAPTER

3

Three months have passed since *The Watch* went down. I take the lawyer's letter out of the envelope and read it again.

Dear Miss Scott,

As you are aware, The Watch's mayday call in December had a negative impact on a scientific study led by Commander Per Amundsen. It is my view that, notwithstanding Law of the Sea requirements regarding rescue, he may have a personal action against you in negligence. This could result in a substantial award of damages.

Commander Amundsen has agreed to a formal mediation. The mediation will enable you to meet face to face, to determine whether this dispute can be settled without recourse to expensive and protracted court proceedings. The commander will have legal representation at the mediation. I strongly recommend that you engage a lawyer to ensure that your own interests are protected.

Please contact me at your earliest convenience.

Yours faithfully,

James Talbot

The maritime authorities weren't satisfied with many of my explanations about what went wrong in Antarctica, but since we hit a berg and the weather conditions were extreme, they didn't prosecute the Scott Foundation or any member of the crew. Per Amundsen was obviously unhappy with that decision. He said I'd regret being rescued. I guess this is what he was talking about.

When Drew jiggles my foot to get my attention I put the lawyer's letter on the side table between us. Then I lean over, straighten Drew's jumper over his shoulders and roll up the cuffs to free his hands. We're sitting on the deck at the back of my house with our feet propped up on the railing. My knee still locks up if I straighten my leg too quickly, and the torn tendons in my shoulder haven't quite healed, but my injuries are nothing compared to what's happening with Drew. His dementia is progressing at a terrifying rate. I'm losing a little more of him each and every day.

'Come on, Harry,' he says. 'Rain's easing. Let's walk along the beach.'

'We'll finish our afternoon tea first.' I hand him his cup, and put a cheese cube on a cracker for him. 'The sister at your care home says you're forgetting to eat. Look at you, you're a bag of bones.'

He smiles. 'Where's Maggie? And Matthew. Where's your father?'

'Mum and Dad died a long time ago, Drew, but they'll always be with us. You know that.'

Just about everyone Drew has ever come into contact with loves and respects him. He has fans all around the world. But his short-term memory is so poor now that within a minute he'll have forgotten what I said. He eats the cracker and takes a sip of tea. Then he rests the mug on the arm of the chair.

We both gaze over the balcony railing out to the Pacific Ocean. It's been overcast and showery all day, and more dark clouds are gathering over the ocean. Waves pound the coarse yellow sand along the shore from the northern end of Avalon Beach, where I live, to the southern end at the heads. The swell is enormous, and every few minutes a wave crashes onto the rocks at the base of the cliff at the south and gushes over the rocks to the ocean pool beyond. The council built the pool decades ago. It's popular in the summer months, but a group of elderly locals—the Avalon Amazons—swim there every morning, summer and winter.

'What are you looking at, Harry?' Drew says. 'You tell me all about it.'

'This cloud reminds me of New Guinea, and the afternoon storms. Remember how you carried me on your back for hours one evening because you wanted to get back to *The Watch* before the rains came? I must've been ten. Mum was cross because I was quite capable of walking.'

Drew smiles, a smile that crinkles his eyes. And suddenly it's as if the last few months of his illness never happened.

'My back went crook for three days afterwards. Couldn't tell your mum about it or we'd both be in the dog house.' He laughs and takes my hand. 'Said I had a sore throat and stayed in bed. Remember that, Harry? Remember that?'

'I brought hot toddies to your cabin, with lemon juice, honey and brandy.'

I reach for my sketchbook when a young kookaburra flies onto the railing. He dips his head to the side and puffs out his chest feathers. My hand darts over the page, trying to capture the image before he flies off again. I'm smiling when I turn to Drew.

'Isn't he handsome? Like the fledgling who used to visit Dad and me at Newport.'

Drew frowns and peers at me as if he's seeing me through a fog. Even before he opens his mouth I know I've lost him again. My throat works to swallow, and I blink back tears as I look out to sea. It's drizzling, and the greys of the sea and sky blend on the horizon.

'We'll go down to the beach for a walk when the weather clears,' I say. 'See any humpbacks out there?'

He frowns. 'What month is it?'

'March.'

'Not likely to see a humpback in March, Harry. Wasn't that in your schoolbooks?'

Mum looked after my education until she died, and then Drew took it on. He filled out the home-schooling paperwork for Dad, and kept an eye on me. And whenever Dad was in respite care or hospital, Drew would send me money so I could join him wherever in the world he happened to be.

When I was fifteen I spent weeks living with him in stilted huts on the banks of rivers in South-East Asia. The village women forced me to eat even though their own children were far skinnier than I was. Drew cried when it was time for me to go home; I bit my lip and patted his shoulder, promising I'd be back before he knew it.

The following year, while *The Watch* was in dry dock, we catalogued the wildebeest migration from the Serengeti in Tanzania to Masai-Mara in Kenya. A few months after that we spent the summer on horseback with Mongolian herdsmen on China's Silk Road. But then Dad's health deteriorated further and he needed twenty-four hour care, and help setting up the Scott Foundation. I was almost seventeen, and it was two years before I travelled with Drew again.

He points out to sea. There's a break in the clouds.

'The worst of the rain is over. Let's go and stretch our legs.'

'You're quite the weatherman today, aren't you? But I'll get our coats just in case. And when we get back we'll organise the invitations for your birthday party.'

Drew is turning sixty-five in a few months. He always joked that the good thing about spending his life on boats was that he had a captive audience for his birthday party. Drew never married and doesn't have children. Dad was like his brother, and Mum like a sister. And then he got me. We were always his family.

The kookaburra preens his chest feathers, and stretches his wings a few times. He flies to a branch on the spotted gum, just a few metres away at the bottom of the garden. I put my sketchbook on the table, on top of the lawyer's letter. The mediation is scheduled for tomorrow after school. I'll worry about it again when we get back from our walk.

CHAPTER

4

The legal firm's conference room is on the twelfth floor of a Macquarie Street building, and overlooks the Botanical Gardens and harbour. Even though I'm on time, the men are there already.

When I was six years old, with no front teeth, we were in Venezuela. Mum was rowing across a piranha-infested river in a hollowed-out tree trunk to pick Dad up; he was abseiling sixty metres down a waterfall. I was photographed frowning. My lips were tight. The shot was used for publicity for years after that. I suspect I have the same expression now.

Per gets to his feet first. He's strongly built yet slender, with broad shoulders and narrow hips. His suit fits him well. When he shakes my hand he looks at my mouth, and then he stares into my eyes. My recollection of the night he treated me for hypothermia on the *Torrens* is hazy, but I remember the rescue vividly, and his gaze is just as intense today as it was in the storm. His eyes beneath his straight black brows are dark like charcoal. And he's tanned, which accentuates the narrow white scar on his cheekbone.

I shake hands with the lawyer, James Talbot, and mediator, Neil Reid, and then we sit at the circular table. It has an aged oak grain and is at least two metres across. Per's legs are long, but even stretched out they're still quite a distance from mine. He's opposite me. His lawyer is on my right. The mediator is on my left.

I'm well prepared for this meeting because the legal studies teacher at school gave me a thorough briefing—on the mediation process, and the principles of negligence. I often sketch when I concentrate, so I pull out a small notebook and reach for my pencil. I attempt to draw Per as the scowling Scar from *The Lion King*. When the good lion Simba takes shape I have to turn over the page.

'Miss Scott, I'm concerned that you don't have a lawyer with you,' the mediator says. 'Have you understood everything so far?'

'Mediation enables the parties to a dispute to formulate solutions that have a greater likelihood of satisfying both parties,' I say. 'As opposed to litigation, in which the judge imposes a decision that may satisfy neither party.'

The mediator nods.

'Which is not to say that Commander Amundsen doesn't have an excellent case in negligence, should the mediation not result in a satisfactory outcome,' the lawyer says.

My hair is in a ponytail. I tighten the band. Then I address the lawyer. 'The inquiry's findings into the sinking of *The Watch* were inconclusive. There was no clear case of negligence. And even if you proved it, I'd hardly be worth suing. All I own that has any value is my house, which is heavily mortgaged. Any money raised from its sale would disappear in legal costs. So why are we really here?'

Per sits back in his chair. He links his fingers together and puts his hands behind his head. He's taken his suit jacket off, and the fabric of his white shirt stretches tightly across his chest. He has enough confidence for ten alpha males put together.

'We're here,' he says, 'as a result of your incompetence. I was on my way to Roosevelt Island when the mayday call went out. My colleagues and I had access to the research facilities at Roosevelt. They're booked up months, years, in advance. I'd also scheduled five days of dives at the Ross Sea Ice Shelf. I had boat crews, lab technicians and other scientists lined up. Some of the dives were for the project I'm working on now. Others were favours for research teams with similar interests to mine.'

I try to speak factually like he is. I didn't mean to muck up his research. Neither did Drew.

'You're looking into ice shelf disintegration rates, aren't you?' I say. 'You need information on those to predict future sea level rises?'

He speaks between his teeth. 'Yes.'

'And I'm guessing none of your friends could step in for you?'

'Correct. Because no one else is qualified to do what I do—dive in Antarctic conditions, and identify the types of glacial formations we're interested in. My training gives me the ability to collect samples. Samples that are used to determine a variety of things, including where we might want to drill ice cores.' He gives me a fake smile. 'Ice cores are used to collect the data we need to further our research. They're hundreds of metres deep.'

'So you'd want to drill them in the right places?'

'*Yes we would.*'

'I'm sorry about what happened.'

He rises to his feet. Then he paces. After a minute, maybe two, he faces me again.

'By your own admissions to the maritime inquiry, you managed to lose vital equipment overboard, steer *The Watch* off its chartered course, and misread weather reports. And that was just the beginning. Sorry isn't going to get you anywhere.'

'So, be specific about what you want.'

Per sits down again. 'I want a ship, on my terms, to get me to Antarctica. And,' he picks up his pen, and rolls it across the table towards me, 'written confirmation that you'll provide it.'

I pick up his pen. It's streamlined and silver, like a torpedo. I sketch a black rhinoceros with it, charging a spindly-legged flamingo.

'Do you find this amusing?' he asks.

I look up. 'I've found nothing amusing since my ship sank three months ago. You threatened me then as well.'

When he raises his brows I turn to the mediator. 'The commander said he'd make me wish I'd never been rescued. That's threatening, isn't it?'

The mediator spreads his arms out wide. 'I suggest we continue our discussion in a spirit of reconciliation,' he says.

I lay Per's pen on the table so it's pointing at his midriff. It shoots quickly over the polished surface when I flick it with my thumb. He catches it between his third and index finger without his eyes ever leaving my face.

'I want a ship to take my team and me to Antarctica this December,' he says, 'and for another two Decembers after that. I need more flexibility than the navy can offer me. And I want to extend my research project.'

'I recall you were sitting next to me when *The Watch* went down,' I say. 'I don't have a ship.'

'It was insured.'

'Yes. But the insurance company is thinking about it like they would an old refrigerator. They're offering replacement value, rather than new for old. The insurance payout would represent around half the cost of purchasing an updated vessel with equivalent capabilities.' I clear my throat to steady my voice. Then I stand. 'I've been trying to convince the foundation to buy another ship. It's refusing.'

I walk to the window and take a few deep breaths. A large motor cruiser and a catamaran plough through the choppy seas towards the heads, and two ferries approach Circular Quay. Once my breathing is steady I turn around and lean my shoulder blades against the window. I'm wearing my usual teaching outfit—slim-fitting jeans and canvas lace-ups with a T-shirt. It matches my eye colour. 'They're cornflower blue,' Mum always said. 'Like alpine lakes, wild lupins and robin's eggs.'

'You're an impressive young woman, Miss Scott,' the mediator says.

I gesture to Per. 'On the *Torrens* he said I was a fraud.'

Per narrows his eyes. 'What else do you remember?'

'That you were an arrogant prick.'

'Miss Scott,' the mediator says, 'that was discourteous.'

Per turns to the mediator. 'I think we're wasting our time.'

'Not necessarily,' the mediator says. 'Because it's my belief that you and Miss Scott have far more in common than either of you care to admit.'

'Yeah,' I say, sitting at the table again. 'We both want a ship. But the foundation's funds are earmarked for other projects.'

The lawyer raises his brows. 'In which case,' he says, 'the foundation will have to find additional funds for Commander Amundsen's project.'

I take a breath, and turn to Per. 'There's no doubt your project is worthwhile from an environmental point of view, but that doesn't mean the Scott Foundation will back it. You know as well as I do that climate variation, and what drives it, is a complex issue. Even scientists disagree on how, and to what extent, certain projects should be funded, especially long-term and expensive ones like yours. The public, including members of the foundation, pick and choose what they want to support.'

The lawyer starts arguing, but the mediator shuts him down. 'We're here to find solutions,' he says. Then he turns to me.

'My daughter is about your age, Miss Scott. She admires you tremendously. You were a tomboy when you were a girl, weren't you? Strong-willed, opinionated. A little precocious, perhaps?'

I grimace. 'More than a little.'

'Our family learnt a great deal from yours about conservation and so on. It continues to learn from the work that you and the foundation are involved in.'

'I'm glad about that.'

'And Commander Amundsen. You have a naval career, and quite a reputation as a scientist as well.'

Per shrugs.

'But, as Miss Scott has explained, your current research project might not appeal to the foundation. Do you have any thoughts on how we could get around this problem?'

Per responds to the mediator's question, but his gaze stays on me. 'No, I don't have any thoughts. Because as you pointed out, I'm a scientist. It's Miss Scott who thinks she's capable of anything.'

It's an effort to keep my voice even. 'I'm a teacher.'

His eyes are icy. 'Which is why your conduct in the storm put your crew's lives, your own life, at risk. I couldn't get a pulse when I pulled you out of the ocean. I pumped your chest for three fucking minutes before you breathed on your own.'

I link my hands together so he can't see them shaking. 'Kat told me.'

He indicates a millimetre space between his thumb and index finger. 'You were *this close* to death. And for what? To maintain the foundation's profile? Your parents are dead. Drew McLeish has retired. It's time you moved on.'

The mediator clears his throat. 'Commander,' he says, 'I don't think—'

'Let me finish. I want her to get the message that the Scott Foundation has two options. It gives me the use of a ship, or a damages payout so that I can fund my own. Because incompetence comes at a price.'

I jump to my feet. 'I'm not incompetent, or an idiot. I was educated about the environment by scores of people, including my parents, and Drew. Yes I'm a teacher, a *geography* teacher, which is relevant to what I do. I'm also a communicator, something you know little about. Because if you did you'd appreciate that most people don't give a shit about ice cores. That's why they need information on how ice cores are relevant to preserving natural environments in Antarctica and predicting sea level rises elsewhere. It's why, even though I'm not a commander with a PhD like you, I need to be out in the world.'

He stands too. 'Thanks for the lecture.'

'You're an arrogant prick!'

'You've already used that one. Got anything else?'

I point to him and my finger wobbles. 'You're an elitist, conceited, patronising ...'

He puts his hands on the table so we're at eye level. His words are spoken softly. 'What, Harriet? Lion? Rhino?'

His lawyer asks him to speak up.

'She heard me,' Per says.

The mediator takes another gulp of water, and suggests that Per and I sit down again. We comply, but Per reaches for his jacket as he does so, shrugging into it and collecting his papers. He thanks the mediator for his time, and tells his lawyer that he'll be in touch.

They're all sitting on the edges of their chairs and staring at me after that. But I'm sketching another image, and refuse to look up until I've finished. I've drawn a bull elephant. The picture is from the perspective of whatever, or whomever, he's planning to annihilate. He's surrounded by dust, beaten from the ground as he charges. His eyes are black and he has a narrow scar, extending from the top of one tusk to just beneath his eye. I refuse to meet Per's eyes. I turn to the mediator instead.

'Can you see what this is?' The mediator peers across the table but he can't make out the image. When I ask the lawyer the same question he puts his glasses on, and then he takes them off. He shakes his head.

I look at Per and raise my brows.

He leans back in his chair, pushing it away from the table and stretching his legs out.

'It's an elephant,' he says. 'African.'

I check the diameter of the table again. Over two metres wide, I'm sure of it. And my notebook is small, not much bigger than my hand. Are Per's senses of hearing, touch, taste and smell as acute as his sense of sight? And what about his other qualities? He's strong, smart, and he swims like a fish. Is he a real life action hero with special powers?

'Does the elephant have any distinguishing characteristics?' I ask.

He doesn't say anything. He simply lifts his index finger and traces the scar on his cheek.

*　*　*

Would the Scott Foundation buy another ship if they had an action hero to sail in her? For months I've been trying to convince

Professor Tan—the chairman of the Scott Foundation—to finance a ship. Could this angle get him interested? I don't have to like Per to see that he'd be extraordinarily marketable. He's clever, exotic, athletic. He'd be photogenic. What I'm planning will result in further embarrassment for me because Per is already notorious for my rescue, but I owe it to Mum, Dad and Drew to do everything I can to secure a ship. There are so many images crowding my mind that I have to write them down. Per frowns; he probably thinks I'm sketching again. He stands and shakes hands with the lawyer and mediator.

'Wait!' I say. 'I have an idea.'

He looks from my eyes to my mouth, and scowls.

'Stop doing that,' I say.

He jerks his head away and stares out of the window.

I tap my pencil on the desk. 'Are you related to the explorer Amundsen?'

He's still considering the view, and he doesn't turn around. 'Remotely. Why?'

'Dad said we were related to Scott.'

He turns from the window. 'What are you talking about?'

I ask the lawyer to search for the foundation's website on his laptop, and bring up a post I did in February. Then I ask him to read the first couple of paragraphs out loud.

The Scott Foundation: Environment Adventure Education

As you all know, The Watch went down in late December. We had trouble getting the lifeboats into the water and, unbeknownst to the rest of the crew, I was left behind. Two people from HMAS Torrens came to pick me up: Lieutenant Katrina Fisher from the Australian Navy, and Commander Per Amundsen from the Norwegian Navy.

A few people have written to me, asking whether I'm aware of the Scott and Amundsen connection. Course I am! I'm a geography teacher. But it's a fascinating story of perseverance and determination, and I'd like to share it with those of you who mightn't be familiar with it.

In December 1911 the Norwegian Roald Amundsen led the team that was the first to reach the South Pole, the southernmost part of the world. Robert Falcon Scott, the celebrated English explorer, and his team, were only thirty-four days behind Amundsen. And, as if coming second wasn't bad enough, Scott's men never made it back to base camp. He was one of the last to die, bitterly disappointed, frostbitten, and starving.

When James has finished reading, Per shrugs. 'So?' he says.

I try to imagine that the three men facing me are a class of thirteen-year-olds on a Friday afternoon. I'll have to be convincing to keep them engaged.

'Amundsen and Scott's race to the South Pole happened over a century ago, but historians still write about the men, the challenges they faced, and the political ramifications of what they did. The data they collected is still relevant today. Imagine what we could do if we had the Scott Foundation and an Amundsen working together, exploring together—not to discover new frontiers, but to save the ones we know about.'

I hadn't exaggerated when I'd told Per that the foundation would only get behind a cause that was likely to attract the support of its members. Contributing to the funding of a study into ice cores and glaciers, involving him and scores of other scientists, would never be of interest. Fundraising targeted to specific and pressing environmental concerns would be a different matter. The mediator raises his brows when I count points off on my fingers.

'Rising sea levels have catastrophic implications for low-lying islands, such as the Maldives, Palau, and Australia's Torres Strait. There are also regions like Bangladesh that are directly affected by ice-shelf disintegration in the Arctic and changes in Southern Ocean currents. The foundation could send a ship and documentary crew to investigate what's happening—how livelihoods, cultures, whole species of flora and fauna are threatened. And we could tie this in with the commander's research into glacial melts in the South Pole, the big picture stuff. Because it's melting ice, whatever the cause, that's resulting in the increased sea levels.'

I'm speaking quickly to get my ideas out. Per's expression is grim. It makes me talk even faster.

'It's the end of March already, so we'd have to start fundraising as soon as we have the foundation's approval. We're not going to get a ship straight away, but leasing one until the foundation has the funds to secure its own isn't out of the question. Maybe we could source a small icebreaker like *The Watch*, which'd be capable of going anywhere? If we can get organised by October, the ship could head to the Pacific, and then return back here in time to prepare for the first of the Antarctic expeditions in December, and—'

'Harriet!' When Per barks my name, the mediator and I both jump. 'Half an hour ago you said a ship was out of the question. Now there's a ship, it's sailing around the world, and taking me to Antarctica. Slow down. Explain yourself.'

The mediator smiles encouragingly. 'Harriet. I may call you Harriet?'

'It's usually Harry.'

'Harry, then.' He smiles again. 'I have a confession to make—I'm having trouble keeping up. Can I confirm you have a project you think the foundation may be interested in? Which means it might, ultimately, finance a ship to replace *The Watch*?'

'Yes.'

'And, contrary to what you said earlier, it may also be prepared to support Commander Amundsen's expeditions to Antarctica?'

'If he cooperates in the fundraising campaign, yes.'

Per curses under his breath and stands. 'I repeat. Explain yourself. Or I leave.'

I flip to a fresh page, and then I pick up my pencil. Per is easy to draw, particularly in profile. Straight nose, well defined jawline, tall and slender with broad shoulders and perfect posture. I include his distinctive widow's peak, but lengthen his hair so a black lock sweeps across his brow. His scar is perfect—a physical manifestation of bravery and resilience. His feet are slightly apart, and his hands are clasped behind his back. I tear out the page and reach across the table to show it to the mediator. He blinks and opens his mouth but nothing comes out. When I show it to the lawyer, he smiles nervously before rising from his chair and handing it to Per.

'What the fuck?' he says.

Per's chest, abdominal and thigh muscles are clearly delineated in my drawing. They bulge against the fabric of his wetsuit. A white sash crosses his torso from shoulder to hip. His hair is dripping with water, his eyes are black, and his expression is grim. Per stares at his image, scowls, and slowly shakes his head. Finally he returns to the table and sits. When he pushes the sketch across the surface towards me it moves so fast I have to slap my hand on it to stop it flying over the edge.

'*Polarman?*' he says.

I'd written the name in the sash. 'I think the action hero idea will be more interesting to younger kids than the Scott and Amundsen historical perspective. We could have a two-pronged campaign.'

'You're joking?'

'No I'm not. I'm just disappointed there's already a *Captain Planet* cartoon character. That name would've been cute.'

He closes his eyes for a moment. '*Jesus.*'

I remind myself I have to stop annoying Per if I want to get him on side.

'If you're uncomfortable about having a superhero name, we could simply use your initials.' I write a stylised version of the word 'polar', highlighting the P and A. He can see it from where he's sitting, but I hold it up so the lawyer and mediator can see it too. 'We could incorporate something like this in the sash instead.'

'You're crazy.'

'And you're a naval officer, eminently qualified—even by your own high standards—to crew on a ship. You'd only have to appear occasionally, and have your details on the website, to ensure your image gets associated with the foundation. Meanwhile, the foundation would fundraise, while simultaneously informing the public, through televised voyages to low-lying regions, about the environmental implications of polar melts.'

The mediator clears his throat and sips from his glass. 'Interesting ideas, Commander. Aren't they?'

Per looks at him as though he's lost his mind. 'They're ridiculous ideas.'

'You don't have to wear a wetsuit if you don't want to,' I say. 'A white uniform could work. Is that what you have in the Norwegian Navy?'

'What?'

'For special occasions. What do you wear?'

He speaks between his teeth. 'Our formal dress uniforms are black.'

'Oh. But what about gold bits—epaulets, stripes on the arms, medals. Do you have those?'

The mediator blinks when he sees Per's expression. Then he turns to me. 'Perhaps we could meet again next week? Once the commander has had a chance to consider your proposal.'

'I have nothing to consider,' Per says. 'I'm a naval officer, not a cardboard cut-out. And after what happened in December I have no faith in Harriet, personally or professionally.'

'Commander ...' the mediator says, 'that was discourteous.'

Per shrugs. 'It's the truth. You know she has a fear of the water? And she can't swim. What sort of rational person goes to sea with a phobia like that?'

I swallow the lump in my throat. 'I can control it.'

'Like hell you can.'

The mediator sighs. 'Commander, please. This is hardly the time or place for this.'

I take a couple of deep breaths before I address the mediator. 'The commander would be dealing with the foundation, not me. All he'd have to do is be associated with it, and maybe take a ship out for a day or two—'

'You're either extraordinarily foolish, or criminally negligent,' Per says. 'I can't decide which, and neither could the maritime inquiry into the sinking. Which means you've never been held properly accountable. And now you want me to volunteer for an imbecilic scheme you've just thought up? Forget it.'

My mouth is dry and I'd like a drink of water, but my hands are shaking so I keep them clenched in my lap.

The mediator stands. 'This meeting wasn't about the inquiry into the loss of *The Watch*, Commander, it was an attempt at mediation.'

The lawyer frowns. 'And in that respect, we'd lose nothing by giving Miss Scott the opportunity to put her ideas to the foundation. In fact, we probably have an obligation to do so as part of the mediation process. Perhaps, Commander, the foundation will adopt the proposal without your involvement?'

Per shrugs, and tells his lawyer that he and the mediator can do what they have to do, but to keep him out of it. He shakes the men's hands. Then he takes mine. His hand is warm. Mine is freezing cold.

CHAPTER

5

The Scott Foundation: Environment Adventure Education

Last month I posted about losing The Watch. Many people will remember the ship, and the important role she played in educating people about our environment, and how we can protect it. I was born on The Watch, so I have a whole lifetime of memories! I miss the ship, and I can't help feeling I've let my parents down. To make things worse, some of the decisions I made before and during The Watch's final voyage put the lives of others at risk. However …

We all (even living breathing action heroes) make mistakes. I'm trying to learn from mine, and doing what I can to make up for the things I could have done better …

Harriet

* * *

I called Professor Tan after the mediation, and told him it was important that we meet face to face. He replied that he could see me in his university rooms on Wednesday afternoon. I'm sitting in the waiting room outside his office.

The professor is a high-profile physicist and committed environmentalist, with excellent contacts in government and media circles. He admired Mum and Dad, and appreciated the fact that their documentaries were based on solid scientific evidence. Dad encouraged Tan's postgrad students, letting them carry out research while crewing on *The Watch*. So Tan was a natural choice as a board member for the Scott Foundation when Dad set it up. A few years ago the other board members—most of them academics—elected Tan as Chairman.

I take out my sketchbook and pencil. When he wasn't in hospital Dad saw a series of specialists as an outpatient—monthly, weekly, sometimes daily. I'd wheel him into their waiting rooms and sit there until he'd been treated, then I'd take him outside to meet whoever was driving us around that day. I must have been fifteen when we were in his neurologist's waiting room. Dad turned to me and said, 'Bring your sketchbook tomorrow, Harriet. It will keep you occupied. And take your mind off Brazil.'

Dad had swerved to avoid a truck overloaded with coffee plantation workers. The road under the front wheel of our four-wheel drive gave way, and the car tumbled eighty metres to the bottom of a gorge. Mum died within thirty minutes and although I got Dad out of the car, he was still unconscious when Drew and the villagers arrived three hours later. I didn't want to talk about what had happened and the locals didn't ask questions because fatal accidents are common in remote regions of South America. But Drew got most of the facts out of me. As did the psychiatrist that Drew sent me to.

Dr Makepeace was funny and kind, and his wife gave me herbal teas while I sat in his waiting room next to a brown-haired girl with beautiful eyes. She was always there before me even though her appointments were later than mine, and she wrote furiously in her notebook while I drew pictures in my sketchbook. Sometimes another girl sat with us in the waiting room. She never smiled, and she walked with a stick, or crutches. Her hair was red-gold and she looked like a Christmas angel.

Professor Tan finally opens the door to his office. 'Sorry to have kept you waiting, Harry.'

The professor is shorter than I am but when we shake hands he always seems to look down on me. And I don't know why he's apologising. He *always* keeps me waiting.

He looks at his watch. 'You have thirty minutes,' he says.

Even before *The Watch* went down, the professor didn't rate me. He sees the world in terms of people who are scientists and people who are not. But he does acknowledge that, through Mum and Dad, and the documentary work I do, I'm very well known and generally liked. It makes me useful for liaising with the public and for fundraising.

He sits on the chair behind his desk and gestures that I should sit opposite. I perch on the edge of the chair and take a deep breath.

'I have an idea, Professor, an idea that might help us get another ship.'

He raises his brows. They pop up above the steel frames of his glasses.

'I see. To replace the one that the foundation previously had?'

Tan isn't convinced by my story about what happened to *The Watch*—that a few silly mistakes were made, which resulted in catastrophe. But I'm not giving him the facts about Drew. Tan's been given the same story as everyone else—Drew's dementia only took hold in January, *after* the Antarctica trip.

I sit up even straighter in my chair. 'I have an idea for a documentary series. One that focuses on low-lying regions around the world and the impact rising sea levels will have on their environments and inhabitants. We'll create a fundraising campaign around the issue and use these proceeds, together with the insurance money we get for *The Watch*, to raise funds for another ship …'

Tan asks me to clarify almost everything I say, and holds up his hand when I speak too quickly or don't give him time to consider my points. After I've finished, he stares over my left shoulder. He rubs his forehead. Then he looks at his computer screen like I'm keeping him from something important.

'This is all very well,' he finally says, 'but the purchase of another ship is a huge commitment. Your ideas are interesting, certainly, but not … inspiring.'

I owe it to Mum and Dad and Drew to get a ship. Per wants a ship too.

'There's something else,' I say. 'Something you might find inspiring. Do you remember the man who rescued me from *The Watch*? Per Amundsen is not only a naval officer, he's a scientist with a PhD. You might even share some research interests. He's into glaciers, glacial melts, things like that.'

Professor Tan wakes up. And he stays wide awake as I outline my plan. I give him the Scott and Amundsen working together angle, the Polarman angle, everything.

'And this is the man who came to your aid in December?' he says.

'That's right. He's capable, professional, and intelligent. He'd be a wonderful pin-up boy for the foundation.'

The professor shakes my hand when I leave. 'Perhaps replacing *The Watch* isn't out of the question after all,' he says. 'There's a long way to go, certainly, but the Australian and Norwegian aspect fascinates me, as do the scientific possibilities. I look forward to discussing it in more detail with Commander Amundsen. You'll tell him to get in touch, won't you?'

⋆   ⋆   ⋆

Four days later, Liam and I are running side by side at the beach.
He got back from a night shift at 6 am and dragged me out of bed.
We're at the very edge of the hard sand because I've regressed since
Antarctica. Just thinking about putting my head under the water
increases my heart rate. It's not likely I'll be dragged out to sea
while running along the sand, but I'm not taking any chances.

'Why are you frowning?' Liam asks.

'Mind your own business.'

He wipes his sweaty sun-bleached hair out of his eyes and shoulder bumps me. I bump him back, much harder, but he doesn't
flinch because he's 184 centimetres tall, solidly built and very fit.
We've been housemates for over two years now but we've known
each other for eleven—we met when he was a medical student at
a rehabilitation centre where Dad was treated. Now he's training
to be a surgeon. We went out a few times but never got serious. I
told him we shouldn't have sex because, with my history, I'd have
to dump him immediately afterwards and never talk to him again.
And that would be a shame because I liked him. He shrugged, and
asked whether that meant he could rent my spare room so we could
live together without 'living together'.

As we run I fill Liam in on the week's events—we've barely
seen each other since last weekend. He laughs when I describe the
Polarman drawing. I'd like to laugh too but I can't quite manage it.
Per was horrified when he saw it. Now Professor Tan knows about
my idea and I have to arrange a meeting between them. Anything
could happen.

I'm doubled over with a stitch by the time Liam and I get to the
southern end of the beach, near the seawater pool. I sit on the sand,
and he tells me if I hadn't talked so much I might have been able to
keep going for longer.

'I was still faster than you, though,' I say, putting my head between my knees.

He sits down next to me and we watch the Avalon Amazon swimming club members while I get my breath back. It's almost eight so they're getting out of the pool and walking along the landing towards us. The mornings are getting colder but none of them wear wetsuits; they're in speedos and one pieces. Everyone is in their sixties and seventies, except for Rhonda who's eighty-two. There are seven women and four men. Allan, the coach of my indoor football team, towers over everyone else. His chest hair is thick and white. Helga is slender and sprightly; her hair is straight and grey, and she wears it in a bob. She wipes her hair from her face and scans the beach. She's probably looking for her grandson Jonty, a boy in my geography class. He's sitting near the surf club, dressed in a hoodie and playing on his phone. Helga locates him, waves, and then she spots me.

'The tide's turning, love,' she says. 'You stay up there.'

Liam pats my leg and winks. 'Good to see Helga's looking out for you.'

'Stop it, Liam. She's been very kind. She wanted me to join the Amazons.'

He laughs. 'Good luck with that.'

I stand and tug his hand until he's upright too. 'I've got to make a call before I pick Drew up,' I say. 'Let's get back.'

'Polarman?'

'Yup.'

'You're determined to stick your neck out over this new ship thing, aren't you?'

'Nothing to lose.'

'Except for your head. Can't you let it go? For once in your life?'

'You sound like Amundsen.'

He ignores me and studies the waves. 'Surfs going to be good. Can't wait to get out there.'

Two young surfers are running towards the sea at the northern end of the beach, near the rock shelf. I sense their excitement, their anticipation. They hold their boards above their heads as they wade into the shallows; white foam churns and froths around their hips. When the water deepens they flip their boards into the ocean, hop onto them and lie on their stomachs, paddling out to the bigger waves that appear and disappear, blue and white like ribbons, as far as the eye can see.

We were moored off Oahu in Hawaii, tracking the migration of giant turtles, when Dad and I took a day trip to Banzai and watched the surfers brave the northern beaches pipelines. I told Dad I was afraid of the rips and the giant surf. He took my hand and led me to the water's edge. Then he gestured to the horizon. 'Be like a dolphin, Harriet,' he said. 'Let the currents take you where they will. I'll always keep an eye on you.'

CHAPTER

6

Per told the mediator he was stationed at the *HMAS Penguin* naval base at Balmoral, so I look up the number as soon as Liam jogs over the dunes to the surf, board under his arm. As the phone rings I perch on a stool at the kitchen bench. How do I convince Per to speak to Professor Tan? Unless I implicate Drew, I can't defend myself against Per's accusations that I'm incompetent. So I have Per's low opinion of me to deal with, in addition to him wanting nothing to do with my plan. I take a breath when the receptionist tells me she'll put me through.

'Amundsen.'

As soon as I hear his voice I jump up from the stool. Liam was right. I am sticking my neck out.

'Commander?' I say, as if there might be another Amundsen there.

'Harriet.'

'Hi.' I can barely get the word out because my mouth is dry. I'm filling a glass from the tap when the phone clatters into the sink. I wipe it with a tea towel and put it to my ear again. 'Sorry.'

He's not there anymore, and the screen is blank. I must have hung up on him. Or did he hang up on me? I'm staring at the screen when the ringtone sounds.

My voice is still croaky. 'Harriet.'

'Per.'

Kat told me Per's name was pronounced like the word pear, but when he says it it's sharper, more abrupt. It suits him when it's pronounced like that.

'What do you want?' he says.

'I saw Professor Tan.'

I tell Per almost everything that happened at the meeting. He tries to interrupt but I talk over him—easier to do when he's not facing me across a table and scowling. I reassure him that if the foundation approves of my proposal I won't be involved in the trips to the low-lying regions, or to Antarctica, and I finish my spiel with a detailed account of the professor's scientific credentials.

'He's keen for you to contact him because he's interested in your research,' I say.

'How does he know about my research?'

'It came up in our discussions.'

'Did you talk about me in any other context?'

I'm hoping Per will be so impressed by Professor Tan's qualifications and enthusiasm that he'll agree to anything the professor suggests.

'No.'

'Liar. You told him I'd be involved in the trips and documentaries you were planning, didn't you?'

'I spoke in general terms.'

'So you didn't mention your idea about the Amundsen and Scott connection?'

Of course I did. And Polarman. But I can't tell him that. 'Speaking of ideas, I've been thinking. I looked you up, and saw most of your research colleagues are scientists at the University of Oslo, so I assume they rely on government and private funding, like most academics. I suppose the navy pays your wages, but I'm sure the university would love it if you had a public profile. It could exploit this in order to—'

'Harriet!'

'I didn't mean to say exploit! I meant if you had a public profile as an environmentalist through working with the Scott Foundation, the University of Oslo could use this profile for its own fundraising activities. And there are additional possibilities as—'

'*Harriet.*'

'Well, there are. I don't know much about Norway, but your armed services are like ours, aren't they? Getting involved in all sorts of worldwide conflicts? Like Afghanistan, and Iraq, and Syria. Which is awful for everyone involved. Obviously. And tragic. So, if someone from the navy, for example, did something different, like sending the world a message that there are environmental battles that can be fought and won if only we could all band together to—'

'Harriet!'

'What?'

He's quiet for so long that I check my phone to see he's still on the line. Then I cross my fingers, willing him to actually think about what I've been telling him—because I've given him a lot to think about. Too much?

When I was ten, we were docked in Lima in Peru, getting *The Watch* ready to head home. I was on the main deck, trying to convince Mum and Dad that we should take a diversion of 2 000 nautical miles to Easter Island, so we could see the Moai statues. Dad suddenly picked me up by my forearms and spun me around and around. Then he put me back on the deck. I laughed as I staggered backwards, dizzy and disoriented. He scooped me up just before I fell, and told me the way I was feeling now was how I made him feel when I talked too much. And then he called Drew over.

'Harry wants to go to Easter Island,' he said.

'Right, Captain,' Drew said, grabbing me and carrying me under his arm. When we got to the bridge he perched me on the chair next to his and I watched silently as he got out his maps and charted a course. Finally he turned to me, his eyes twinkling. 'Hi ho, Harry, ready to set sail?'

'Harriet?' Per says. 'Are you still there?'

'Um. Yes.'

'Professor Tan called me last night. He asked me to attend a cocktail party given in honour of the Swedish Ambassador.'

My heart skips a beat. 'That sounds nice. Is the Swedish Ambassador a friend of the Norwegian Ambassador?'

'I have no idea. You set this up, didn't you?'

'I did not! If I'd known you already had a date with Professor Tan, I wouldn't have wasted the last fifteen minutes trying to convince you to call him, would I?'

Per tells me he still hasn't given up on the idea of suing me, and possibly the foundation as well. And then he warns that if I cause any more trouble for him he'll personally throw me overboard from one of the navy's biggest ships, the *HMAS Adelaide*.

'And this time,' he says. 'I'll let you drown.'

* * *

Dad and I never spoke about what happened immediately after the accident in Brazil, and how it led to my fear of the water. He continued to communicate intelligently and thoughtfully on environmental issues, just like he always had, and although he'd lost his mobility and couldn't go to sea anymore, when he was well enough he gave support and advice to Drew and the crew. But the part of his brain responsible for emotions like affection and empathy was damaged, and the only thing he appeared to really care about was his ship. He established the Scott Foundation, and transferred *The Watch* and most of his other assets into that. He gave me his apartment in Newport. Drew wasn't happy with how Dad set things up because I hadn't even finished my schooling yet, but I didn't mind. I loved what the ship represented just as much as Dad did.

On a warm February evening he told me he was sick of the drugs and tubes that were keeping him alive, and that he was ready to die. And then he made me promise not to call an ambulance. I moved his bed into the corner of the living room in the apartment so he could see a strip of ocean between two pine trees, and I propped him up on pillows. It was after seven, and the sun was a giant blurry ball of saffron. The ocean was unusually calm. There were no surfers, only paddling children.

He pulled the cannulas out of his arms, took off his oxygen mask, and reached for my hand. 'Harriet for ingenuity, Hillary for perseverance, and Amelia for pluck,' he said. His eyes were half closed, and perhaps I was imagining it, but for the first time in over four years I thought his expression softened, so that he was looking at me in the same way he used to look at me before the accident. He was struggling to breathe, so he wheezed his instruction that I was to take out a boat with Drew and scatter his ashes off the coast of Palm Beach, in the same spot we'd put Mum's.

I rested my head on his chest and wrapped my arms around him. He rubbed his chin against my forehead. When I closed my eyes it was like I was fourteen again and at the bottom of the gorge—exhausted, frightened, bereft. It was then that I'd lost the kind loving father who had inspired and adored me. At last I could say goodbye.

CHAPTER

7

I was named after the geographer and explorer Harriet Chambers Adams, but I'm not sure my parents imagined I'd become a geography teacher. It's the last period of the day and my Year 7 class of twelve- and thirteen-year-olds is waiting for the bell. Most of them are slumped over their desks, or leaning back in their chairs and staring out of the windows.

I'm dreading the bell. Two weeks have passed since the first mediation. The second is scheduled for four this afternoon. Jonty waves his arms around to get my attention.

'Harry!'

'It's Miss Scott when we're at school, Jonty. You're well aware of that. You have a question?'

Jonty grins. 'Can you tell us a story, Miss?'

I often tell my students adventure tales set in the Andes, or the Galapagos Islands, or up north in the Daintree. They learn about things like sustainability without knowing they're doing it.

'One with *The Watch* in it,' he says. '*Please,* Miss.'

Two girls at the back of the class exchange glances. Many of my students will have seen me burst into tears on national television just after I returned from Antarctica—a journalist had asked how I'd felt when my ship had gone down. I send the girls a weak smile. Then I address Jonty.

'Have I told you the story about my father being arrested when he boarded a Japanese whaling vessel?'

Jonty grins. 'No, Miss.'

'*The Watch* followed the Japanese boat all the way back to Japan. Meanwhile, Mum gave interviews to people all around the world about the commercial whaling industry, and how it was threatening species like the Blue and Sei whales.'

'You did interviews too!' Lucy says. 'I've seen that show.'

The media couldn't get enough of the story. I was a cute chatty kid with long fair plaits. Mum was an articulate anthropologist and biologist. She was clever, passionate and beautiful.

'How long was your dad in jail?' Jonty asks.

'Just a few weeks.' I stand and tap Amber's desk until she turns off her phone. Then I draw a few polar bears and a cub on the white board. They're stranded in the ocean on a narrow patch of ice. 'But by then it was March, and summer was over in the south, so we headed north to Sisimiut in Greenland, close to the Artic Circle.' I go to the world map and point out our route.

Amber continues to look at the board, and raises her hand. 'Miss Scott?'

'Yes?'

'What's going on with the bears?'

The bell sounds but no one packs up.

'We'll look at that tomorrow. C'mon, collect your things. I have to get to the city.'

★ ★ ★

It's pouring with rain when I hop off the bus near Wynyard Station. I contemplate buying a cheap umbrella at the pharmacy, but there's a queue, so I reconcile myself to getting wet. It's not like I have to impress anyone at this mediation anyway—even if Per decides to assist the foundation he won't want me to be involved. My boots are flat-heeled and mid-calf length; I tuck my jeans into the tops, hold my backpack to my chest, and dash into the rain.

Ten minutes later I cross Hunter Street against the lights. Then I walk further up the hill towards Macquarie Street. I'm almost there when I see Per standing on the corner, watching me. He's wearing a thin grey jumper, dark trousers, and suede lace-ups. And he's holding a black umbrella. His hair, brutally short, is dry.

'Hey,' I say. Most of my hair is tied up in a bun but the shorter strands at the front are plastered to my face; I swipe them out of my eyes and scrape as much as I can behind my ears. My long-sleeved T-shirt is sticking to my skin and hanging off one shoulder. I pull it up so my bra strap doesn't show. I don't know what Per's thinking as we walk together under the cover of his umbrella, being careful not to touch each other. Neither of us speak until we step into the foyer of the lawyer's building. Then I remember the parcel I want to give him, and reach into my bag. My hands are cold and clumsy, and I struggle to find it.

'Can you give Kat something for me?'

He looks at his watch as he folds his umbrella. 'I'm meeting James before we convene. I'll take it later.'

I'm muttering 'Piss off to you, too,' as I walk towards the bathrooms on the far side of the lifts. When he says my name, I turn around to face him.

'What?'

'I heard that.'

* * *

Neil Reid, the kindly mediator, smiles when I walk into the conference room. 'Hello, Harry,' he says, as I shake his hand.

James Talbot stands. He shakes my hand too.

Professor Tan is sitting at the round oak table sorting through his papers; he looks up and nods. When I called him to ask what he and Per had talked about at the Swedish Ambassador's cocktail party, he only mentioned complementary research interests. I presume that means fundraising didn't come up.

Per gets up from the table and holds out his hand. His fingers are long and his grip is firm. I've spent the past fifteen minutes in the bathroom thinking up ways *not* to annoy him. I will not speak unless I am asked a question. I will not call him names. I will not mutter swear words that might be overheard by an action hero.

'What's so funny?' he asks.

'Nothing!'

The mediator sits in the same position at the table that he sat in last time. The lawyer is to his right. Per is sitting next to the lawyer, opposite me, and Professor Tan is on my left. Things get off to a bad start when Tan hands out a detailed proposal that, on page one, refers to Scott and Amundsen's South Pole voyages, and how their names, and my and Per's names, will be used in the fundraising campaign for a ship to replace *The Watch*. As Tan starts summarising, Per mutters and tips his head back, so he's looking at the ceiling. When Tan asks whether there's a problem, Per fills him in about what happened at the first mediation. Then they're *both* furious—at me, not each other.

'I'm afraid you've been wasting your time, Professor,' Per says. 'We both have. I made it clear to Harriet that I wanted a ship, not a fan base.'

Tan already suspects I'm hiding something about the sinking of *The Watch*. Being evasive about Per's reaction to my proposal won't improve his opinion. He purses his lips.

'I suspected the commander got a sanitised idea of your plan, Harry,' he says, 'but you led me to believe he was prepared to commit to the fundraising component of the proposal.'

'I didn't say he was prepared to commit to it, just that he knew of it. And I got the impression he was particularly opposed because I'd be involved. But if I'm not involved, and you're in charge, I'm hoping ...' I glance at Per. He's scowling. '*Praying* that he'll change his mind.'

Tan's brows draw together so they meet in the middle. 'What do you mean you won't be involved? That's ludicrous. You're the public face of the foundation. And you're a Scott.'

'It's not like I don't want to be involved.' I gesture to Per. 'He doesn't want me involved. That's why I'm putting the interests of the foundation first. Anyway, Mum and Dad were Scotts, and they're much better known than me. And if you had Per he'd be incredibly marketable, even if he refuses to be Polarman.'

At the mention of Polarman, Per drops his pen on the table. It's the solid silver one. The sound reverberates through the room. I mentally kick myself for making him even crosser than he was before.

'Sorry!' I say. 'Really! Forget Polarman. Just focus on Scott and Amundsen, like Professor Tan has. Or Amundsen and Scott, in that order. Amundsen did get to the Pole first, after all. And try to be open-minded about this. Surely having Professor Tan involved changes everything? Just think about how great it'll be for you to have access to the foundation's ship for a few years. Think how it'll help your research.'

Per's jaw is clenched tight. 'Don't tell me what to think.'

'I'm not! It's just that you want a ship to conduct your research. I know—'

'Harry!' The mediator clears his throat. 'Perhaps it would be better if you let Professor Tan speak for the foundation.'

Nobody says a word and the silence stretches interminably. But then Tan shifts his chair, so he's facing Per.

'My apologies, Commander,' he says. 'Harriet's … enthusiasm can be trying.'

I take a pad and pencil out of my bag. 'Please don't apologise for me, Professor. I get the message.'

Tan presents his arguments to Per rationally and persuasively. It's an impressive performance. I'm sketching, but I don't miss a word. Whenever *The Watch* is mentioned Tan gives me a dark look, which probably endears him to Per as well. By the end of an hour, even though Tan is using my idea of engaging the public by getting them interested in Scott and Amundsen's expeditions—and relating this to research into current-day issues like polar melts—Per is listening and asking questions. And then they discuss their research projects and talk about scientist colleagues they both know.

Per gets to his feet. I keep my eyes down, but I sense that he's looking at my sketch. I've drawn a small waterhole and three giraffes. The adults are keeping an eye on a newborn. She's nuzzling her mother's belly.

'Can giraffes swim, Harriet?' Per says.

I blink up at him. Is he having a dig at me because I can't swim?

'Digital simulations have shown that giraffes could probably float, and possibly swim, but not well,' I say. 'No one's seen a giraffe actually doing it.'

'Why hasn't the theory been tested?'

'By dropping a giraffe into water? Out of its depth? You're the scientist. You know that's impossible from an ethical point of view.'

Seconds pass as he looks at me. I can't read his expression. He turns away eventually, and addresses the mediator. 'May we take a break? I have calls to make. James, can I use your office?'

Tan and I make coffees from the machine on the sideboard, and the mediator pours himself a glass of water. None of us refer to Per. It's like we're afraid we'll jinx the outcome of the meeting if we do. I take my coffee to the window; it's still raining and pedestrians are dashing along the footpath, dodging each other's umbrellas. Neil walks around the table and looks at my pad.

'Remarkable,' he says, smiling, and gesturing to my sketch. 'So that's why Per asked you about giraffes.'

I shrug. I'm not sure why Per asked his question, but something about the way he did it makes me uneasy.

* * *

When Per and James return to the room we all sit down again. I'm trying to read Per's intent as he takes his seat. Tan looks like he's doing the same. Meanwhile, Per's gaze travels from the mediator, to Tan, to me. He refers to the issues he'd face—costs, hassle and uncertainty of success—if he brought a personal action against the foundation, or me. He agrees that the use of a ship would make working with the foundation an attractive proposition. Then he praises Tan and his faculty's exceptional research work. Finally, he tells Tan that he's spoken to the University of Oslo, and Norwegian Navy personnel. They like the Scott and Amundsen angle in principle, and think it can work in all sorts of ways, with minimal personal involvement from him.

'But Harriet's other idea is out of the question,' he says.

'Agreed,' Tan says. 'No Polarman. But Harry will have to be involved with the Scott and Amundsen campaign, including the documentaries. It won't work without her.'

I hold my breath when Per hesitates. 'I expected that,' he finally says. 'And I'm prepared to tolerate it. Provided two conditions are satisfied.'

'Name them,' Tan says.

'Firstly, I don't want Harriet on my Antarctic expeditions.'

Tan looks at me.

Antarctica is the last place I want to go to with Per. 'I accept that.'

'Good,' Tan says. 'We'll save you for the other voyages.'

'Secondly ...' Per looks pointedly at Tan. 'I presume you know that Harriet can't swim?'

I jerk upright. The mediator looks at me sympathetically, and shifts uncomfortably in his chair.

'Yes ...' Tan says. 'Which is why those travelling with her ensure, as far as is possible, that she's kept out of danger.'

'She wasn't wearing a life jacket when I took her off *The Watch*. And she was the only one on the ship.'

'We were a life jacket short,' I say. 'And there was a mix up with the lifeboats. What are you getting at anyway? I'm not proud of it, and the foundation doesn't publicise the fact, but it's no secret I can't swim.'

Tan clears his throat. 'There was an incident many years ago, in Brazil. Harry—'

'Professor! If the commander wants my history he can google me.'

Per stands. 'I don't need to read about your history. I've seen you in action. It's not *just* that you can't swim, is it? That doesn't explain your behaviour in Antarctica. You have aquaphobia, something far more serious. Which begs the question, why were you allowed anywhere near *The Watch*?'

I stand too, and hold on to the table with both hands. 'Like I said in our last meeting, I can control it.'

He slowly shakes his head. 'You can't. The crew on *The Watch*, Kat, and other personnel on the *Torrens*. Their lives were put at risk because of you.'

My hands are shaking in earnest now. 'I wasn't planning to go to Antarctica. Everything went wrong.' I swallow down nausea. It's not going to help my case if I throw up on the lawyer's oak table. 'Ships are all right because they're big, and I'm not too close to the water. I only do transfers to shore when the weather is calm.'

Per narrows his eyes. He speaks softly.

'You're very pale, Harriet. Have things got worse since Antarctica? Been paddling in the ocean lately?'

I only just make it to the bathroom at the end of the corridor before I start retching. I haven't eaten much, and I don't have a migraine. I'm not having a full-on panic attack either. Even so, it takes a while until I'm breathing evenly again. I drink water from the tap, and lean my forehead against the wall tiles. At least five minutes pass before I open the door.

Per is waiting for me. His arms are crossed over his chest.

'Are you all right?' he says.

I stop directly in front of him. 'You mentioned a second condition. What is it?'

'We don't have to do this—'

'Tell me!'

His lips tighten. He doesn't like it when I raise my voice. He wants to be the one who issues commands. Not that he'd shout them. He's too controlled for that.

'My second condition is this—if you can prove yourself to be a competent swimmer in the next few months, I won't object to you going on the ship. If you can't swim, there are two possible outcomes. One, you stay on shore. Two, you travel on the ship, and I'm no longer involved. Meaning Professor Tan will have to choose between us.'

'You're giving me an ultimatum?'

'I'm giving you a choice.'

I shove my shoulder into his chest as I push past him. And I almost get to the meeting room door before my leg locks up. It's the knee I hurt in Antarctica—the one that I carefully stretch out before I go for a run. I gasp, and grasp it. I teeter on my good leg while I will the other one to do what I want.

The corridor is deserted except for Per and me. I hear the murmur of voices on the other side of the door. And then Per is behind me, gripping the tops of my arms and pulling me upright.

'Is it a cramp?'

'Yes. Let me go.'

'Lean on me. Ease it straight. Don't force it.'

His hands slide from my arms to my waist. I feel the imprints of his fingers and thumbs through my shirt. And then my shoulder blades are resting on his chest and my bottom is touching the tops of his legs. I feel his belt buckle against the small of my back. His torso is rock hard. I'm hot all of a sudden, and my good leg is wobbly. His breath stirs the hair at my temple.

'You can't rush this,' he says. 'Tell Tan you won't swim. That you'll pull out.'

Per doesn't want to be associated with me. He sees me as a liability. The only reason he suggested a second condition was to please Tan. It makes it look like he's prepared to compromise.

'I'll do what's right for the foundation.'

When he takes a deep breath I *feel* it. I'm leaning against his body, just like he told me to. I don't even have a cramp anymore.

When I jerk my elbows into his stomach he doesn't react. Except to release me slowly and deliberately. I think he wants me to know that he could have kept me exactly where I was for as long as he liked if that's what he'd chosen to do.

He opens the door wide so that I can precede him into the meeting room. I sit on my chair but he stands behind his. His face is grim and his eyes are darkest grey—I can barely distinguish the pupils from the irises. James and Neil appear to be concerned about me. Tan ignores me as he rifles through his folder.

Per tells the others about his second condition. 'Harriet is reserving her decision on it,' he says.

When the men look my way I refuse to meet their eyes.

The mediator clears his throat. 'It's been a long afternoon,' he says. 'But undoubtedly a productive one. And I think it's only fair we give Harry some time to consider her response to Per's suggestion.'

'It's not a suggestion,' Per mutters, as he walks behind my chair and studies my giraffe sketch again. He holds out his hand, palm up. 'You said you had something to give me, for Kat.'

I stuff my pad into my bag. 'Forget it.'

Tan clicks open his briefcase fastenings. 'I've got a plane to catch on Friday morning. Can we meet on Thursday evening? Six o'clock in my office at the university?'

After Per nods, Tan turns to me. 'Brazil was ten years ago, Harry. Maybe it's time to move on.'

I'm at the door when I reply. 'It was twelve years ago, Professor. Yesterday.'

* * *

The Scott Foundation: Environment Adventure Education

Professor Tan recently posted an item about the anniversary of Mum's death. Thanks everyone for your messages. Mum would be delighted the Scott Foundation continues to support the environmental work she and Dad were committed to.

Thanks also to those who've been asking after The Watch's former Captain, Drew McLeish. He's been unwell since January but in typical Drew fashion, he's optimistic about the future. Please say hello to Drew and me when you see us out and about. Drew loves to chat just as much as he ever did!

Harriet

CHAPTER
8

'Have a shot!' Allan shouts.

My indoor football team plays a game every Wednesday evening at the Avalon community centre. When I kick and the ball flies over the goal, hits the back wall and crashes back to the floor, Allan throws his arms in the air.

'Sorry!' I say.

He laughs. 'No worries.'

I'm playing above my skill level, but women are difficult to find for the mixed teams. One of the physical education teachers from school roped me into the team last year. I go home stiff and bruised every Wednesday evening.

'Keep your head up, Harry!'

Someone in the small crowd standing on the sidelines yells the words. Most of the people watching the game are the partners of the players, or they're players themselves, waiting for the next game to start. Suddenly I'm uneasy. I know that voice, and when I scan the crowd I see him, tall and attractive, standing at the back of the hall. Grant Reid.

His uncle runs the local veterinary practice and his parents live in Avalon, so it's not the first time I've seen him around the village, but he usually avoids me. At most we nod to each other. We haven't spoken for years.

The final whistle blows. We've lost—again. But the whole team high-fives each other anyway. Then we shake hands with the opposing team. Allan gives us a pep talk, reassuring us that we'll thrash them next time we play. But I'm conscious of Grant being close, so I'm barely listening. He looks much the same as he used to. More mature maybe—broader shoulders and thicker bristle. He's wearing a football kit and warming up, but he keeps looking my way; it's obvious he's waiting for me to come off the court. Allan is having a chat with the referee so I join them, pretending I'm interested in their discussion on throw-in technique.

I was eighteen when Grant and I were together. He was twenty-one, and studying veterinary science. I'd been living at Newport for the past few years with Dad, so Grant and I had seen each other around, but Dad's funeral was the first time we'd actually spoken. The funeral was a turning point in all sorts of ways.

Mum and Dad were celebrities, and I was born into that life. But we were on *The Watch* most of the time, or living overseas, and I never went to school. People recognised me whenever we came home, but that was no big deal. And after the accident Dad was so unwell that the public and media left us in peace.

After Dad's death, the image of me, six years old and frowning into the camera, popped up again in the media. In another more recent shot, taken at Dad's funeral, I was frowning as well. Only then I was eighteen. I had the same blue eyes and blonde hair, but I also had breasts—and long legs. The media's perception of me changed overnight. Suddenly I was public property, the daughter of renowned adventurers, who grew up in front of the cameras.

It was unfamiliar, and unsettling. I couldn't talk to Drew about it because, since the week before Dad's death, he and *The Watch* had been stuck in sheet ice off the Finnish coast. So I turned to Grant. He was smart, handsome and fun to be with. I thought I was in love with him, and I didn't mind the odd photograph of us in the papers. But then Grant spoke to a journalist. She twisted his words and misrepresented things he'd said, but that didn't make her report any easier to read. Grant had told her that he'd taken my virginity in the back seat of his car, and he thought I was immature and insecure, but he was happy to put up with me anyway.

I cried for a couple of days. And then I conceded that Grant might have had a point. Until the accident I'd spent most of my life surrounded by adults who watched out for me—Mum and Dad, the scores of friends and colleagues they had around the world, the crewmembers and documentary makers on *The Watch*. It was time I grew up and took control of my life.

In retrospect, I didn't do too well at first. Within a week of breaking up with Grant I started hooking up with men I was vaguely attracted to. When I took them to the Newport apartment I thought I was doing what eighteen-year-olds did. The sex was no worse than it'd been with Grant. It sometimes hurt because I wanted to get it over with as quickly as possible. At best it was uncomfortable. And as soon as it was over I sent the men away. I didn't want to wake up with them.

I'm not sure how things would have turned out if not for Drew. He knew about Grant, and I suspect someone had told him about the other men as well, because within a day of *The Watch* coming home he was banging on my door, and waggling a boarding pass under my nose.

He bought me new hiking boots because I'd grown out of my old ones, and he filled my backpack with clothes and camping gear. Then he rustled up an old camera and reels of film. There were only the two of us. For six weeks straight we hiked in Tasmania— the South Coast Track, the Overland Track, and the Three Capes Track along the sea cliffs of the Tasman Peninsula. Drew never mentioned Grant and neither did I. But every once in a while he patted my shoulder. And he relit the fire and made me hot chocolate when I had nightmares about Dad's death.

Towards the end of our trek we came across a school group. There were two teachers and ten adolescent boys. One of the teachers recognised me, and asked whether I'd talk to the boys about the Tasmanian wilderness. My education was unconventional, but I knew a lot about the environment. So I told them about temperate rain forests, and how habitat destruction had led to the extinction of the Tasmanian Tiger.

The next day at dawn I took the boys on a hike. We got back to camp—exhausted, bruised and exhilarated—at the end of the day. I woke with a start a few hours after I'd crawled into my sleeping bag. I'd always imagined sailing the world like Mum and Dad. But now they were gone, and the foundation owned *The Watch*. I was as passionate as I'd ever been about what the foundation stood for, but I had to control my own future. Meaning I needed a career of my own. I did a bridging course to get into university, and then I enrolled in a teaching degree. And as soon as I got a permanent job I sold the Newport apartment, took out a mortgage and bought my house on the beach. My fear of the water was the same as it'd been for years, but I still loved the ocean. I wanted it close.

Allan puts an arm around my shoulders. 'Come off the court, Harry lass. Ref's blown his whistle. It's time to start the men's game.'

Grant smiles as he walks past, but I act like I haven't seen him. I was vulnerable and alone when I was eighteen, and looking for something he wasn't capable of giving. He should never have pretended to love me.

* * *

Dr Makepeace's letter is waiting for me when I get home from football. When I spoke to him over the phone he said that even though I hadn't seen him in years, he'd be happy to look at my file again and give me his considered opinion.

Dear Harriet,

It was marvellous to speak to you this morning. My wife, children and grandchildren follow your career with a great deal of interest. We were saddened The Watch was lost in your recent adventure, but relieved that you and your crew arrived home safely.

Now to the matter at hand. There is no physical reason that stops you from swimming but, as a result of your childhood trauma, you have a phobia. Hence the panic attacks and the debilitating physical responses they trigger, such as the migraines.

You are welcome to lie on my couch again (not that you ever stayed still the first time around!) but you don't have a mental illness, or a personality disorder, and you're not suicidal, so I don't know that I'll be much use. Your hypnotherapist may be worth seeing (incidentally, he's still wearing hemp shirts and trousers, and is currently sporting dreadlocks). A psychologist who practises behavioural therapy is also an option. Or a sensible swimming instructor.

In conclusion, Harriet, by all means go back in the water. But not without assistance, and never alone.

Kind regards,

Gordon Makepeace

It takes me a while to find the folder I labelled 'Crazy Harry' when I was sixteen. There are notes on breathing exercises, and advice from the numerous psychologists Drew dragged me to. At the second mediation Per said, 'I'm giving you a choice.' He's bound to ask about my decision when we meet Professor Tan tomorrow afternoon. I lie on my bed and visualise putting my head under the water. Then I take a deep breath and do my best to suppress the nausea that starts in my pit of my stomach and travels to the back of my throat.

CHAPTER
9

At least Per has dangled a carrot at the end of his stick—if I can swim, he won't oppose Tan's plans to involve me in a voyage later in the year. Tan has a point too: a long time has passed since the accident.

I sit in the waiting room outside Professor Tan's office for half an hour before he opens the door and waves me in. A minute later, Per appears.

All his clothes are black—T-shirt, trousers, boots. His hair is roughed up and streaked with salt. He's damp. The smell of the ocean clings to him. Tan jumps to his feet and holds out his hand. They shake, and Tan grips Per's upper arm with his other hand and squeezes it, the way politicians do. At the mediation Per told me that he refused to be a cardboard cut-out, but Tan is looking at him as if he's measuring him up for size. Perhaps he's picturing Per on a giant billboard? How would he dress him? Special Ops headgear and fatigues, or an officer's uniform?

Per looks at me critically as he shakes my hand. 'Why are you smiling like that?' he says.

'No reason.' I turn to the professor and smooth my jumper over my hips and bottom. 'Can we get started? I have something on at eight.'

Tan gestures that we sit in the chairs facing his desk, and takes a seat opposite. Then he asks us to look through folders marked 'OVP Proposal'. I've only got halfway through my folder before I realise why he's looking so pleased with himself. He's found a ship that has the potential to replace *The Watch*. It's an Offshore Patrol Vessel, not an icebreaker like *The Watch*, but with a strengthened hull and cold climate capabilities. It's only fifteen years old, and is owned by the New Zealand government. It even has helicopter landing capacity. And best of all, it's available on lease short term, with an option to purchase by early next year. It's expensive, but perfect.

Suddenly I'm not fed up because I've been writing school reports all day. And I don't mind being the prize in a charity auction this evening. I'm not even angry with Per for being a prick, arriving late, and smelling so nice. I jump to my feet, run around the desk and wrap my arms around Professor Tan's neck. He laughs, and then disentangles himself.

'Calm down, Harry,' he says. He's still smiling though, and I can see he's excited too. 'Commander, your thoughts?'

Per has an elbow on the desk and his chin in his hand. He's still reading, and is about two-thirds of the way through the folder. His eyes don't leave the page when he answers Tan's question.

'I'm in the process of assembling them,' he says.

I perch on Tan's desk with my legs stretched out in front of me and my toes on the carpet.

Tan raises his brows so they appear above his glasses. 'Yes, Harry?' he says.

'Let's start lobbying! I'll be seeing the Environment Minister tonight, so I'll let him know you'll be in touch. The universities will be keen to send postgraduate students to sea with us like they always have, so we'll get additional funding through them, and plenty of volunteers. And I'll put together a proposal I think will work with breakfast cereal companies, so they can tie in educational information about what the ship will be used for, and how this relates to the pioneering work Scott and Amundsen did. Which reminds me, I'd better do another post, to keep Scott and Amundsen in people's minds. We should start planning for the October voyage straight away. I think it should be Palau, because that'd be a great follow on from a trip I did with Mum and Dad. We'll get backing for the documentaries from pay TV or free-to-air channels, and the tourism industry. The UN environmental organisations will be interested as well, and then—'

Tan clears his throat. 'Harry,' he says. 'I think the commander would like a turn.'

Per watches silently as I get off the desk and sit next to him again. 'Sorry.' I grin. 'You should've butted in.'

He sighs and closes his eyes for a moment. Then he goes back to his folder and spends fifteen minutes cataloguing the specifications of the class of ship Tan has in mind—the positives and negatives. He compares it to the smaller and larger ships he's sailed in for the past number of years and concludes that the OPV ship would, in his view, be eminently suitable for the type of voyages the foundation is contemplating.

'The core crew would be large, around fifty, with half of them in essential roles. That's excluding the *Seasprite* helicopter personnel, who I'm assuming you won't need. It's a fine ship, better than *The Watch* in most respects.'

Tan beams. 'I'm delighted it has your support.'

Per nods. Then he turns to me. 'Which brings us to Harriet. What have you decided about learning to swim?'

I feel sick. I even glance at Tan's wastepaper basket and work out how many steps it'll take for me to get there. Then I remind myself there are a million good reasons why I should get back in the water. One of them is that if I don't do it, Tan will be forced to choose Per over me because there'll be no ship without him. It might take years before Tan would allow me on it.

'I'll do it.'

Tan leans over the desk and shakes my hand. 'I'm glad to hear that.'

Per's eyes haven't left my face. He speaks quietly. 'Your pupils have dilated. You're pale. Your heart rate is up; it shortens your breaths. The prospect of swimming terrifies you.'

Sight, hearing, smell, touch and taste. Per must have a sixth sense as well. He's already made my hang-up a part of his deal with Tan. But that's not enough for him. He has to let Tan know, as if he didn't know it already, that the thought of swimming *terrifies* me. Per has more or less agreed to work with the foundation. I can be as nasty as I like.

'Professor,' I say. 'Now the commander has agreed to join us, hadn't we better check him out properly?'

There's a note of warning in Tan's voice. 'Harry … I'm sure the commander didn't intend to—'

'What? Humiliate me?'

'I made a factual statement,' Per says.

I take a deep breath. Then I address Tan again. 'The commander's past is relevant. He may have a history of bullying, for example. Or misogyny. What about academic misconduct? Then there's his sexual history. You'd like to have him as a poster boy, wouldn't you? Are you sure he's clean enough for that?'

'That's quite enough,' Tan says.

'Why? He likes to think he knows all about me. How *terrified* I am.'

'I made a comment based on personal observation,' Per says.

'Well, how about I make a personal observation about you?' I say. 'Your scar, for example.'

He stiffens.

'In an interview, you said you got it before you joined the navy, but you refused to go into detail. Did a drug deal in an Oslo back alley go wrong? How did you get it?'

Per jumps to his feet and walks to the bookcase on the far side of the room. He scowls at the spines of the books for a while, then he turns and addresses Tan. He speaks through his teeth. *'Deal with her.'*

He didn't react when I suggested he might be a bully or cheat or misogynist. He did when I mentioned his scar. Now his mouth is so tight that he's white around the lips. He's not merely angry. It's worse than that. His eyes are particularly dark. They're troubled.

I sit down again and link my fingers together. 'I'm sorry.'

Per nods formally. He returns to his chair. He speaks as if nothing has happened. 'Professor,' he says, 'I presume you did check me out?'

'We had to, of course,' Tan says. 'You have an extraordinary military record, exceptional academic credentials. And,' Tan glares at me, 'an unblemished personal reputation.'

There's no point hanging around. Even sticking up for myself makes things worse. So I stand again and fumble in my bag. Finally I locate the present for Kat. It's wrapped in brown paper. Inside is a piece of stone, carved into the shape of a penguin. An indigenous villager from Chile gave it to me as a farewell present. It must have been captured in one of the documentaries because one night on the *Torrens,* Kat told me how disappointed she'd been when she'd asked her parents for something similar for Christmas, and they gave her a stuffed toy penguin from a Disney movie.

'Catch,' I say.

The parcel is an awkward shape, small but heavy, and it spins drunkenly in the air when I toss it to Per. He raises a hand and catches it, just before it hits him.

★ ★ ★

Sandstone buildings surround the central lawn of the university quadrangle. They cast thick dark shadows across the dimly lit path. When I hear someone behind me, I stop jogging and look over my shoulder. It's Per. We're the only two people in sight. White clouds of condensation escape from my mouth when I speak.

'What do you want?'

He holds up Kat's gift. 'What is this?'

'A thankyou present. Kat was kind to me.'

For a fleeting moment the expression in his eyes changes, but it's only a flash, and gone before I can identify it.

'And I wasn't?' he says.

'You may have saved my life but no, you weren't kind.'

His gaze shifts to the package. He throws it high in the air and catches it one-handed. Then, as his eyes meet mine again, he holds out a hand.

'Can I?'

'What?'

'Touch you.'

'If you must.'

He grasps my chin. The pad of his thumb skims my mouth.

'Be kind to yourself, Harriet Hillary Amelia Scott,' he says. His thumb moves gently along my bottom lip and sets off a tingling sensation. Last time it felt like that I was naked and lying in a hospital bed on the *Torrens*. 'Stay on dry land.'

I blink. And then, as if it's a perfectly natural thing to do, I rest my hand on his chest. It's warm, and firm. His heart thumps against my palm. I breathe in the ocean smell of him and it's intoxicating. The gentle pressure of his thumb on my lip increases, and his eyes get brighter. My breath catches in a gulp. I fight against moving even closer, finally jerking my face to the side. His fingers skim across my cheek to my earlobe. But then, as if he's never even touched me, his hand is by his side again.

My palm is still on his chest. How can I tell him to keep his hands to himself when the heat of his skin is warming my fingers? I touch my bottom lip with my tongue and taste the salt from his thumb.

Finally I find my voice. 'Why did you do that?'

He hesitates. 'On the *Torrens* your lips were cracked and bleeding. I assumed they were swollen. They weren't.'

'I've seen you staring before.'

'Are you fishing for compliments, Harriet? You have a beautiful mouth.'

'I've got two crooked teeth. Why do you call me Harriet? Everyone calls me Harry.'

'I like the name Harriet.'

I take another step back. I leaned my back and bottom against his body on Tuesday. I put my hand on his chest tonight. Why did I let him touch my lip? Is he aware that I like the feel of him?

'I have to go.' As I turn away he reaches out and takes my hand. I freeze, and then stare silently as he gives Kat's present back, closing my fingers around it. The action is intimate, but the expression in his eyes is distant.

'I'm not a messenger boy,' he says. 'Kat's stationed at Balmoral this week. Give it to her yourself.' He spins on his heel and strides across the quadrangle, back to Tan's office. I watch him until, like a panther, he blends into the shadows and disappears.

* * *

The Scott Foundation: Environment Adventure Education

Following the post I did in February, a number of people have posed questions about Robert Falcon Scott and Roald Amundsen's journeys to the South Pole. I'll address some of these today.

Many historians have looked at why Amundsen's journey to the Pole (and all the way back again!) was a success, and why Scott had a far more difficult time of it. Scott largely relied on ponies, dogs, and man-hauling in his quest to reach the Pole. In contrast, Amundsen relied solely on dogs. Amundsen's team's skiing prowess and dog driving skills were superior to the skills Scott and his team had. Amundsen's men could move more quickly behind the dogs on their skis; Scott had to slow his dogs down because he and his men couldn't keep up.

There were also problems with the tins of cooking fuel Scott's team had left at depots near the base camp earlier in the year. Some of the fuel vaporised and escaped through cork stoppers, meaning Scott's men had to eat frozen food on the return journey, and had less fuel to melt water, leading to dehydration. Amundsen didn't have a problem with evaporation. He soldered his fuel lids closed!

Another factor was the weather. Scott and his men expected tail winds towards the end of their journey (these would have enabled the men to attach sails to their sleds) but these winds never eventuated. Rations dwindled, leading to malnutrition, and this slowed the men down further. Amundsen and his men had sufficient rations and fuel. They gained weight on their way back from the Pole!

On the bright side, the fact we know so much about what happened to Scott on his journey is attributable to his excellent communication skills. He recorded everything in his journal until the very end.

Harriet

CHAPTER

10

'I have a gift for Kat Fisher. Can I drop it over?'

'Sure,' says the man at the Balmoral base who answers the phone. 'But I saw her five minutes ago. I'll check her room so you can speak to her yourself. Who's calling?'

'Harriet Scott.'

'*The* Harriet Scott? From *The Watch*?'

I take a breath. 'That's me.'

After one ring Kat picks up. She tells me she's on shore leave, and bored. And when I tell her I'd like to drop something over to her, she asks if I'd mind if she came to me. I'm busy with Drew and the foundation over the weekend, so I invite her over on Monday evening.

I'm sweeping jacaranda leaves off the front path when she arrives. She's on a motorbike, dressed in leathers and wearing a full-faced helmet. She pulls the helmet and jacket off and runs her fingers through her vibrant red hair. It's still short, but her fringe has grown in the past four months; it feathers into her eyes. Freckles cover her face and arms. She's tall and toned. I don't want to like her because of her connection to Per, but her smile is infectious. I hug her, grabbing her helmet in one hand and her arm in the other.

'C'mon in,' I say. 'I'll get you a drink.'

She whistles when I take her onto the deck and she sees the expanse of ocean, sparkling blue and silver as the sun goes down.

'*Jesus*,' she says.

Does she use that expression because Per does? Or is it just a naval thing? I stand next to her and lean my hands on the railing. The paint is flaking.

'Fancy a walk? We'll eat later, when my housemate Liam gets home.'

Even though the tide is out, I put Kat between the shore break and me. I'm only half-listening to what she's saying as I warily contemplate the ocean.

Dr Makepeace said I could get help from a psychologist before I go back in the water. But I don't want to talk about the accident any more now than I did years ago. He also suggested swimming lessons, but they were a disaster when I tried them last time. Roger was a sports psychologist and coach. He agreed to take me on because, as he told Drew, he was bored with dealing with Olympic swimmers and wanted a new challenge. For the first few weeks we met at a toddler's pool at a leisure centre and, in between panic attacks, he made me blow bubbles on the surface of the water. The next month he held me under my arms, so my face stayed above water, and pulled me along. Then I did breaststroke, with my knees scraping the bottom of the pool. A couple of weeks later he told me I'd graduated to a deeper pool. We faced each other across the water. I could *just* stand. He walked backwards so he was treading water, and then he held out his arms.

'You can do it, Harriet!' he said.

I was sixteen. I wanted to please him. But as soon as I was out of my depth I panicked, thrashed around, and kicked him in the face, breaking his nose in two places. Then the flashing lights of a migraine took over and I passed out. Drew had just arrived to pick me up. He jumped into the water and dragged me out of the pool. Then he laid me on my side and thumped the water out of my lungs.

Drew was furious with Roger, and accused him of making a lot of fuss over a piddling broken nose. What Drew was really upset about was seeing me face down in the water. It was clear he was shaken. His face was ashen.

'Giraffes don't swim, so far as I know,' he said as we walked to the car park. He put his arm around my shoulders. I barely reached his chest because I hadn't had my growth spurt yet. 'So you'll be all right, Harry. I'll keep an eye out. You'll be all right.'

★   ★   ★

On our way home Kat and I meet Allan, walking his golden retriever Dougal. The dog breaks free, jumps at my chest and slobbers on me. When I laugh, Allan gently chastises me for being too soft on him. Meanwhile, Kat snatches Dougal's tennis ball and throws it into the shallows, and Dougal chases after it, and then her, as she darts in and out of the water. Her jeans are rolled up to the knees but within minutes she's wet to the thighs, and she's been splashed so often her shirt is sticking to her back.

When we were at the lawyer's office, Per asked me whether I'd been paddling lately. He clearly thought that I hadn't. And he was right. I can't paddle, and it's getting increasingly difficult to watch other people paddling. Kat is laughing but I'm frightened for her. I swallow down the nausea and take deep breaths.

'Dougal!' Allan calls. 'Time to head home, laddie.'

By the time Kat and I get home Liam is there. Kat looks him up and down when I introduce them, and sends him an appreciative smile. I suppose he's good-looking for a doctor. I ask her questions through dinner, about Perth where she grew up, and what attracted her to the navy. She gives us an outline of all the remarkable things she gets up to, and then complains how difficult it is to keep up with her boyfriends.

'I have one in every state,' she says.

She's open and confident when she talks about men. Why can't I put a youthful infatuation and all the stupid decisions I made afterwards behind me, and be more like Kat? I wouldn't hand over my mind and body again, like I did with Grant. And I don't want casual sex. But surely there's a middle ground?

★ ★ ★

Liam drapes an arm around my shoulders as we watch Kat stow the carved penguin in the storage box of her bike.

'Per said you might be getting another ship,' she says.

It's the first time she's mentioned Per. I hold up both hands and cross my fingers. 'Hope so. She's *beautiful*.'

'Yeah, Per said that too. We're back at sea next week. Working north of Darwin. We'll be gone for a month, maybe longer.'

'Right ... Take care, then.'

Kat is fiddling with the buckles on her jacket, and avoiding looking at me. 'He said I should find out what's happening. You know, about the swimming.'

'Tell him I'll contact Professor Tan when I have something to say.'

She grins. 'Yeah. Thought you'd say something like that.'

★ ★ ★

Ten minutes later Liam and I are standing side by side at the kitchen sink.

'You kissed my mouth when I got back from the beach,' I say. 'Ewww!'

He laughs and flicks me with the tea towel. 'I'm a good kisser. It must be you who sucks. Anyway, it was only a peck. And we have kissed before, Harry. With tongues and everything.'

I shoulder bump him. 'Yeah. But we were going out then. Sort of.'

He laughs again, and tells me not to worry. Although he and his smart, beautiful, on-again-off-again doctor girlfriend Rachael are *almost* definitely over this time, he won't be visiting my bed unless invited.

'So why'd you kiss me? To put Kat off you? That'd be stupid. She's great.'

He shakes his head. 'She has a crush on you, not me, you idiot.'

'It's just the celebrity thing. She'll get over it. So why did you kiss me?'

He shrugs. 'Don't know. Just figure you've got Tan and Polarman hassling you to get back in the water, so she should know there's someone in your corner.'

I stare at him, open-mouthed. Then I find my voice. 'It's my decision to swim, Liam. All Per has done is force me to do it at a time that suits him. And I'm warning you, he'll kill you if he hears you call him Polarman. And then he'll kill me because I told you about it.'

'I'm not scared of him.'

'You should be. He's an action hero, remember?'

Liam knows about my meeting in Professor Tan's office. But I'd never tell him what happened in the quadrangle afterwards. Even though Per had salt in his hair and smelled of the ocean, it was stupid to let him touch me.

It's been well over a month since I met with Professor Tan and Per. Soon the foundation will be ready to launch the Scott and Amundsen fundraising campaign for the new ship. I promise my Year 7 class that if they work quietly for the next hour, I'll tell them a secret. Then I pin butcher's paper to an easel and get to work. The kids can't see what I'm doing, but I can keep an eye on them.

First I sketch the OPV ship. Professor Tan left me a message that he'd secured funding to lease it until the end of the year. And he's got an option to purchase it early next year. Which gives us a deadline—by then we'll need to raise funds to add to the insurance money the foundation will get for *The Watch*. Tan has agreed to lobby the government, institutional investors and media outlets. My role is to engage the public so they get behind the project too.

Next I sketch Per. He looks like Polarman—without the sash. He's standing on the deck of the ship, at ease. The wind ruffles his hair. *How am I going to convince him to grow his hair longer?*

Finally, I draw a classroom of Palauan children. They're sitting at their desks. One little boy is looking out of the window, frowning as he watches palm trees bending in the storm, and fishermen hauling in their boats.

It was sixteen years ago that I was last in Palau, but I still remember the marine life, reefs and rock formations. And the diving, snorkelling and climbing. Footage shot by Dad will be useful as background material for the new documentary. Particularly as I haven't changed much, other than getting taller. Palau—now that it has tides so high they threaten villages and livelihoods—has changed a lot.

'Finished yet, Harry?' Jonty says.

Lucy swivels in her chair. 'Shut up! Or she won't tell us the secret.'

'Lucy,' I say, 'face the front. Jonty, I'll speak to you later. Class, would you like to see my sketches?'

I tell them about my trip to Palau when I was a child, only a few years younger than them. And I give them details about the new ship, and how the foundation will use it for a documentary series. Jonty meekly addresses me as Miss Scott. He asks about Commander Amundsen's scar.

'Did he get it in the Middle East?'

Per's eyes were troubled when I referred to his scar. I'm still not sure why that worries me so much.

'I'm not sure how he got it,' I say.

Jonty taps keys on his laptop. 'He's on the foundation's website. I'll email and ask.'

'I don't know that such a personal question is appropriate. Ask about Antarctica instead. He'll be on the ship for that voyage.'

We talk about the best way to educate people about global warming and sea temperature changes, and the impact of these on the world's environment. Then I outline my ideas for competitions for school children, and we think up names for the ship to replace *The Watch*.

'What about *The Watch II?*' Jonty says.

'That's boring,' Amber says. 'What colour's the ship?'

'Mostly white, some black.'

'What about *The Polar Bear?*' Lucy says. 'Because the ship's going to the South Pole with Commander Amundsen.'

'To rescue the polar bears!' Amber says.

'Except ...' I say, 'there aren't any polar bears in the South Pole. They live in the North Pole. Any other suggestions?'

'How about *The Penguin?*' Lucy says. 'There are penguins in the South Pole.'

'There are heaps of ships called *Penguin* already,' Jonty says.

Lucy slumps in her chair. But only for a moment. 'The Adélie! That's an Antarctic penguin. You can call the ship *The Adélie*.'

The kids are making so much noise discussing names that we don't hear the bell until the final ring. We're clearing our desks when Jonty asks another question.

'Will you go to Palau with the ship?'

I've completed hundreds of sets of breathing exercises, but I'm no closer to swimming than when Kat came to dinner.

'I'd like to go.'

'Will you be the captain?'

'I'm not qualified to be the captain.'

Lucy turns towards Jonty again. 'She's not allowed to be the captain because *The Watch* sank,' she whispers.

'I hope to be a gofer on the ship, and work with the documentary crew,' I say.

'You had plaits last time you went there,' Lucy says. 'They were *so* cute. Will you have plaits again?'

I laugh. 'If I do get to go, I'll think about it.'

* * *

The Scott Foundation: Environment Adventure Education

Professor Tan recently announced that the foundation has leased a ship—a 1,900-ton OPV. For now she's going to be named The Adélie (thanks to my Year 7 Geography class for their fabulous suggestions!). With your support, the foundation is hoping to buy her next year.

As modern day Scott and Amundsens, Commander Per Amundsen and I will be keeping you up to date. We'll be telling you about the polar explorers who went to the remotest regions of the world in the 1900s, and what's happening in the North and South Poles now. Because oceans are warming worldwide, with serious environmental implications …

Harriet

* * *

Per and I exchange emails the day after the post appears on the foundation's website.

Harriet. I saw your post. Don't send anything out that mentions my name without my written approval. Per

I won't say Roald Amundsen was a control freak, without letting you know first. Harry

I won't tell anyone Robert Falcon Scott was an accident waiting to happen. Per

CHAPTER

12

A few days ago Jonty asked whether I was going to Palau. I'll never get there if I don't progress more quickly.

I walk along the beach at least twice a day. This evening I'm on the rock shelf at the northern end of the beach. Sometimes I walk to the rock shelf at the southern end, close to the pool. But I haven't felt confident enough to put a toe in the water yet. I won't do it today, either. It will be dark soon, and Professor Tan and I are representing the foundation at a function tonight.

I twist my hair into a knot at the back of my head and secure it with my hair band for the third time. It's not surprising it's blowing around everywhere because there's a stiff breeze tonight.

I come to this spot at dusk whenever the tide is out. The northern rock shelf is sandwiched between a towering sandstone cliff and the sea. The rock pools nearer the cliff face, where I am, are roughly circular and puddle depth. They dry out when the tides are low and the days are warm. The rock pools where the waves break are deeper and darker, and irregularly shaped. They're fringed with black and white barnacles, lime green algae, and limpets. My heart thumps as I approach the narrow crevice. It's less than a metre wide but filled with seawater that ebbs and flows with the tides. I could almost step across it but instead I back up and take a running jump, clearing it easily.

I've only taken a few steps past the crevice when I hear a bark. It's Dougal, Allan's dog. He's at least thirty metres away, near the waves that break on the rocks. There's no sign of Allan.

'Dougal! Come!'

He looks at me and barks again. He's agitated about something; it's obvious even this far away. When I call again he yelps. Why won't he come?

There are two surfers in the distance, sitting on their boards. I call out, hoping they can check on Dougal, but they're too far away to hear me.

As Dougal continues to bark more and more frantically, I make my way towards him. I keep a close eye on the foaming whitewash and reassure myself that it's metres away from where Dougal is. I skirt around myriad rock pools, avoiding them all, shallow or deep. The algae and seaweeds are slippery under my feet but finally I'm standing opposite Dougal with the crevice between us. It's no wider than it is near the cliff but the water is turbulent and flows over the edges. One of Dougal's front legs is wedged to the first joint, between two rocks. His eyes are fearful. He's sopping wet; drips fall from his long golden coat.

'Hey, Dougal. What've you done with Allan?' I hardly recognise my own voice. It's high pitched and shaky. I'm standing on a narrow section of rock between two rock pools, each a couple of metres wide. There's a crevice directly in front of me. 'This is a pretty shitty situation, isn't it?'

He yelps again. I look towards the cliff. I could walk back the way I came, cross the crevice where I usually do—where the rocks are smooth—and navigate my way back to Dougal. But traversing the rock shelf on the other side of the crevice would be just as perilous as doing it on this side. And the tide is coming in. The waves could reach Dougal at any time. I look for the surfers again, but they've gone. There are a few walkers on the beach but they're too far away to hear me when I shout.

I lock gazes with Dougal. He wags his tail. 'Don't know I'm the right girl for this job, boy.' He wags again and whines. I swallow down the nausea.

I can't wade across the crevice. It's too deep. I could sit on the edge of it and ease my way into the water, and then reach for the ledge on the other side and pull myself up. Great in theory, but I'm likely to have a panic attack halfway through the exercise. My only other option is to jump it. But there are no flat rocks here like there are close to the cliff, only rock pools and scattered rocks, some big, some small. I can't do a running jump. I'll have to do a standing one.

I take a few deep breaths, aim for a spot on Dougal's right, bend my knees, and spring. I can't risk slipping into the water either side of me, or the water in front of me, so my jump is long and high. I anticipate losing my balance and falling, but I don't expect Dougal to free himself a moment before I land. He careens into my airborne body in a joyous welcome and we roll together over the rocks. There's a burning sensation on my face and side, and a shooting pain in my shoulder. Then I'm lying flat on my back. I'm winded. There's a sea lion on my chest and I'm fighting for every breath.

Only it's not a sea lion, it's Dougal. I push him off as I roll onto my side but he continues to lick my face as I get my breath back. It's wet under my hands when I stretch them out. The waves are close. I roll onto my stomach and stagger to my feet. The cliff is in front of me and the waves are behind.

'Dougal!'

I think that's Allan's voice. I'm shivering. When I wipe my hair from my face it sticks to it. I think I have blood on my cheek. It's almost dark now but my eyes adjust to the half-light. I inch my way towards the cliff, skirting around the rock pools like I did before. Dougal follows. I stop when I have to, breathe deeply, and rest my hands on my knees. I only retch a couple of times, but my head is throbbing.

Allan is standing on the sand at the edge of the rock shelf. He sees me and waves. I continue to take tiny steps as I make my way towards the cliff and finally reach the smooth rocks where I usually walk. Dougal follows me all the way on three legs. By the time we reach Allan I've warmed up a little, and my breaths are more regular. He holds out his hand as I step from the shelf to the sand.

'Careful, Harry,' he says. 'Dougal, what were you thinking, lad? Running off like that.' Dougal's tail swishes against my leg when we reach the sand. Allan embraces me tightly. My shoulder hurts, but I hide my wince. The two surfers run up. I recognise one of them from school. He's sixteen and his name is Luke.

'We saw you and the dog from the car park,' he says. 'You okay, Miss Scott? You've got blood all over your face.'

I wipe my cheek on my sleeve. 'Just a few scrapes.' I get onto my haunches and my hip twinges. My pants are torn; they rub uncomfortably against my thigh. I pull Dougal's ears. He whimpers, and Luke picks him up, laughing when he slobbers in his ear.

'Gross!'

We're walking slowly towards Allan's car, parked in the car park behind the low dunes, when I remember my date with Professor

Tan. The second surfer, who's not much older than Luke, is the only one with a phone. My hands are too cold to use it so I give him Tan's number and ask him to dial for me. He waits for it to start ringing, and then he hands it over.

'Harry,' Tan says. 'Your ears must be burning. The commander is here. We were just talking about you.'

So Per is back. 'I have to bail tonight,' I say. 'I had a fall.' My teeth are chattering. It's hard to hold the phone. My fingers are frozen.

'What? I can barely hear you.'

'I'm at the beach. I'm all right, just a bit sore.' The phone slips out of my hand and Luke's friend catches it just before it hits the ground. When I tell him I don't need it back, he puts it to his ear.

'She can't talk. Says goodbye.'

I reassure Allan that Liam will patch me up, and then I ask the boys to help Allan get Dougal to the vet. The shivering gets worse as I walk down the few steps from the car park to the dunes. I'm probably in shock. The wind is whipping my hair around, and the thumping in my head beats in time to the pounding of the surf on the sand. I force myself to put one step in front of the other until I get to the house.

At least Liam's not home yet. If he saw me like this I'd burst into tears; it's obvious I've fucked up again.

CHAPTER
13

I can't help grimacing when—after my shower—I look into the full-length mirror behind my bedroom door. These aren't injuries I can explain away by saying I ran into a tree branch while I was adjusting the volume on my phone. The graze on my face is superficial but it extends from my left temple to my cheek, and it's fire-engine red. The cut on my chin won't stop bleeding. And I've wrenched the shoulder I hurt in December, so I have to hold my elbow by my side to support my upper arm. My pyjama top is damp because I can't get my arm high enough to tie my hair up, so it's dripping down my back.

I'm sitting on the sofa when someone bangs on the front door. It's probably Jonty, asking whether Drew will be here tomorrow. I've just got my hip into a comfortable position, and I can't muster the energy to get to my feet.

'Come in!'

The front door opens and clicks shut. Then I hear footsteps. A man's footsteps in hard-soled shoes. I'm staring at the entrance to the living room wondering who it is when Per strides in. He must've been expecting to see me, but he stops dead and stares when he does.

I'm speechless too. And I'm not sure whether it's because I'm so surprised to see him, or because of what he's wearing. When I thought Polarman up at the mediation, I asked Per whether he had a white dress uniform. He told me, grumpily, that the Norwegian dress uniform was black.

I'm guessing he's wearing it now. He shrugs out of the jacket and throws it over a kitchen stool. The rows of decorations on the front of the jacket and the thick gold stripes on the sleeves sparkle under the lights. His gaze locks with mine as he walks to me, hitches his trousers and squats. His shirt is starched white, and tight across his chest. It smells ... lemony, and has a stiff pointy collar. I suppose he should be wearing a tie but he must have taken it off.

He puts his hand to the uninjured side of my face. His fingers are warm against my cheek. I'm sure I'm not meant to find the gesture comforting but I do. Probably because I'm even colder than usual, and my teeth are chattering. He closes his eyes for a moment. And then frowns when he opens his eyes, and catches me staring at his inky black lashes. He puts his other hand to the back of my neck and tips my head upwards so he can stare at me more thoroughly. His fingers are threaded through my hair. He's so close I can see myself reflected in his pupils.

'*Jesus*, Harriet,' he says. 'You're a mess.'

I twist away, and poke my elbow into his chest. It hurts my shoulder but it's worth it because he lets me go. Now I'm used to the sight of him and he's not touching me anymore I get my voice back.

'Leave me alone.'

'Wish I could. What happened?'

'What are you doing here?'

He rubs his chest where I elbowed it, and wraps his other hand around the back of his neck, like he has a headache.

'Tan sent me. We both made a calculated guess you'd done something stupid. Were you in the water?'

I massage my shoulder. 'I was walking on the rock shelf, and then Dougal got his foot stuck in a rock pool near the waves. I fell while I was helping him.'

'Who's Dougal?'

I hesitate for a moment. 'Allan took him home. He's okay.'

There's another knock on the door. Per tightens his lips and stands to attention.

'Come in!' I shout.

It's Allan. He's pale, and looks every minute his seventy-three years. His gaze moves from Per to me.

'Hey, Allan. This is Per, Commander Amundsen. Per, this is Allan Lane.'

The men shake hands. Then Allan sits on the edge of the sofa, and clears his throat.

'How are you feeling, Harry? I'm terribly sorry about what happened.'

'I'm fine, Allan. Per, you were just leaving, weren't you?'

'No. Why did you say you were sorry, Mr Lane?'

Before Allan can answer, I butt in. 'Allan's had a shock, Per. Leave him alone.'

Allan pats my hand. 'I don't mind answering the commander's question, Harry.' He slowly shakes his head, and then he turns to Per. 'Dougal was chasing seagulls, you see, and then he got carried away. I had no idea where he'd gone. But then I saw Harry, walking across the rocks towards the sea. Well! I knew she'd never do anything as dangerous as that unless something was amiss, and—'

'Dougal was chasing birds?' Per says. He looks at me accusingly. 'He's a dog, isn't he?'

'It's in the genes,' Allan says. 'Him being a retriever.'

I'm twisting my fingers together, refusing to meet Per's gaze, when Liam runs up the back steps and into the house. He pushes past Per and Allan to get to me.

'What happened?'

'It wasn't her fault,' Allan says. 'She's been walking around the rock pools for weeks without incident.'

The scratch on my chin must be bleeding again. Liam, tight-lipped, finds a tissue and presses firmly against it. He barks questions at Allan until he gets a disjointed account of what happened. Meanwhile, Per walks onto the deck. He rests his hands on the railing and looks out to sea. There's a half moon and no cloud cover; the white caps on the waves shine silver.

I'm sure Per is listening in. So I try to distract him and Liam by questioning Allan about Dougal. The vet thinks he has a fractured leg, so he's keeping him at the surgery to do X-rays tomorrow.

'Dougal and I can convalesce together,' I say. 'I might have to take Monday off. Meaning I can finish marking assignments. And I can post on the foundation's website, and I can also—'

'Shut up, Harry, you're jabbering,' Liam says. 'What the hell have you been up to?'

Per comes back inside. He and Liam don't *quite* look each other up and down, but I'm certain they're sizing each other up. Per is slightly taller, but Liam is more solidly built. When they shake hands they have serious expressions on their faces. I'm relieved about that because it makes it less likely that Liam is going to call Per 'Polarman'.

'Per Amundsen.'

'Liam Johnson-Barton.'

'You're a doctor, aren't you?' Per says. 'The grazes could've been from oyster or barnacle shells. So … antibiotics? Will you tape her chin, or does it need a stitch? She must've hurt her shoulder again. And what about her hip? She's done something to that too.'

'It's nothing!' I say. 'And I'm sitting here in front of you. Talk to me, not Liam.'

'You can't sit straight,' Per says, giving me a fake smile. 'And you've skinned your thigh.'

'He's right,' Liam says.

I follow his gaze. My pyjama fabric has a pink background, with white sheep in the foreground. A sheep at the top of my leg has red splotches on it from where I've bled through the flannelette. I carefully turn so both feet are on the floor, and smile at Allan.

'Thanks for coming. I'll drop round tomorrow. Maybe we can visit Dougal together?'

Allan looks up at Per and Liam. It's hard to tell which one of them is crankier. But Allan must conclude that neither is going to kill me imminently, because he gets to his feet.

'Sleep well then, lassie. I'll see myself out.'

★   ★   ★

I made myself a mug of cocoa before I sat down and it's sitting on the side table. In order to pick it up I'd have to ask Per to move out of the way. Or risk touching his leg as I reach for it. It must be cold by now anyway.

'I'm going to bed,' I say.

'I'd better examine you first,' Liam says. 'You can follow up with your own doctor tomorrow.'

It's not easy, but I shuffle my bottom to the edge of the sofa, ready to get up. Per comes closer. I think he's going to offer his arm or something horribly gentlemanly, but when I glare he puts his hands behind his back and stands at ease next to Liam. They're like an impenetrable wall in front of me. I take a breath, and stand. They both have shoes on and I don't, making the height differential worse.

'I'm fine,' I say. 'I've put antiseptic on everywhere, and my chin is only scratched. The shoulder needs rest. My hip is bruised. No big deal.'

Liam and Per exchange glances. Then Per looks at me. 'Like I said, you need antibiotics because there's a chance of infection. And you're risking a scar if the cut on your chin isn't treated.'

I'm risking a scar? I'm sore and tired and not game to ask him about his scar again. So I ignore him and turn to Liam. 'Back off!'

Liam suppresses a grin. Then he shrugs and says, 'He's right, Harry. But I'm not going to force you to do anything.'

'I'll do it then,' Per says. 'It's not like I haven't treated you before.'

My face is suddenly hot. I have a horrible feeling I'm blushing. I was naked when he treated me last time.

Finally I find my voice. 'I'm going to bed.'

There's an underlying threat in Per's tone. 'Don't annoy me *too* much, Harriet, because I'm the man who gets you your ship. So do you want him,' he gestures to Liam, 'or me to examine you? Either way I'm staying because I haven't finished with you yet.'

* * *

I'm lying on my bed wearing a sports bra and boy-leg underpants. Liam is leaning over me and sticking tape on my chin. I have an ice pack on my hip. My thigh is stinging because he cleaned it with an antiseptic wipe.

'I don't want to talk to Per. Send him away.'

Liam grins. 'I don't know that I'm *capable* of sending him away.'

He finishes with my chin and admires his handiwork. Then he leans down and kisses my mouth. It's not a peck; it's a proper lingering sort of kiss that lasts for a few seconds. After he finishes he stands and peers down at me. Then he grins again.

'Liam!' I point to my mouth. '*What* has got into you lately?'

'Just checking I'm still straight.'

'What?'

He winks. 'Reckon I've got a boy crush on Polarman.'

I'd like to shout some sense into Liam, but Per is in the living room only a few metres away and the walls are thin. I hiss instead.

'Don't you dare! Have you gone mad? Pass me my pyjamas. Now!'

I slap Liam's hands away as he tries to help me dress. And it's only as I'm doing up the buttons of my clean flannelettes that I realise I should be wearing proper clothes when I speak to Per. The pyjamas cover me from neck to ankles though, and they're comfortable, so I decide to keep them on. I awkwardly tighten the drawstring waist with my left hand because I can't move my right arm properly.

'Sling,' Liam says, reaching into his doctor bag and pulling out a piece of gauze fabric that he folds into a triangle.

'I don't need one.'

'Shut up.' He stands opposite me, positions my arm with the sling, and ties a knot at the back of my neck. 'You'll sleep easier.'

Our eyes meet. Suddenly I'm teary. 'Per will want to talk to me about the water. He has a thing about it. Maybe you should tell him I'm not going to do it anymore, so he'll leave me alone? Even though I don't want to give up, because I do want to swim. For myself, I mean, not him.'

Liam combs his fingers through his hair and sighs. 'I want you to be safe in the water,' he says, 'but I'm not happy you've been taking risks. Needless to say, neither is Polarman.'

'I shouldn't have gone to Dougal.'

He flicks me under the chin. 'It was a stupid thing to do.'

I wrap my good arm around Liam's neck and hug him. 'Thanks for that.'

I was around fifteen when Liam and I met at the rehabilitation unit. He was in second or third year med, on student prac. For the first few months I followed him around the wards like a puppy because he was friendly, windswept, super-smart, and I had a giant crush on him. He came to Dad's funeral. He'd only just graduated and he told me later he'd wanted to ask me out then, but he didn't think it was appropriate because I was on my own, and only eighteen.

'You haven't really got a crush on Per, have you?' I say. 'He scowls all the time.'

Liam turns me around and pushes me gently towards the door. He whispers in my ear as he opens it. 'He's an *action hero*, Harry. And I'm only human. Course I've got a crush on Polarman.'

*   *   *

As soon as he sees Liam and me through the open back doors, Per steps inside from the deck to the living room.

Liam walks past him. 'I'm going for a walk. Harry's sore. Don't keep her up too long.'

When Liam closes the door it muffles the sounds of the surf. Per and I face each other across the room. His sleeves are neatly folded to the elbows; his forearms are tanned and muscular. He rolls the sleeves down and does up the cuff buttons. He seems perfectly comfortable. I can't stand the silence.

'How long have you been out there? It's freezing. And windy. But it is winter, after all. Aren't you cold? Though I guess it's not as chilly as Norway.' Liam said I was jabbering before. I fear I'm jabbering again. When I point to his jacket, thrown over the stool where he left it, my hand isn't quite steady. 'Do you want to put that on?'

He looks at me quizzically, but walks to the stool and picks up his jacket.

'I didn't get a chance to drink …' I glance to where my hot chocolate was when I left the room. It's not there anymore.

'It was cold,' he says.

My gaze follows his to the kitchen. The mug is there, sitting on the bench with all the crockery that was in the sink before.

'You washed and dried my dishes?'

He ignores my question, and puts his jacket on. 'Are you always cold? Is that why you wear pyjamas made out of winter sheets?'

Don't they have flannelette nightwear in Norway? The pyjamas I'm wearing now are light blue with white clouds and navy buttons. I walk past him and close the door from the living room to the hallway. Then I pull out the old electric heater that's wedged between the bookcase and wall, and turn it on. The three bars make clunking noises as they heat up.

'That thing's a fire hazard,' he says. 'And environmentally unsound.'

I need to be doing something, so I go to the kitchen and line up my mug, and another one, on the bench. 'Do you want a drink?'

He follows me. 'Coffee. I can make it.'

Has he been through all my cupboards and memorised where everything is kept? Or is he planning to use his X-ray vision to look through the doors?

'I'll do it. Instant okay?' I point to the dining table and four chairs. 'Please sit.' I refuse to move until he does as I've asked, but even though he's now on the other side of the kitchen bench I'm still horribly aware of him. Is it the uniform? Do I have some sort of officer fetish? I've never had one before. I pick up the jar of instant coffee. The cocoa box is still on the kitchen bench. He filed it neatly between the sugar bowl and the tea canister when he tidied up.

'How long have you known Liam?' Per has pushed his chair back from the table and his legs are stretched out. When he folds his arms and turns his body towards me the gold braid on his jacket collar glistens.

'Is that what you're hanging around to ask me about? Liam?'

'No. What I want to talk about is your aversion to water. But you're edgy. I'm making conversation.'

My hands are so shaky I can't get the teaspoons out. And I feel sick. At first I head for the table, but I don't think I can sit comfortably on a hard chair, particularly if he's opposite me. So I go back to my position on the sofa, sitting sideways with my back to him, one leg straightened and a cushion under my knee. I pull two cushions onto my lap and rest my slinged arm on them. Then I comb my fingers through my hair; it's almost dry. I speak over my shoulder.

'Get it over with, then.'

He curses under his breath. At least I think he's cursing because he's speaking in Norwegian. Then I hear him in the kitchen— boiling the kettle, opening and shutting cupboards, and the fridge, warming up Liam's coffee machine, and grinding beans. He positions a side table close to where I'm sitting and a dining chair on the other side of it. Two mugs appear. One hot chocolate. One black coffee. And a plate with two cheese and tomato toasted sandwiches, cut into triangular halves.

'Eat,' he says.

When I awkwardly reach for the mug he picks it up and hands it to me. Then he goes back to the kitchen and comes back with another plate, puts one of the sandwiches on it, and balances it on the sofa next to me so it's within my reach. He takes half a sandwich from the other plate and eats it silently.

I keep my elbow on the cushions to support my shoulder, and cradle the mug with both hands. He watches me blow into it. It's strong and bitter. I must have grimaced because he puts down his own mug and sandwich and reaches over to take my mug back.

'Sugar?'

'Please.'

I pick up a sandwich half and take a bite. Suddenly I'm ravenous, and it's the best food I've ever tasted. It has ground pepper and sea salt and everything. As I eat my sandwich, and the half of his that he adds to my plate, he tells me he's come to certain conclusions based on personal observation and information he's gleaned from Kat, Tan and internet searches—that I was obviously traumatised by the accident I had when I was fourteen, and ever since then I haven't swum. He theorises that I must've tried most things by now to remedy the situation (he even mentions the disastrous swimming lessons with Roger) and then he lists, pretty accurately, the sorts of medical professionals I must have seen by now. Finally, he asks a question.

'I assume you're suffering from some sort of post-traumatic stress associated with the accident. And that what happened on *The Watch* exacerbated it. Kat said watching her in the shallows made you nervous. Are you on any medication for anxiety?'

I'm feeling much better after the hot chocolate, and one and a half sandwiches. 'No. Anxiety wasn't a problem till I met you.'

'Same here.' He's leaning forward, holding his mug with both hands and studying what's left of his coffee. He's not trying to be funny. He's as grim as ever.

'I think I can help you to do it,' he says.

'What?'

'Stop you frowning all the time? What do you think?'

'I haven't a clue.'

'Swim, Harriet. I think I can help you to swim.'

I propel myself off the sofa so quickly that I knock the table onto its side. Then I trip over it. Per catches me before I hit the ground, grabbing my body in such a way that he hurts neither my shoulder nor my hip. My breaths are coming in short spurts. As soon as I have my balance I push against his chest. He hesitates before letting me go. For a moment I just stand there, my mind a maelstrom of thoughts. Like how cold the Southern Ocean was when I panicked and dived into it, and how the water in the crevice on the rock shelf was deep and dark. And how Per's eyes are grey like the stormiest of seas. When I close my eyes against the images, memories of Drew take their place. I think about him taking me to Dr Makepeace, and the hypnotherapist, and countless psychologists. I went to them all just to please him. And every time I failed he patted my shoulder and said, 'Not to worry, Harry, you did your best. You'll be all right. I'll keep an eye out.'

The happiness I associate with Mum and Dad and Drew and *The Watch* is tangled up with the despair I feel about losing them. And the joy and heartache is inexorably linked to the sea and rivers and streams. Yet Per, who probably thinks less of me than anyone I know, is arrogant enough to believe he can fix me.

I step over the mugs and plates and shove the heater out of the way. He follows me; I hear him turn off the heater as he passes it. Then I'm in my bedroom and so is he. When I turn away from the wall and face him, he's only a metre away.

My voice is croaky. 'I don't want help from you.'

He takes a step towards me. I'm not sure what he's thinking. 'I know that, Harriet,' he says, putting his thumb under my eye. 'Don't cry. The salt will sting.' He ignores my flinch, and wipes tears into my hair before they reach the grazes on my cheek. I stand mutely and twist my fingers together. After a while my tears stop and my nose starts to run. I swipe it with the back of my hand. Then I do a huge shuddering hiccough. He looks around, finds tissues on the bedside table, and hands me the box.

I blow my nose. 'Go away.'

He speaks quietly. 'Should I get Liam?'

'Why?' I wipe my eyes.

He comes closer again, and although he's not quite touching me, I smell his lemony shirt. And something else. Surely not salt and ocean again? I lean in and take a deep breath.

'What are you doing?' His eyes crinkle, just a little, at the corners.

Suddenly my heart is thumping double time.

'Nothing to say?' he says. 'That's unusual.'

When I straighten my pyjama top, he watches.

'Those pyjamas are the same colour as the T-shirt you wore to the mediation.'

Why is he talking about my pyjamas again? He waits for a response. I hardly recognise my own voice when I answer. It's husky.

'Cornflower blue. My mother liked it because ...' I don't want to chat with Per. He seems to be closer than he was before. The buttons of his jacket are undone; one of the front panels juts out and brushes my collar.

'Because?' he says.

'It doesn't matter.'

'It's your eye colour?'

'Yes.'

He straightens and jerks his head in the direction of Liam's room, across the corridor.

'You don't sleep with him, do you? Kat didn't think so.'

Is he observing my responses to him, so that he can draw conclusions about my relationship with Liam? I could tell him to mind his own business. Or tell the truth. Or not. Per is honourable. If he thinks I'm with Liam he'll keep his distance. He won't touch my lip with his thumb like he did in the quadrangle, or wipe beneath my eye when I'm in tears. Which will make it much more likely I'll survive being attracted to someone who doesn't like or respect me.

'Have sex with him, you mean? Sure I do.'

He frowns. Looks from me to my bed. It's not a large bed, just a king single because my room is so small. Liam has the big bedroom.

'I don't believe you.'

'He kissed me before, when he was patching me up. Maybe you'd like to check for his DNA?'

Per is silent for a minute at least. I'm sure he's calculating whether Liam would have had time to check me over, tape my chin, and kiss me.

Finally he says, 'What sort of kiss?'

Has he concluded it was just a kiss on the cheek? Is the fact that I haven't had sex for eight years, and never enjoyed it even then, written all over my face? Does he think it's impossible anyone could find me attractive? That Liam would *want* to kiss me?

Before I lose my nerve I take a giant step forward and link my good arm around Per's neck. The arm in the sling lies against his chest.

'Can I touch your mouth?' I ask.

His eyes flash silver, like they did when he touched my lip with his thumb. He hesitates. Then, 'Yes.'

I'm relieved I can surprise him. I'm sick to death of him thinking he knows everything about me.

'You asked what sort of kiss,' I say. '*This* sort of kiss.' I stand on tiptoes and press my lips against his.

He moves his hands to my waist but the rest of his body is solid and immoveable like a statue. I'm not even sure that he's breathing. I pull back a millimetre. I have to show him that Liam kissed me properly. So I run the tip of my tongue along the line of his firmly closed lips. Finally he reacts. Not by opening his mouth, but by making a growling sound deep in his throat. It reverberates through his chest and I feel it against my breasts. It encourages me, so I pull back a little and feather my fingers against his mouth, as if I can soften his lips that way. I trace the contour of his top lip with my index finger, and feel the texture of his bottom lip with my thumb. Finally he exhales, and his breath as he opens his mouth dampens my fingers. The sensation sends a tingling feeling through my body. It intensifies when he grasps my fingers in his and runs them along his lips again.

'I don't want the same kiss you gave him, Harriet,' he murmurs. '*I want my own.*'

His eyes aren't flashing silver anymore, they *are* silver. He's staring at my mouth. Waiting for me. I grasp his lapel and stand on tiptoes again, but I don't kiss him like he's expecting me to. I take his bottom lip between my teeth. Slowly and gently I bite it. Once, twice, three times. When he moans, I pull back.

'Did that hurt?'

His voice is raspy. 'Not sure. Do it again.'

I speak against his lips. 'It wasn't meant to hurt.' I run my tongue over his lip, back and forth, and he makes the growling noise in his throat again. My nipples are so sensitive they're uncomfortable so I press them even closer to his chest. I'm putting to the back of my mind all the reasons I don't like him, and thinking about how nice and warm his body is, and how it was kind of him to make me a cheese and tomato sandwich, and give me half of his. But he's not initiating anything and I'm not sure what I should be doing next. Pushing back, I pretend to be fascinated with one of the stripes on his collar and run my finger over the golden embroidery.

'I don't think I could hurt someone deliberately,' I say.

He dips his head and kisses my neck. He rests his cheek against mine. 'You've elbowed me a few times,' he says. 'And you threw a rock at me.'

'It was a penguin. And I missed. Anyway ... I've never bitten anyone before.'

'Harriet?'

'Yes.'

'*Du. Er. Trøbbel.*'

'What?'

He wraps his arms around me so firmly that when he pulls me tightly against his body I'm totally off the ground. One of my legs slips between his and he clamps his legs together to hold it there. When I lean forward the tingling sensation between my thighs intensifies and I gasp. He swallows the sound because even though our lips aren't quite touching, he's breathing in all of my breaths and I'm breathing in all of his. I want to kiss him so badly I ache with it.

But then he jerks his head away and puts me on my feet again. He steadies me when I sway. Then he takes a step back and drops his hands by his sides. It's as if we've never touched. His face is set and his eyes are arctic cool. My heart is hammering against my chest and my breaths are coming in short sharp gasps. He looks over my shoulder. He raises his brows. His tone is even.

'Yes, Liam?'

Liam is leaning against the doorframe. His eyes move from Per to me, and back to Per. It's obvious he's been there for a while. One leg is crossed casually in front of the other. He has a book in his hand.

'Sorry to interrupt,' he says. 'Wanted to return this.' He walks very deliberately between Per and me and puts the book, which he borrowed about a year ago, on the bookshelf with my other books. 'You okay, Harry? Thought I told you to take it easy.'

'Yes.' My voice squeaks. 'All good.'

Per stands at ease. 'Harriet and I may be spending a lot of time together in the next number of weeks. You don't have a problem with that, do you?'

He knew Liam was there. He held me like that because he wanted to see Liam's reaction. To ascertain whether he would be jealous, or angry. Liam isn't either of these things, which means we don't sleep together. Per glances at me. He raises his brows as if he can read my thoughts. I don't think he's attracted to me at all. He couldn't have recovered so quickly if he was. He merely wanted to catch me out because I'd lied to him.

Liam stands next to me. 'I'll have a problem with it,' he tells Per, 'when Harry does. Until then you can do whatever you want.' He adjusts the sling knot at my neck 'Night, Harry.' When he gets to the door he turns briefly. His eyes meet mine. 'I'll be in my room if you need me.'

* * *

A minute passes, and then another. Per is facing the window and holding the windowsill, but there's nothing for him to look at because the blind is down.

'I want to go to bed,' I say.

He turns. His eyes are back to normal. Basic grey. 'I shouldn't have come in here. Or let you kiss me. It complicates things. I apologise.'

'Piss off!'

He puts his hands in his front pockets, tips his head back, and stares at the ceiling.

'I'm on shore leave, most of the time, for the next few months,' he says. 'It'll take a week for you to get over your injuries. We'll start the Monday after next. Six every morning so I can be at work by eight thirty. Here is as good a place as any.'

'I'm a liability, remember? A danger to anyone who has anything to do with me. Why are you doing this?'

'You're exhausted. We'll discuss it next week.'

My voice is uneven but I'm determined to get the words out. 'I want to get it over with now.'

'Sit down, then.'

I can barely stand so I do as he says, perching on the side of my bed. Then I listen silently as he explains how attempting to get me back in the water will benefit the foundation, Tan and him. Because when I do stupid things, like I did today, it reflects badly on all of us. He confirms that I can be involved with the Palau trip if I learn to swim. And this, as a result of my marketability, will improve the foundation's chances of buying the ship.

'I want that ship for three Antarctic expeditions,' he says. 'I agreed to the Scott and Amundsen idea on that basis. You owe it to Tan and me.'

'What if I don't agree?'

'You risk Tan questioning the strength of your commitment to the foundation. And you'll further compromise your credibility. Sinking *The Watch*, being unable to travel to Palau … Tan knows you'll stick around. But maybe he'll find someone else as well—to take the risks that you can't take.'

'You?'

He shakes his head. 'If we get the ship he already has me.' He hesitates. 'It'd be more likely to be a woman anyway. Someone capable. Gutsy. Someone like Kat.'

Per has pinpointed all my vulnerabilities—my fear of the water, guilt about losing *The Watch*, passion for the foundation. And I appreciate he's insulting me as a means to an end—he thinks if I can swim I'll be more useful to the foundation. My eyes are burning so I switch off the light on the bedside table. When he stays in the shadows I turn my back on him and lie down. My shoulder aches and my hip is uncomfortable. My chin stings when I rest my face on the pillow.

I want to say I'll see him on Monday week so that he'll leave, but it's impossible to hold the tears in. All I can do is swallow, and make muffled whimpering noises. It's pathetic. After a while he walks to my bed. When he touches my hair I jerk away, and then make a squeaking noise because my shoulder pulls.

He takes a step back and speaks in a gruff whisper. 'Harriet? What's your answer?'

Grant was young and thoughtless when he humiliated me. Per is acting deliberately. He's powerful. He has to be in control. Finally I manage a reply.

'Like you said, *sir*, it seems I have no choice.'

CHAPTER
14

Allan is facing a group of Amazons, and supervising their stretches. It's sunrise, and I'm walking along the beach in their direction. My leg is stiff and sore, and my face is red and bruised, but my shoulder is feeling much better. Liam grunted as I tiptoed down the hall at six o'clock. He told me he'd serve breakfast on the deck in two hours, so I'd better be back in time. I've taken the sling off my arm because I need my right hand. I walk up the steps to the paved area in front of the surf club and sit on a bench. The easterly breeze has flattened the surf so there are more paddle boarders than surfers out in the swell. I watch them for a few minutes before opening my sketchbook.

I rarely do self-portraits, but I have to get these images out of my mind and onto the page. I'm wild-eyed and angry in the first sketch. In the second I'm in the sea. Lifeless eyes stare back at me. My mouth is open.

I have no idea that Jonty is behind me until he speaks. 'Hi, Harry. What're you drawing? Who's that?'

'You gave me a fright. And I'm insulted. I'm drawing myself.'

He tilts his head to the side and gives my face a once over, and then he glances at the sketch again.

'How come she hasn't got gravel rash and a black eye? That'd be deadly. How's Dougal? Gran said he's got a broken leg.'

'He has. I'm in much better shape than him.'

'Can I come to your house today? Else I'm stuck with Gran. She locks me up in the afternoons. Like prison.'

Jonty lives with Helga most of the time because he's not getting on well with his father. When I give him a schoolteacher look, he curls his lip. Perhaps his dad is right— Jonty has been spending too much time hanging around with older kids, the ones who smoke dope and skip school.

'Your mum and dad want you to go to another school, closer to where they live, and further away from the beach. Helga is helping you out by letting you live with her. She's the one stuck with you, isn't she?'

'Guess,' he says.

'Drew will be at my house this afternoon. I'm sure he'd be happy to see you. And maybe you can surf with Liam later, *if* it's okay with Helga.'

I give Jonty money for a coffee and a Coke at the surf club café and then I look at the page in front of me. All I see is a lousy derivative of Munch's *The Scream*. In the scheme of things—drought in Bangladesh, the highest tides ever in the Maldives, armed militia killing innocent civilians in Sudan—going back in the water is no big deal. Because all I'll have to endure is heart palpitations, migraines, panic attacks and nightmares. In the meantime, I'll continue to raise funds for *The Adélie* whether I get to go to Palau or not. I rip out the sketch, scrunch it into a ball, and throw it into the bin a few metres away. A man holding a little girl's hand is walking past. He must have seen my throw because he gives me a thumbs up. I don't know him, but he recognises me.

'Harriet Scott! What've you done to yourself, then?'

'Had a fall last night. Nothing serious.' I wave at the little girl. She's about four, with long black hair. When she stares at me the man tugs her hand.

'Don't gawp, Ava. Say hello. You know Harriet. From the television.'

The girl's eyes widen. I smile at her. 'Hi, Ava. My face is swollen. Have you ever hurt yourself and got a bruise?'

'I fell off my bike and my knee had blood and I had to go to the doctor.'

'Were you speeding down a mountain?'

'I was at the bike park. I like your long hair.'

My hair is blowing around everywhere—I can't put my arms behind my head to tie it back.

'Thanks,' I say, patting the space next to me. 'Come and tell me about the bike park. Any ramps or jumps?'

After Ava has filled me in, and I've said goodbye to her and her dad, I contemplate the first sketch. Why did I get so upset last night? I don't like the idea of Tan questioning my commitment to the foundation. I don't like the way that he and Per are forcing me to swim on their terms. I'm sick of being told I'm incompetent. But there's no need to be wild-eyed angry like I am in my drawing. Cool-calm angry is much better. I tear out the page and rip it into eighths. Then getting up carefully, I walk to the bin, and watch as the pieces of the sketch flutter through my fingers.

★ ★ ★

Jonty gobbles down two poached eggs and three slices of toast. Then I send him to Helga's house to ask if it's all right for him to spend the day with me.

Liam is poking at my chin. 'Looks okay.'

'Can I take the plaster off?'

'No. Like Polarman said, it'll scar if it's not taped up.'

I shake my head. 'You're the medical doctor. You don't have to defer to him.'

Liam goes to the kitchen when the toaster pops up. He comes back to the table and throws a slice of toast on my plate, and one on his.

He sits, and shrugs. 'Reckon he's had experience on the battle-field though. You know, bullet wounds, land mine victims, that type of thing.'

I'd like to argue but it wouldn't feel right. I can see Per all too easily in that setting.

'You're not over your crush, then?' I say.

'The way I wedged you into bed last night was his idea. Bloody good solution for hip and shoulder injuries where there's no hospital bed to jack you up.'

I roll my eyes. After Per walked out of my room, I heard him knock on Liam's door. They talked for a few minutes in an under-tone before Per left. After I'd been to the bathroom, Liam came and made me comfortable with cushions and pillows.

'Okay,' I say. 'I concede it was a good position.'

'What about the position I interrupted?'

'Please don't bring that up.' I move my plate out of the way, rest my hot face on my forearms on the table, and look at him side on. 'He wanted to find out whether you and I were together, that's all.'

Liam nudges my arm until I raise my head. 'He could've just asked,' he says. 'Why did he care anyway? Why did he kiss you?'

'I'm not sure that he did.'

Liam laughs. 'You're not sure?'

'Shut up, Liam. It was complicated. And your fascination with him is driving me mad.'

'Polarman doesn't know that you're tough. He's just concerned.'

'Concerned he won't get his ship. Other than that, there's nothing.'

'So why'd he have an erection?'

'What!' I jump up to clear the plates away. 'Liam, please stop.'

'Just stating a fact. When he … may or may not have kissed you, he had an erection.'

'How would you even *know* that?'

Liam puts on a serious face and deepens his voice. 'I'm a doctor, Harry. Trained to observe subtle changes in the human body.'

I put my hands over my ears. 'Liam!'

'Even though this particular change wasn't at all—'

'Liam!' My face is really hot now. Did Per have an erection? I guess men get them all the time so it's no big deal. But … I close my eyes. *Oh God.* Is that what I was rubbing myself up against when my feet were off the ground and I was straddling his leg?

I throw the cutlery into the sink and swish the water around. Images of Per and the water are all mixed up. I'm breathing too fast and then I'm light-headed. Liam must see it. He puts his hands around my waist and pulls me away from the sink.

'I agree he's a control freak, Harry,' he says. 'But he's also an action hero. At least he'll keep you safe.'

★ ★ ★

The Scott Foundation: Environment Adventure Education

Robert Falcon Scott was en route to the South Pole on his ship, the Terra Nova, when he received a telegram from

Roald Amundsen. The telegram read, 'Beg to inform you Fram proceeding Antarctic.' Amundsen, on learning two Americans had made it to the North Pole before him, had decided to venture to the South Pole instead.

Fram means 'forward' in Norwegian—a fitting name for Amundsen's ship because once Amundsen had decided on a course of action he pursued it aggressively. Even though going to the South Pole in Scott's wake, largely unannounced, was thought to be an ungentlemanly thing to do, Amundsen would not be deterred …

Harriet

* * *

Harriet. Only from the British point of view was it thought that Amundsen acted inappropriately. I repeat—don't post anything without checking with me first. Per

CHAPTER
15

The bruising on my face is hardly noticeable by Wednesday, and the graze is settling down. The only mark on my chin is a short red line, covered by a narrow strip of plaster. I'm not fit to play football yet but I've agreed to stand in for Allan as coach. He's staying home with Dougal. My hand is on the front door knob when someone knocks.

'Hey, Harry.'

Kat is wearing leathers, and running her fingers through her hair to spike it up. She grimaces when she sees my face, but I think she's more interested in my football boots than my grazes.

'Per said you were a mess. Sorry to gate crash. What's with the gear?'

Anything I say to Kat will be reported back to Per. She told him that I was frightened when she splashed in the waves, and that she didn't think Liam and I were together. I knew she and Per were close. It was stupid to have been so open with her, walking on the beach, sharing a meal. I've learnt my lesson.

'I'm on my way out,' I say.

She shuffles her feet. 'Sure. No problem.'

Neither of us speaks as I throw the kit bag into the back of my car. Her bike is parked behind it in the driveway.

'You'll have to move your bike.'

'Per warned me you'd be mad.'

I turn and face her. 'The work I do for the foundation is my public life. The rest of my life is private. I made a decision to keep it that way when I was eighteen. I only mix with people who respect that, who don't gossip about me.'

'Yeah,' she says. 'I get that now.'

She can fearlessly pilot a boat in a Southern Ocean storm. But now she's flustered and awkward.

'I'm grateful for what you did in Antarctica, Kat. I'll always be thankful to you and Per for that.'

'But you don't want to see me again, right?'

I shrug. 'Sorry.'

Her shoulders lift when she sighs. 'It's all Per's fault. He sits me down and asks me questions like he already knows the answers.' She slowly shakes her head. 'It gets me every time.'

It's impossible not to like her. 'I hope you have a suicide pill,' I say. 'You'd be useless in enemy hands.'

'I'll try harder next time, Harry. I promise.'

She must think I'm weakening. 'There won't be a next time. You and Per talk, you're friends, but that's okay.'

'We're not friends officially. He's too high ranked for that. Why are you wearing footy gear? They're indoor boots, right? Don't know that Per would think you're ready for a contact sport—'

'I have to go. My team's waiting.'

'I've got something for you.' Kat opens the storage compartment on her bike and takes out a large black backpack with a small red, white and blue Norwegian flag embroidered on the top. 'Per thought this might be better coming from me. It's the best you can get. Full body, leak-proof, welded seams. Back zip with internal neck seal. Four-millimetre thickness for warmth and flexibility. It's hard-core naval, so he had to get a sign off from the quartermaster.'

I swallow. 'I already have a wetsuit.'

'It won't be as good as this one. Not for the ocean in the middle of winter.'

So we will be at Avalon. I'll be able to make a fool of myself on home turf. When I don't make a move to open the bag, Kat takes it out of my hands and pulls out a wetsuit, wrapped in plastic, and then she burrows some more, and shows me thermal skins—mid-thigh bike pants, and a long-sleeved shirt. She measures the thermals against my chest.

'It cost a couple of thousand all up,' she says.

'Two thousand dollars?'

She shrugs. 'That's what they cost. Per paid for it, he didn't care.'

'I care!' I grab the gear out of Kat's hands. It's difficult to cram everything back into the bag but I manage it eventually. Then I zip it up. She's watching me, and grimacing.

'You don't like it?' she says.

'I hate it. And you're welcome to pass that on. Then he won't have to get his water board out.'

She frowns. 'That's pretty offensive. Waterboarding's torture, you know.'

'Yeah … well, so is what he's doing to me. Just tell him I have my own wetsuit. I don't want his.'

'What's he going to do with it?'

'He can shove it down his throat for all I care. Assuming he's capable of opening his mouth. Or,' I thrust the bag at her midriff, 'he can give it to the foundation's new poster girl.'

'Who's that?'

'Ask him!'

Before Kat can say anything else I get behind the wheel and start the car. She has no option but to move her bike out of the way.

It's a five-minute drive to the community centre. I spend every minute of it kicking myself for losing my temper. Why didn't I tell Kat I didn't want the wetsuit because I want to wear Mum's? And why didn't I say that in any case I don't want Per buying me things? Why did I talk about his mouth? She's bound to tell him everything. Will he connect what I said to what happened in my bedroom? To the way I ran my tongue along the crease between his lips? It's *worse* than mortifying. And raising the issue of an alternative poster girl wasn't much better. It'll sound as if I actually care about him speaking to Tan about replacing me. Of course I do, but why did I risk letting him know that?

*   *   *

I'm pretty sure Grant is watching out for me at the door to the community centre because as soon as I approach he looks the other way. He's still blocking the entrance though, so I'll have to deal with him. Do I tell him to fuck off? Or would that be making a fuss over nothing? We were together a long time ago, and his reputation suffered more than mine did after we broke up. Bragging about a fling with a recently orphaned eighteen-year-old was never going to endear him to the locals.

'Hi, Grant.'

He turns around. 'Harry!'

I step into the light.

'What the hell?' he says.

'Dougal knocked me over. Your uncle's looking after him.'

'Heard about Dougal. Didn't realise you were involved.'

'Are you visiting your parents?'

'Worse than that. I'm living with them for a couple of months.' He grins. It's the same boyish smile he had eight years ago, the one that used to turn my knees to jelly. 'I've bought an inner-west practice with a couple of colleagues. I'm working for my uncle and doing locum roles around here until the place is ready. Then I'll move back to the city.'

'How'd you get into a football team midseason?'

'That's a locum role too. One of the guys did his Achilles a couple of weeks ago.'

'Right. Better get my team warmed up.'

★   ★   ★

I'm still congratulating myself on how calmly I handled Grant, and looking forward to telling Liam about it, when the whistle blows to start the second half. Grant appears a few minutes later, joining me on the sideline.

'So you're teaching now?' he says.

'Yes. Geography.'

'I can see you doing that. I bet the students love you.'

'They're great.'

'You haven't changed much, Harry.'

'What do you mean?'

'Still beautiful, even bashed up.'

Grant has kept his distance, not saying anything about me publicly since that one indiscretion eight years ago. And if it hadn't been him who'd forced me to grow up, it would have been someone else. But seeing him gives me an ache deep in my chest because it reminds me of everything I lost at eighteen. My virginity didn't matter much. My innocence mattered a lot. He took away the part of me that used to see the good in everyone.

'Maybe we could have a drink one night?' he says.

'Thanks. But I'm pretty busy.' When I offer him my hand he hesitates, but then he shakes it. I give him a wooden smile, and take my hand back. Then I walk away.

* * *

Kat mustn't have waited long to fill Per in about the wetsuit. When I check my phone after yet another loss in football, there's a text on the screen.

Harriet. Confirming Monday 0600. On your rear balcony. Before we do anything we need to talk. Per.

CHAPTER
16

The tide is out so I can barely see the ocean from the top step of the back deck. It's 5.45 am and I'm waiting for Per to arrive.

Mum's wetsuit fits me reasonably well. If she had lived I'm confident we would have been able to wear each other's clothes. Slim build, long legs and medium height. I'm not sure why I kept her wetsuit for so many years. It's not like it's been useful to me. Maybe it was because—besides the books and photographs she kept on *The Watch*, and her pearls—she didn't leave many personal items behind.

We were at Farnando de Noronha, a mountainous archipelago off the north-east coast of Brazil, the week before Mum died. She and Dad had joined other environmentalists lobbying the UN to declare the region a UNESCO heritage site. There's a lot of footage of Mum and me proudly wearing our matching wetsuits— black neoprene with yellow zips—and diving with hammerhead sharks.

In an attempt to keep the cold out I tighten the voluminous yellow beach towel I've wrapped around my shoulders. My teeth are chattering. I turn my head when I hear a rustle of leaves at the side of the house. The lilly pilly hedge has taken over the path and it's hard to get through, especially in the dark.

Per walks to the foot of the steps and stands feet apart in front of me. Action hero personified. His wetsuit is matt black and fits him like a glove. It shows off the muscles in his chest and his six-pack. His quad and calf muscles are clearly delineated too. He has a backpack slung over one shoulder. I suspect it holds the wetsuit Kat tried to give me last week. He's wearing black sheepskin boots—they should look ridiculous because he has a wetsuit on, but somehow they don't.

I focus on his boots as I stand and walk down the steps. As I pass him I say, 'Let's get this over with.'

His hand shoots out. It's like a vice on the top of my arm and stops me in my tracks. I must be imagining the warm imprint of each of his fingers because it would be impossible to feel them through Mum's wetsuit.

'Like I said in my text,' Per says, 'we need to talk.'

I wrench my arm away. My shoulder pulls a little. 'What about?'

He steps in front of me. 'To start with, you look like a bumblebee.' His hand finds a route through the folds of the yellow towel. He flicks the wetsuit zip tag that lies at my throat. 'And this is too big.'

I gather the towel tightly around my shoulders again and step out of his reach.

'I want to wear it. It's fine.'

'It's old, and off the shelf. This one is custom made.' He drops the bag at my feet. 'Put it on.'

'No.'

The neutral expression he's been wearing evaporates. He clenches his jaw. His nostrils flare. 'It will keep you dry, and warm. You're already freezing and pale and you're not even in the water yet.'

The words 'dry' and 'warm' don't match up with the word 'water'. Before I went to Antarctica I was happy to sail on *The Watch* whenever I took a break from school. Rough seas didn't bother me too much. I avoided the bridge in stormy weather and stayed below deck. Getting to shore in an inflatable boat was manageable—even when I got splashed. And I could watch the surfers and swimmers at the beach without my heart rate increasing. If my feet got wet in the surf I walked up the beach to a safer stretch of sand.

In the past few months just thinking about the water has taken me back to where I was years ago. I clear my throat.

'Thanks for telling me how I'm feeling. I repeat, let's get this over with.'

He blocks my path when I try to walk around him.

'Can we get this over with? *Please sir?*'

'Stop it, Harriet. Put on the wetsuit.'

I throw the towel on the steps and spread my arms wide. 'I'm wearing one already. See? It's not custom made, but I can't think how your wetsuit is either, since I've never been measured for it.'

He takes a giant stride, and grasps my shoulders. Then he looks me up and down. He spits his words at me.

'Your weight,' he narrows his eyes, 'is about 54 kilos. You're a little over 172 centimetres tall. Waist diameter,' he spans it with his fingers, 'roughly 70 centimetres. BMI 22 per cent. Do you want to hear the rest?'

I'm too surprised to answer. I don't know my waist measurement, but the other things are spot on. He's still staring at my body but when I lift my hands to his chest to push him away they freeze. His wetsuit fabric is nothing like I've ever felt before. It's soft, pliable, and silky against my fingers, like the skin of a dolphin. Per slowly inches closer until my hands, palms flat, are splayed on his chest. He's still firing statistics at me. He tells me what my arm span is, and my hip measurement, and makes a calculated guess about the breadth of my shoulders.

'Your legs are about ten centimetres shorter than mine,' he says.

We both look down and compare. From our knees to our hips our legs are only a few centimetres apart. I have the same tingling feeling at the tops of my thighs that I had the last time he held me. I try to think of something else.

'Maybe it's less than that.'

'It's not.' He's so close that when he speaks, his breath ruffles my hair. It's loose; I still can't put my hands behind my head to tie it back.

A kookaburra, the young male that Liam feeds, flies above our heads and perches on the railing. He looks at us and we look back at him. Behind me the sea roars; I hear the waves as they crash against the sand. I'm sure Per would let me go if I pushed against his chest but I don't even try to get away. I'm even more afraid of what's on the other side of the dunes than I am of the way I feel whenever we touch. I think it's me who leans in closer.

'Harriet?'

Our eyes meet. He runs his hands up my arms and over my shoulders. He touches my chin. The cut I got on the rock shelf barely shows now, and the grazes have healed. I like the feel of his fingers.

'You're always cold,' he says, coming so near that our noses almost touch. When I close my eyes he softly growls my name. And then he says something in Norwegian, like he did when he was in my room. I recognise one word. '*Trøbbel.*'

'You're not saying I'm troubled, are you?' I ask.

He takes a breath. 'No. I'm saying you *are* trouble.'

'Oh.' I turn my head to the side so my ear is resting against his chest. His heart thumps. He wraps his arms around me. I should move away but he's so warm.

His thumb moves to my bottom lip, and he presses down on it. He runs a finger along it, back and forth, and whispers. *'Don't clench it.'*

Which reminds me of when I bit his lip in my bedroom, and the argument we had. It suits him and the Professor to get me back in the water at a time that's convenient to them. When I jerk away I hit beneath his chin with the top of my head. He releases me and I stagger, and then we're far apart.

I get my balance, and cross my arms over my chest.

He rubs his chin, looking at me suspiciously.

'I didn't mean to headbutt you.'

'Didn't you?'

'No. But,' I take a breath, 'please stop touching me.'

I turn my back on him and neither of us speak for a while. I listen to his breathing. He probably listens to mine. Now it's my heart that's thumping. I start blowing out breaths like smoke rings, and watch as the white condensation forms gossamer circles in front of my eyes. It's getting lighter now. It must be six thirty. If I can delay him for another hour maybe he'll leave me alone.

It's like he's read my mind. 'I'm not leaving, Harriet. And we may as well deal with this before we start.'

I turn around and face him. 'With what?'

'I'm attracted to you.'

I close my eyes for a moment to gather my thoughts. When I open them again I'm just as flustered as I was before. He doesn't seem to respect me in any way that matters. He thinks I'm incompetent. So surely he wouldn't *want* to be attracted to me physically.

In which case, why bring it up? The silence is never-ending and I have to say something.

'I'm sorry I bit your lip! I don't know why I did it.'

'Because you're attracted to me.'

This is excruciating. He's just standing there.

'You made me a sandwich,' I say. 'And before … I was cold. And anxious. I don't like you. I mean, why would I?'

He blows out a breath. Then he shrugs. 'Have it your way. If you're too immature to acknowledge the attraction, it probably doesn't matter anyway.'

Immature? That's what Grant called me, though it didn't seem to worry him when we were having sex.

The kookaburra is still on the railing. He's looking through the glass to the kitchen, waiting for Liam to appear with his breakfast.

Per picks up the wetsuit bag and throws it on the deck. 'We've still got an hour,' he says. 'I won't take you out of your depth. Not today.'

He doesn't respect my strengths, or understand my weaknesses. I've let him touch me, and allowed myself to feel safe in his arms. My teeth are chattering again. I'm light-headed. He'll tell me I'm pale any moment.

He frowns and holds out his hand. 'Harriet?'

He'll force me to walk over the dunes and down to the sea. He'll do things on *his* terms. I take a deep breath—and run.

CHAPTER
17

Whenever we could, we'd anchor *The Watch* off the coast and set up camp, sometimes for weeks at a time. We'd explore the coastline, talk to the people who lived there, and stretch our legs. Drew would organise an exercise regime for the crew. We'd play games, and race each other. By the time I was a teenager the fastest of the crew could outrun me on the straight, but it was almost impossible to catch me on uneven terrain. Dad once told me I ran like a gazelle. 'If a doe is threatened, she flies over the ground helter-skelter exactly like you do,' he said.

I'm not as fit as I've been in the past, my shoulder is sore, and my hip is stiff, but I have a head start because Per has to kick off his sheepskin boots. I hear him cursing as he does it. I'm heading for the ocean via the dunes. The twisting paths are familiar even in the half-light, and I know where the fences are lowest and easiest to hurdle. I leap over native grasses and shrubs, jump down the steps—two at a time—that lead to the beach, and land on the soft sand just before he does. I swerve, avoiding his hand by a hair's breadth. Then I sprint as fast as Mum's wetsuit allows towards the sea.

★ ★ ★

My quads ache, and my lungs are on fire. Per runs alongside me once we're on the beach. He knows I can't escape with the water in front of me and sand all around. I pull up a few metres from the shore break and catch my breath. The wind is coming in from the east and the waves are over a metre high. There's a rip to the south—the whitecaps are irregular and choppy. A sandbar fifty metres out appears and disappears with the swell. When I turn my back on the ocean I see a figure in the distance walking towards the pool—it'll be one of the Amazons. Otherwise the beach is deserted.

'Why did you run?' Per says. He's not panting like I am, and his voice carries easily over the pounding waves and the stiff breeze coming off the sea. His hair is so short that it barely lifts in the gusts. Mine is flying around everywhere.

'I needed to think. I have to tell you stuff.'

He takes a step towards me. I can't afford to back away or I'll be even closer to the waves, so I hold out my hand and he pauses. If I don't take control of this situation, he will. Even though my voice is shaky, my words are clear enough.

'The water. Even thinking about putting my head under. It frightens me.'

'I see it in your eyes.'

His tone is measured. Is this the voice he uses with the men and women under his command when there's a crisis and he has to calm them down? The one that makes them do what he wants?

'Quit looking at my eyes.'

He looks at my mouth. Then he shifts his gaze to the dunes, and then out to sea. He's breathing deeply; I watch the rise and fall of his chest. He shrugs. 'All right.'

'The fear, it makes me vulnerable. I don't want to be like that, doing things like ...' I wave my arm towards the house, 'like what happened back there. And before.'

He opens his mouth like he's going to argue, but doesn't say anything.

'So if I let you help me with this water thing ...' When I point to the ocean my hand shakes. 'You can't touch me. Or say there's an attraction between us, or anything like that.'

His fists open and close, and his mouth is a thin angry line. I've somehow infuriated him.

'Are you suggesting I'd act inappropriately?' he says. 'That I'd take advantage of your fear for some sort of ... What, Harriet? Sexual gratification? Is that what you mean? *Jesus.*'

'I'm not saying that. I just ...' All of a sudden I'm exhausted. I hardly slept last night. I've been on tenterhooks with Per for what seems like hours. I'm barely three metres from the ocean and my breathing is uneven, my head hurts, and I'm on the cusp of a panic attack. I don't know what I'm thinking or saying anymore. And to top it all off, I was the one who bit him, not the other way around, so maybe I'm making a big fuss over nothing. But he called me immature. I don't trust myself. Or him.

'You have to promise,' I say.

He tips his head back and curses some more. Then he looks me up and down. His eyes are icy grey. 'I will not touch you in any manner inconsistent with getting you to swim. Happy?'

I nod.

'Well I'm not. I'm fucking offended.'

'Yeah, well. Sorry.'

He lifts his wetsuit cuff. He's wearing a fancy black watch. 'We'll start tomorrow,' he says, turning around and walking a few paces. When I don't follow he turns again. Then he runs a hand through his hair and massages his neck. 'I'm meeting the Chief of Navy at eight thirty. He's kind of important. Can we get back?'

The wind suddenly drops. I hardly need to raise my voice. 'Just one more thing. You and Tan, now you're best friends, are forcing me to do this, right? So that I can go on the ship.'

He takes a breath. 'Tan has realised it's not safe to have you near the water. And I don't want the inconvenience of resuscitating you again.'

'Getting me to swim is not going to be as easy as either of you think. I want your word that if you can't fix me in the next few weeks, you and Tan will leave me alone.'

'If you can't swim I won't let you on the ship.'

'I get that. But once you finish your research, I get to do what I want again, like I used to. Do you agree to convince Tan that that's okay?'

As I'm speaking I'm taking tiny backwards steps towards the sea. I don't want to chicken out, so I keep my eyes on Per. The sand is increasingly wet against the soles of my feet. Then the water rises to my ankles. At any moment a wave will rush in. I was hot after running down here. Now I'm freezing again, but sweating too. I wipe the hair out of my face and feel the clamminess of my skin. My heart is racing—it feels like it's about to burst through my rib cage.

'Do you agree? Say it!'

He's watching me walk backwards. 'All right. If you still can't swim when I've finished with the ship, I'll talk to Tan.' He's using his calm voice again. 'You're hyperventilating, Harriet. And so pale it's ... I think you're about to pass out.' He extends his arm. 'Take my hand. We'll do this tomorrow.'

I look over my shoulder. There's a wave twenty metres out. 'You should know what you're in for. I'm worse now ... worse than Antarctica.' The water level is around my knees. It gets lower as the wave gets closer. Words leave my lips in fits and starts. 'I don't only ... retch ... pass out ...'

The wave hits the back of my legs and whitewash froths up to my hips. It splashes my stomach and chest. There's a drag on my lower body as the water is sucked out to sea again. I'm ready for it, and brace myself. Per stands behind me. He's yelling but I can't make out the words. I can see that his hands are on my arms but I can't feel them. At first I'm conscious of the rivulets of water that run down my body, and then all I'm aware of is the roaring in my head.

Per pulls me out of the water and drags me up the beach. As soon as I feel the soft sand under my feet I collapse onto my hands and knees. He must suspect what's about to happen because he twists my hair into a rope and wedges it under the neck of Mum's wet-suit. Then his hands are on my shoulders. For a moment I freeze, then I scurry out of his grasp like a crab. I yell obscenities at him and I think he backs away but I'm not sure because that's when the migraine really kicks in.

Lights flash in front of my eyes. They're brighter than I've ever seen them, but that's what I always think. I count and wait, until the pressure behind my temples builds and my brain explodes into a million colliding fragments. Bile fills my throat. I gag and retch. My chest muscles cramp and my breath comes out in wheezy gasps. I vomit a stream of foul-tasting yellow. Then green. And then foamy white. Tears and snot and saliva run down my face. My teeth chatter; my arms and legs quiver and shake.

I'm aware of voices. What's Helga doing here?

As I struggle to sit she wraps a towel around my shoulders. She tries to brush my hair back from my face but I twist away and do it myself. So she turns her attention to Allan and bosses him around. He gives me a bottle of water so I can rinse my mouth, and passes me Helga's wrap, the one with bright blue and green peacocks on it. I bunch the fabric into my hands.

'Use it for your face, Harry,' Helga says.

I rock on the sand until the pain in my head eases and I can breathe without sobbing. Then I send Helga a weak watery smile.

'I'll ruin it.'

'Don't be silly. It washes beautifully. So blow your nose, there's a good girl.'

★ ★ ★

Per stands a couple of metres away, arms folded across his chest, watching what's going on. The sun is up. It must be well after seven. If his meeting is in Balmoral it'll take more than an hour to get there in the traffic. And he'll have to change first.

'You'd better get going.' My voice is croaky.

His face is grim. 'I have time,' he says.

He crouches by my side and rests his arms on his knees, and Helga and Allan step back. I study his widow's peak. It comes to a perfect point in the middle of his forehead, as if it's been carefully drawn there.

I meet his gaze. 'Sorry.'

'No you're not. You did it deliberately.'

'You didn't have to hang around after you got me out of the water.'

'But then …' He glances over his shoulder at Helga and Allan. They can't hear him, but he lowers his voice anyway. 'I'd have missed your performance.'

I pull Helga's towel more tightly around my shoulders. I'm still shivering. Why did I have to show him what he was letting himself in for? Was I hoping he'd be put off and leave me alone? Or did I want him to see I was so badly broken that he wouldn't be able to fix me? I'm afraid of crying again so I close my eyes tightly. But then he grabs my chin. I'm so surprised I open my eyes and the tears escape and run down my cheeks. He takes a deep breath. And snarls.

'You want us to feel sorry for you? After what you just did?'

'No! I didn't know Helga and Allan were there.'

He grasps under my arms and hauls me to my feet. He hisses his words. '*You knew I was there.*'

Once I have my balance he lets me go. I jerkily turn my back and wipe my face with the wrap. There's a wet patch on the sand where I vomited so I methodically spread layers of sand over it until it disappears. I'm dimly aware that Helga and Allan are talking to Per. They tell him about the Amazons, and he asks polite questions about midwinter temperatures in Avalon, and wind chill factors.

And then he walks away without saying a word to me.

I refuse to let Helga and Allan walk me home. 'I'm fine,' I say. 'Go and have your swim.' I feel their eyes on my back as I head for the dunes. I look over my shoulder and shout. '*Please* go. I'll see you at the party tonight.'

It's a cloudless morning and the sun warms the sand underfoot. A silver soft drink can discarded on the path catches the light. The reflection, just for a moment, shines into my eyes and blinds me.

*   *   *

The Scott Foundation: Environment Adventure Education

A few people have asked me why Robert Falcon Scott wasn't rescued. This isn't an easy question to answer.

A week or so before Scott died, two men from the British base camp restocked One Ton depot (a scheduled stop in the final leg of Scott's journey). While the men were there, Scott was only eleven miles away, too exhausted and malnourished to leave his tent.

The actions to be taken in the event that Scott didn't make it to One Ton depot or base camp (within the expected timeframe) had never been clearly defined. Scott put the fact that a dog crew had not arrived to meet him as 'a miserable jumble'. It appeared he thought there were no dogs available to do the task, when in fact there were. Could Scott have been rescued? Were the men charged with coming to his assistance at fault? If they were, Scott didn't bear a grudge, seemingly attributing their failure to the inherently dangerous conditions in Antarctica. In one of his very last journal entries Scott wrote that 'no one is to blame'.

Scott accepted his fate. He and his men were on their own. In a blinding wilderness of white.

Harriet

CHAPTER

18

My house is packed to overflowing for Drew's sixty-fifth birthday party. The chatter and music is loud and cheerful. Most people here are Drew's regular weekend visitors. Many are around his age, others are younger—sailors he's worked with on *The Watch*, and environmentalists he's mentored over the years. Drew seems to be enjoying himself, even though he can barely remember who most of the guests are. Thank goodness he hasn't forgotten me yet, or Mum and Dad.

'Within a year he'll lose all of his memory,' his doctor has said. 'Shortly after that, you'll lose him altogether.'

Drew sees me across the room and smiles. I smile back, and then pirouette to remind him I'm wearing a dress. Our eyes meet again and he laughs. He turns to the woman next to him, one of the documentary producers we've worked with before, and takes her hands and bows. She follows him when he leads her to the corner of the living room where I've cordoned off a dance floor. Spotify is set on shuffle. Liam and the other men complain whenever a seventies disco song or a ballad from the eighties or nineties blasts out of the speakers.

There's a lot of footage of Drew and me dancing together—with Ghanaian drummers, North American boot-scooters, Turkish belly dancers. He used to say he only got into trouble when I *wasn't* dancing with him, like the time he waltzed with a dictator's mistress in Cuba, and did the tango with a Geisha in Japan.

Helga puts her hand on my arm. 'Take the quiches out of the oven,' she says. 'Allan, pass around the dips. Liam, go to my house and get four more bottles of sparkly from the fridge. Turn down the music please, Jonty.'

We all grumble, but do as she asks. She corners me between the oven and the kitchen bench. She doesn't notice that Jonty turns the music up again.

'It's a lovely party, Harry,' she says. 'And I'm glad you put a dress on.'

'Told you it'd look fine with the jumper over it.'

Helga lifts the baggy black jumper above waist height and surveys my body. 'I'm using my imagination to picture you without the camouflage. Are you feeling better now?'

I've been refusing to answer her questions all evening. 'I'm tipsy.'

'But you've only had a sip of cider.'

'I talk too much when I drink.'

'You should be enjoying yourself at your age, not working all the time. When you're not at school you're doing something for the foundation. And now there's this swimming business with Commander Amundsen.'

'I like to be busy. And I enjoy what I do. Mostly, anyway. Sorry about this morning.'

'Have you apologised to the commander?'

'Sort of.'

'Maybe you should do it properly. You told him to keep his hands off you, even after he'd been good enough to pull you out of the sea. And you called him a freak.'

Besides wishing I could die—immediately—I can't remember much about what happened after the wave hit.

'Did I call him a control freak?'

She nods.

'That's not so bad, then.'

Helga purses her lips. 'Harry ...'

'Okay, I'll think about it.' I take Helga's arm and lead her out of the kitchen. 'Want to dance with your favourite girl?' I call to Drew.

He watches me approach, and holds out his arms. The song has a dance club beat—Jonty's choice—but Drew and I dance slowly. The others on the dance floor step back, form a circle, and watch us. One of the crew has a word to Jonty, who finds Rod Stewart's 'Sailing' on my phone. I'm weepy as Drew and I sway together. He pulls me tighter and pats my shoulder.

'You'll be all right, Harry. I'll keep an eye out. You'll be all right.'

★   ★   ★

We're tidying up when Liam tells me that Per called.

'Drew was holding your phone when it rang,' he says. 'He told Per you were here, and wearing a dress. And that you had a queue of men waiting to dance with you.'

'*Liam!*'

He laughs. 'I took the phone away from Drew. It was difficult to hear what Polarman was saying, what with the music and drunken laughter in the background, but I got the distinct impression he wasn't expecting you to be dancing.'

'He can't control everything I do.'

Liam shakes his head and sits on the sofa, pulling me down next to him. 'I think he called to see you were okay, Harry. Anyone'd think you *wanted* him to think the worst of you.'

'He wasn't suspicious about Drew I hope.'

It's not easy to perpetuate the lie that Drew was in tip-top mental health before *The Watch* went to Antarctica. Particularly as he's deteriorated so dramatically in the past few months. I tell people that dementia set in from January, but I'm careful to keep Professor Tan away.

'You shouldn't have lied about the date of his diagnosis,' Liam says. 'Or about what happened with *The Watch*.'

'I wanted to protect him. I still do.'

Forging documents to hide what Drew had neglected to do to prepare *The Watch* for Antarctica was wrong. I lied under oath. And I misled the maritime inquiry. But now it's done. No one will ever be able to say, 'He was a brilliant sailor in his day, *but then* …'

I look at my watch and yawn, trying to hide the tremor in my voice. 'Is Per coming at six? Is that why he called? No point going to bed if he is.'

'Off the hook for now, Harry. Said he had things to reassess in light of what happened this morning, and that Tan would be in touch.'

★ ★ ★

Harry,

Can you meet with me at the university on Friday, seven o'clock? Per will join us shortly afterwards.

There are two agenda items. Firstly, the commander wants medical confirmation that going back in the water won't harm you. Secondly, he wants your agreement that you'll follow his instructions.

You know I want you on board for the October voyage, so I trust you'll do your best to reassure the commander he has nothing to worry about on either count.

I appreciate you have a function at Taronga Zoo at eight the same evening, so I won't keep you long.

Xiao Tan

CHAPTER
19

I arrive early to the university. There's no point going to Tan's office because he keeps me waiting even when I'm on time.

The Ancient History museum is near the main quadrangle. The museum is closed, but the curator is working in his office nearby. I tell him my name, and he lets me in.

'Your mother was a graduate,' he says. 'As was your father.'

The old bones and artefacts remind me of Mum, and the bits and pieces she'd dig up. She never kept anything. She'd convince local museums or elders to take her treasures, and then she'd worry about whether they'd have the resources to care for them properly. Dad used to tease her about it.

'Harry's quite small. You'd better not put her into storage by mistake,' he said one day. The three of us were on our hands and knees in a hut in Thailand, cataloguing pottery fragments. Someone had pilfered them from Angkor Wat.

Mum smiled at Dad. She had a really big smile, like mine.

'Harriet's the most precious thing in the world,' she said. 'I'd never leave her behind.'

*   *   *

Tan reads the letter from Dr Makepeace. 'Thanks for this,' he says, nodding. 'Precisely what we needed.'

He's sitting behind his desk and peering at me over his glasses. I'm perched on a chair opposite. He wasn't happy when I walked into his office at five past seven and told him I had to leave by seven thirty, but he's looking very pleased with himself now.

'You don't mind me showing it to the commander?'

'After he put you up to this? Slap his face with it for all I care.'

Tan barks a laugh. 'Strange how you two don't get on.'

'It's not surprising, given how we met, and what's happened since. Not that our antipathy seems to bother you. Why is that, Professor?'

He blinks a couple of times. 'Sometimes, Harry, you're *too* direct. Let's just say I'm a physicist. I enjoy making sense of all sorts of things. You and the commander have the potential to work well together for the benefit of the foundation and, by extension, the environment.' He rests his elbows on the desk and props his chin on his hands. 'That's my primary focus. And yours, I presume?'

'Yes.'

'The other agenda item—will you follow the commander's instructions?'

'Sure. Within reason.'

'So you agree to wear the wetsuit he provided?'

I wanted to wear Mum's wetsuit. When I got home from the beach on Monday I rinsed it in the laundry tub and hung it on the line to dry. And then I carefully folded it and packed it away.

'If that's what he insists on.'

Tan frowns when he sees the tears in my eyes. 'He mentioned it specifically, Harry. He said he'd had it made for you.'

I have a jumble of images in my mind. Per's hands on my body, confirming the lengths of my limbs. Per standing over me, accusing me of *performing*.

I get to my feet, fiddling with my bag strap. 'I hope the foundation's not paying for it.'

'I don't believe so.'

'Right, then. Better go.'

'Just one more thing. I understand you've negotiated other matters regarding the commander's assistance. Care to tell me what they are?'

Per agreed that he wouldn't touch me unless absolutely necessary. He also agreed that once he'd finished with *The Adélie*, even if I couldn't swim by then, he'd help me to convince Tan to let me on board. I can't think how I can tell Tan about the first condition without sounding like I can't handle myself, or the second without it seeming like I'm going behind his back. If Per hasn't said anything, I'm not going to either.

'Nope.'

Tan only has a moment to be annoyed before there's a knock at the door. I glance at my watch. It's seven thirty. Time to go.

* * *

Per smells of soap. I try not to breathe in too deeply but it's an effort not to because it's a nice, fresh, clean sort of smell. Not ocean, but almost as good. His hair is damp. And just like last time we met here, all his clothes are black: V-neck long-sleeved jumper, trousers and canvas shoes. I'm suddenly self-conscious about my white sneakers, blue skinny jeans, and blue and white striped jumper. Am

I wearing a sailor suit? He's breathing slightly faster than usual. He must have walked quickly to get here. He looks at me again. Then he looks away. Just like he did at the beach.

Tan places another chair next to the chair I was sitting in, and gestures for us to sit. Per waits for me.

'I'm leaving,' I say. 'The professor will fill you in.'

'Stay, Harry,' Tan says. 'I won't keep you long.' He turns to Per. 'Harry's agreed to follow your instructions, Commander. And she's provided a letter from Gordon Makepeace, the adolescent psychiatrist. He's an excellent fellow, known him for years. The letter states that there's no physical or physiological reason that stops Harry from swimming.' He pushes the letter across the desk as he speaks. 'Read it for yourself.'

Per asks for my permission.

'Like I have a choice?'

'Is that a yes?'

'Yes, *sir*.'

He reads the letter and hands it to me, narrowing his eyes. 'It says you shouldn't go into the water alone. So why did you go onto the rock shelf?'

'I wasn't intending to go in the water.'

'Like you weren't intending to be incompetent, and sink *The Watch*?'

When Tan clears his throat and suggests we look to the future, Per gives me a fake smile.

'Sorry,' he says. 'Badly phrased. Just one more question though. Have you been back to the therapists referred to in the letter?'

'I'm not answering that.'

'I'll take that as a no, then. Which makes sense. You never ask for help when you need it.'

'Piss off.'

Tan looks at me over his glasses. 'That will do, Harry. The commander's agenda items have been satisfied. You can go now.'

I'm putting Dr Makepeace's letter into my bag when I think up my own agenda item.

'The accident in Brazil,' I say. 'If we do this, I don't want Per badgering me about it, asking personal questions.'

'I have no *personal* interest in you,' Per says, 'after what you said on Monday.'

'You can barely look at me. Why are you insisting on doing this?'

His eyes, darkest grey, bore into mine. 'Like I've said before, you're dangerous yet marketable. It's in the foundation's interest, and my own, to keep you alive until we secure the ship. Preventing you from drowning is a means to that end.'

It's like there's not enough air between us anymore. I take a step back. I'm cold, and the tips of my fingers are white. Tan grimaces. I think he's wondering whether it'd be more worthwhile to stick up for me, or side with Per.

'Thanks for the letter, Harry,' he says, 'and for agreeing to toe the line with the commander. We'd better let you get to the zoo.'

Per wins.

My hand is on the doorknob when Per speaks again. 'Harriet?'

I don't turn around. 'Yes?'

'I'm at sea for the next two days. We'll start again on Monday morning. Six o'clock. I'll get the wetsuit to you beforehand.'

I'm too choked up to articulate anything sensible in reply.

★ ★ ★

Taronga Zoo is twenty minutes from the other side of the Harbour Bridge, and the traffic is still heavy so I'm half an hour late. The woman who meets me at the door shepherds me into the bathroom. When I look into the mirror I understand why.

I have a wild-eyed look. So I take a few deep breaths. Then I smooth down my hair, and smear lip gloss over my mouth. Thinking about Per and Tan and the meeting will have to wait. One of my laces is undone so I do that up, and then I pull my stripy jumper down over my hips.

When I'm led to a table next to the stage, a man with bushy brown hair and a red beard gets up, smiles widely and pumps my hand.

'I'm Robbie Matheson, a vet working on the orangutan-breeding program,' he says. 'I understand we have a mutual friend, Grant Reid. We were at uni together.'

I swallow and smile. 'What made you specialise in orangutans? Is it an advantage that you have the same colouring?'

He laughs. 'Yes!'

The CEO of the zoo takes my arm and we walk to the stage together. He tells me I'm the third and final speaker at the orangutan fundraiser, and I only have a five-minute slot. Then he whispers that he suspects the guests have heard more than enough about orangutans from the other speakers in the past thirty minutes, and they're keen to eat their main courses.

The waitstaff move from table to table, putting plates in front of the guests, as the CEO talks about the zoo's animal sponsorship program. Some guests pick at their food while pretending to listen to what the CEO is saying. Others fill their glasses, or talk to each other.

Finally I'm introduced. I put my orangutan speech in the back pocket of my jeans, rest my arms on the podium and speak into the microphone.

'People far more knowledgeable about orangutans than I am have already spoken to you about them, so the CEO suggested I talk about something else. When I asked him for direction, he said, "Say whatever's on your mind".'

Two camera guys come closer to the stage. A beautiful russet-haired woman in a sparkly red dress sitting at a table in front fiddles with her phone; I see the recording light flash red.

'What's on my mind tonight is that things don't always turn out the way that we intend. For example, I was reminded only an hour ago that even though I didn't intend to sink *The Watch*, I had to take responsibility for doing so because it was my fault that the ship got stuck in the storm in the first place.'

Guests put down their knives and forks.

'Losing *The Watch* was a personal tragedy for me. But far more importantly, it was a loss to the environmental movement. The ship, and my parents, and Drew McLeish, and others who supported them and their causes over the years, were inspiring. They encouraged ordinary people like me and you—nurses, tradesmen, teachers, lawyers, shop assistants, mums and dads—to care about the environment, and be prepared to stand up and take responsibility for what the human race, through carelessness and ignorance, has done, and continues to do, to destroy it.'

Orangutan vet says, 'Hear, hear.'

'In the past few months I've been called incompetent and foolish. Whether intentionally or not, we all make mistakes. But we also have the capacity, individually and collectively, to learn from the things that we've done wrong so we can do better in the future. Yet we continue to burn fossil fuels that pollute the air, use chemicals that poison the soil, over-crop and over-stock the land. We destroy the habitats of vulnerable primates like the orangutan. We fish and hunt species to extinction. Our winters are colder, and summers are hotter. Polar ice is melting in the Arctic north and the Antarctic south. Our planet is facing challenges that it's never faced before ...'

I tell the guests that the foundation wants to get people thinking about new environmental frontiers. Then I outline some of the fundraising plans we have, and how we'll tie them in with visits to regions at risk, like Palau and Antarctica, and make a documentary series. When I finally take a breath and look at my watch I see that twenty minutes have passed.

'Questions, anyone?' the CEO says. 'If Harry doesn't mind.'

Quite a few people hold up their hands. The woman in the sparkly red dress stands up. I finally place her—she's a television journalist.

'Who was it that accused you of being foolish and incompetent?' she asks.

'Unfortunately for me, someone who knows what they're talking about.' When everyone laughs, I laugh too, as if being insulted by Per hardly matters. Because it's not like I can name him, after talking so enthusiastically about the Scott and Amundsen connection. 'Next question?'

The orangutan vet stands. 'You mentioned a trip to Palau in October. Do you have any suggestions about what people can do to help you get there?'

★ ★ ★

Liam knocks on my bedroom door on Saturday morning.

'Go away,' I say, burying my head in the pillow. 'It's still dark.'

He opens the door, walks in, and pulls up the blind. 'It's after eight, lazy bones. Let's go for a run. And look what I've got. Someone loves you after all.'

Liam is holding a giant bunch of roses. They're red and unfurled, wrapped in cellophane and tied with a ribbon. He hands me a gift card. *Professor Xiao Tan.*

I give the card back. 'He feels guilty.'

Liam laughs. 'It's a little more than that. Wait till you see the newspaper.' He pokes me in the back. 'C'mon, get up. I've got to be at work by eleven and I want to get a surf in.'

Seeing my smiling face in the paper is a surprise. I didn't mean for last night to be the unofficial launch of the fundraising effort. Luckily there's a picture of an orangutan as well, though it's not quite as big as the photo of Per. His image is the same as the one on the foundation's website—he's wearing his black dress uniform with the gold braiding and the peaked cap that hides his face.

'It's good publicity,' I say, as Liam and I run along the soft sand near the dunes. 'A bit embarrassing though. Quoting my speech like that.'

★   ★   ★

Kat is sitting on the steps to the back deck when Liam and I get home. The Norwegian flag backpack is sitting at her feet.

'Hello, Kat,' Liam says, grabbing his board. 'I'll see you later.'

'Hi, Harry,' Kat says. 'You didn't answer the door. Thought you might be at the beach.' She holds out the bag and grimaces. 'Sorry 'bout this.'

I walk past her. 'Per sends you on a lot of shitty errands, Kat. Pretty hypocritical really, when he says he's not a messenger boy himself.'

She follows me inside. 'He's gone up north for a couple of days. I wanted something to do.'

The new wetsuit is lighter than Mum's; I hardly feel its weight in the bag. I'm sure it's also warmer and fits me better. It will be superior in every way that Per thinks is important.

Kat opens the fridge and gets herself a glass of milk. Then she flops onto the sofa. Her colouring is beautiful. Her skin tone is ivory, and her freckles are a washed-out version of her hair shade. I'd love to draw her in pastels.

'So … what's up?' she says.

I should have as little to do with her as possible. But she's smiling. And she piloted the boat that saved me. I put two mugs on the bench top. Tomorrow morning Per will be here instead of her. I'll have to wear his wetsuit. And I'll have to go down to the beach.

CHAPTER
20

Per is sitting on the top step of the deck, his long legs stretched out in front of him. He's wearing his black wetsuit and sheepskin boots. A small backpack is sitting on the ground at his feet.

I'm glistening like a dolphin because I'm dressed in my wetsuit too. It's a dark silvery grey colour, and although the fabric is much thicker than silk it has a similar texture. It clings to my body; there's not a wrinkle anywhere. The zip is at the back; I had to wake Liam so he could do it up for me. He tied my hair into a ponytail too, complaining as he bunched it into a hairband that he was still half asleep and couldn't see properly in the light from the hall.

Something flashes in Per's eyes as he looks up at me from the step. Then he blinks and it's gone. It could have been admiration, or maybe it's just relief that I'm wearing the wetsuit and he doesn't have to drag me out of bed. He frowns at my bare feet, and kicks off his boots. Then he walks down the steps, shrugs the backpack over a shoulder, and folds his arms across his chest.

'I didn't say you were foolish.' His tone is gruff and accusatory.

He must have read my speech. I walk down the steps and brush past him. 'You've called me incompetent plenty of times. Foolish is much the same thing.'

'The word incompetent is objective.' He narrows his eyes. 'Foolish is more judgemental, critical, subjective.'

I suspect he's studied the English language far more thoroughly than I have. And I don't feel like arguing anyway. I've barely slept, and even though I got out of bed an hour ago and made a slice of toast, I couldn't face eating it. If I don't leave now I'm afraid I'll run inside and hide under my bedclothes.

'Whatever. Let's go.'

He follows me across the lawn towards the dunes. We jump over the low fence that leads to the path. The sun is rising but the shadows are deep and dark. I hesitate when I get to the top of the steps that lead to the beach. The ocean, blacker than the sky, stretches out in front of me, all the way to the horizon. Whitecaps fringe the water close to shore. The beach is deserted. I close my eyes and tip my head back, swallowing. Per moves to my side. My face was colourless when I looked into the mirror thirty minutes ago. It's probably grey by now.

'You have to trust me, Harriet. Totally. For this to work.'

When I open my eyes he's staring into them. His eyes glide to my mouth. My lips are tightly closed. He takes my hand, holding it firmly when I try to pull it away.

'I promised, remember? I gave you my word I wouldn't touch you *inappropriately*.' He takes a breath. 'But I have to touch you while we're here. And you have to touch me. There is no other way.'

I look at him—arrogant and confident. Then I look at the water—beautiful and frightening. When I shove my elbow into his stomach and turn away he releases me. But the sudden movement makes my head spin. I double up with my hands on my knees and retch. It's not a full-blown panic attack and there's nothing in my stomach. All I spit out is saliva.

'Sit,' he says when I've finished. I'm happy to put my head between my knees as he reaches into his backpack and takes out a water bottle. When I've finished rinsing my mouth he stands behind me and hoists me up to my feet. For a moment I lean against him, but then I pull away. What do I want from him? Sanctuary?

My voice is low and shaky; I hardly recognise it. 'This isn't me. I hate what it does.'

'I would too.'

I search his face. He's not laughing at me.

'We're going to walk along the beach,' he says, 'adjacent to the dunes. And then we'll go down to the pool.'

I stiffen.

'Not in the water,' he says. 'I just want to talk to you.'

'How's that going to help?'

'It'll do for today.'

'And tomorrow?'

'Tomorrow we'll do something else. And when I decide what that is, I'll tell you about it. Because I'm not going to trick you, or force you, or make you do anything that you don't want to do. I won't lie to you, either. But there's a price to pay for that. You have to take my hand. You have to let me hold you. I want your body to learn that you're safe when you're with me.'

'My body?'

He nods.

'What about my head?'

His mouth twitches. It softens the shadowy planes of his face. '*Bli med meg,*' he says, holding out his hand.

I hesitate, but take it. His hand is much warmer than mine. He changes his grip and links our fingers together as we walk down the steps to the sand.

My voice is shaky. 'Did you just say, "You must do as I command"?'

'No, Harriet. I said, "Come with me".'

I feel a little better after retching and, like Per said, we're walking near the dunes away from the water. We pass the surf club, with its shower block and toilets. The café is locked up at this time of the morning. He asks me questions about why I chose to live in Avalon, and how long I've been here, and where I work. I'm conscious that he's talking in order to distract me, even though he doesn't have to because holding my hand is distraction enough. I don't want to like the feeling of his warm fingers threaded through mine. I answer in monosyllables and focus on the squeaking noises our feet make as we step through the sand. Before we reach the cliff and pool he veers towards the ocean. I baulk.

'Not much further,' he says.

He stops about ten metres from the waves and I tug my hand away. I sit, bending my knees close to my body and resting my chin on them. Per sits next to me, very close, so our calves, thighs and arms are touching. The breeze is coming from the south, but he's much bigger than me and blocks it.

'Are you warm enough?' he asks. 'That's important.'

I wrap my arms around my legs and rub my feet. 'You know I am. I've got your wetsuit on.'

'It's your wetsuit.' He sweeps up sand and covers our feet. 'I could've got boots and gloves as well. But it'll be better if you feel the water against your skin from the start.'

He frowns when I take a shuddering breath and swallow.

I hear laughter, and look over my shoulder. It's Helga, Allan and some of the other Amazons. They're stretching on the sand. Per sees them too, but he doesn't acknowledge them.

'See the seaweed?' he says.

It's lighter now, and easy to make out a big billowing carpet of seaweed a few metres from the shore, drifting towards the rock shelf and wall that borders the pool.

'*Hormosira banksii*,' I say.

'What?'

'Common brown algae. Up close it looks like little beads joined together. What about it?'

'It's floating.' He points to a couple of seagulls bobbing further out, looking for fish. 'So are they.'

Half an hour ago he said he'd never called me foolish. Does he realise he's treating me as though I am? I stretch my legs out in front of me and create some distance between us.

I lift my chin. 'I already know what you're going to say. That most things can float, and that includes me.'

Per opens his mouth and closes it again. He seems to be choosing his words carefully. 'It's a fact.'

'You're good at facts. Which is why you're going to give me a lecture now, all about people like me, people terrified of sinking. How they try to grasp onto the water.' I send him a fake smile. 'They're so irrationally, pathetically and insanely scared that they thrash around, instead of—'

'Stop it, Harriet. I get it.'

'Instead of lying back and floating. I've already heard that one.'

He curses under his breath. 'Do you want to go home?'

'No!' I turn and face him. 'Because now you've started I'd just as soon you finished. Otherwise I'll have to put up with your hypotheses all week. You'll be lecturing me while I'm throwing up and passing out. What if I miss something?'

He tips his head skywards. 'I appreciate there's no formula for this.'

'But you think you're qualified to give it a try anyway? Without asking me what's been tried already.'

'That's unfair. When I asked you questions after you fell on the rock shelf, you refused to answer any of them. You're bloody impossible to deal with.'

'You could've asked again.'

'My apologies.' He pretends to smile, just like I did before. 'We could have a drink together tonight, maybe dinner, and discuss this sensibly, like *adults*.'

'Fuck off.'

He's quiet for ages. I think he's trying to get his calm voice back again. 'I know about post-traumatic stress disorder. I don't believe you have that.'

'Are you sure, *Doctor*?'

'But some of the symptoms are similar. Do you get nightmares?'

'Yes.'

'Would you care to elaborate?'

'No.'

'Slowing your heart rate—'

'Will stop me panicking and puking. Right?'

He speaks through his teeth. 'It might.'

'But I can only slow my heart rate if I feel safe and comfortable. I know all this! I'm good on the theory. So there's no need to patronise me, or treat me like an idiot.'

He frowns. 'I haven't—'

'Yes, you have. You talked about seaweed and seagulls and floating. And I'm pretty sure I know what's coming next. Psychoanalysis.'

He closes his eyes. 'Let's not talk about this now.'

'I want to get it over with.'

He waves his hand as if he's giving me the floor. 'Go ahead.'

I clear my throat and try to keep my voice steady. 'As a result of a childhood trauma, I have a fear of the water, and that's why I avoid it. While this coping mechanism keeps me safe, it means I'm unable to move forward in my life.'

I'm at eye level with him. He's thoroughly pissed off. 'Are you done?' he says.

We stand at the same time. And then he reaches for my hand. When I put it behind my back he swoops in and grabs it. He tugs—hard—and I stumble, barely getting my balance before he picks up his backpack and marches along the beach. Sometimes I have to jog to keep up. We're slightly closer to the waves than we were on the way here, and every once in a while he strays even closer, and then lets me steer him away. Our fingers aren't linked together, he's firmly holding my fist in his hand instead. My nails are pressed into my palm, but if I open my fingers I'm afraid he'll think I want to hold his hand properly again. He doesn't say a word until we're close to the dunes, where he halts, mouth tight and nostrils flaring. He releases my hand and glowers down at me.

'Congratulations, Harriet,' he says. 'You've been foul tempered, childish and fucking annoying, generally all at once. I'll see you tomorrow morning. We'll go to the pool. Bring your phone and earbuds, then you won't have to listen to anything I have to say.'

I watch his departing back as he strides through the dunes. My anger and resentment and fear are all mixed up with the emotions I have whenever he takes my hand.

A seagull stands one-legged on a fencepost near the dunes. He's a handsome bird, very well groomed, with a bright yellow beak. I study him for a while.

'What would you do if you were me?'

He stares. Then he blinks and flies away.

CHAPTER
21

Liam and I are up at three the next morning.

'It's unfair of you to keep this from Polarman,' he says, pushing his fringe out of his eyes. He still has a crease running down the side of his face; he must've been fast asleep when I woke him. We're sitting on the sofa in the living room, cradling mugs of ginger and valerian tea.

'He asked if I had nightmares,' I say. 'I told him I did, but I wouldn't tell him anything else.'

'He'd get a better understanding if he knew the details.'

'You don't know the details.'

'I have to put up with your screams. I have an idea.'

I squeeze his leg. 'Sorry. But I think I'm showing him enough of me already. Panic attacks, vomiting, everything else.'

'You're giving him a hard time. You need as many excuses as possible.'

'I want to go into the water on my terms, not his. He's only got this power over me because of Professor Tan, and Palau.'

'Hate to point it out, Harry, but your terms weren't working for you. And don't forget he's an action hero. Meaning he has the capacity to help, whether you want him to or not.' Liam taps my nose. 'You'd usually be practical enough to see that. It's doing your head in, not sleeping well.'

It's not unusual for me to dream about the accident, but it's been happening nightly since I fell on the rock shelf. Liam took me by the shoulders this morning and shook me until I opened my eyes. He wrenched me upright and I sobbed all over him, crying like a baby.

'What time do you have to be at the hospital?' I ask. 'Go back to bed.'

He yawns. 'Seven. May as well stay up and get some reading done.' He shudders and puts his mug on the coffee table. 'This tea is awful.'

'It's meant to settle the stomach and calm the mind. Sorry I woke you up.'

'That's okay.' He winks. 'Least I get to see Per in his Polarman costume.'

I elbow him. 'Shut up. I hate your man crush. Is my face blotchy?'

He studies it. 'Eyes like a puffer fish. Same dream?'

It's always the same dream. Though it's more a re-enactment than a dream, because everything I dream about actually happened. The four-wheel drive went around the bend and swerved because of the truck in its path. Then the road gave way, and suddenly we were airborne, and crashing down the gorge like a ball in a pin-ball machine. I'm not sure how long I blacked out for, but when I opened my eyes it was quiet, eerily so. I imagined feeling the dampness of the forest in the car. Dad was unconscious. The car was lying on its side and he was on the high side, still strapped to his seat, suspended from his seatbelt. He had a gash in his head; blood was running down his forehead and dripping off his face. I couldn't look away.

'Dad?' The sound didn't come out properly. It was barely a croak.

'Harriet?' Mum said. I couldn't see her, but she sounded close.

'I'm here, Mum.'

'Thank God.'

Mum was in the front passenger seat, and I was behind her. Our side of the car was on the ground; all I could see out of my window were rocks and murky green shapes. I leaned forward, trying to see Mum. The car shifted and tilted forward, like it was going sideways down a steep hill.

'No sudden movements, darling,' Mum said.

I found out later she'd broken her arm, pelvis and a leg. But you wouldn't have known it. Her voice was calm, patient. It was the same tone of voice she used when she was braiding my hair and telling me not to fidget.

'Is your seatbelt still on?' she said.

'Yes.'

'Undo it if you can, or slip out of it. Can you see Dad's toolbox?'

It was still strapped to the back of Dad's seat. 'Yes.'

'Good. The window above you, Harriet, behind Dad's window, you have to smash it open. That's how you're going to get out. Find something in the toolbox—a spanner, or screwdriver, or use the box itself.'

I glanced at the window. Everything outside was blurry. I couldn't think why that was.

'Dad can't get out that way,' I said. 'Why can't I open the door above me? Then I'll open his door. I can pull him out, and you can push.'

Mum hesitated. 'I've hurt my arm, Harriet, and I can't undo my belt.'

The door I was wedged against was wet. What had been a trickle of condensation running down the inside of the windscreen was now a stream of water, making it even more difficult to see outside. But I still didn't understand what had happened. Everything—my thought processes, my speech—was laboured. Then Mum went quiet. I could hear her breathing but she wouldn't answer me when I asked about the windscreen. I thought I had to think things through for both of us.

'I'll get Dad out. And come back for you. Is that all right? Don't worry, Mum, Dad's not dead. He's still bleeding, so he can't be. Drew will be here soon, and get him to the hospital in Brasilia. Won't he? He was only an hour ahead of us. He'll search when we don't turn up.'

'Yes,' she finally said. 'Drew will come.'

There were scraping noises then, and a whining sound. The car shifted again, tilting even further forward. Then Mum said, very quietly, so I had to strain to hear her, 'I love you, Harriet. So does Dad. Have you taken your seatbelt off yet? Do that, and then get the toolbox. Hold onto something when you break the window, because you'll be forced backwards. The car may move again. It doesn't matter. Get to the surface and Drew will come. Quickly, darling.'

I undid my belt, struggled to my knees, and grasped the strap that attached the toolbox to the back of Dad's seat. I'd just got the buckle open when the windscreen shattered. There was no explosion, just a relentless crackling sound. And then, as water flooded into the car, everything made sense—the blurriness outside the car, the dampness within. The car had been under water all that time. And now the water was coming in. It reached my chest within seconds, a bubbling churning mass, and then I was kicking my way through it, squeezing my body between the seats to the front of the car. By the time I got there Mum was underwater. Dad was still hanging from his seatbelt. There was a pocket of air above his head but most of his face was submerged. I tasted his blood in the water. I tried to lift him higher but I wasn't strong enough to keep him there, so I had to let him go. I screamed for Mum but of course she couldn't answer me. I took a breath, and dived—

'Harry?'

It's an effort to open my eyes and focus on Liam. He's squatting next to me. 'Let it go,' he says, grasping the tops of my arms.

'Sorry.'

'Want a hot chocolate? To get rid of the taste of the tea?'

I give him a shaky smile. 'Better not. Throwing up milk might get messy.'

He strokes my cheek with his index finger. 'Go get dressed then, Polarwoman. I'll do up your zip, and tie back your hair.'

'You can't call me that. He won't let me go to Antarctica, remember?'

*   *   *

I open the back doors as soon as I see Per on the deck. Liam pushes me out of the way and walks outside first, even though I told him to stay inside.

'Greetings,' Liam says, shaking Per's hand.

'Morning.' Per nods in my direction as he kicks off his boots. 'Harriet.'

Liam puts an arm around my shoulders. He smells of coffee. 'Take care,' he says. 'See you tonight.'

Per walks down the steps and across the lawn. I have to run to catch up. He stops dead when I grasp his wrist. I take a deep breath as I link my arm through his and thread our fingers together.

'I'm sorry about yesterday,' I say. 'And for going into the surf when Helga and Allan were there.'

He looks at me suspiciously. 'You're apologising?'

'Liam said we're on the same page, that I should be practical. I'd like to go into the water again. You want to please the professor. We both want *The Adélie*.'

It's still dark. We're standing under the washing line. The waning moon casts stripy shadows over Per's face. He's frowning.

'You've been crying,' he says. 'Why?'

When I blink up at him, he raises his brows. Is this a test? I'm sure he knows I want to tell him to mind his own business, or to piss off. I straighten my shoulders.

'The thought of going under the water gives me nightmares. I can't stop the crying when I'm asleep.'

'What do you dream about?'

'The accident. And you've promised not to ask about that. Remember? In Professor Tan's office.'

Now he's cross, but he's trying to hold it in.

'So let me understand this,' he says. 'One, I can't touch you *inappropriately*.' He looks at our hands, still joined. I see the incongruity as clearly as he does. Holding his hand makes me feel safer, just like he said it would, but there's an undeniable physical attraction between us as well.

'That's right,' I say, tightening my grip.

He doesn't say anything for ages. Then he takes a breath. 'Two, you don't want to hear anything from me that may be categorised as a *lecture*. Three, I'm not allowed to speak about the accident.'

'Yes. They're my conditions. But point two is tricky. I don't like long silences—they make me uneasy. But I'm not likely to have much to say because,' I gesture towards the ocean, 'you know, the nausea. So while I don't want you to lecture me, you can still talk.

If you want.' My nose is cold and my teeth are chattering. 'Can we walk now, while you talk?'

I have to tug his hand to get him going.

'What do you want me to talk about?' he says.

'I don't care. Anything, really, just nothing personal about me. You're an environmentalist. So am I. Talk about that.'

'I'm an environmental scientist,' he corrects.

'Whatever. What was your PhD topic?'

'Climate variability and anthropogenic factors in polar regions, with a specific focus on the internal dynamics of glaciers.'

'Well, then. There you go. Fascinating stuff.'

I'm dimly aware of him smiling as we reach the top of the dune and the steps that lead to the beach. But then the taste of the ginger and valerian tea takes over. It's rising up to the back of my throat. I have to keep swallowing it down. The surf isn't large today but the waves are dumpers, unpredictable and dangerous. Even experienced surfers avoid waves like these. They can break boards. And bodies.

I jerk my hand out of Per's grasp moments before I retch into the grasses. It doesn't take long. He hands me the water bottle once I'm upright again. Then he takes my hand and we walk down the steps together.

'Your conditions are ridiculous,' he says.

'You have to agree to them.'

'No I don't. But I will. Because like I said yesterday, you have to trust me.'

I take a deep breath. 'At the beach?'

'That will do for now.'

My steps slow as Per and I, hand in hand, step onto the concrete landing at the southern end of the beach. The landing is like a deck, and overlooks the pools. The pool closest to the sand is the children's pool. There's also a much larger, deeper, rectangular pool. It's too early for the Amazons, but this is where they swim their laps. The large pool is bordered on the short sides by the children's pool, and the southern rock shelf and cliff. The landing, and a rocky wall that leads to the ocean, border the long sides.

Seawater floods into the pool when the tides are high, or the waves are big, or the weather is stormy. Today the surf is small and the tide is out. The water in the pool is still, except where it's ruffled by the breeze. Even so, I'm swallowing compulsively. What if I throw up on the concrete? How will I wash it away without going near the water? What if people step in it?

I freeze when we approach the pool steps. There are five of them, each about a metre long and a ruler-length wide. There's an aluminium railing either side.

Per is still talking. He's speaking calmly and without expression about how difficult it is to extract and transport core samples, notwithstanding significant developments in coring technology. He's been on the same topic since we stepped onto the sand.

'Analysing ice core samples allows for the measurement of climate variation over millennia,' he says. He tugs my hand. When the only move I make is to lean backwards, he stops talking about ice. 'Harriet?'

My eyes lock with his. They're darkest grey. They're probably reflecting the colours of the ocean but I try not to think about that. He prises his fingers away from mine and puts his hands on my shoulders. Then he moves so close that I have to tip my head back to keep my eyes on his.

'I'm going to be sick,' I say.

He jerks his head towards the pool. 'You're not getting wet. I'll sit above the top step. You can sit next to me. We'll work our way down.'

'You said you wouldn't force me.'

He frowns. 'I won't.'

'I can't walk.'

'I'll pick you up.'

He slides one arm beneath my shoulder blades and the other behind my knees as he scoops me up. He takes one step, and adjusts his grip.

'Per!' I launch myself out of his arms.

'Jesus!' he says, bending his knees and catching me. 'What are you ...'

My body convulses in a giant retch. He swears, puts me onto my feet and drags me to the far end of the pool, where the rock shelf is. Moments later I'm on my hands and knees. I've already vomited the ginger and valerian tea so there's nothing much left. I dry retch for a while.

Per stands back and leaves me in peace until my breaths have quietened. When I sit he gives me a chamois to wipe my face. He squats in front of me.

'Sorry.' I swallow. My words are a jerky series of croaks. 'I thought you were going to throw me in.'

He's terribly serious. He shakes his head. 'I would never do that.'

The thumping in my head is settling down. So are the flashing lights. 'You said if I made trouble you'd throw me off the *Adelaide*.'

'When?'

'On the phone. When you told me you were going to the Swedish Ambassador's cocktail party.'

'I've changed my mind. Now I want you to trust me.' When he holds out his hand I take it, and he pulls me to my feet. 'Should we make a second attempt?'

When I take a shuddering breath and nod, he picks me up again.

'Tighten your arms around my neck,' he says.

It's not like he has to ask, I'm holding on like a barnacle. I haven't been held like this since I was a little girl, and Dad or Drew lifted me into their arms. When Per sits down he takes me with him. I'm not sitting next to him. I'm on his lap.

'Åpne øynene dine,' he says. 'Open your eyes.'

I'm not in the water. But when I see that his feet are resting on the first step of the pool and he's wet to his ankles, my stomach rebels all over again. He tips me forward and rubs my back as I spit saliva into the pool.

CHAPTER

22

Per and I have been at the beach—excluding the weekends—every morning for the past four weeks. We must be up to day twenty.

I'm sitting on his lap on step three of the pool, breathing into the warm soft skin where his collarbone meets his shoulder. He smells fresh and salty, just like he always does. If I lift my face a little higher, up against his neck, there's a hint of pine as well. He's always cleanly shaven when he arrives on my deck.

'You know it's fashionable to have a three-day growth?' I say.

'Not in the Norwegian Navy,' he says. 'Unless you're on leave.'

I press in closer and he tightens his arms around me. I hear the Amazons laughing as they warm up on the sand, and the waves as they crash on the shoreline. Neither of us speaks until he says, 'Are you falling asleep, Harriet, or struggling for breath?'

He's more aware of when my heart rate goes up or down than I am, so he must know I'm doing neither of these things.

'I'm just breathing like a normal person,' I say. 'Stop micro-managing me.'

When I'm relaxed like this, which doesn't happen often, I try to hide my awareness of his scent, and the feel of his body as it holds onto mine—the way his hands move up and down my spine, and the way he sometimes rubs his cheek against the top of my head. Being comfortable in his arms makes me feel safe. He'd be happy about that. But I've banned him from thinking inappropriate thoughts. He might have a problem with me taking pleasure from lying here, breathing him in.

'Stop wriggling. *Du er umulig.*'

I sit up straighter, and look into his eyes, narrowing my own. 'I am ... what?'

'Impossible.'

I shrug and rest my face against his neck again. Then I stretch my legs out so they float on the top of the water. I move my feet up and down in a careful kicking motion.

'Should I put my hand in?' I move one of my arms from around his neck, and rest it on his chest. His heart thumps. My hand quivers. He puts his hand over it.

'You've had enough for today.' He rubs my hand. 'You have the coldest hands on the planet.'

'It's been weeks and I'm only waist deep. I'll never get to Palau at this rate.'

He rests his chin on my head. 'Stop chasing deadlines. You've got to be in control of your heart rate before you move on.'

'I have to overcome my fear of the water before I learn to swim. Not the other way around, right?'

'You said it, not me.'

He hasn't lectured me since the day we sat on the sand and argued. Not in English anyway. I'm pretty sure he does it in Norwegian, particularly when I'm throwing up into the rock pools, or refusing to do what he says.

I link my hands behind his neck. After a while he stops scowling.

'It's humiliating how I do what you tell me to do. I'd rather be disobedient, like Dougal.'

The corner of his mouth twitches. It's the first time he's smiled today.

'Your heartbeat, Harriet,' he says. 'Focus on that. On Monday we'll come to step three again. If you can match your breathing to mine within the first half hour, you can put your hands in the water.'

I didn't get wet for the first three mornings we came to the pool. I sat on Per's lap on the landing above step one. I listened to his heart and the slow regularity of its beats. On day four I put a foot into the water, and on the following day, both feet. Eventually my calves got wet and we moved to step one. Then it was step two, where sitting on Per's lap the water reached up to my thighs. We started on step three at the beginning of this week.

I trace his scar. 'Why won't you tell me how you got this?'

He should be used to me asking about his scar by now. But he can't seem to stop himself stiffening and blanking his expression. 'You know I don't talk about it.'

'It's because you can't tell a lie, isn't it? A normal person would just make something up.'

'It's a personal matter.'

'Like swimming's a personal matter to me.'

'Heartbeat, Harriet. Focus on that. We've still got two steps to go.'

I study step four. The water will be up to Per's neck by then. Say he slips? He may be an action hero but he's got a scar. Something or someone has hurt him. I can't breathe under water. *But neither can he.*

The tide of nausea is sudden and overwhelming.

'Harriet!'

I don't need to say anything when this happens. Per feels it in my heart rate.

He stands with me in his arms, walks up the steps and strides along the landing. Then he supports me around the waist as I drop to my knees. He shields me from anyone who might be able to see me from the beach as I heave into a rock pool. When I've finished I sit on my haunches and lean against him while I catch my breath. I scoop water from another rock pool and rinse out my mouth.

'I shouldn't have eaten anything before we left. It makes it go on longer when I do.'

'It's better that you eat.'

Sometimes I have a glimmer of hope that I'm improving, but then it's obliterated. We could be back on step one on Monday morning. When I was with Roger, I could swim with my head above water. And then I fucked it up. If I do the same thing this time I'll be letting Per, Tan and the foundation down. It won't do my self-esteem any good either.

'Can we go?' My voice is croaky.

Per's still standing behind me. He speaks quietly. 'Tell me what set you off.'

I silently shake my head. Then I get up and walk along the landing to the top of the steps, and pick up his backpack. I'm drinking from the water bottle when I turn and bump into him.

He takes my arms above the elbows and frowns into my eyes. 'Harriet. Tell me.'

Tell him what? That it was the image of his head going under the water that tipped me over the edge? That I was concerned about him? It adds another level of craziness that I'm not sure I want to share.

When I twist in his arms he releases me. The Amazons are still warming up. I worry that sometimes they'd like to be in the pool earlier than seven, but they don't want to interrupt me and Per. Helga is lying on her back, leaning on her elbows. She smiles when she catches my eye. She lifts her legs in the air and points her toes. All she's wearing is a one-piece swimming costume.

'Morning,' I say, sitting next to her and wrapping my arms around my knees. 'Aren't you freezing?' The temperature can't be much more than eight degrees. That's not bad for winter, but the wind off the ocean is cool. It's less sheltered here than it was at the pool.

'I'll warm up soon enough. I saw you on step three again. Well done, dear.'

Per appears. He stands at ease with his hands behind his back. 'Good morning, Helga,' he says.

'Hello, Commander,' Helga says, beaming at him.

'If you insist on calling me that, I'll have to address you as Mrs Lamont.'

'You'll do no such thing. I enjoy calling you Commander. It impresses my friends at bridge when I tell them you've joined the Amazons.'

He frowns. 'I'd prefer you didn't mention me. Or Harriet.'

Helga rolls onto her side, then stands and scoops up her towel. She looks up at Per in an imperious way.

'I'm not a gossip, young man. None of the Amazons are.' She touches my shoulder. 'Goodbye, Harry.' Per and I stare after her as she walks to the pool.

'Harriet?' Per holds out his hand. 'Let's head back.'

'What were you thinking?' I say, taking his hand and pulling myself to my feet. 'As if Helga would talk?'

'I was warning her in order to protect you.'

'Liar! You were protecting yourself.'

He tips his head back. I imagine him counting, so I say the numbers out loud, the ones he uses with me when he's encouraging me to match my heart rate to his.

'*En, to, tre, fire* …'

'Stop it.' He links our fingers together. 'Let's walk.'

'All right. But it's true—you were protecting yourself. I guard my personal life, but I don't hide away from people like you do.'

Other than letting the foundation use his official navy photo, where his peaked black cap obscures his eyes, Per has refused to get involved in any of the foundation's fundraising efforts. Tan and I didn't have high expectations of him doing so, but we were both hoping he'd get more comfortable with the idea and show up at some of the functions. But all he's agreed to do is limited publicity relating to the December trip to Antarctica. And he tolerates the foundation linking his name with Roald Amundsen in my posts.

'If I was prepared to argue with you,' he says, 'I'd dispute that.'

'And if I wasn't being civil to you, I'd tell you I don't need your protection because I'm perfectly capable of looking after myself.'

He squeezes my fingers. I'm not sure whether it's an acknowledgement, an admonishment or because he wants to shut me up. But as we're only a couple of metres from the surf now I don't much care what he's thinking. There's hardly any wind and the ocean is relatively calm. There are always breakers at Avalon, but they're less than half a metre high today. The whitewash dawdles to the shoreline, sinks into the sand, and disappears.

We always walk home this way, on the hard sand close to the waves. And then we stop at the northern end, near my house and the rock shelf where Dougal knocked me over. Sometimes we sit close together and watch the waves. Other times Per stands directly behind me. Whenever I flinch at the approach of a wave he pulls

me against his body. I'm always too jumpy to say anything much, so
he talks about his research. I'm wondering whether we'll be sitting
or standing today when he interrupts my thoughts.

'Tell me why you panicked at the pool.'

I close my eyes for a moment. 'I'd rather not.'

He changes direction immediately. We walk onto the soft sand
and head for the dunes. From the stiffness of his fingers I can feel
that he's angry, but I'm not going to tell him I was worried about
him. When we get to the steps I pull my hand out of his. He follows me in silence until we climb over the fence that leads to my
garden.

'Thanks,' I say, reaching behind my back for the zip tag of my
wetsuit. 'See you Monday.' My shoulder pulls. 'Ouch.'

'I do your zip every morning,' Per says, moving behind me.
'Why is today any different?'

When his fingers touch my neck he sets off thousands of nerve
endings all down my spine. I shiver. He freezes for an instant, and
then he comes closer. I feel his warmth against my back and the
movement of his chest when he expels a breath.

'I wish you'd stop asking questions.' My voice is uneven.

He must have dipped his head because now I feel his breath on
my neck. '*Du tar livet av meg.*'

'You've said that before. What does it mean?'

He hesitates. 'It means "I'm going to have to kill you".'

I turn. 'No it doesn't. You said the same thing a few days ago,
when we were on step two. You weren't angry then.'

His hands are clenched and he's scowling. 'Angry? Do you think
that's what I am now?'

'What else?'

He closes his eyes. Then he opens them again and stares into
mine. '"*Du tar livet av meg*" means "You are killing me". Happy?'

I shrug. 'You've said much worse. And I can't really blame you, having to put up with me vomiting all the time.'

He searches my face, and then his hands go to my shoulders. He touches my neck with his fingertips. When my legs wobble I lean forward and rest my hands and forehead against his chest. His fingers thread through my hair and he tips my head up. Then he puts his mouth and nose against my cheek. His breaths are just as jerky as mine. They warm me.

'We can't do this.' His voice is raspy.

My fingers glide over his chest. I wish I was touching his skin. 'You said I had to touch your body.' My voice is barely a whisper. 'That's how I'd feel safe.'

He laughs but it's more like a groan. 'This isn't safe.'

'It's not?'

I want him to hold me closer. An ache spreads through my body. My breasts are sensitive. I stroke the side of his neck, and his cheek. I touch the hair near his temple, and then I trace around the rim of his ear. When he shudders I take a tiny step, lining my body up against his so we're touching almost everywhere. He tenses—I feel it from his chest to his knees.

He takes a deep breath as he pushes me backwards, holding me at arm's length. 'Something like *this*,' he slowly runs a finger over the rim of my ear, and back again, 'can *never* be safe.'

His grey eyes stare into mine. I know I'm in the wrong so I look away before I turn and dash up the stairs to the deck like a startled possum.

'Harriet.'

I watch him pick up his sheepskin boots. His bag is over his shoulder. His expression is perfectly neutral, as if nothing even happened. And maybe it didn't. Because he's given his word not to behave in a manner that would suggest he's attracted to me. I'm the one who set the rules. I should be happy.

'I understand you have a function tonight,' he says.

I clear my throat. 'The UN dinner at Government House. You refused Professor Tan's invitation, so I have to go instead.'

Other than tightening his lips, he ignores my comment. 'You'll be late home,' he says. 'But we could go for a walk on the beach tomorrow morning. Eight?'

It's not the first time he's asked about Saturdays and Sundays over the past number of weeks. Perhaps it's because he's back at sea in a few weeks' time—he needs to work out whether I'm a lost cause before he goes. That would explain why, even though he's unfailingly patient while we're at the beach, he's invariably grim on the walk home. I'm progressing so slowly he must get fed up.

Not that I can help him with that, because I can't do any more than I already am. My heart skips a beat when he smiles. I like listening to his voice, even when he's talking about glaciers. His self-control infuriates me. I want to kiss him. And I want him to kiss me back.

'I'm tied up tonight, and Saturday night,' I say. 'And I have to catch up on sleep and schoolwork during the days.'

'You're committed all weekend?'

I salute. 'Yes, Commander.'

He takes a step towards me. But then the kookaburra swoops in front of him and lands on the railing a few centimetres from my hand. I jump.

Per is startled too, but he recovers more quickly. '*Løgner*,' he says, giving me a fake smile before turning and walking up the side path.

I'm not sure what it means. Liar?

★   ★   ★

Twenty minutes later I'm showered and dressed, sitting at the table on the deck eating my cereal. I have a blanket over my knees, a spoon in one hand and a pencil in the other. My sketchbook is open but I know it's unlikely I'll be drawing the kookaburra even if he does come back. I'll be watching Per.

After he walks me home he must take his boots and bag back to his car, which is parked near the surf club. Then he runs along the sand and dives into the waves at my end of the beach. His long strokes take him straight out to sea, fifty metres or more, until he's behind the break. He swims the length of the beach, all the way to the pool. When the sea is calm he swims freestyle. In stormy weather or rough seas he often swims under the water. Sometimes he disappears for a minute or more before he reappears, takes a breath like a dolphin would, and dives out of sight again.

He's already in the ocean when I see him, black and long and lean. His strokes are powerful and so are his kicks. When he dives beneath the swell I hold my breath, and only breathe again when he comes up for air. If I weren't sitting down I'm not sure my legs would support me. My heart pounds and my palms sweat.

He's the only one out there today—even surfers avoid the midwinter swells. Finally he reaches the southern end, catches a white frothed wave to shore and runs up the beach. He looks in my direction. It would be impossible for him to see me from where he is but all the same I pack everything up with shaking hands and walk inside the house.

The Scott Foundation: Environment Adventure Education

Busy weekend! Professor Tan has already filled you in on our dinner at Government House on Friday, and the shindig at the Vice Chancellor's residence last night, so I'll just tell you what Drew and I have been up to.

We had a fantastic day at Taronga Zoo on Saturday. Robbie Matheson, primate vet at the zoo, was kind enough to show us around the new orangutan enclosure. You can get information on the orangutan orphan sponsorship program on the zoo's website.

Today we drove to Newcastle, a few hours north of Sydney, to see The Adélie. Her captain, Tom Finlay, gave us a tour. The fit-out is amazing. Have a look at the photos—the ship is magnificent!

We can't wait to put The Adélie through her paces on her maiden voyage for the foundation—a trip to Palau, a tiny island in the Pacific Ocean. We hope you'll all join us on that trip—on your screens anyway—as we explore firsthand the devastating effects rising sea levels are having on low-lying regions of the world …

Harriet

* * *

Five minutes after I've posted, I get an email message from Per.

Harriet. Løgner means liar. I'll call you tonight.

I pick up a stack of marking and go in search of Liam. It's his turn to cook.

'When will dinner be ready? I'm starving.' I stand on tiptoes and look over Liam's shoulder to see what's in the saucepan.

'Get out of the kitchen,' he says, bumping me away and consulting his cookbook. He adds pepper. 'I'm concentrating.'

I leave him alone, and warm my hands in front of the heater. 'Long day.' I yawn. '*The Adélie* was worth it though. You should've seen Drew's face when he saw her. Brilliant.'

'Did Polarman get onto you? He called this morning.'

'I was driving. Didn't pick up.'

'You told him you'd be home today, sleeping and marking.'

'He sent me an email. Didn't sound happy. Said he'd call me. What do you think he wants?'

Liam sucks in his breath. 'Tell you over dinner.'

I narrow my eyes. 'Tell me now.'

He stops stirring and rests his hands on the kitchen bench, grimacing. 'Polarman and I are worried about you.'

Liam is intelligent, and besides Drew, he's the closest I have to family. So why can't he get over this crush on Per? He puts on a serious doctor voice and repeats everything Per told him about me. That I should be resting on the weekends because the weekdays are traumatic. That I'm feeling the cold even more than usual because I'm losing weight. That he suspects my sleep is still troubled.

'Told Polarman the nightmares get worse with every step you go down in the pool,' Liam says. 'He wasn't happy about that.'

I'm too angry to speak to Liam while we're eating. But he's gone to a lot of trouble with dinner so by the time I go to my room to finish my marking we're on civil terms again. He wakes me up when he sticks his head around the door.

My light is still on and I have papers all over the bed. 'What time is it?'

'After twelve. Polarman couldn't get you on your mobile so he called the landline. When I told him you'd gone to bed, he said I should pass on a message.'

'0600 hours?'

'Nope. He's going to sea tomorrow. Said he'd call again later in the week.'

I'm still half asleep, and not sure how I feel about Per not coming. It would have been awkward seeing him again because of the way I behaved on Friday, leaning against him in the garden and touching his ear. And he would have been angry that I lied to him about my plans for the weekend. But I want to continue with step three of the pool. Has he given up on me? Do I have to do the rest of the steps by myself?

'Is there an emergency at sea?' I say. 'Or was it planned?'

Liam shrugs. 'No idea. Though he did make a point of saying that if *you* go anywhere near the sea, or the pool, or the rock shelfs, he'll kill you.'

So he is coming back. 'He's quite funny sometimes.'

'He wasn't laughing. And neither was I, when I said I'd help him do it.'

★ ★ ★

The Scott Foundation: Environment Adventure Education

Preparations are complete for our annual fundraising dinner, to be held at the Intercontinental Hotel on Saturday evening. I look forward to seeing many of our friends there, as do Professor Tan and the other members of the board. The dinner gives us the opportunity to discuss the foundation's work with environmental colleagues, sponsors, parliamentarians and media organisations.

I'm looking forward to briefing everyone on how the foundation and our modern day Amundsen and Scott—Per and me—are working together through scientific exploration and education to preserve the polar environment. And Professor Tan will give an update on fundraising efforts for The Adélie.

See you Saturday!

Harriet

★ ★ ★

It's Wednesday afternoon and there's been no word from Per. I've missed three days at the pool. Professor Tan calls when I'm on my lunch break, supervising the canteen queue.

'Hey, Professor.'

'Afternoon, Harry. I wanted a word about Saturday.'

'Sure.'

'I'd like Drew to be there.'

Drew comes to many of the foundation events—when I'm around to look after him. That won't be possible at the foundation dinner because hundreds of guests will be there. I doubt Drew would say anything incriminating about what happened before *The Watch* sank, but every so often he lets something slip. A few weeks ago he talked about the need to check the ballast tank seals, a detail he'd forgotten all about in the lead up to the Antarctica voyage. I don't trust Tan not to question him when my back is turned.

'There'll be so many people,' I say. 'Drew might not enjoy it.'

'He enjoyed the AGM a few weeks ago.'

'You're going to the Maritime Museum gala at the end of the month, aren't you? We'll see you at that. And you're welcome to come to Avalon. Drew's with me every weekend.'

There's a silence. 'Commander Amundsen wants to meet Drew.'

'What?'

'As you know, he's been refusing to attend the dinner. But he called an hour ago and said he'd consider coming if you and Drew were there. I assured him you would be.'

'You had no right. Tell him I'll be there, but not Drew.'

'He already knew you'd be there. He obviously wants the two of you.'

'Meaning he wants Drew. What's he playing at?'

'He's asked to meet him a number of times, ever since you had the fall at the beach. I've explained that Drew hasn't been well, that I've barely seen him either. I think that's why he's been holding back. Seeing Drew splashed all over the papers last weekend might have prompted this.'

Per wouldn't want to question Drew about *The Watch* going down—he decided I was to blame months ago. Does he want to ask him about Brazil, in the hope I'll progress in the pool more quickly?

'I think Per wants to use Drew to get information on me. The answer is no.'

'Think it through, Harry. Drew was in fine spirits last weekend. And he'll like the commander. You know he will.'

'Why didn't Per tell me this himself?'

'Probably because you always think the worst where he's concerned. He wants me to get back to him and confirm everything tonight. He called by satellite phone, off the coast of Darwin.'

Per told Liam he'd call me later in the week. I assumed he wanted to talk about going back to the pool. Maybe I was wrong. Perhaps he wanted to talk about Drew.

'I don't like to be manipulated. If he wants to see Drew, he can see him at Avalon.'

'Harry. Why complicate things? The commander has made a simple request to meet Drew, a famous mariner and founding member of the Scott Foundation, at an important annual event. If you can't accommodate that, he'll want to know why. *I'll* want to know why.'

There's a lump in my throat. 'He always gets what he wants.'

'Look on the bright side. The fact he's coming to the dinner will benefit the fundraising effort. And I'll personally pay for a driver to pick up you and Drew and take you home afterwards. Then you can have a champagne or two without worrying about driving home.'

* * *

My geography class must see from my expression that I'm upset. They work silently at their desks while I type an email to Per.

> Per. I'm preparing a post on Amundsen's character traits. The way I see it, Amundsen was arrogant and dictatorial, and (at the very least) cruel and unfeeling. What do you think? Harry

Harriet. Amundsen was firm in his beliefs. He focused on what had to be done to achieve his objectives. He was also practical—eating his sled dogs (I presume your 'cruel and unfeeling' refers to this) got him and the rest of his party back to base camp alive. This was an outcome Scott and his team were unable to achieve.

I'll see you on Saturday. Per

Per is waiting for Drew and me in the valet area of the Intercontinental Hotel. He's wearing his dress uniform, his shirt starkly white
against the black of the jacket. His hair is shorter than when I last
saw him—he must get it cut every fortnight because there's never
a hair out of place.

The doorman opens my door and I wait on the footpath as Per
helps Drew from the car. He puts a hand under Drew's elbow to
steady him. Then he introduces himself, and holds out his hand.
Drew responds, shaking vigorously. He notices the red, white and
blue insignia embroidered on Per's tie, and tells him he spent three
wonderful weeks in the Lysefjorden region in the 1980s, while a
problem with *The Watch's* bilge tank was being sorted out.

Drew looks around until he finds me, standing behind Per. He
grins. 'I thought I was smart in my penguin suit,' he says. 'But this
young fella puts me in the shade.'

Per finally turns and faces me. He's much too polite to look me up and down, but he stares at my face for a moment. My straightened hair is in a ponytail; it's smooth and glossy, and swings from side to side when I move. He glances at my shoes. I'm taller than usual in my heels. His eyes go to the V-neck of my dress.

I frown. 'What are you looking at?'

'The dress,' he says.

It was inexpensive but it suits me. The slinky fabric clings to my breasts and hugs my bottom. It's midnight blue and above-knee length, with shoestring straps. I'm wearing Mum's necklace—a rope of tiny natural pearls. They disappear into my cleavage.

'What about it?'

'You're cold.'

'Piss off.'

Per closes his eyes.

Drew looks from Per to me. 'Now, now, Harry,' he says. 'Maggie won't approve of language like that. Neither will Matthew. Not that I'll tell them. But it is chilly out. If you get a cold you'll have to stay in your cabin. You'd rather be on the bridge, wouldn't you?' He takes off his coat. 'So put this on, there's a good girl.'

My hands shake when I take Drew's jacket and drape it around my shoulders. I can't even look at Per.

'That's better,' Drew says, winking at Per. 'Maggie calls Harry her little ice-block.'

Someone touches me on the shoulder. It's Professor Tan. He kisses my cheek.

'You look lovely, Harry,' he says.

I take a breath and give him a bright smile. 'Thanks.'

Tan shakes Per's hand, and Drew's. He tells Drew how delightful it is to see him again and they chat away like old friends, even though Drew has forgotten who Tan is. After a couple of minutes they walk together, arm in arm, through the doors to the foyer.

'Harriet?' Per's voice is a rumble near my ear. I smell his fresh pine smell. '*Jeg er lei meg.*'

Our eyes meet. His are so dark the irises and pupils appear to merge together.

'I'm not in the mood for games,' I say. 'Especially with you. What does that mean?'

'It means I'm sorry. Sincerely sorry.'

'Why?'

'You're close to Drew. This must be extremely difficult for you.'

'Is that all? You weren't apologising because you forced me, *blackmailed me,* into bringing him here? Knowing if I didn't do as you asked, Tan would make my life difficult? You wanted to question Drew. Didn't you? About Brazil?'

He hesitates. 'Not specifically. But I thought he might be able to assist me. Yes.'

'He can't!'

'I see that now.'

When he takes my hand our eyes meet and his expression softens. He's my least favourite person in the world right now but it's all I can do not to bury my face against his neck—just like I do at the pool.

When a car door slams behind us, I jump. Per tightens his grip on my hand.

'*Bli med meg,*' he says, threading his fingers through mine. 'Come with me.'

The feel of his hand is familiar and comforting. Too comforting. I'm not frightened, I'm not at the beach. I don't want my stomach to flutter because he apologises. I don't want to be weak and vulnerable and needy.

It's not easy to get him to relinquish my hand. Pulling it subtly doesn't work, so I stop in the middle of the foyer and wrench it back. 'Why didn't you call me during the week? Liam said you would.'

He reaches for my hand again.

'Don't touch me.'

'Harriet, for fuck's … After Friday, I thought we needed a break from the pool. *I* needed a break.'

'Why?'

He blinks. 'Can't you see what's happening? You're impossible.'

'*Du er umulig*? Right?'

We're not far from the ballroom and people are milling around. Some are smiling at me. Many are staring curiously at Per. He's scowling, and probably counting to ten, but when I walk away he follows. We gather with the other guests and stare at the notice-board. It's silly because I know we're on table one, and I'm sure Per knows it as well.

Our table is at the front of the room and we pass scores of people as we walk towards it. Most know who I am, and I know quite a few of them. Many shake my hand, or kiss my cheek, or hug me, and I introduce Per to every one of them. He's reserved and formal, but courteous as he answers their questions. He recognises Robbie from the photograph taken at the zoo, and asks him about the orangutan-breeding program. Tom Finlay has obviously talked to Per recently about *The Adélie*. They discuss the fit-out and readying her for Palau. Occasionally Per smiles stiffly at someone and says, 'Please, call me Per,' but hardly anyone does. Just like Helga told him on the beach a month ago, people like addressing him as 'Commander.'

⋆ ⋆ ⋆

'What happened to me again, Harry?' Drew says.

Per and Professor Tan, and the others at the table, have heard my response numerous times in the past two hours. I'm telling the same lie over and over.

'You had some health problems Drew, back in January. It affected your memory.'

'Well, fancy that. I feel perfectly well now.'

'Course you do. You're as fit as a fiddle. Just like you were when we did our Silk Road documentary. Why don't you tell Professor Tan about that?'

Drew frowns. And before he opens his mouth I sense this is going to be one of those times when he remembers something clearly.

'It was a good break for us, wasn't it, Harry?' he says. 'Your dad was in hospital again. And you'd been going through a tough time with Roger, and the nightmares—'

'Excuse me, Captain McLeish,' Per says, standing and gesturing to the table where Kat and the *Torrens* crew are sitting. 'I have some colleagues who would like to meet you. Would you mind?'

Drew and I are on the opposite side of the table to Per. I thought he'd been engrossed in his conversation with the woman sitting next to him. When I send him a grateful look his lip twitches, and all of a sudden I'm not nearly as resentful as I was. He'd like to know about Brazil, but he doesn't want Drew to tell everyone how crazy I am.

Per excuses himself to the woman he was talking to, and stands behind Drew's chair. 'Are you ready, sir?' he says.

Lisa Toohey—the TV journalist who wore the red sparkly dress to the orangutan function at the zoo—drops into Drew's seat once he's left with Per. She's wearing a short black sparkly dress tonight, and looks just as beautiful up close as she does from a distance. She and her producer are thinking of running a few segments about Scott and Amundsen's polar expeditions, and are interested in what the foundation is doing.

'Professor Tan gave an inspirational speech tonight,' she says. 'Impressive man.'

'He is.'

'And Commander Amundsen is *extraordinary*.'

'We were lucky he made it tonight because he's often at sea. Make sure you get plenty of photos.'

'We already have!' She takes a sip of wine. 'Does he happen to be the man you referred to in the speech you made at the zoo? The one who was critical of you because of what happened with *The Watch*?'

I force a smile. 'I grew up in front of a film crew, so I know better than to answer a question like that.'

'Are you and Per ... close?' She touches my arm. 'I saw you two outside.'

Was that when I was holding Per's hand, or accusing him of blackmail? I sip from my glass.

'My teaching, my home life, my relationships, are private. I stopped answering questions about them years ago.'

'I'm aware of that. But you and Per must spend a lot of time together. Anything could happen, surely?'

After we've finished at the pool, whichever way it turns out, I won't see much of him at all. So there'll be no arguments, and there won't be a mind-numbing physical attraction that makes me weak at the knees. Meaning there'll be nothing that journalists can gossip about.

'I'll be doing what I've always done—working with the foundation to educate people about the environment, and supporting fundraising for research into environmental issues. Per will crew on the ship for a few Antarctic expeditions and carry out his research, which happens to be in line with the foundation's interests.' I reach for the wine bottle and top up her glass, smiling stiffly. 'If you want access to me, or Per, it would be best if you asked questions about our work.'

Lisa holds up her hands, and laughs. Her amber eyes are beautiful. I'd draw her as a leopard if I had the chance.

'All right, Harriet,' she says. 'I get it.' She looks over my shoulder.

I don't need to follow her gaze to know that Per has come back to the table. He's not even touching me but the hairs on the back of my neck are standing on end.

He sits on my other side, in Tan's chair.

'Where's Drew?' I ask.

Per frowns. 'Liam's just arrived. They're on their way over.'

Liam said he'd get here as quickly as he could after his shift at the hospital, so that he could take Drew back to his care home.

'Drew gets tired in the evenings,' I tell Per, as Drew walks to the table and kisses me goodbye.

'What are we up to tomorrow, Harry?' he says.

'We'll have breakfast at Palm Beach and then walk to the lighthouse. I'll see you at eight.'

'What! Six at the latest.'

I laugh. 'Seven.'

Liam throws his arm around me, and begs a lift for him and his surf ski. 'I'll paddle while you walk.' Lisa's eyes have been glued to Liam since he got to the table. He's wearing loose-fitting hospital garb that brings out the blue in his eyes, and his doctor ID is pinned to his chest. He needs a haircut. He grins at Lisa and shakes her hand. 'See you on the telly,' he says.

We watch Liam and Drew leave the room. It takes a while because so many people chat to Drew on the way out. Lisa clears her throat.

'Commander,' she says, 'the fundraising effort for *The Adélie*, I'm keen to know how you're involved.'

Per looks from Lisa to me. 'Should I answer that, Harriet, or leave it to you?'

He doesn't want to be involved in anything to do with the foundation. All he wants is the use of the ship. But it's not like he's opposed to what the foundation is doing, and it's important that he *seems* interested.

'The commander does a lot of work for the Scott and Amundsen posts. I couldn't cope without his input. This isn't fundraising as such, but it raises the profile of the foundation and highlights the polar melt issue.' I turn my back on Lisa and put my hand on Per's arm, opening my eyes wide. 'That's right, isn't it, Per?'

He tenses up everywhere. His arm is rock hard. He stands, nods abruptly to Lisa, and gives me an arctic smile.

'Harriet,' he says. 'May I have a word? In private.'

He ignores everyone who looks our way as he strides from the room.

'Your comments on my drafts for the website *sort of* help,' I say. 'So what's the big deal? Why make such a fuss? You're so ... so ...'

'Truthful?' Per says, jutting out his chin. 'Honest? Are those the words you're searching for? The words you're not *familiar* with?'

We're facing each other in the only place the concierge could come up with when Per marched to his desk and demanded somewhere private. It's the 'bride and groom's retreat', reserved for newlyweds who have their receptions in the ballroom. In the middle of the room there's a spindly-legged chaise lounge upholstered in silver-grey and light blue satin. Two heart-shaped cushions are propped against the armrest. The only other furniture is a standard lamp and a narrow table. A white candelabrum, festooned with crystal baubles, dominates the table top.

'You're *too* truthful,' I say.

'There's no such thing. You're either truthful or you're not. I am, you're not. You lied to that journalist. And while we're on today's transgressions, Tan thinks you're hiding something. Something to do with Drew.'

'Bullshit.'

'Liar.'

I turn my back and walk the few steps to the window. The curtains are drawn. They're made out of the same material as the chaise lounge and are overly long, so the fabric pools on the floor. Their ropes and tassels hang on hooks either side of the window. I reach for a tassel and run the long silver and blue threads through my fingers until I can trust myself to speak calmly.

'What Tan suspects is of no real importance now, anyway. And I can handle it.'

'Like you handled *The Watch* going down? And your fear of the water? You've been trouble since the moment we met.'

I turn and face him. 'You're going back to Antarctica in December, aren't you? I'm not all bad news.'

'You were lucky. The foundation backed your ideas, and so did I. It wouldn't have happened otherwise.'

I turn my back on him again, twisting the tassel threads together. 'Yeah, well, I'm a team player. Not a *commander* like you.'

Within a heartbeat he's behind me, breathing down my neck. 'You have an impeccable environmental pedigree. You're smart and passionate. The people here tonight would follow you just about anywhere.'

'You wouldn't.'

'I wouldn't because you're impetuous, reckless ...'

'Is that all?'

'No. You scare me half to death.'

I swallow the lump in my throat. 'Stop lecturing me.'

'Gladly, when you stop diving in at the deep end.'

Without any warning, an image of the pool comes into my mind. The water will be at my chest if we go to step four. It'll lap around

Per's throat. Lights flash before my eyes so unexpectedly that I don't realise what's happening at first. But then the nausea starts and it's all I can do to stay upright.

'*Jesus,*' Per says, pulling me backwards against his body and crossing his arms around my middle, cocooning me. 'Easy, Harriet. Breathe.'

My back is warm against his front. The side of his face rests on mine. I'm not under the water and neither is he. We're here, safe.

He counts slowly. '*En, to, tre, fire, fem.*' A few minutes pass and we're breathing in time. I'm aware of Per rhythmically stroking my sides from the base of my rib cage to my hips, and back again. The nausea has gone.

I shift in his arms. 'I'd better get back.'

He sighs and stands up straighter, but he doesn't let me go. 'Soon.' He points to a tassel. 'What's that thing called? In English.'

My voice is croaky. 'There's no need to distract me. I'm okay.'

'I'm curious, that's why I asked.'

He didn't know about flannelette pyjamas so he mightn't know about this.

'It's a tassel.'

He turns me around so we're facing each other, then he reaches for my ponytail. He threads the strands of hair through his fingers, again and again, and then smooths them down. I can't take my eyes from his face. He's looking at my hair as if it fascinates him.

'What are you doing, Per?'

'*Gyllen dusk.*'

'What?'

'*Gyllen dusk.* Golden tassel. That's what your hair is.'

I'm terrified I'm blushing, so I take a deep breath and step away. 'You're just being kind to me so I don't puke on you.'

He crosses his arms over his chest. His eyes are silvery grey, like the stripes on the chaise lounge, as his gaze travels from my face to my neck to my breasts.

'Those pearls suit you.' His voice is husky.

'They were my mother's.'

His hands are nowhere near my breasts but my nipples tingle. And there's a warm ache that extends from my belly to my thighs. When he reaches for me, I step straight into his arms and rest my cheek against his chest as if this is a rational thing to do, even though we've been at loggerheads for most of the evening. His heart is thumping like crazy. I put one hand over my left breast, just like he's taught me to, and compare our heart rates. I look up in surprise.

He swallows. 'What?'

'Your heart is beating quicker than mine.'

'So?'

'That's never happened before. Maybe you're having a heart attack.'

'I told you a week ago, you're killing me.' His face is tense and drawn, and when I smile at him he doesn't smile back.

'You can be funny,' I say, fitting my body to his. His erection is pressed against my stomach.

He stares at my face for a moment and then he groans, reaching between our bodies for my hands. 'I gave you my word not to touch you,' he says. 'Not to act *inappropriately*.'

I've never desired anyone before, not properly. I liked it when Grant kissed me but I didn't like having sex with him. What I really wanted him to do was just to hold me, but I was so desperate to please him that I went along with what he wanted.

This is different. Per is different. I'm attracted to him even though I don't like him a lot of the time. He's attracted to me even though he thinks I'm incompetent and reckless.

'We're not at the beach,' I say. I'm looking at his mouth, and he's looking at mine.

'It doesn't matter.'

When I kissed him in my bedroom he was the one to pull back. I free my hands and shove him in the chest. 'Right, then. Don't worry about it.'

He closes his eyes for a moment. 'We can meet tomorrow, walk along the beach.'

'No, thanks.'

His jaw is tight. He's white around the mouth. It's the same shade as his scar. He moves me aside to get to the door but instead of storming out like I expect him to do, he locks it. Then he rests his forehead against the doorframe before turning around and facing me.

He takes his jacket off and throws it over the back of the chaise lounge. 'You wanted this,' he says, 'so you can't accuse me of acting inappropriately. Is that understood?'

He's angry. But sexy-angry. I'm not sure how to handle him.

'You're the one in control,' he says, undoing his cuffs and rolling up the sleeves of his shirt. 'Just like in the pool. So I'm not making you do anything you don't want to do. I'm not taking over. Got that?'

I don't know whether I'm nervous because he's taking off his tie and undoing the button at his throat, or because the ballroom is only twenty metres away—on the other side of the door and down the corridor. Is anyone looking for us? Professor Tan, or Lisa Toohey? Maybe Kat, or someone else from the *Torrens* table?

He drapes his tie on the hook where one of the tassels hangs and gestures that I sit on the chaise lounge. I'm ramrod straight in the middle of the seat when he kneels in front of me. We're at eye level.

'If you intend to kiss me, Harriet, you'd better stop frowning and pressing your lips together.'

When I smile, he touches my bottom lip with the pad of his thumb. Which is when I look at him properly and see that he's not nearly as calm as he's pretending to be. His eyes are bright, his face has more colour than usual, and his breaths are short, even a little ragged. I touch his face, skating my fingers over his cheekbones, jaw and chin. I kiss his scar and then draw back.

'You have wonderful bone structure. Your face is almost perfectly symmetrical. And you have a widow's peak. That's very unusual.'

'I'm an identical twin. My brother looks the same.'

'Do you have to have an answer for everything? What's his name?'

'Tør.'

I run my fingers through his hair. It's thick and smooth. He presses his face against the inside of my arm.

'Does Tør have longer hair than you? Is he in the navy too? What does he do?'

'Yes. No. Diplomat. Are you going to kiss me or not?'

'Will you join in properly this time?'

His hands rest on my upper arms, and his fingers clench and unclench. His voice is gruff. 'Yes.'

I take his hands and hold them on my lap. Then I study his forearms. His skin is tanned, and the muscles are firm.

'I like your arms,' I say, running my hands over them.

'Kiss me,' he says.

At first I use my fingers to touch his lips, and then I kiss him gently, but thoroughly. He sighs deeply when our tongues meet. I think he's relieved I've finally got around to it. I touch the corner of his lip with my tongue, and his mouth slides across my mouth to do the same. I suck tentatively on the tip of his tongue and he finds mine and mimics my action. His hands feather over the back of my neck as I hold his face between my palms. When we're both breathing unsteadily I ease away, and then I lick his bottom lip and take it between my teeth, like I did months ago. I loosen my hold and mumble against his mouth. 'Shall I bite it?'

His voice is so croaky I can hardly understand his words. *'Jesus.* Yes.'

The sensation of having him moaning into my mouth as I play with his lips and tongue arouses me more than I'd ever have thought possible. He's still kneeling in front of me. I undo his second button, and the next one, and slide my hands inside his shirt. The skin of his throat is smooth, and the muscles of his neck and the exposed part of his chest are warm and hard. When I trail kisses over them he mutters words in Norwegian. I kiss my way back up to his mouth and speak against his lips.

'What's *"Jeg vil ha deg*?" What else did you say?'

'I want you. Like crazy.' He kisses me, briefly and hard. Then he looks at his watch. 'It's almost eleven.'

I nuzzle his neck. 'Tan wants me to thank everyone for coming.'

He grumbles. 'Fuck Tan.'

'My car will be here at twelve.'

He turns his head to search for my mouth and then we're kissing all over again. I think he must've liked it when I touched his mouth with my fingers because he keeps pulling back, and running his fingers over my lips. When I softly bite his thumb his breath catches in his throat. I drag his shirt out of his trousers and open all the buttons so I can see him properly. But when I try to take the shirt off he looks towards the door and shakes his head, so I have to be content with opening the crisp white fabric as wide as I can. I've seen the shape of his body plenty of times in his wetsuit so I know he's slender and muscular, but this is different. His nipples are flat and dark brown. His navel is neat. He has hardly any hair on his chest, but there's a line of hair running down his stomach to the waistband of his trousers. I think he knows I'd like to see more of it because he says, '*Nei*, Harriet,' in a gravelly voice when my hand goes to his belt.

I give him a shaky smile as I stroke his stomach. 'I know what that means.'

He cups my face with one hand and wraps my ponytail around his wrist with the other.

'*Du er vakker*,' he says.

'I am … what?'

'Beautiful.'

I sit back and study his body again. I'd like to draw him, just like this. I dip my head and kiss his nipple. He tenses immediately, which encourages me to sweep over his other nipple with my tongue. That makes him even tenser, so I run my finger over one wet nipple while I lick the other. I'm smiling when he grasps the tops of my arms and sits me up straight. At first he stares at my mouth, but then he holds my face firmly in his hands and stares into my eyes.

'Can't.' His voice is rough. His gaze sweeps down to my breasts. My dress is gaping at the front and my breasts are rising and falling with each breath I take. He lowers one hand and it hovers over my body, but then he brings it back to my face. It's a little shaky. 'Can't do …' He looks over my shoulder.

'Can't do what?'

Suddenly I'm aware of how warm his hands are. His palms and fingers are hot like he has a fever. But his eyes aren't feverish. They're determined and …

He's holding back. I don't know why I didn't see it earlier, but that's what he's doing. And that's also why—even though he must be far more experienced than me—he hasn't initiated anything. He told me at the start that I'm responsible for this, and that I'm in control. So he's determined not to lose control of his own responses.

Kissing me was obviously manageable. But touching my breasts? Would that be more difficult?

I narrow my eyes. 'You said I was in control, didn't you?'

He exhales on a shaky breath. 'Yes.'

I swivel around so my back is to him, and then I turn my head to the side. 'Can you pull my zip down?'

He's silent for ages. I imagine him counting. Then he groans, and buries his face at the side of my neck.

'Don't do this, Harriet. Please. We're in a fucking cupboard here. Tan will be looking for us. This bench thing—it won't even hold my weight.'

'This,' I pat the seat, 'is called a chaise lounge. And you promised to participate. You gave me your word. I want you to touch my breasts.'

'*Fuck, fuck, fuck, fuck, fuck,*' he says, as he slowly draws down the zip. When I slip the straps over my shoulders the dress slithers down to my waist. He grumbles. 'This is not a good ...'

I'm not wearing a bra. The air is cool on my skin. I shiver a little, but within seconds I'm warm again because he puts his hands on my shoulders and kisses all the way down my spine to my waist, and then up again to the base of my neck. Then he pulls me back against his body. He runs his fingers down the strand of pearls until his hands meet, just above my navel.

'*Vakker,*' he says, cupping my breasts and gently rolling his thumbs over my nipples.

I tip my head back and make murmuring noises against his throat. I'm weak with desire when he whispers against my ear. 'Turn around?'

I do as he says but once I'm facing him I feel self-conscious. My breasts are nice enough but they're not very big.

As if he can read my mind he dips his head and kisses one nipple, a slow lingering kiss. Then he kisses the other one. 'Perfect.'

He kisses my mouth. 'Everything. Perfect.' He carefully takes my necklace off and puts it on the floor.

I wrap my arms around his neck. 'Thank you.'

He rests his forehead against mine and we both watch his hands as they explore my body, from my collarbones to my breasts and stomach and hips. Then I kiss him again. We're both taking jerky breaths when he pulls back and lays the heart-shaped cushions on the end of the chaise lounge. His chest muscles ripple when he moves.

He looks at me uncertainly. 'Would you like to lie down?' he asks.

It's ludicrous for him to pretend that I'm in control because I haven't done anything like this in eight years. And even then I merely endured what happened next.

'Do you want to have sex?' I say. 'Is that it?'

He tips his head back and stares at the ceiling—like he always does when he can't believe what I've just said. 'Harriet Hillary Amelia Scott,' he mutters, and lays me down. He drapes himself over the chaise lounge, so that one of his legs is between mine. 'Just kiss me for now.'

I stroke over his shoulders and down his back. 'How do you say "bossy" in Norwegian?'

He takes a breath. 'You mean as an adjective?'

'In the sense of, "You are very bossy".'

He smiles. '*Sjefete.*'

'That doesn't sound anything like "bossy".'

He rests his hand on the inside of my knee. I bend it immediately, and wriggle down the lounge.

'Nevertheless, that is what it means,' he says, grimacing when my dress rises up to my thighs. He pulls it down again.

I push it up. 'You think I'm being impetuous, don't you? Impulsive?'

'Worse. Reckless.'

I stroke his hair. 'You probably want emergency provisions. Water. Flares. Things like that. Matches too. And contraception.'

I'm not sure whether he's groaning or laughing against my neck. But then we're kissing again and I can't think about anything at all except for how good he smells and tastes, and how wonderful the texture of his skin feels beneath my hands. His fingers finally rest right at the top of my thigh. My mind goes totally blank when he looks into my eyes and says, very seriously, 'Would you like to come, Harriet?'

I manage a nod. And then I gasp because his fingers slide into my underpants and move against me, and I've never felt anything like it before. His breath against my mouth is laboured, and he's shaky, and I think that excites me just as much as anything else. Finally he zeroes in on just where I want him to be. He circles and strokes and plays. When I moan he smiles against my mouth. And then he slips a finger inside me.

Memories come flooding back—of Grant, and all the men I picked up at the pub. Without meaning to do it I clamp my legs together and dig my fingernails into his shoulders.

His hand freezes. He searches my face. 'I won't hurt you,' he says. 'I couldn't.'

'I've had sex before. With lots of men.'

'Not with me.'

He kisses me—a long, possessive, thorough sort of kiss. And when I'm kissing him back as frantically as I was before, he touches between my thighs again. His fingers soothe and calm, they gently glide, they tease until I press against his hand. And before too long I'm lifting my hips because I want him inside me. I want him to touch me everywhere. But each time I'm about to climax he pulls back a little.

'Please, Per.'

'Do you want me?' His breathing is harsh. '*Say it.*'

I wrap my arms around his neck. 'Yes, Per. I do.'

There's something subtly different in his next kiss, a fierceness I haven't felt before. And soon the waves of sensation take over and I'm trembling. He smothers my sounds against his mouth, and strokes until I'm limp and breathless. He nuzzles my neck, and then rests his face between my breasts. I stroke his hair and hold him tightly.

★   ★   ★

Per eases himself off the chaise lounge. He avoids looking at me as he takes my hands and pulls me into a sitting position. His face is set, and grim. He turns his back as I struggle to adjust my dress, pulling my arms into the straps, and pushing down the skirt so it covers my thighs. My underpants are damp.

I'm flushed and cold all at the same time. 'Are you all right?' I say.

He nods. It's a brusque *I don't want to talk about it* kind of a nod.

Is he angry with me because I've made things even more complicated than they were already? Or with himself for doing something he didn't really want to do? Most likely it's a combination.

He does up his buttons. Then he puts his tie back on, and his jacket. When I stand he gives me my shoes. I can't even remember taking them off. He hands me my pearls.

'Turn around,' he says.

I do as he asks. He doesn't touch my skin when he fastens my zip.

'Get your bag and I'll drive you home,' he says.

I focus on straightening my dress again. 'The professor wants me to wind things up.'

'I'll wait.'

'Could you look at me, please?'

He faces me. 'What?'

'I don't need a lift home. I'm tired. I want to go home by myself.'

'I'm taking you home, not asking for sex.'

'I said no. I don't want you, or sex.'

Maybe he flinches. I'm not certain because there's an enormous ache in my chest and all I can think about is the way that I'm feeling. He opens the door and gestures that I precede him. Then we walk silently side by side down the corridor. He turns sharply left, towards the men's bathroom.

I see him briefly back in the ballroom, shaking hands with the people seated at our table.

He catches my eye and mouths one word. 'Monday.'

He's long gone by the time I give the closing address, and thank the guests for coming.

CHAPTER
26

Liam *desperately* needs a haircut. He swipes his hair from his face and grins.

'Is he a good kisser then, Polarman?'

We're at a Palm Beach café, across the road from the beach. A wide stretch of fine-grained sand extends from the southern end near the café to the northern tip of the peninsular, marked by Barrenjoey Lighthouse at the top of the cliffs. The sea shimmers bright blue in the early morning sunshine. Drew has finished his breakfast. He's sitting on a bench, gazing through binoculars at the ocean.

'That's none of your business.'

'Yes it is. I'm jealous.'

'Since when?'

He winks. 'About you getting to kiss Polarman, not the other way around. Take pity on me.'

Liam wouldn't have known anything if I hadn't been stupid enough to poke my head around the door to the living room to say goodnight to him and Rachael early this morning. They were lying on the sofa together watching a movie. Rachael's hair was sticking up everywhere, so I think they'd been to bed and got up again.

'I have nothing to tell you.'

Liam orders more coffees before I can stop him. He takes my chin and looks at my mouth. 'Last night your mouth was red and—'

I wrench my face away. 'Shut up!'

'Puffy. This morning it's back to normal. Which is entirely consistent with my diagnosis of prolonged kissing. Any other symptoms, Miss Scott?' I clamp my lips together and, without thinking, cross my arms over my breasts. He zeroes in immediately. 'Aha!'

The waiter brings the coffees and asks whether he can take a photo of himself with Drew and me. I make Liam get up to take the photo. Then I settle Drew again, and rest my head on my arm. Liam can't see my face but he can hear me.

'I'll only tell you stuff if you promise not to talk about it ever again.'

'Patient confidentiality, Harry. Spill the beans.'

I give Liam a sanitised account of what Per and I did in the bridal room. How I almost had a panic attack, and forced him to kiss me, and how afterwards he acted as if nothing had happened.

'Per only did what I asked him to do,' I say. 'I'm ashamed of myself. I should have let him take me home, even if he was bad-tempered.'

Liam shrugs. 'Don't worry. He's an action hero, accustomed to adversity. He'll live.'

'I find him exhausting.'

It was me who asked him to unzip my dress. He was considerate and generous. He let me take control—even though he was the only one of us who knew what to do. I screw my eyes shut.

'It doesn't have to be such a big deal, you know,' Liam says.

'What?'

He grins. 'Sex. It can be fun.'

Liam and Rachael aren't together anymore because they want to go out with other people as well as each other. Yet they have sex all the time. Are they in love? Can they be, when they seem to be happy together, but just as happy apart?

'Do you love Rachael?'

'I guess. We're mates.'

'What about me?'

'Definitely love you. And Polarman.'

'I wish you'd take this seriously.'

'I wish you'd give him the opportunity to convince you that he cares. Like I said, have some fun. Be happy with whatever happens.'

When Per was touching me I said I wanted him. But I wanted him even more afterwards. I didn't want to let him go. Ever.

It's like a chill passes over me. Mum and Dad loved me absolutely. So does Drew. I loved my parents, and I love Drew, in exactly the same way. I thought I loved Grant. Is this the only kind of love I'm able to feel? The kind of love that hurts so much when you lose it that you don't want to experience it ever again?

'Harry?' Liam says. 'You okay?'

I stare at him across the table. 'You make me happy. So do lots of other people, like Helga and Allan, my friends from football, and the kids at school. Tom and the crew too. I quite like the orangutan vet as well. He makes me laugh. Maybe I'll go out with him.'

Liam raises his brows. 'Can't Polarman make you happy?'

The kind of love that hurts so much when you lose it that you don't want to experience it ever again.

I shake my head. 'Not Polarman. He's not for me.'

★   ★   ★

'Harry,' Jonty yells from the deck, 'Drew wants to know where Maggie is.'

I'm cutting onions, and wiping my eyes on the sleeve of my jumper.

'Tell him the truth. Mum's not around anymore, but she still keeps an eye on us.'

Kat is perched on a stool facing me. She and Jonty were sitting on my doorstep when we got back a couple of hours ago. Her eyes are watery too.

'Are the onions worrying you?'

She gives me a shaky smile. 'Nah. I cry easily. Cute kids. Movies. Kind of worshipped your Mum.'

I wipe my eyes again. 'Now you're setting me off. Pity you're such a nice person, Kat.'

'Per tells me I should toughen up.' She sees my expression. 'Shut up about Per, right?'

I shrug. 'Whatever. Have fun last night?'

Kat details everything that went on after the dinner at the hotel, how she and a number of the *Torrens* crew went clubbing and only got home at six this morning. And how she thinks she might have found herself a Sydney boyfriend. Then she fishes for information about where Per and I disappeared to last night, and tells me that Professor Tan was looking everywhere for us.

'For Per more than me, though?'

'Yeah. That guy *loves* the commander.'

I put the tuna casserole in the oven and fetch Drew's oilskin coat. There's a storm moving in from the south. The wind coming off the sea is bitterly cold and it'll be dark in an hour. Drew gets into his coat, and I help him with the press-studs. He's wearing a thick shirt and a jumper, but up close like this I feel how thin he is. I'm glad he came to the dinner last night. All afternoon we've teased him about how handsome he looked in his dinner suit.

'Hurry up, Harry,' he says. 'Stop your fussing.'

We're walking along the beach when we meet Allan and Dougal. Dougal has his cast off now, but he has to stay on the lead for a few weeks so he doesn't jump around too much. Kat takes Dougal's lead from Allan and runs down to the shoreline, and she and Dougal dart in and out of the waves together. Jonty sprints down the beach to join in. I'm not sure how long he and Kat were on the doorstep together, but he's begun to idolise her now, just like he idolises Per. It'll make him even more determined to join the navy.

'You have to wait until you're eighteen,' I told him last week, 'and finished with school.'

'Commander Amundsen didn't wait,' he said. 'He was sixteen.'

A few details about Per's naval career are on the foundation's website now. He did join up at sixteen, and finished his schooling, and university, while he was in the navy. I explained to Jonty that things are done differently here, but he didn't want to hear it. 'What would you know?' he said. 'You never even went to school.'

Allan is talking about our strategy for Wednesday night's football game when Kat screams Jonty's name. He ignores her—he's mucking around, collecting handfuls of seaweed to throw at her. The wave rises up behind him. It's a freak wave, much larger than the others. Allan calls out and swings his arms above his head. Drew does the same. Kat runs towards Jonty, laughing, and Dougal runs after her, his tongue lolling out.

I gag on the saliva that races up my throat. I don't move or call out as the wall of water sweeps Jonty off his feet and sucks him into the sea. He disappears. And then I see bits of his body tossed about like flotsam, until the wave spits him out and dumps him on the shore. He's sodden, and coughing. Kat is still laughing. She grabs him under the arms and yanks him further up the beach. Dougal licks Jonty's face, and he splutters and laughs. He pulls at the clothes that are plastered to his body. His words carry on the wind.

'It's me best jumper!' he says. 'Nan's gonna *crucify* me.'

I've been dizzy and nauseous countless times. I'm always throwing up. But this is the first full-blown panic attack I've had since I ran into the surf to show Per what he was in for. The lights in front of my eyes blind me before I even get to my knees, and when I lower my head to vomit my skull explodes. The colours behind my eyes are brighter than they've ever been before.

* * *

Mum tried to send me away when I dived under the water and tugged at her seatbelt strap and buckle. She gestured towards the shattered windscreen and pleaded silently that I swim to the surface. But then she lost consciousness, and although her eyes were still open she couldn't see me anymore.

I knew she wouldn't die for a while, that she'd have enough oxygen in her brain to stay alive even though she'd stopped breathing. So I kept diving to her to try to set her free. But then the black mists would appear in front of my eyes and blur my vision, and I'd swim back to Dad and the air pocket above his head. I lifted his face out of the water as I gulped in air, but once I had my breath back I let him go again and swam back to Mum.

I didn't want to leave Mum there all by herself. I didn't know whether Dad was alive or dead. The only thing I could do for either of them in the end was to keep swimming between them. Up and down, up and down, up and down.

CHAPTER

27

The only light in my room is coming from the kitchen, so the shadows are deep and dark. I'm sitting up in bed and my face is wet. I'm gasping. And crying. Someone's sitting next to me but I don't think it's Liam. I hiccough when I breathe in.

Per pulls me onto his lap and whispers words I haven't heard before. '*Stakkars liten*,' and '*Det går bra*.' He's holding me so tightly that I'm pinned to his chest. I'm not sure how long I breathe in his scent. Last time I saw him we were on the chaise lounge. I'm stumbling from disaster to disaster.

I wriggle out of his arms and snatch tissues from his hand. I swipe them across my cheeks and blow my nose. 'I'm sorry. Why are you here? Where's Liam?'

'He left half an hour ago. It's after seven.'

I look around for my phone. 'Why didn't my alarm go off? It's set for five thirty.'

'Liam turned it off. He said you'd been up all night and needed to sleep.'

I scramble off the bed. 'I'll get my wetsuit.'

'Tell me what's going on.'

I'm almost at the door. 'Just a nightmare.'

'Liam told me it was worse than usual. That something happened yesterday afternoon.'

'Didn't Kat tell you about it?'

He stands. 'No.'

'Well.' I sniff. 'Good on her.'

He stares at the ceiling for a moment. Then he frowns. 'Drew knows your history, but he's not capable of helping you anymore. Liam won't talk. Tan suspects you're hiding things from him. Now Kat's clamming up. You've got so many secrets it's no wonder you can't sleep. Have you been back to the psychologist?'

'No. I was doing perfectly well until you came along, and I'll be fine once you're gone.'

I hear him muttering as I walk down the hall to the bathroom, but I can only identify one word. '*Trøbbel.*'

★   ★   ★

When I walk into the kitchen a few minutes later Per is standing at the kitchen bench. He's rifling through a stack of sketches. Most are of the kookaburra, but there's a picture of a dolphin at the top of the pile.

He doesn't look up when he holds a slice of toast in my direction.

'No thanks,' I say.

He shrugs, and takes a bite. 'Why didn't you become an art teacher?'

'I didn't have a portfolio, or any formal training, so I wouldn't have got into university that way. Anyway, I like geography, anthropology, things like that.'

'Didn't your parents see how talented you were? Come here. I'll fix your wetsuit.'

After Saturday night, I'd wanted to prepare myself before seeing him again. I wasn't ready to wake up to his fresh pine smell, or have him talk about my secrets. I don't want him in my kitchen like this, moving my ponytail out of the way when he pulls up my zip.

'My parents were like most parents—they thought I was good at everything.'

I see his troubled look before he can hide it. I'm not sure what I've said to upset him. He turns away abruptly. 'Hurry up. We're already late.'

I guess he's taking us back to the way things were ten days ago, when we were on step three of the pool. He wants to behave professionally and put the swimming first. I walk past him, he follows me out, and I close the doors behind us. After we step over the fence at the bottom of the garden I reach for his hand at the same time he reaches for mine. Our fingers entwine. My breath catches.

He looks down at me. 'You can trust me at the beach. We know what to do when we're here. You're safe.'

The wind whips my hair around my face as we climb the rise over the dunes. The sun is almost up. Long low clouds streak across the pale blue sky. The ocean is navy and white, the waves rough and fierce. When I stop, Per peers into my face. It's bound to be pale. Clammy. Afraid.

He takes me by the shoulders. 'We're not going into the pool, Harriet. Not today. Got that?'

I swallow. And nod.

We sit on the soft sand in front of the surf club. Per sits behind me with his legs spread out, and I lean against him. My legs are straight. When I turn my head into his chest I hear the slow steady thuds of his heartbeat.

Waves crash over the rocks and into the pool. Sea spray shoots skywards. The water is heaving. The steps are covered with white-wash and so is the landing. I point. The pitch of my voice is high.

'Look at the pool.'

Per tightens his hold on my body. He leans over my shoulder and whispers, 'Would you like me to tell you about the calving fronts of ice shelves?'

I nod. And then I shut my eyes in the hope it will erase the images of the pool and the steps. By the time I open my eyes again the sun is even higher in the sky. I must have slept.

'What time is it?'

'Almost eight.'

'You'll be late. *I'll* be late. Why didn't you wake me?'

When he whispers against the nape of my neck, it sets off a tingling sensation. 'Your heartbeats were good.'

I pull him upright after I've got to my feet. He follows me along the soft sand as I rehearse in my mind what I want to say. It can't be put off any longer. I have to present my arguments like Professor Tan would, sensibly and rationally. I wait for Per when we reach the steps to the dunes.

'If I put something to you, do you promise to hear me out?' I say.

He narrows his eyes. 'Within reason.'

'You're going back to sea in a few weeks, and it'll be mid-September by the time you get back. And I won't be able to go to the pool for a few days after that because a mining magnate has paid $10 000 for me.'

'What?'

'I was a prize at a fundraising auction. I'm going hiking with Malcolm Curtis in the Blue Mountains. The foundation is putting the money towards the fit-out of *The Adélie*.'

Per frowns, but doesn't say anything.

'The trip to Palau is in October. I only have a two-week school break and anyway, I don't want to leave Drew for too long. Which is why I plan to travel to Palau on *The Adélie*, do the front of camera work on the documentary for a day or two, and then fly home again. The documentary crew will stay longer. When they get back, I can do voiceovers and anything else that needs to be done.'

Per narrows his eyes. 'You said you wanted to put something to me. What?'

'Palau can't be put back because *The Adélie* will need to be home in time to prepare for Antarctica in December.' I point towards the pool. 'But I don't think I'll be swimming by October.'

'You won't.'

'I want to go to Palau anyway.'

'No.'

'At least think about it! I'm better than I was, you know I am. And Professor Tan has approved it.'

'Has he?' he snaps.

'Yes … subject to your okay.'

When he strides towards the dunes, I scamper after him.

'I promise to wear a life jacket the whole time I'm on board. I'll even *sleep* in it if you want me to. I'll stick to Tom and the rest of the crew like glue. *Please*, Per. It makes sense. You have to say yes.'

He doesn't say anything until we climb over the fence to my garden.

'Turn around, Harriet.'

I let him undo my zip. 'Well?'

'No.'

I spin around, swallowing a couple of times so I don't do something stupid like burst into tears. 'I made mistakes in Antarctica. I've taken responsibility for them. This isn't fair. I'm capable. I'm competent.'

He shrugs. 'I'm here, more or less, until December.'

'That's too late for Palau!'

'I won't change my mind. You're not going on *The Adélie* unless you can swim. Not while I'm involved with the foundation. That was what we agreed.'

'On Saturday night you said I had an impeccable environmental pedigree. You were talking about my parents, weren't you?'

'Yes.'

'You said I was smart.'

He hesitates. 'You are. But that doesn't get you to Palau.' He looks at his watch. 'I have to go.'

'Sorry for wasting your time.'

'Drop this, Harriet. I'll see you tomorrow.'

When I refuse to even look at him he picks up his boots and walks back to the beach. Will he swim today? I tell myself I don't care what he does. But before I rinse my wetsuit I climb the deck stairs two at a time to watch him.

He doesn't bother taking his bag to the car this morning. He dumps it on the sand and then he runs into the surf, diving through the waves until he gets behind the break. When he disappears beneath the water I hold my breath. He's an action hero. He's a sleek black shadow in the swell. He belongs in the ocean. But that doesn't stop me worrying about him.

* * *

It takes a week to get back to step three. The following day I want to go to step four.

'You're already nauseous,' Per says. 'That's never a good way to start.'

I sit straighter in his lap. 'I want to try it.'

He frowns over my shoulder as he puts his hand on my chest and checks my heart rate. It's much faster than his, but I must pass his test because he holds me firmly and stands.

'Are you sure about this?' he says.

I swallow. 'Yes.'

He sits on step four. I don't want to see how close his mouth is to the water so I bury my face in his salty damp hair. My arms are wound tightly around his neck.

'All right?' he says.

'Yes.'

He smooths my hair away from my face and rubs his cheek against mine. 'How long are you going to stay angry about Palau?' he says.

'Forever,' I say.

I'm getting used to the feeling of weightlessness. If Per didn't hold me down I'd float above his knees. He's telling me about water mass transformation beneath ice shelves. Over two weeks have passed since we argued about Palau and now we're on to step five. In two days' time, he'll be back at sea.

I point to the bottom of the pool. 'Tomorrow you'll have to stand up. We've run out of steps.'

'*Slutt å avbryt.*'

'Are you insulting me?'

'It means "stop interrupting". I was about to tell you about tide-water glaciers.'

'Not everyone loves ice like you do, you know.' I run my fingers through the water.

He pulls me closer. 'You said I should talk about the environment.'

'But you're *such* a scientist.'

'Did you tell Roger what happened in Brazil?'

I hesitate. 'You're not supposed to talk about Brazil.'

'I'll rephrase my question. Did Roger ask what triggered your fear of the water?'

I sit up straighter in his lap and narrow my eyes.

When his lip twitches I relax against his chest again. 'Drew wanted me to tell Roger what happened. I refused.'

'By breaking Roger's nose?'

I touch the end of Per's perfectly straight nose with the tip of a finger. Then I trail my hand across his cheek to his scar. 'Why won't you tell me what happened?'

He stiffens, lifts my hand and puts it on his shoulder. Takes a deep breath. His words when he finally speaks are clipped.

'I was a child.'

'And?'

'It was the worst fucking day of my life.' He narrows his eyes. 'Until I met you.'

It hurts, the way he shares so little. I push myself off his lap and stand, and he stands too. The water swirls around my hips and waist. A few drops hit my face. I'm light-headed all of a sudden. He must see it because he grasps my elbows, holding them firmly.

'Why did you stand so abruptly?' he says.

'To get away from you.'

He jerks me up against his chest. 'Do you think I enjoy this?'

'Seeing me fail?'

He speaks quietly. 'Seeing you *suffer*.' When I try to pull back he holds me more tightly. 'You're always cold. You're deathly pale. Your hands shake constantly. You—'

'Stop it!'

His face comes even closer to mine. His eyes are inky grey. 'You fight for every breath when we walk along the sand. Your pupils dilate when the whitewash gets close.'

'I get it!'

'Do you? You fall to your knees and sob because the pain in your head just won't go away. You're frightened all the time. And when you vomit? *Jesus*. It kills me.'

I have to swallow twice before I can speak. 'I want to go home.'

He puts his hands on my shoulders and mutters swear words in Norwegian. And then he feathers his thumb across my cheek, stroking.

I'm holding back tears. 'I'm sorry.'

He takes a few deep breaths, and rests his forehead against mine.

'Sorry isn't enough, Harriet. I want more than that. It's been twelve years now— almost half your life. So for Christ's sake, tell me. *What happened in Brazil?*'

*　*　*

It's like Per has opened a door and I can't force it closed again. Thoughts crash through my mind and I try to get them in order. A car tumbling over a cliff. Deafening noise. Silence. The vines and the shrubs and the trees and the river. So many shades of green.

'Lime, avocado, bottle, apple, emerald, olive, sea,' I say. 'That was what I saw.'

Once I've started talking I have to tell Per everything. How I didn't realise we were under the water until the windscreen shattered. How I tasted Dad's blood every time I came up for air. How he used to say I should swim with the tides. How Mum had promised she'd never leave me behind. How frightened she was. How my eyes are the same colour as her eyes.

I can't see Per through my tears. He's a blur. And he's squeezing my hands so tightly he's hurting them.

'I swam and I swam and I swam. I promise I did. Up and down, up and down, up and down.'

The hair that's come loose from my ponytail is sticking to my face. Per lets go of one of my hands to lift the strands and put them behind my ear. Then he holds my hands again, and we walk up the steps together. His hands are probably cold too, but they're warmer than mine.

'You're shivering,' he says. 'It's time to go home. I'll make you toast. *Ost og tomat*. Can you guess what that means?'

I can barely hear him. He's either whispering, or the roaring in my ears is muffling his voice. When I don't reply he answers his own question.

'Cheese and tomato.'

He lets go of my hands to gets the chamois out of his bag. I wipe my face and blow my nose. My throat hurts and I can't think why. It's light now. Our bodies cast shadows over the water. The Amazons are walking towards us. It must be well after seven. I've kept them waiting.

Helga puts her towel down on the landing. 'Are you all right, Harry?'

I nod. 'Late. Sorry.'

She raises her brows as she looks from me to Per. He meets her eyes and shakes his head. I've noticed their friendliness lately. I think they chat when I'm not around. Do they talk about me? I don't like the thought of them doing that. Per, the Amazons. They see me at my worst, when I'm vulnerable, afraid, and pathetic.

Vulnerable. Afraid. Pathetic.

I've dreamt about the accident often enough but it's been years since I really *thought* about it. I held my breath and swam in a car filled with water. I dived countless times to Mum. She was under the water but I didn't give up. Dad weighed 90 kilos. I undid his belt, pulled him through the shattered windscreen, dragged him to the surface and hauled him onto the riverbank. I rolled him onto his side to get the water out. Then I resuscitated him.

It was hours before Drew found us. They took Dad to the hospital but I wouldn't leave the riverbank. Not until we got Mum out.

It was getting dark. Drew paid three local men to dive for her body. I straightened her limbs and her clothes. I tidied her hair. I told her she was beautiful. And that she didn't need to be frightened anymore because I'd done what she'd asked me to do, and got myself out of the car. I made her a promise that I'd look after Dad.

Per holds out his hand but I refuse to take it. He walks silently by my side but when we get to the steps to the dunes he crosses in front of me and blocks my path. I look towards the cliffs at the northern end of the beach. That was where I fell on the rock shelf. Where all of this started with Per.

He puts his hands on his hips. 'We always hold hands. What the hell is going on?'

I take a deep breath. 'You said I was frightened all the time. Well, maybe I'm sick of being scared. And weak. And incompetent. Maybe I'm sick of caring what you think of me, and how you think of me. Maybe I'm sick of worrying about everyone. Even you.'

'Why would you worry about me?'

'Why do you think?' I point to the ocean. 'You swim out to sea!"

I can't stand still any longer so I push past him and run up the steps and over the dunes. He catches up as I jump over the fence to the garden. His sheepskin boots are at the bottom of the steps where he left them. The kookaburra watches as I pick them up.

Per frowns when he takes them out of my hands. 'We have to talk about what happens next,' he says.

'No we don't. There's no point floating, or even swimming, if I can't hold my breath. I learnt that from Roger. So I'm going to put my head under the water, to see if I can do it without blacking out.'

Per adopts his calm voice. 'We'll get to that.'

'When? At the end of October? After *The Adélie* has sailed? That's not good enough. I'm doing it at a time that suits me.'

'When?'

I lift my chin. 'Tomorrow.'

'No.'

'Yes! It can be our last swimming lesson. I'll take someone else if you won't come with me.'

His eyes are darkest grey. He narrows them. 'No you fucking well won't.'

Per thought he had a duty to rescue me when he suspected the *Torrens* wouldn't get to *The Watch* in time. No one takes out an inflatable—even one with a fibreglass hull—in six-metre waves. But he did. And once he'd decided to teach me to swim he had to look after me too. He thinks I'm vulnerable and afraid and pathetic. Scared and weak and incompetent. I'm not really like that. I wasn't like that in Brazil.

* * *

I'm hanging my wetsuit on the washing line when Rachael walks onto the deck.

'Liam's gone already,' she says. 'Time for a coffee?'

'That'd be nice.'

I'm sure my eyes must be red, but Rachael doesn't say anything when I walk into the house.

'I'll be out of the shower in ten,' I say.

I organise cereal and toast while Rachael operates the coffee machine. I'm feeling better now that I'm dressed, and my hair is washed and tied back. My mind is surprisingly clear. Tomorrow will be the last time Per and I go to the pool. My fear when I'm with him isn't only because of the water. I care about him. The idea of losing him frightens me more than it should.

The wind is picking up and my wetsuit swings around on the washing line. It spooks the kookaburra and he flies off his perch on the railing.

'It's going to get cold later today,' Rachael says. 'Speaking of which, what've you been up to with Polarman?'

I take another mouthful of cereal. 'He'd so hate it if he knew Liam called him that.'

She laughs, and tells me she's heard so much about him from Liam that she fantasises about them having a threesome together. Then she gives me an inquisitive doctor look, and asks again what happened this morning. I'm non-specific when I answer, telling her I told Per some personal stuff I haven't thought about in years.

'Now it's time to move on,' I say. 'I'm not going in the water with him anymore.'

People thought I'd been brave, dragging Dad out of the car and resuscitating him. But they didn't know the truth—that he mightn't have had a brain injury if I'd saved him straight away. I made a mistake. Every day that he lived I was reminded of that. And when he took off his oxygen mask and told me not to call an ambulance because he'd had enough, I did as he said. I always wondered whether I let him die for his sake, or for mine.

Rachael clicks her fingers in front of my face. 'Want to talk about it?'

I take a breath. Things are clearer now. I think Dad wanted to die for both of our sakes. I did what I was told because that was what Dad wanted. He knew I loved him. He knew I was courageous. He had faith in me.

I give Rachael a shaky smile. 'No, thanks. I think I'm good.'

'Sure you're not going too far with this? Not seeing Polarman in the water doesn't mean you can't see him at all.' She raises her brows. 'Don't forget, I saw those lips of yours after the dinner.'

'Shut up.' I slap vegemite on my toast. 'And enough about me, anyway. What about you and Liam? What's going on there?'

Rachael's not expecting my question, and doesn't quite manage to get the sadness out of her eyes before I see the truth. How could I not have noticed earlier? She cares for Liam. A lot.

'No!' I say.

At first she denies it, but then the words spill out. It was like me in the pool—except that Rachael's eyes stay dry and her nose doesn't run. It seems she's pretending to be happy with an open relationship because that's all Liam is offering. But she's thirty-three; she wants much more.

How can Liam not realise what she feels for him? Or does he know, and having an open relationship is his way of being honest with her? I don't like telling her that Liam's being a shit but I don't have much choice.

'You're clever and gorgeous and nice and … you're wasting your time with Liam. Dump him. I'll do it for you if you want me to.'

She groans. 'I know the theory, Harry. The practice is much more difficult. And to be honest, I thought he might be prepared to commit to me once you found someone. But you being with Polarman didn't make any difference at all.'

'I'm not with Per. And even if I were, Liam wouldn't care.'

Rachael picks up her bag. 'Promise you won't say anything?'

I've already told one big secret today. I'll do my best to keep hers to myself.

CHAPTER
29

Per and I exchange texts at recess.

> Harriet. Don't go to the
> beach without me. Per

> > No, sir!

> Don't call me that.

> > Do you think Scott would
> > have survived if he'd been
> > luckier with the weather?

> If he'd been better prepared
> for the realities that lay ahead,
> he wouldn't have needed to
> rely on luck. I'll see you
> tomorrow at six.

* * *

The end of the day can't come quickly enough. All I want to do is climb into bed and sleep. Lucy raises her hand but I can't remember what we've been talking about. Climate variation measurement?

'Yes, Lucy?'

'Commander Amundsen said Robert Falcon Scott mapped the Ross Sea in the *Discovery,* and kept journals when he was on the *Terra Nova* expedition. Scientists can look at what Scott mapped and wrote about in Antarctica, even when he was dying, and then look at what's there now.'

Lucy has woken me up. 'Good answer. When did Commander Amundsen say that?'

'Last week, on the science camp. Mrs Latimer set up a Skype session.'

A number of the kids start talking at once, telling me Per told them all about glaciers. It's the first I've heard of it.

'So Mrs Latimer got in touch with him?'

'I asked him if it'd be all right,' Jonty says. He looks around to make sure he has everyone's attention. 'I saw him with Gran at the beach.'

'Mrs Latimer said Commander Amundsen is hot,' Lucy says. 'Do you think he's hot, Miss Scott?'

Mrs Latimer is retiring next year. She must be sixty-five at least. 'I'm sure Mrs Latimer didn't say that, Lucy.'

Lucy shrugs. 'She said he's a honey. That's the same, isn't it?'

'I think it was an excellent idea to ask him about ice formations,' I say. 'He's got a PhD on those.'

'I don't want to be a scientist,' Jonty says. 'I want to be an officer in the navy. But the commander said I have to finish school for that too, which sucks. He joined up early because he couldn't live with his dad anymore. They hated each other's guts, that's what I reckon.'

I'm not sure how to respond to this. I'd like to sit Jonty down after the class and ask him to repeat every word that Per said. The kids are silent all of a sudden. Maybe they sense how much I want to know about Per's childhood. How he got his scar. Whether he's close to his twin. Why he left home at sixteen. All I've got out of him is heart-rate statistics and information about glaciers. I should have made him talk about his family when we first started going to the beach. It's too late now.

Thankfully the bell rings. 'Pack up, class. I'll see you all tomorrow.'

Lucy shouts over the chatter. 'Can we Skype the commander? So he can talk to our class too?'

The class quietens again. 'He's very busy,' I say. 'And he's a scientist. This is a geography class.'

'But he knows about continents like Antarctica,' Lucy says. 'That's geography.'

'He swims at Avalon all the time,' Jonty says. 'You could bring him in.'

If Jonty knows that Per swims lengths of the beach, he probably knows he holds my hand. He shuffles his feet when I give him a teacher look.

'Tomorrow's the last time he's coming to Avalon,' I say. 'He's going back to sea.' I pick up my bag and walk to the door. 'C'mon, let's get going.'

★ ★ ★

It's 3 am and I'm sitting on the sofa, drafting a post for the foundation's website.

The Scott Foundation: Environment Adventure Education
'I am just going outside and may be some time.'
  This is what Laurence Oates was reported to have said when he walked out of Scott's tent and into a snowstorm. Suffering

from frostbite, exhausted, and weak with malnutrition, he didn't want to slow the progress of his colleagues, so ended his life. Shortly afterwards, Scott wrote, 'He went out into the blizzard and we have not seen him since.'

Scott and his remaining two men were only 18 kilometres from food and fuel, but the storm was unrelenting …

Harriet

* * *

There's a drumming sound on the roof when I wake up. Rain darkens the timber on the deck and dense clouds obscure the waning moon. And it's windy; the lilly pilly branches scratch against the kitchen window. Per walks onto the deck in his wetsuit and sheepskin boots. He faces me, his back to the storm.

I open the door. With a whoosh of damp cold air, he steps inside. His dark hair is dripping. I'd like to run my hand across his forehead to wipe the moisture away. My knees weaken at the thought. What would he do? Press his face against my hand? Or scowl? Do I know him any better than he knows me?

'I parked out the front.' He examines my pyjamas—the blue flannelettes with white clouds. His eyes meet mine. 'We're staying here?'

'No.' I point to the sofa where my laptop is sitting on top of a doona and pillows. 'I got distracted. I'll get ready now.'

When a plastic chair on the deck crashes against the railing, I jump. Our eyes meet again.

Per jerks his head towards the beach. 'You're not ready yet. Don't do this.'

I raise my chin. 'I want to try.'

His mouth is set. 'Why end things now, when I'm just beginning to understand?'

'It was me who needed to understand, not you.' Whenever I did think about the accident, usually in my dreams, all I focused on were the things that I did wrong. Now I can see that I did some things right. When I get to the door of the hall I turn and face Per again. 'I almost had a panic attack when we were at the dinner because you said something about me diving in at the deep end. But that's what I have to do now. I have to be brave.'

CHAPTER
30

I chose a terrible day to be brave. The waves are enormous. I'm nauseous. My hands are shaking.

Per takes my hand when we get to the dunes. His grasp on my fingers is much too tight but I don't complain. I like the feel of his skin against mine.

'I'm totally opposed to this,' he says.

'I've done difficult things before.' I raise my voice over the roar of the ocean. 'Why aren't you talking about glaciers?'

'You promised to follow my instructions. You've gone back on your word.'

'You went back on your word first. You asked about Brazil.'

'Did you have nightmares last night?

'No.' I squeeze his hand. 'Thank you.'

I'd like to re-fasten my hair. Strands fly into my eyes and mouth. The rain is relentless. The tide is out but the occasional wave crashes against the rocks and washes into the pool. I can't stop swallowing.

When we reach the landing Per puts his bag near the base of the cliff. He turns and faces me. His mouth is a grim hard line. 'We can sit on the steps,' he says.

'I want to go under the water. I want to hold my breath.'

At the top of the steps he pulls me against his chest and puts his hand on my heart to feel my heart rate. His breath is warm on the side of my face. '*Du får meg til å skade deg.*'

I take a shaky breath. 'What?'

'You're making me hurt you.'

I push against his chest until he takes a step back, and then I take his hand. I tug, and we walk down the first three steps. A wave crashes over the rocks and sweeps into the deep end of the pool. A moment later the water rolls towards us and laps around my hips. I shudder. I'm trying so hard to breathe steadily that it's almost impossible to speak, but it seems important to say the words out loud.

'I held my breath in Brazil. And I was only a child.'

We walk down to steps four, and five. I don't look down but I feel the water at my waist. The wind stirs up the surface, making it choppy. The rain and the seawater splash me.

Per stares at my profile. 'You're not a child now.'

There's something in the tone of his voice that makes me turn towards him. His gaze locks with mine.

'I want you, Harriet. *So fucking much.*' There are molten silver flashes in his eyes. His lips are wet like mine. He'll taste of the sea.

I wrap my arms around his neck. He grasps my bottom and pulls me against his body. Then we explore the surfaces of each other's lips and tongues like we're searching for something elusive and can't get deep enough. We're both gasping for air when he raises his head. His breaths are short and sharp against the side of my face. I'm standing in the water and the waves are crashing onto the rocks but all I want to do is kiss him again.

I touch his face. 'Per?'

'Harriet,' he says, kissing my wrist. 'Harriet Hillary Amelia. Why are you called that?'

I have to gather my thoughts. 'Harriet for Harriet Adams. The explorer, geographer. Imaginative.'

He takes my bottom lip in his mouth and pulls on it with his teeth. Then he trails his lips over my chin, across my throat and up the side of my neck to my ear. He bites my earlobe. He whispers words I don't understand as he collects raindrops with his lips and kisses them into my mouth.

'Hillary,' he says. 'Is that for Sir Edmond?'

How can he string a sentence together? 'Yes.'

Another wave crashes into the pool, and little waves lap against the small of my back. I take a jerky breath. 'He was for determination.'

He holds me by the hips and lifts me. 'Wrap your legs around me.'

When I do as he says he kisses me again, a hard possessive bruising kiss that's difficult to keep up with. I don't realise he's standing at the foot of the steps until he raises his head.

'Amelia?' he says.

'Earhart.'

He's a few metres into the pool now. 'What does it stand for?'

'Courage.'

He presses his forehead against mine. 'Can we go home yet?'

I slowly shake my head. Then I look over his shoulder to the deep end. Every nerve in my body is on high alert. I'm aroused. And terrified.

'I want to hold my breath.'

Per growls as he pulls me closer. He walks backwards until he's almost at the end of the pool. The water is up to our necks. His breath is warm on my face.

'You're sure?'

I nod, and take a breath.

But that's not what he wants. He presses his lips against mine again. He opens my mouth with his tongue and mutters, 'Breathe. Through. Me.'

He bends his knees and we go under the water together. His breath is in my mouth. Then the sea is there as well. But I don't breathe in until we break through to the surface again. I can't think how he's still kissing me because my lips are frozen and my teeth are chattering. The rain falls in thick heavy drops on our faces and the sea spray casts foggy mists around us.

He talks against my mouth. His lips are gentler now, persuasive. '*Vakker*,' he says, before we go under again. This time I kiss him back. My lips and tongue slide against his while I hold my breath. One, two, three seconds, and then we break the surface again.

'Enough,' he says.

I take my legs from around his hips and hold on to his arms.

'Again. By myself.'

When I go under, the water swirls around me. I hear the underwater echo sounds I'd almost forgotten. The salt stings my eyes. The light is soft, and green. My hair floats and tangles.

Per links his arms around my waist when I come up for air. I whisper in his ear. 'Listen to the rain with me?'

We stare at each other under the water. His face is blurry but his eyes are fixed on mine. My heart thumps in my chest. He said he wanted me. I know that I want him.

* * *

He sits on step three of the pool as I lie on my back and kick slowly off from the wall. He lunges after me, and lifts me into his arms. The wind has died down and the rain has eased to a drizzle. I wipe the drips from his widow's peak.

'You're as cold as ice,' he says. 'And you promised to stay within reach.'

I smile. 'Sorry.'

'*Løgner.*'

When I bury my face in his neck he mutters. '*Trøbbel.*' He carries me up the steps, kissing me silent when I complain. After he carefully lowers me to the ground he looks up, and I turn around. Helga, Allan and the other Amazons are approaching. It must be seven already.

'Good morning, Harry,' Helga says. 'Hello, Commander.'

Per nods abruptly. 'We're done.' He grabs my hand as if he's concerned I might be tempted to stay with the Amazons.

Allan continues his warm-up. He swings his arms out wide and then crosses them over his chest. He rolls his shoulders and smiles. 'Morning, lassie,' he says, 'Morning, Commander.'

They must have seen Per kiss me. I look at my feet. 'Morning, everyone. Awful weather.'

As we walk along the coarse yellow sand, our hands swing in unison. We've never held hands like this before.

CHAPTER
31

Steam from the shower fills the bathroom. Per is behind me, drawing down my wetsuit zip. His eyes meet mine in the cabinet mirror as he reaches over my shoulder and traces around my lips with his finger.

'You've made them puffy,' I say.

'*Vakker.*'

I remember what he said in the quadrangle of the university. *You have a beautiful mouth.*

When I take his finger and bite the knuckle, he kisses my neck. Then he peels the wetsuit from my arms and yanks it down to my waist. He pulls me backwards so I'm leaning against his front and cups my breasts over my thermal top, gently stroking my nipples. I tip my head back and put my hands over his, pressing my bottom against his thighs. He spins me around and pulls the wetsuit down further, past my thighs, exposing my leggings.

He gets onto his knees. 'Hold my shoulders.'

When I do, he rolls the wetsuit down over my calves and feet. He runs his fingers up the outsides of my legs and grasps my waist. Then he finds the gap between my thermals and nuzzles my stomach, searching for my navel. He circles it with his tongue.

His voice is muffled. 'I think about you all the time.'

I sink to my knees and we share salty impatient kisses in the steam. Then he pulls my top over my head and draws my leggings down. We both yank at them until I'm free. He runs his hands over my body and kisses me while I tug at his wetsuit. But my hands are clumsy and I'm much too slow, so he strips it off himself and hauls me to my feet. His thermals are gone in even less time. He faces me.

I'd love to draw his body like this. Bones and muscles, angles and curves. He holds his breath while I study him. Everything is fascinating. I touch his face and his chest and his flat stomach, and when I take him into my hands he groans. Then he reaches around me to test the water, and eases me backwards into the shower.

His erection nestles against my stomach. He strokes my bottom with an open hand as I wrap my arms around his waist and listen to his pounding heart. We're so closely bound together that the water cascades over both of us. My skin tingles. When I wash my hair he steals the foam and lathers it over our bodies. He gazes at my breasts when I wash his hair.

'Please don't cut it so short,' I tell him, tugging at the hair of his widow's peak. 'There's no fringe at all.'

When I comb conditioner through my hair, he dips his head and suckles my breasts. I drop the comb to hold him there.

'It'll serve you right if you get soap in your eyes,' I say.

'Look,' he says.

My nipples are erect again. He seems to be pleased with himself. I graze his collarbone with my teeth.

'Harder,' he says, cradling my head and running his fingers through my hair.

'No. I might hurt you.'

He stills. Then he takes my face in his hands. The water blinds me. He kisses me so hard that our teeth clash. He's frantic again, like he was when we kissed on the steps of the pool. I stroke his erection, tentatively, not sure what's next. He covers my hand for a moment and squeezes, but then he turns away. His breathing is harsh.

'Per? Tell me what you want.'

'Can't,' he says, closing his eyes. He takes a breath, steadies himself. He feathers his hands down my body and puts one hand between my thighs; his breath catches when he strokes, and feels the slipperiness. His tongue moves against mine, slowly, in time to the slide of his fingers. He lifts his head. His voice is raspy. 'I have to kiss you there.'

I try to keep him upright but he pushes my hands away and crouches at my feet. I watch the water splash onto his shoulders and run in rivulets down his back as he burrows between my legs and kisses the insides of my thighs.

'Hang onto my shoulders,' he mutters.

'No. I want to hold you.'

He frowns as he nudges me up against the tiles. 'Let me, Harriet,' he says, as he runs his hands up my legs, spreads them a little, and holds me steady. He looks up, asking permission to go further.

I smooth the crease between his brows with my fingertips. He's blinking against the water that's splashing into his eyes. This is the way he wants me for now. I run my hand through his hair.

'I guess.'

His lips explore, and so does his tongue, like he wants to discover places in my body that are new to him. The warm water caresses my breasts and stomach, and flows over his sleek dark head. My legs quiver and I grip onto his shoulders with unsteady hands.

My voice is soft and shaky. 'I want you inside me.'

'I *am* inside you.'

He searches with kisses until the warmth between my legs spreads throughout my body. He grasps my hips to stop me from falling when I climax. He soothes me with slow gentle touches of his tongue when I tremble. He stands and drapes my boneless and compliant body against his. He turns off the taps with shaky hands and reaches for towels. He wraps me up and pulls me close.

I nuzzle against his neck and yawn. The ceiling fan whirs and clunks. There's hardly any steam now.

'Let's go to bed.'

I feel the movement of his jaw when he smiles. 'To sleep?'

I shake my head. 'Sex.'

'I could've been sleeping around, doing drugs in Oslo back alleys.'

I kiss his chin. Then I stroke his chest. 'I didn't really think that. You're careful and noble.'

He tips my chin up with a finger. 'I don't have a condom.'

'You're a commander. You should be better prepared.'

'I bet you're not on the pill.'

'No.'

'So you want to have a baby straight away?'

I'm not sure what to say to that. A couple of seconds pass, before he throws a towel over my head and rubs briskly. It's easier to talk to him like this.

'I haven't had sex since I was eighteen.' The rubbing stops, and then it starts again. 'Liam has condoms. We can use his.'

When he pulls the towel off my head, our eyes meet. His are serious.

'I don't want another man's condoms,' he says. 'And we have to talk.'

I *shouldn't* be cold. I'm wrapped in two towels. My skin is pink. He said he wanted me. Why doesn't he want to have sex with me?

'I shouldn't have said what I said before, should I, about being eighteen? I don't have a problem with sex.'

I don't want to have sex just to please someone. That's what I did with Grant. I don't need to have sex to prove I have control of my life. That's what I was trying to achieve with the one-night stands. I'm desperate to have sex with Per because I want to hold him inside me. Only him. But how can I tell him that?

He frowns. 'You've had a difficult few months.'

'Because of the swimming?'

'And other things.'

I inch backwards and he loosens his arms. 'You think I'm careless because I didn't ask about condoms, afraid because I haven't had sex for a while, and mixed-up because of the water. Don't you?'

'I don't want an argument.'

'Neither do I!'

'Get dressed then. We'll eat, and then we'll talk about what happens next.'

I have goosebumps all over my body but I don't want to get dressed. I don't want to talk. Or eat. So I skirt around him and open the cabinet. The bottom two shelves are mine. Liam, with shaving gear and twice as many toiletries as me, has the other four. I have to stand on tiptoes to reach the box of condoms on the top shelf. There's a strip of six inside. I shove them at Per's midriff.

He keeps his hands by his sides. 'I said no.'

'You'd better go back to Balmoral then.'

He unleashes a string of expletives in Norwegian—I'm familiar with all of them. Then he tips his face to the ceiling.

I count for him. '*En, tro, tre*—'

'Stop it, Harriet.'

We stare at each other. His lips are firm. They're not soft like they were before, when he kissed me in the shower. The thought of that flusters me. I have my hand on the door handle when I turn and face him again.

'You are like Roald Amundsen. The way you're so disciplined. The way you have to be in control.'

Something flares in his eyes. He speaks between his teeth. 'Are you getting dressed, or not?'

'No. I don't take instructions from you.'

'For fuck's sake!' He snatches the condoms out of my hand and kicks the door open. Then he takes my other hand. He curses all the way down the hall. He's sexy-angry, like he was the night of the foundation dinner.

Within a minute of coming into my room he's ripped off our towels. He kisses me briefly, groans, and then we tumble onto the bed. The blind is still drawn. The light coming in from the hall throws shadows on his body.

'Does this constitute control?' he says. I'm on my back and he's lying half on top of me, one leg draped across my hips. His hand runs over my stomach and rib cage. 'Does this?' He cups my breast and rubs my nipple with his thumb. When he takes the nipple into his mouth and rasps it with his tongue I arch my back and moan. He caresses the top of my leg, and then rests his hand between my thighs. I dig my heels into the bed and press up against his fingers. 'What about this?' He holds my wrists and pulls my arms above my head. He teases my lips and neck with hard impatient kisses.

I open my legs and wrap them around his body. He releases my arms and I grasp his shoulders.

My voice is husky. 'That's *loss* of control. I like that a lot.'

He slowly shakes his head. Then he rolls off me and puts on the condom. He holds my hip and pulls me onto my side. We face each other.

My muscles clench when he nudges his erection against me. So he strokes with his fingers and tells me how soft and sweet I am. How he'd never hurt me. He kisses my breasts with slow sweeps of his tongue. When he finally enters me I welcome the pressure, and the stretching. He shakes with the effort to go slowly. We're halfway there when our eyes meet and I see the strain on his face. I can't help laughing. He groans against my lips.

'Don't *do* that. You're so fucking tight already.'

'I'm sorry. How do you say that again?'

'What?'

'Sorry. In Norwegian.'

He takes a breath. '*Jeg beklager.*'

'But that's different from when you said it last time.'

'That was a different sorry.'

'How can there be different sorts of sorry?'

'Harriet?'

'Yes.'

'I can't have sex. And talk.'

Finally he's all the way inside. He kisses me. A slow, wet, tender kiss. He pulls back and searches my face. 'Are you all right?'

Ever since he touched me on the chaise lounge, this is what I've wanted. To hold him like this. I pull him even closer.

'Yes.'

The rain flurries against the window. There's a steady drip from the leak in the downpipe near the front door. He trembles when he moves inside my body. I taste the salty sweat on his shoulder and run my hand over his back. Soon his breathing is laboured. It's like no matter how hard he thrusts he can't get close enough.

I can barely make out his words. 'I'm rushing you,' he says.

I don't want him to slow down. His desperation, his ferocity, is intoxicating. I grasp his hip and roll onto my back, pulling him on top of me.

He stills, his eyes black in the half-light. He frowns and kisses my eyes. Then he draws back and feels with his hand how deeply he's buried inside me. He groans. 'I'll go too fast.'

I wrap my legs tightly around his waist, and lift my hips until our navels touch.

'Please, Per. I want to hold you like this.' I nip along his collarbone and he shudders. I match the strokes of his tongue when we kiss. He whispers words against my neck that I don't understand. And as he climaxes he claims my mouth again, like he's starved of the taste of me. When he collapses against my breasts I feel his heartbeats, fast and irregular. I stroke his hair, and tell him to breathe in time with me.

I'm not sure how long it is before he wakes. He has his breath back. My body is warm where he's touching me, but a draught blows in from the hallway, cooling my arms and feet. When he tries to pull out I clench my legs to keep him where he is, and wrap my arms more firmly around his neck. He raises himself up on one elbow and brushes my hair away from my face. His eyes are heavy. 'If I lose the condom, it's risky. That all right?'

An image forms in my mind. Of a little boy with straight black hair that falls into his eyes. It frightens me. Imagine how much it would hurt to lose something as precious as that?

I push against his chest. 'Don't be long.'

When he gets back he leans over me, kisses my shoulder, and mutters, 'We need a bigger bed.'

He lies down and pulls up the covers. He kisses my mouth, hard and deliberately, before he falls asleep in my arms again. I put the image of the little boy aside. Now I imagine Per and me in my cabin on *The Watch*. The wind is picking up. Gulls screech, so we can't be far from land. Sea spray splashes against the porthole. I explore his body as the ship rocks on the swell.

The textures of his skin, the firmness of his shoulders, the soft hair on his forearms, the scar on his cheek. His capable hands. I'm lying on my back and he's on his side, facing me. His arm lies flat on my belly and his fingers splay over my breast. His breath is warm against my throat. His long limbs are heavy, and trusting, in sleep.

CHAPTER
32

Per sleeps for an hour in my arms, and then he stretches. 'I'll make toast and coffee,' he says.

I stretch too. 'We can go back to the beach after that.'

After breakfast we pull on our wetsuits. They're still wet because we left them in a sandy pile on the bathroom floor.

Per grumbles as we walk through the garden. 'We've done enough for today. I'll be back in two weeks. There's no need to do this.'

I take his hand. 'I want to do it.' I open my mouth to try to explain about the accident, how I'm stronger than I thought I was, but the words get stuck in my throat.

'Don't rush it,' he says. 'It will come.'

I give him a shaky smile. 'Thank you.'

A washed-out yellow sun breaks through the clouds as we walk over the dunes. Per peers at my face when the ocean comes into view. He's checking that I'm okay but I'm studying him as well. His

scar is long, and the edges are uneven. When I fell on the rock shelf
he insisted I get tape on the cut.

'You didn't get stitches, did you?' I say.

He frowns. Then he sighs. 'Harriet …'

'Tell me.'

He shakes his head. 'No.'

'Why not? It must have been serious. How old were you?'

'Ten.'

'Who was looking after you?'

'I lived with my father.'

'What about your mother, and your brother?'

'My parents separated when Tør and I were two years old. Tør
went with my mother to France.'

'What? But you were just a baby. Why did—'

He squeezes my hand. 'Leave this.'

I take a breath. 'Okay. Just tell me how you got hurt.'

'I fell through a roof.'

'At ten?' Why didn't you see a doctor?'

'I hid the wound from my father.'

'What! How?'

'Enough questions, Harriet.'

'Does anyone know what happened?'

'My brother.'

A surfer walks past, a board under his arm. He's tall and wiry
with scruffy hair. He grins. 'Hey, Harriet. Great to see you. How're
you doing?'

I smile. 'Fine thanks.'

Per glances at me. 'Do you know him?'

I shrug. 'I don't think so. You're leaving tomorrow, aren't you?'

'Yes. First thing.'

'I'm going to swim with the Amazons.' When his hand stiffens I squeeze it. 'I have to be competent in time for Palau.'

The sun disappears. A few minutes later, just as we get to the pool, the rain comes back—a drenching shower that soaks our hair. Per runs his thumb along my lip when we stand at the top of the steps. I press his frown lines smooth. I feel sick and my heart is thumping as I hang onto the railing and walk down the steps. But when I extend my arms the water holds me up, and I swim with my head above it. After a while I duck dive, and swim a few strokes underwater. That worries Per because he refuses to be more than an arm's length away, and it's difficult to spot me in the deep end.

Occasional waves flow over the rocks. We hang on to the edge of the pool and hold our breaths. We're covered with foamy white-wash, and our bodies are tossed around.

Per is behind me with his hand on my waist. 'Give me your word that you won't do this with the Amazons,' he says.

I turn, wrap my arms around his neck and kiss him. His salty taste is addictive. 'I promise.'

After we leave the pool we walk back along the beach and stop near the rock shelf at the northern end. I'm not ready to brave the surf yet so we sit on hard sand near the break. Per is behind me. He wraps his arms around my middle as occasional waves lap against our feet. We watch the ocean together. The colours of the sea and sky merge on the horizon—when I turn and look into his eyes I find the same shades there.

'What are you looking at?' he says.

I smile. 'Do you appreciate how nautical your eye colour is?' I count on my fingers. 'Steel, gunmetal, cadet, battleship, silver.'

He shrugs. 'They're grey. Yours are *blå som nordlys*.' He kisses the tip of my nose. 'Blue like northern lights.'

'Nice.'

When I nibble along his jawline and put my hand on his thigh, he stands and hauls me to my feet. We're kissing hungrily and tugging at each other's wetsuits by the time we get to the deck. I spread towels and cushions on the floorboards in the living room and even though I'm shivering I keep the doors to the deck open, so we can hear the waves crashing on the shore and the sounds of the wind whipping through the trees. I straddle him, and before long we're wild and ferocious like the stormiest of seas.

'You taste like the ocean,' I say.

After we shower again and go back to bed, I lay on his chest and we kiss slowly and lazily. When I nuzzle his neck he rolls me over and runs his hands and mouth over my body, as if everything is new and he has to chart it over again. He murmurs against my breast when we finally collapse, our warm limbs entangled.

'We have to talk,' he says. 'Plan.'

I yawn and close my eyes. I stroke his hair, damp with sweat. 'Later.'

'It scares me, leaving you.'

'What do you mean?'

He doesn't answer for a while, and when he finally speaks I can barely hear him. His words are slurred with sleep.

'*Du er trøbbel.*'

* * *

I'm not sure whether it's the dream that wakes me, or the landline phone jangling in the kitchen. We're in my bed. Per was hugging my back when I went to sleep. He's still behind me, but now he's leaning over my shoulder. It must be midafternoon, and it's finally stopped raining. Weak rays of sunlight creep into the room either side of the blind.

He strokes my hair, and speaks quietly. 'Harriet? What were you dreaming about?'

If I had been dreaming about the accident, I might have told him about it. But I was dreaming about him, diving under a wave and never resurfacing. I was running along the beach, calling his name.

'I don't want to talk about it.'

I can't see him but I hear his indrawn breath. 'When I get back,' he says, 'I'll take you to someone I know—a post-traumatic stress psych. You can't go on like this.'

I roll over and face him, pulling up the sheet to cover my breasts. He makes an exasperated sound, but then he strokes my arm, circling my wrist with his fingers. He's perfectly comfortable being naked. His chest is broad and smooth, his stomach flat.

'I don't want to see someone you know,' I say. 'I'm doing well on my own.'

He narrows his eyes. 'You're not on …' He pulls himself up mid-sentence. He's clearly reluctant to argue with me, but he's not prepared to capitulate totally. 'Just tell me about your dream then. Before I go.'

'I said no.'

He's reaching for me when the phone rings again. I scurry to the end of the bed, taking the sheet with me. He heads me off, and puts a hand on my arm.

'Leave the phone.'

Our eyes meet. His are guarded. He's not sure what I'm up to. Neither am I. It's tempting to fold myself into his arms and let him take care of me and tell me what to do. But that wouldn't make me happy, not for long. I was awake for ages thinking about what he'd said before he went to sleep, that he was afraid to leave me alone.

I force myself to say the words. 'Will you tell the professor I can go to Palau?'

His lips firm. 'It's too early to decide.'

'I need to know now, to settle things with work, and Drew.'

'Before this morning you had no chance of going. Why the hurry now?'

'Why not? The documentary producer is finalising the schedule. And it'll give me something to work towards while you're gone. I'll swim with the Amazons for the next two weeks, and with Liam if he has time. *Please*, Per. You have to tell Tan.'

He runs his fingers through his hair and massages the back of his neck. He growls his words.

'Don't do this, Harriet. Not today.' When he puts my hair behind my ears I have to use all my willpower to pull away and wriggle off the bed.

'I want to get dressed,' I say. 'I have things to do.'

He silently watches as I struggle to keep the sheet around me. I must be moving too awkwardly to stare at for long though, because he puts on his thermals, and gets his suit carrier out of the car. By the time I'm dressed in jeans and a sweatshirt he's wearing black trousers and a crisp white shirt. There are golden stripes on each of his shoulders. Even though he hasn't tucked the shirt in, or done up the top couple of buttons—and his shoes are in his hand—he's back in commander mode.

When our eyes meet in the hallway I'm certain our thoughts are the same. We're not wearing wetsuits, or naked. The rules have changed about touching each other.

★ ★ ★

Half an hour later, Per is eating his sandwich. I'm picking at mine. He makes an effort to converse.

'We're doing a joint operation off the east coast of Tasmania. Half the Australian fleet will be there, and a number of US Destroyers. Fourteen days straight.'

'That'll be cold,' I say. 'Being that far south.'

'I'll be in Darwin next month. That's warm. Meet me there?'

'I'll be busy. End of term. And Palau.'

He reaches across the table and takes my sandwich. It flusters me when he holds my gaze as he bites all the places I've nibbled at. Finally he drains his coffee. He bangs his mug on the table so loudly that I jump.

'I have to report to Balmoral,' he says, giving me a stiff smile. 'But I'll be back here around eight. Maybe you'll have found your voice by then, and your appetite.'

'I've got something on.'

'Cancel it.'

'It's for the foundation. Potential sponsors will be there. We need their money to finance *The Adélie*.'

He pushes his chair back and stalks to the back doors, opening them wider like he needs the air. Then he steadies his breathing, and faces me.

'Were your parents obsessed with the foundation like you are? Putting it above everything else in their lives?'

'I'm committed, not obsessed. And the foundation didn't exist until just before Dad died.'

'You father put all his personal assets into it, didn't he?'

I hesitate. 'Most of them, yes.'

'My lawyer looked into what happened. You were eighteen. Your father was wealthy. But all he left you was the apartment in Newport, and a few thousand dollars in your bank account. Not enough to last until you'd finished your degree. Drew had to help you out.'

I don't respond.

'You work two jobs now, but only get paid for one. And all your teaching income goes into paying your mortgage.'

'The foundation supports causes I believe in. Most of its workers are volunteers.'

'You're exploited. You didn't have a choice about the way you grew up, but you don't have to live that life now.'

'I had a wonderful childhood. And I enjoy my life now. None of this is any of your business.'

'You've made it my business.' He narrows his eyes. 'Have dinner with me.'

'I told you, I'm busy.'

His patience evaporates. He's ramrod straight. He balls his hands into fists. When he speaks his voice is glacier cold.

'Why did you have sex with me?'

I study my hands. My fingers twist together.

'Well?'

I was desperate to hold you inside me.

I can't tell him that. He didn't even *want* to have sex with me the first time we did it. He thinks I behave recklessly, impulsively. He thinks I'm vulnerable.

I swallow. 'I was happy about holding my breath, I guess. And—'

'Were they thankyou fucks?'

'What …? No!'

'What sort then?'

I don't want to think about what sort of sex it was, any more than I want to think about the image of our little boy with dark hair.

When the phone rings I race for it, snatching the receiver like a lifeline. 'Hello!'

'Harry,' Professor Tan says. 'Where have you been all day? I need to talk to you about *The Watch*, and about Drew.'

Per gets up from the table after I hang up the phone. 'What was that about?' he says.

'Professor Tan wants me to meet him on Monday night.'

'You're upset.'

'I'm not.' There was a steely note in Tan's voice that I haven't heard for a while. It makes me uneasy. I clear my throat. 'I have things to organise before I go out tonight, that's all.'

Per washes our plates and mugs while I pick up the towels and cushions strewn on the living room floor. When he's ready to leave he stands in front of me. His face is drawn. 'Kiss me goodbye,' he says. 'You owe me that.'

I've hurt him. I owe him far more. He's standing stiffly to attention with his hands by his sides. I'm on tiptoes because that's the only way I can reach his mouth. My hands are on his chest. He's warm, and his heart is thumping. After a while the feel and the scent and the taste of him fills my senses.

He scowls when he pulls me closer, lining our bodies up. 'It would be impossible to overstate how furious I am with you,' he says. '*Rasende*.'

'What does that mean?'

'Furious.'

Jonty interrupts us, clumping up the back steps.

'Hey, Harry. Where were you today?'

Per glares at Jonty, takes my hand and drags me to the front door, slamming it behind us. When he kisses me his mouth is hard, unyielding. I stroke his face to imprint his features on my mind. I don't want him to play war games off the coast of Tasmania, where the seas are rough and cold. I want him to stay safe in my bed with me. No sooner has the thought entered my mind than he straightens. He swipes his thumb over my bottom lip, and then he walks away.

CHAPTER
33

Professor Tan opens the door to his office on Monday evening, thirty minutes after our scheduled appointment. Last time I was here Per arrived late. All weekend I've been trying to get him out of my mind. The happiness I feel about holding my breath is tempered by the unhappiness I feel about him going away. Two weeks at sea.

I shove the assignments I've been marking into my bag and stand. 'Hello, Professor.'

He nods but doesn't say anything. There are papers all over his desk. And even looking at them upside down I can see they have nothing to do with physics. As soon as I'm seated he picks up a wad of pages held together by a bull clip. He reads from the transcript of evidence I gave to the maritime inquiry into the sinking of *The Watch*.

'"The captain's conduct was exemplary. I lied when I told him there was room for me on the second lifeboat. I did it because I felt responsible—the winches had failed on the other lifeboats, and the ones we managed to get into the water were overloaded already".'

Tan flicks through more pages, summarising and quoting and giving me pained looks.

'"Yes, I was aware of the satellite problems we'd had on our previous trip. No, I didn't get advice from anyone on how they ought to be addressed".'

He purses his lips when he gets to the next section.

'"Yes, we were one life jacket short, even though we should have had at least ten extras on board. Captain McLeish had ordered new jackets and asked me to collect them. I'd forgotten to do that. It slipped my mind to do a gear audit before we left Sydney".'

He finishes with a quote from the final day of proceedings.

'"It was too late to avoid the storm by the time I'd got accurate weather readings. Yes, I am now aware that, had I downloaded appropriate software and taken other precautions, we may never have lost *The Watch*."'

'This is sworn evidence,' he says. 'You appreciate the potential consequences of lying to the inquiry? You could be prosecuted for perjury. And contempt.'

I'm trying to hide my nervousness from Tan. I lift my chin. 'Who says I lied?'

He slaps the pages onto his desk. 'Don't insult my intelligence!'

As if raising his voice is some sort of signal, his PA opens the door. She brings in a coffee plunger and two cups and saucers and puts them on the desk. Tan sends her home for the day. He pours the coffee and pushes a cup and saucer across the desk towards me. I don't like black coffee, but there doesn't seem to be any milk.

'I encountered one of the documentary producers last week,' Tan says. 'She told me she often sees Drew at Avalon, and at his care home.' He's speaking more calmly now, but he still has a steely edge to his voice. 'I'm sure she didn't realise she was giving you away when she told me his dementia was diagnosed last December, before *The Watch* left for Antarctica.'

'What are you getting at, Professor?'

He takes off his glasses and cleans the lenses, then puts them on again. 'What I'm *getting at* is that I've pieced everything together. All the elements that never added up—your interviews with the captain on the *Torrens*, the inconsistencies in your evidence at the inquiry. Drew was methodical in everything he did. And in your own way, you are too. You wouldn't have *forgotten* to pick up life jackets or download software. It was Drew, wasn't it?'

'It was my responsibility.'

Tan acts as if I haven't spoken. 'The type of dementia Drew probably has could have affected his ability to function months before he or anyone else knew of his impairment. I'm cognisant of the type of confusion and confabulation that could have occurred. He would have believed that something had happened because it *should* have happened.'

I hold myself back from responding. I have no idea where Tan is going with this.

He looks over his glasses. 'I've confirmed a number of things with other members of the crew. They weren't sure what had happened with Drew, but they suspected you were lying to protect him. Their loyalty to you ensured they kept quiet about it.'

I take a deep breath. 'Even if you're right, none of this matters. The inquiry is over. No one is interested anymore.'

Tan purses his lips, and taps one of his folders. 'You're wrong about that. Fundraising for *The Adélie* isn't going well. You're still popular with the public and other environmentalists. The Scott and Amundsen angle is attracting a lot of interest from schools and community groups. But the money they're contributing isn't nearly enough.'

'Corporate sponsorship?'

'Is a problem. As are the universities, and the private benefactors who have been generous in the past. They want reassurances before they hand over their money. You lost the last ship, so why should they give you money for another?'

I take a breath. 'Fair enough, I suppose. Doesn't Per's involvement help?'

'On the rare occasions he makes an appearance, yes. But our real problem is you. You're the public face of the foundation.'

'I can't change what happened on *The Watch*.'

He smiles stiffly. 'Except that it didn't happen like you said it did, did it? *You lied to the inquiry.*'

'This isn't getting us anywhere. Why did you want to see me?'

He takes a sip of coffee. Then he looks at me over his glasses again. 'We have to correct the record for the foundation's sake, and so that we get *The Adélie*. You have to tell the truth about Drew.'

'No!' When I slam my cup into its saucer, coffee slops onto the desk. I fumble in my bag for a tissue. As I mop up the drips I try to calm myself down. I have to be measured or Tan won't listen to me. I meet his eyes. 'Drew deserves our protection, Professor. He's earned it. He dedicated his life to *The Watch* and its causes.'

Tan tidies his folders again. 'Drew made errors of judgement because he was unwell. We'll approach the maritime authorities and make sure they understand the circumstances. You were traumatised after a near-death experience in Antarctica. You were grieving over Drew's diagnosis. And you were the only one harmed by your evidence.'

'I said no! It's not the way I want Drew remembered.'

Tan links his hands together and rests them on the desk. 'We need *The Adélie*,' he says. 'So the ship and her crew can engage people like *The Watch* did. But we'll never get her permanently if we don't change our strategy. We have to recast your image—as a competent and worthy successor to your parents. There are all sorts of things we can do. A profile in one of the weekend magazines will be a start. How you risked everything, your reputation and your credibility, to protect a beloved mentor. And how you're back on track, fighting for the things that are important to you and the planet.'

I jump to my feet. 'Listen to me!'

He stands too. Purses his lips.

'Sorry I yelled,' I say. 'But ... I'll work harder with the corporate people and the donors who've been generous in the past. Show them I'm competent. I'm going to Palau. That will help.'

He raises his brows. 'The commander has given his permission?'

'I can swim.'

He methodically stacks his folders, forming two neat piles on the desk.

'Please, Professor. Just give me some time.'

Finally he looks up. 'Very well, Harry. But not too much time, until the end of the year at the latest. I want *The Adélie*, and if I have to *un*-tarnish your reputation to get her, then that is what I shall do.'

CHAPTER
34

Per. Helga told me you emailed her, and asked how I was going in the pool. Please direct your questions to me. Harry

Harriet. I tried that. You told me to mind my own business.

Helga said you'd been sick. Did you catch a cold at the beach?

I'm always warm. Remember?

I'm doing another post about Scott and Amundsen. Any ideas?

Amundsen was trustworthy and dependable, with weak communication skills. Scott took unacceptable risks. He was a good leader, but his judgement was poor.

*   *   *

'Liam? Do you think I have poor judgement?'

We're walking up the beach towards the dunes. I swim with the Amazons every morning, and since Liam's been on night shift I go to the beach with him in the afternoons. He surfs while I swim in the pool—he doesn't need to watch me anymore. When the waves are small we paddle in the surf.

He grimaces. 'Are you quoting Polarman?'

'Yes.'

'You've been on your best behaviour for the last week and a half. Why don't you let him know about that? He might worry less about you.'

'I doubt it.'

'Are you going to tell him about Drew?'

'Why would I do that? Per would hate that I lied. Maybe that'd be even worse in his eyes than my supposed incompetence losing *The Watch*.'

'Drew wouldn't have wanted you to lie either. He was sick, that's why he made mistakes. So stop covering for him. You did the same for your father.'

Dad wasn't capable of supporting me emotionally after the accident because of his brain injury, but I knew that the man he had been couldn't have loved me more. And I'd promised Mum I'd look after him. As for Drew, there's nothing I've done for him that he wouldn't have done for me.

We're at the steps to the dunes now. Before I turn to face Liam, I go up a couple of risers to get a height advantage. 'I know what I'm doing, Liam.'

He shakes his head. 'You sure about that? You take things on for people. Your father, and Drew.'

I poke him in the chest. 'I'd stick up for you too.'

'Yeah. Got that. But what about Tan? He's being an arsehole threatening you, but you're still supporting him, attending events most nights.'

'I'm supporting the foundation, not him.'

He raises his brows. 'The foundation comprises sponsors, thousands of regular donors and a million or so kids. That adds up to … what? Around ten per cent of the population? No wonder you never take the rubbish out.'

There's an ice-cream wrapper on the sand. I pick it up and wave it at him.

'Fix up your own life before you meddle in mine. You're going away to Byron soon. Is Rachael going with you?'

Liam doesn't say anything. He walks past me and keeps walking until we get to the garden. Then he turns and faces me. 'You told me to fix up my life,' he says. 'Then you referred to Rachael. Care to explain the connection?'

'I can't. That would be breaching a confidence.'

'So? Have you been talking to her?'

'You are *such* an idiot! Why won't you commit?'

'Does she want that?'

I cross my arms over my chest. 'I'm not at liberty to say.'

We stand near the washing line after we've hung up our wetsuits. The kookaburra is perched on the railing. He's an adolescent now; shades of teal blue peep through the cream and grey feathers on his wings. He looks hopefully at Liam, who ignores him, and puts a hand on my arm.

'C'mon, Harry. Give.'

He follows me up the steps to the deck and we sit side by side, staring through the foliage to the ocean beyond.

I nudge his knee with my foot. 'Casual sex, at this stage in your relationship, is not what Rachael wants.'

He laughs and pokes me in the arm. 'You had sex with Polarman. Using my condoms, no less Was that appropriate *at this stage in your relationship?*'

Every night when I go to my room I imagine Per is waiting for me. He's sprawled on my bed. His arms are linked behind his head.

'This is about you, not me. You have to be honest with Rachael. She deserves that.'

'Does she want kids? All that palaver?'

'I think so.'

He shrugs. 'That's not for me. I'll talk to her. Now back to you—what's going on with Polarman?'

'He's at sea.'

'Yeah, like that's what I want to know about.' He gets up and stretches. 'I saw you a few times, Harry, after you broke up with Grant. At the surf club in Newport, and the pub.'

Liam never looked at me disapprovingly when I was pretending to have fun with whatever man I'd picked up for the night. It was worse than that. He looked … unhappy for me.

I stand and face him. 'At first I was regaining control because Grant had let me down. And then I was punishing myself for being so stupid. But since then … there hasn't been anyone I've ever really wanted.'

'Until Polarman?'

'He thinks I'm high-risk and nothing but trouble. And maybe he's right. Maybe, so far as it applies to men, my judgement *is* poor.'

'I doubt Polarman wanted you to question your judgement in regards to your feelings for him. And high-risk could be a good thing if it means you'll give him a chance.'

It's been ten days since Per left. Nobody's bossed me around, talked about glaciers, or held my hand. The beach feels different without him—the salty breezes, the way the waves race each other to shore, and the early morning light as it dances on the surface of the ocean.

★ ★ ★

The Watch was anchored off the West Australian coast in the year I turned twelve. Dad, Drew and I spent long days scuba diving in an underwater cage. One morning I unlatched the door and dangled fish guts from the end of my flipper to attract a great white shark. Dad was filming, facing the other way. He nearly had a heart attack when he turned around and saw a shark barrelling towards us. Drew laughed so hard he couldn't breathe into his mouthpiece. He had to signal Mum to take us up.

A few weeks later I grabbed a dolphin's dorsal fin near the reefs off Shoalwater and let him carry me out to sea. Mum wasn't even aware I was out of my bunk. She happened to hear me squealing, went to investigate and spotted the wake that trailed behind me. She followed me in the outboard dinghy and hauled me on board.

'Harriet is grounded!' she said to Dad when we got back to *The Watch*. Drew laughed at that too, because we were about to head off on a three-month voyage.

I'll never be fearless in the water like I used to be. I can't imagine scuba diving or swimming in open waters. But I'm determined to snorkel the reefs in Palau. Saturday and Sunday I'll be hiking with Malcolm Curtis. Monday and Tuesday I'll swim with the Amazons. Then I'll call Per.

He thinks I'm reckless. I'll have to prove to him I'm not.

He thinks I'm a liar. That worries me. When we were at the foundation dinner he said *you're truthful, or you're not*. I'll try to be truthful from now on.

He thinks I'm afraid. The only thing I've been fearful of lately is losing him.

He needs to trust me, and trust that I'm strong. Will he nod abruptly when he sees me swimming laps? Will he hold my hand on the beach? If the waves are small I'll lead him into the surf. We can tread water. I'll kiss his salty mouth.

I shouldn't have sent him away like I did. I'll do what Liam suggested. *I'll give him a chance.*

CHAPTER
35

The overnight mists have dampened the eucalypts; their leaves glisten brightly in the early morning sunlight. The escarpment glows red and burnt orange in the distance.

'How much further, Harry? I need a break.'

Malcolm Curtis is in his late thirties. He's full of himself, and used to bossing people around. And if he has trekked the Kokoda Track and hiked at Machu Picchu like he says he has, someone else was carrying his pack, organising his gear, erecting his tent and feeding him, because he seems to have no idea how to do anything for himself.

'Another twenty kilometres in total,' I say, smiling broadly like it'll be a stroll to the boardroom for him. 'But once we're out of the valley we can rest.'

We'll be climbing most of the day, up towards Narrow Neck, and then Katoomba, where I left my car. We could've done an easier route but Malcolm insisted he wanted a challenge—to get his money's worth for the $10 000 he paid for my company.

After dinner last night he patted the space next to him. 'C'mon Harry,' he said, holding out his hand. 'Keep me warm?'

Billionaire or not, the thought of even taking his hand turned my stomach. I don't want anyone touching me except for Per.

'I'm making hot chocolate,' I said, adjusting the billy can on the fire. 'That will keep you warm.'

*   *   *

It's clear by 2 pm that I'm stuck with Malcolm for a second night. We're only three hours away from Katoomba but I don't trust him to pick up the pace, and there's nowhere suitable to pitch our tents in the last couple of hours of the hike. To make matters worse he's got blisters, even though he promised me he'd worn in his boots. I've dressed his feet a number of times but he's still complaining about them. And the weather is closing in. I chose a route with no river crossings, but there's a narrow creek up ahead. It's unlikely to have much water flowing through it, even in bad weather, but I don't want to pick my way through it in the rain.

'I brought plenty of food, and we're fine for water,' I say, dropping my pack on the ground and surveying the clearing around us. A cliff face reaches skywards on the eastern side, and a couple of substantial boulders and a giant scribbly bark eucalypt will shelter us from the west. 'There's plenty of kindling around here, so I'll make a fire as soon as I've pitched the tents.' My pack must be thirty kilos—it has most of Malcolm's stuff in it. I roll my shoulders around to loosen the knots.

'Don't you have a beacon?' Malcolm says. 'To get us rescued this afternoon.'

'Yes, but that's for emergencies. Do you really want a helicopter hovering overhead because you have blisters? They wouldn't be able to land here anyway. And even if they did get to us today, they'd see we were safe and send out a team tomorrow. Then, quite reasonably, because we're not lost and would meet them halfway, they'd complain we'd wasted their time.'

He grumbles, and throws down his pack. 'I was seeing friends tonight. Maybe they'll send out a search party.'

'I doubt it. I registered our walk with the rescue service. I told them we'd be back tonight but they wouldn't do anything until tomorrow morning anyway. They'd assume there was no emergency or we'd have activated the beacon.'

'You're enjoying this.'

'Not really. I organised to have tomorrow off so I could spend the day with Drew McLeish. But we may as well make the best of things. Take off your boots and I'll have another look at your feet. Then I'll tell you a campfire story. You can tell me one as well—about rich people you know who care about the environment. I'll ask them for money when I get home.'

Malcolm laughs, and offers to give me the personal details of anyone I'd care to name. He gets his phone out of his pocket and takes a photo of me tending his feet.

'I'll post it when we get back to civilisation,' he says.

★ ★ ★

Close to Katoomba we meet up with the track that leads to a clearing, and the car park beyond it. I'm not sure why there are so many people here—at nine on a Monday morning it's too early for the tourist buses that stop at the lookouts. For some reason there's a television helicopter resting on the tarmac.

'There's Harry!' A woman and a man, the man holding a camera in front of his face, walk quickly towards us. I recognise the woman—Lisa Toohey, the journalist with the sparkly dresses, only today she's wearing red trousers and a white shirt. Her thick auburn hair bounces on her shoulders

'Malcolm!' the cameraman shouts. 'You okay, mate?'

Malcolm hoots, pumps the air in a victory salute and throws an arm around me. My knees buckle and I stumble. Isn't it enough that I'm carrying half his gear without him exaggerating his limp and leaning on me?

I've just steadied myself when I see Per jump to the ground from the cockpit of the helicopter. He's dressed in tightly fitting black fatigues. His dark hair and panther body is unmistakable. He looks up and talks to someone who's still inside, presumably the pilot. I'm not sure what I feel—whether the sudden pressure in my chest is relief because he's safely back from sea, or trepidation because I don't know what he and all these people are doing here. Lisa Toohey shoves a microphone in my face. The crowd gathers around us.

I answer Lisa's questions patiently—a smile plastered to my face—as I explain that we weren't lost and didn't need rescuing. But it was raining and misty yesterday afternoon, making it safer to camp overnight. Malcolm details the hardships he's endured. He shows off his scrapes and scratches, and takes off one of his boots to display the tape that covers his blisters.

I'm hot and sticky, and dismayed that this excursion has somehow become a media event. Per is still standing next to the helicopter, talking on his phone. Even though I've decided to take a chance on him I didn't plan to see him today. What's he doing here?

The crowd eventually disperses. Seven-year-old twins, a girl and a boy, ask for a photo. After their mother has taken it, I point to Per. 'Commander Amundsen's a twin. Go and say hello.' The children race away and the cameraman follows them.

Lisa clears her throat. 'If you didn't need rescuing, Harry, can I ask why Commander Amundsen believed that you did?'

'What do you mean?'

'The commander called me last night. He told me you and Malcolm Curtis hadn't returned from your hike at the scheduled time.

He requested the helicopter to get him up here first thing. And in case we needed it later on.'

'What for?'

She shrugs. 'In the event you didn't show up. Our chopper's used for rescues all the time.'

'But I didn't need rescuing!'

She touches my arm and smiles. 'Go with the flow, Harry. This is a good news story. You and Malcolm have been found safe and sound, so there's cause for celebration.' She smiles in Per's direction. 'The commander is the icing on the cake.'

'There was nothing to worry about.'

'Tell that to the commander.'

Per squats in the shadows of the helicopter as he talks to the children. Then he gets to his feet and shakes their hands. The girl hugs his leg before she waves goodbye.

I can barely hold onto a neutral expression. 'Thanks for filling me in, Lisa. I'll have a word to the commander before he heads back.'

I take my keys out of my pocket. 'Malcolm! Catch.' I shoulder my pack and walk towards Per.

★   ★   ★

He's lost weight. His cheekbones are prominent and his scar is more pronounced. His eyes are glinting black. When he helps me off with the pack, our hands touch. He's particularly warm. Helga said he had a cold. He may have a temperature. The realisation troubles me, but I put it aside.

'Why are you here?'

'Because you are,' he says, reaching for me.

'No.' I step back. 'The press is still here. They'll take photos.'

He frowns, and rests a hand on my arm. I shove it away.

'I said no. They think you came to find me. To save me again.'

'I did.'

The lump in my throat gets bigger. It's an effort to speak. 'You shouldn't have contacted Lisa.'

'I needed her help. I told her the facts.'

'That I'm an accident waiting to happen?'

His smile is tentative. 'You are.'

It would be easy to lean my head against his chest. He wouldn't care that I'm dirty and weary. He'd hold me tightly and nuzzle my neck, trail kisses to my mouth. My knees would go weak with wanting him. I could trace the shadows under his eyes and take him home. I'd make him a cheese and tomato sandwich.

But what would be the point of any of that? He came here to *rescue* me?

'Liam wouldn't have been worried about me,' I say. 'Neither would the rescue services, so long as I was back this morning. I had a beacon, supplies and a planned route. When the mists roll in, it's stupid to keep going.'

'You planned a two-day hike. Anything could have gone wrong.'

'I've been hiking, climbing ... abseiling, since I could walk. No one would have been worried if you hadn't alerted Lisa.'

He rubs his neck and closes his eyes for a moment. 'Yeah, well, maybe people don't know you like I do.'

Grant didn't mean to harm me when he blabbed to the media. Neither did Per. But their thinking was similar—someone immature or incompetent like I am, someone who's vulnerable, has to be managed, protected. I take a long slow breath as I straighten my shoulders.

'You don't know me at all.'

He tips his face skywards and brings it down again so his nose is only centimetres from mine. 'I know you sink ships. And you have secrets.'

'Thanks.'

He runs his hand around the back of his neck again. '*Jeg har savnet deg.* That means I've missed you. I haven't slept.'

'Am I supposed to say thank you? Maybe Lisa can add *ungrateful* to my character profile?'

He straightens. Blows out his breath. 'She doesn't matter.'

'Yes she does!' My lips must tighten because he zeroes in with his thumb. I jerk my head away. 'I told you not to touch me.'

'*Jesus*, Harriet. I've waited two fucking weeks to touch you.' His voice is low, gravelly.

'My personal life is private.'

'What? When half the fucking country has a piece of you?'

I clear my throat and try to speak calmly. 'I deal with the media to support my causes, and I do it on *my* terms. This is the first time you've engaged willingly with them, and what do you say? *Harriet Scott's in trouble again.* I care about my reputation, and my professionalism, just as much as you do.'

'Your reputation went down with *The Watch*. And professional? When you sell yourself for weekends?'

It's like I've been punched in the stomach and the air has been forced from my lungs. I was giving him a chance to get to know me better, to learn to trust me and have faith in me. My dreams were stupid and girlish. The silence between us is interminable. I'm trying to get my breath back. He's trying to get his temper under control. Finally he speaks.

'Harriet, I didn't—'

'Oh yes you did. And it's not for the first time either. You think I'm the foundation's whore. It doesn't matter anyway, because—'

'I didn't—'

'No!' I reach for my pack. 'I have to get back to Malcolm. He's *paid* for my services.' My voice is unsteady. 'And like I said, it doesn't matter. It's not like we have to see each other. I can swim now, and you never turn up to functions.'

'Are you saying we're over? For fuck's—'

'If we were ever together, then yes.' I shoulder my pack and shift my weight around until I get it balanced. I'm careful not to meet his eyes so he can't see the tears in mine. We both turn when we hear the crunch of gravel. Lisa and her cameraman are driving away in their van. My car door is open. I see the bottom half of Malcolm's legs; he must be lying down on the back seat.

'Harriet?' Per's eyes are darkest grey. 'The professor, he wants a meeting about Palau.'

'Why?'

'Friday afternoon at five. I can't do it any earlier. Or later. I'm going away again.'

'But Friday's four days away.'

'Complain to Tan, not me. He's the one who wants both of us there.'

We stare at each other. He can't apologise in a way that has meaning because in similar circumstances he'd behave in exactly the same way, say exactly the same things, all over again.

*   *   *

Malcolm wants to watch the helicopter take off. He won't shut up, telling me he flies on choppers all the time in the Pilbara, and up north at Bowen Basin. Then he talks about navy helicopters, like the *Seahawks* Per must get to fly in. As the helicopter disappears over a ridge I start the car. Malcolm continues to talk, shooting me encouraging glances. Thank goodness he doesn't ask questions about Per and me, because I don't know what I'd say if he did. That only a couple of weeks ago Per made love to me like I meant everything to him? And I held onto him as if my life depended on it?

CHAPTER
36

Lucy raises her hand. 'The commander's like Spiderman. He always comes to your rescue.'

'Can we get back to work, please?'

'He's more like an Avenger,' Jonty says. 'Or a vigilante.'

'Was it scary in the bush?' Lucy says.

'No … because nothing went wrong.'

'Then why were you on the news last night?' Jonty says.

'I was a little late back, that was all.'

'Why didn't you come back home in the helicopter?' Lucy says. 'I would've. How old is Per? Does he want to go out with you?'

'That's inappropriate, Lucy. Move on to the next workbook if you've finished the first one.'

'He's almost thirty-one,' Jonty says. 'His twin's a bit younger. Tør had asthma when he was a baby and almost died.'

Jonty is much better at finding things out than I am. I presume Tør is well now. I googled him. He looks the same as Per only his hair is longer.

I clear my throat. 'Let's return to the curriculum. Has everyone read my Antarctica post from Tuesday?'

The Scott Foundation: Environment Adventure Education

Scott's motorised sleds (which looked like a smaller version of the snow mobiles we use today) were developed specifically for the Antarctic expedition. The first and heaviest of the sleds fell through the ice as it was being unloaded from the Terra Nova; the other two sleds were discarded due to mechanical failure before the trek to the Pole had even begun. The loss of the sleds, combined with the failure of Scott's Siberian ponies, and insufficient dogs, meant that man-hauling—where Scott and his team were pulling the sleds themselves—was increasingly necessary. This was exhausting work, particularly in light of dwindling food supplies. But notwithstanding the hardships he endured, Scott never lost sight of the scientific objectives of his mission. He continued to collect rocks for the purposes of geological study even though it increased the weight of his sled ...

'What an idiot,' Amber says. 'His fingers are falling off with frost-bite and he's picking up rocks.'

'You don't lose your digits immediately,' I say. 'It takes a week or two.'

'If you're dead you don't lose them at all,' Jonty says. 'Not if you're in the deep freeze.'

'Be quiet, Jonty. Didn't you read the rest of the post, Amber? The reason Scott kept collecting was because he planned to take the samples back to England. The research aspect of his earlier work had inspired a lot of interest from institutions like universities and geographical societies. So his work in the field was important from a scientific perspective, and it helped him raise funds for later voyages.'

'Roald Amundsen just wanted to get there first,' Jonty says. 'That's what he cared about. Even if he could've rescued Scott I don't reckon he'd have bothered.'

'Not everyone's like the commander,' Lucy says. 'He *loves* to rescue people.'

I take a breath. The innocent smile Lucy had at the beginning of the year isn't looking so innocent now she's thirteen.

'Can we get back on point please, Lucy? Scientific enquiry?'

'Will you collect rocks when you go to Palau?'

'No, but I'll have plenty of other things to keep me occupied. Because in addition to being threatened by risks associated with global warming, Palau was the first country in the world to create a shark sanctuary in its waters, and it's also working on fishing exclusion zones to protect vulnerable species like Big Eye and Bluefin Tuna.' I nod towards the board where I've sketched a school of fish. 'Sustainable management of resources. Let's have a look at that now …'

* * *

Two days later Drew and I are walking together near the shore break. I picked him up from his care home after I finished at school. The waves gather around our ankles and our feet sink into the sand. Halfway along the beach we stop and face the horizon.

He links his arm through mine. 'It's a lovely evening, Maggie,' he says.

I squeeze his arm. 'Hey, I'm Harry, remember?'

He looks at me closely. 'Course you are. Confuses me a little, you looking so like Maggie.'

Most things are confusing to Drew now. He calls at six every morning wanting to know where I am and what he should be doing. 'Get dressed, have a chat to the night nurse, and then help out with the other residents until breakfast,' I tell him. 'Don't go outside until George or one of the other carers arrives at nine, or you may get lost again.'

'Harry! Drew!' Allan and Dougal are running down the surf club steps to the beach. Dougal is fully fit again, and gallops over the sand. I brace myself when he gets to me but he doesn't jump up; he rubs himself against my legs like a giant cat.

'Hey, boy,' I say, running my hands over his long curly coat. 'Nice to see you too.'

'Missed you in the second half of the game last night,' Allan says. 'How's the head?'

I thought I'd got used to seeing Grant on Wednesday evenings, chatting on the sidelines about the animals he was treating, or what was going on with the foundation. But last night he asked me out. He said he remembered how much I liked Thai food, and told me a bunch of people from his team had booked a table at a local restaurant. He smiled his boyish attractive smile. 'Will you come with me?'

It was half time. I looked down at my football socks and shorts. 'I'm hardly dressed for it,' I said.

All of a sudden he was serious. 'You're beautiful whatever you're wearing.'

Maybe it was the use of the word beautiful that upset me. *Vakker.* Within a heartbeat I was so choked up I could hardly speak. I said something about having a headache and leaving early, and could he pass a message onto Allan. It was another half an hour before I could see clearly enough to drive home.

★ ★ ★

Allan walks with Drew while I paddle. Dougal runs circles around me, and darts in and out of the ocean. We both spot the seagull. It's perched forty metres away on a piece of driftwood that's washed up on the shore.

'Race you, Dougal,' I say, taking off in a sprint. The wind is behind us and we fly over the ground.

I ran with Mum when I was small. When I could outrun her I ran with Dad. The first time I was faster than him we were on a beach in Cornwall in the middle of winter. *The Watch* was moored off shore; when we sat down to catch our breaths she was a blurry black shape in the distance. The coarse grey sand was rough between my toes, and I was so puffed I could barely breathe. 'Beat you!' I said.

Dad smiled, and shoulder bumped me. Thinking about it now, I can't recall that he was panting like I was. Maybe he'd let me win? The tide was out, so it was easy to follow our tracks as we walked back to the outboard. It was tied up to a jetty near the headland. I stepped in Dad's footprints, and he stepped in mine.

By the time we walk back to Drew and Allan, Dougal's and my footprints have been washed away. Per's were obliterated weeks ago. After tomorrow we'll barely see each other. I'll be heading to Palau in *The Adélie* towards the end of October. In December he'll take the ship to Antarctica. One day I'll thank him properly for giving me this gift of the ocean. I'll write him a letter to tell him what it means. When he's back in Norway. And when I'm sure I'm not in love with him.

CHAPTER
37

On Friday afternoon I bang on Professor Tan's door, ignoring his PA's instructions to stay in the waiting room until I'm called. When he opens the door he gives me one of his long-suffering expressions.

'Weren't you told to wait outside, Harry? I'd like another few minutes with the commander.'

Per is standing at the window with his back to me, gazing at the view of the university quadrangle. Even though I've psyched myself up to see him again, my heart threatens to burst through my chest. My words are stilted.

'I'll work on my sketchbook. Just pretend I'm not here.'

Per relinquishes his hold on the windowsill and turns. Our eyes meet. He doesn't appear to be unwell like on Monday. Or maybe he just looks particularly good because he's wearing his dress uniform. 'Harriet.'

He says my name as if it has three t's on the end.

I nod. 'Per.'

'Please take a seat, Commander,' Tan says. 'Sit, Harry.'

I take my sketchbook out of my backpack and flick through the pages, opening it wide on a picture of the kookaburra. I don't usually mix pencil and crayon but the splash of blue on the kookaburra's wings had to be captured somehow. He sat on the railing and stared back at me as I sketched.

My pencil stills on the page when Per sits next to me and studies my profile.

'We can start now,' he says.

The professor clears his throat. 'Have you recovered, Harry?'

I steady my breath. 'I had nothing to recover from.'

'Getting Lisa Toohey to play things down wasn't easy,' Tan says. 'She had numerous ideas for a much bigger story.'

I look at Per, and then back at Tan. 'I bet she did.'

Tan gives me a stiff smile. 'Irrespective of what you think of the commander's actions, they wouldn't have been necessary had you briefed him appropriately.'

'I didn't have to—'

'Let me finish. The weekend's events reflected badly on you, and by extension the foundation. It's been a difficult year all round, with the loss of *The Watch,* and lacklustre fundraising for *The Adélie.* The last thing we needed was coverage of you walking out of the bush sixteen hours late. Particularly with a foundation donor in tow.'

I walk my fingers down the spiral binding of my sketchbook and count the rings. By the time I've finished, my breaths are a little more even. The men are watching me.

'There is some good news,' I say. 'We have the use of *The Adélie.* For now, anyway. And I can swim, meaning I get to go to Palau for the first episode of the documentary series. That should generate publicity.'

Tan looks from me to Per. 'Commander?'

Per shrugs. 'She can swim, just. I still have fears for her safety.'

My voice is remarkably steady in the circumstances. '*The Adélie* leaves in less than a month and I'll be on board. Tom says it'll take six days to get there. I'll spend a day or two on shore. Then I'll fly home to Drew. Most of the footage in Palau will be shot after I've left, but we've got our regular producer and film crew, and they know what they're doing. We'll put the footage together and do most of the commentary in Sydney.'

'Only a week?' Tan says. 'Is it worth you going?'

I jerk upright in my chair. 'Yes! Because this is what we've been working towards. Finding a ship to replace *The Watch*. Fundraising. Swimming. *Everything.*'

Tan makes a pyramid with his fingers. He won't look at me.

'You're not going to like what I'm about to say, Harry, but hear me out, hmmm?'

My voice wavers. 'What?'

'I don't want another incident. The commander said he had fears for your safety.'

'I don't care what he said! I can swim. He *knows* that.'

'It's still risky—to you personally, and to the foundation should anything go wrong, particularly given our recent discussion.' He raises his brows. 'About your *reputation* and so on.'

He's bringing Drew into this? I can feel Per's gaze on the side of my face again. I grip the seat of my chair to keep me in it. I force myself to speak slowly and quietly.

'You promised not to say anything, Professor. You promised.'

'For the time being. In the meantime, I don't want to jeopardise our chances of turning people's thinking around. I don't believe you should go to Palau.'

When I stand, my sketchbook slides onto the floor. My jaw is clenched so tightly I can barely get my words out.

'This isn't fair.'

'Sit down, Harry.'

'No!'

'The change in plans will free you up to do other things,' Tan says. 'You could start by telling the commander what this is all about.' He smiles at Per. 'It may even encourage him to increase his involvement in the foundation's activities.'

Does he seriously believe Per may be more willing to help out if I'm not quite as incompetent as he's been led to believe? Even though he'll find out I'm even more of a liar than he thinks I am?

'I'm not telling the *commander* anything.'

Per stands, and leans down to pick up my sketchbook. He puts it carefully on the desk in front of me. Our eyes meet. He slowly shakes his head and sighs. He walks back to the window and looks outside. Eventually he faces the desk again.

'Professor,' he says, 'will you give me five minutes? I'd like to have a word with Harriet. Alone.'

I scamper to the bookshelves as Tan leaves the room. My hands are shaking so I stuff them into the back pockets of my jeans. But that pulls my T-shirt tight across my breasts. My nipples are taut. Surely breathing in Per's scent when he picked up my sketchbook isn't enough to arouse me? Not when I'd prefer to be anywhere else but here. I put my hands in my front pockets. That doesn't feel right either.

Per crosses the room and stands so close that I smell him again.

His lip twitches. '*Nervøst hoppeføll.*'

I stare at my feet.

'Harriet? Do you want to know what I said?'

I shake my head.

'Nervous filly. You have the colouring of a palomino fjord pony.'

I tighten my ponytail. But that emphasises my nipples again. I remind myself he would've had training in this—extracting information. Torture.

'Don't let Tan manipulate you,' he says. 'Tell me your secret. There can't be much I don't know by now.'

'No. It has nothing to do with you.'

When he rests his hand on my arm, it's like the fire that's been smouldering low in my stomach ignites. My breath catches. I shudder when I exhale. My breasts *almost* touch his chest.

His breathing is unsteady as well. His hand moves to my neck and he strokes the fine hairs that always escape from my ponytail. When he dips his head it's like the heat of his breath seeps into my bones.

'*Jesus.*' His voice is raspy. 'You told me it's over but … oh fuck, Harriet. It can't be. *Trust me.*'

I shake my head. 'I can't.' I lied to a maritime inquiry—on oath. I falsified evidence. I neatly forged documents in Drew's careful script. Per would never commit perjury. He'd be compelled to report someone who had.

He runs his hands down my sides, lightly, using the tips of his fingers. He makes a sound deep in his throat. He rests his cheek against mine, buries his nose in my hair, grazes the rim of my ear with his teeth. My hands are pressed flat to his chest. I slip two fingers between the buttons of his shirt and touch his skin, warm like it always is. He holds my hand in place.

'*Fortell meg,*' he whispers. '*Tell me.*'

Drew deserves protection. His reputation is all that he has left.

When I shake my head and step back, Per clings to my hand for a moment, but then he lets it go. He drops his hands by his sides and opens and shuts his fingers. His jaw is tight.

I take a deep breath. 'I want to go to Palau. You more than any-one else know how hard I've worked to get there. You said I could go if I could swim.'

He spins on his heel and walks to the window. He has his back to me but he turns his head to the side so I can see him in profile.

'I said if Tan let you go on the ship even though you couldn't swim, he had to choose between us. The final decision was always his. We assumed he'd support you going.'

'You can threaten to pull out of Antarctica. To force his hand.'

He turns, and frowns. 'What?'

'It would just be a threat. Of course you can go, whatever he decides.'

He lifts his chin. 'I wouldn't make a threat I had no intention of carrying out.'

I force my words past the lump in my throat. 'The information Tan's got has nothing to do with Palau. It's not relevant to my abil-ity to do the trip. I'm not even a proper crewmember. I'll just be doing the documentary, that's all.'

Per tips his head up to the ceiling. I'm sure he's counting but I don't say a word. I even hold my breath. Maybe he has a little faith in me?

'I can't judge whether the information is relevant or not if you refuse to tell me what it is. And I'm not going to stick my neck out for you when I don't think you're ready for the ocean yet. You were a mess only a few weeks ago.' In two strides he's standing in front of me. 'Like the professor said—wait.'

'I've been banned from your Antarctica voyage, and there'll be no trips next year if we can't raise more money. Please, Per, help me get to Palau.'

His hands are still by his sides. His body is hard, immoveable, just like he is. He thinks he's always right. He's so frustrating and intractable he makes me want to ...

I put my hand on his rock-hard body to push him away. Besides narrowing his eyes, he doesn't react. I clench my fist.

'Harriet?'

'Everyone calls me Harry!'

He grasps my wrist with one hand and opens my fingers with the other. Then he dips his head. He kisses the base of my thumb, and trails his lips over my palm. He kisses the pulse at my wrist. When I let out a shuddering breath he releases me, and stares into my eyes. His are silver.

'I'm not *everyone*,' he says.

There are tiny lines on the outside corners of his eyes. He has lost weight, just like I thought when I saw him on Monday. There are shadows beneath his cheekbones. I'm suddenly teary.

'I've never pushed anyone. I shouldn't have—'

'Or bitten anyone?' He wraps his arms around me and kisses my neck, and then he nuzzles behind my ear. So many thoughts are running through my mind that I can't get a single one out. I hate what he's doing to my life. I like being with him. He smells nice. His breath is warm against my face. Occasionally he makes me laugh. He doesn't know me.

'I want to go to Palau.'

He takes hold of my bottom lip with his teeth and tugs. When I gasp he lets it go and licks it. Slowly, and softly. 'Did I hurt you? *Beklager*. Sorry.'

'I know what *beklager* is.'

We stare at each other. I touch his mouth. The tingling sensation in my fingertips travels down my arm and into my chest, and then it sinks lower and settles between my thighs. My fingers tremble. What sort of sorry do I want to hear from him? What sort of sorry does he need to hear from me?

When our breaths are so sharp we're almost panting he yanks me even closer. Finally we kiss. Our tongues push, our lips fuse, our teeth clash. His hands are rough and possessive. They move down my back and over my hips to my bottom. He lifts me so I'm barely on my toes. But then we hear footsteps outside, and he pulls back a little.

'Harriet Hillary Amelia,' he says, stroking my back. When he rests his cheek against mine his eyelashes brush my temple. He turns and walks backwards, pulling me with him. He leans against the door. Then he stands with his legs apart so we're about the same height. He holds me still with his arms banded behind me. He whispers words against my mouth. I don't recognise any that I understand, but it's clear he's asking me something.

I pull back. My voice is hoarse. 'What do you want?'

His eyes are dark grey and inky, like the colour of the ocean at night. 'I want you,' he says.

I want him more than I've wanted anything in over twelve years. But I'm tongue-tied.

'Harriet? Do you want me?'

I swallow. Shake my head. 'It won't work.'

'So why do you kiss me like that?'

I can't look at him. 'I'm attracted to you. But that's not important.'

He lifts his hands so abruptly that I stumble. My T-shirt is twisted at my waist and my hair is on my face. I tie it back while he watches. I touch my tender mouth.

He walks to the window. Then he comes back again and grasps my shoulders. His fingers open and shut. 'You have no idea,' he says. 'No fucking idea what's important.'

Releasing me, he blows his breath out in a long angry rush. He rubs both hands around the back of his neck.

When Tan walks in, Per stands to attention. 'We're finished,' he says. 'Harriet's not going to Palau.'

*   *   *

Liam and I are walking back from the beach on Saturday morning when I see Kat sitting on the top step of the deck. She's wearing tiny denim shorts and a yellow strappy top, and her long pale legs are stretched out in front of her. My sketchbook is on her lap, and she's flicking through the pages.

'Jesus,' she says. 'Per said you were good, but these are *awesome*.'

I snatch the sketchbook. 'What are you doing here? How did you get this?'

She flushes, her eyes wide. 'Sorry, Harry. I was just looking. I didn't know it was private.'

It isn't private. The sketches are being auctioned tomorrow afternoon to raise money for the school's art scholarship program. I called Tan's PA last night when I realised I'd left the sketchbook behind, and asked her to courier it out to me.

Liam comes up behind me and undoes my wetsuit zip. 'Easy, Harry,' he mutters. 'Don't shoot the messenger.' He grins at Kat. 'Harry's had her future put on hold. Her trip to Palau's been canned, so she's a little uptight.'

Liam makes coffee, and the three of us sit side by side on the deck so we all get to face the ocean. I shouldn't have snapped at Kat. It makes her determined to give me all the details of how she came by my sketchbook.

'When you called, Per was still with Professor Tan,' she says. 'His PA couldn't get a courier at that time on a Friday night, so Per said he'd sort it out. He saw me at the base last night. He was picking up his gear. He asked if I felt like a drive up the coast.' She smiles. 'Course I said yes. Hate shore leave.'

'Didn't you pick up a boyfriend a couple of months ago?' Liam says.

Kat frowns as if there are too many men to remember. 'You mean party boy? That's over. Suspected he was too good-looking to wait around. What are you doing this weekend? We could go out.'

Liam shrugs. 'Sorry, party girl. Can't. I'm heading off to Byron.'

'But you would go out with me otherwise, right?'

'Sure I would,' Liam says. 'Give me a call when you've run out of good-looking men.'

Kat strokes his arm. 'You're not bad for a doctor.'

They're only mucking around, but ... Liam was with Rachael for a year. Kat liked party boy a lot. Shouldn't they be just a little bit heartbroken?

'Per shouldn't have made you come all the way out here,' I say. 'If he'd contacted me, I would have picked up the sketchbook.'

'But I wanted to do it.'

'You obviously think a lot of P... *Per*,' Liam says. 'Why is that?' He's hiding a smile. I'm sure he's only asked the question to get at me.

Kat shrugs. 'He's great. He doesn't bullshit. That's important. And he treats you the same whether you're a seaman or an admiral. And he's smart, athletic. He's hot too. *Fantastic* body. Though we're not allowed to say that.'

'When will he be back?' Liam asks.

'He went to Darwin last night. He'll be there for a few days, and then he'll be on the *Hudson*, a US ship, for a couple of weeks. That's why he gave me the sketchbook.'

★ ★ ★

After Kat leaves, I help Liam pack. He's spread most of his things on the sofa in the living room.

'You going to miss me while I'm at Byron?' he says. 'I'll be gone for weeks.'

I throw him a pair of boxer shorts. 'I won't miss sorting your washing.'

The kookaburra laughs. He's been doing it quite regularly. 'That bird's in love with you. You know that, don't you?'

Liam shakes his head. 'Since Rachael left me, I only have eyes for Polarman.'

Rachael split up with Liam after he told her that he didn't see them having a long-term future together.

'You haven't been moping so much lately. I think you're moving on from Rachael.'

'I didn't realise how much I liked having her around.'

'You can be friends again when she's happily with someone else. She'll pity you because you'll be miserable and alone.'

Liam could say he's been living with someone like that since I got back from the mountains. But I must look too unhappy to tease, because he puts a hand on my head and roughs up my hair.

'You okay, Polarwoman?'

'Guess I'll have to be.' I sniff. 'I miss him though.' I look out over the deck to the sea, and then back at Liam. 'I told him it wouldn't work. I think I was right, wasn't I? How can I be happy with some-one who thinks I'm pathetic, who questions my judgement? He doesn't trust me at all.'

*   *   *

The Scott Foundation: Environment Adventure Education.

Last week one of my students said he didn't think that Roald Amundsen would have helped Robert Falcon Scott if he'd come across him on the way to the Pole. I believe Amundsen would have given Scott food, clothing, fuel, and maybe a husky or two. But he wouldn't have done so without a lecture. Perhaps he would have said something like this:

'Your motorised sleds were an accident waiting to happen. So were the ponies. My men and dogs are better prepared. I'm concerned for your safety. Go back to the Terra Nova. There'll be other opportunities. Leave the Antarctic to those who know what they're doing ...'

Harriet

Within an hour of posting on the website, I get an email message from Per.

Harriet. If you go into the surf while Liam's away I'll inform the professor you're behaving in a way that puts the foundation's reputation at risk. Another negative report from me and he'll tell me whatever it is that you don't want me to know.

Your post pissed me off—as you intended it would.

I'll see you in a week and a half. I hope I get some sleep before then.

Per

CHAPTER
38

'Harry?'

Kat must be calling from a satellite phone. Her ship left for New Zealand two days ago.

I speak through a yawn. 'It's four in the morning. You okay?'

'It's Per. He's been airlifted off the *Hudson*. Bacterial pneumonia. The hospital he's at is called ...'

While she's searching for the name I jump out of bed and drag on a pair of tracksuit pants. 'What?'

'Royal North Shore. Can you see that he's okay? He's got a thing about hospitals.'

*   *   *

I buzz at the locked door of the hospital's emergency ward. A few minutes later, a nurse appears.

'I'm Harriet Scott. Can I see Per Amundsen? The front desk said he'd be here.'

'Immediate family members only,' she says, smoothing her short brown hair. 'You'll be able to visit once we've admitted him to the respiratory ward. Visiting hours start at eleven am.'

'His family are in Norway. Katrina Fisher spoke to someone here, then she called me and asked me to come straight away.'

'This isn't something to do with one of your television shows, is it?'

'No. It's nothing like that.'

Her gaze runs over my football shirt, tracksuit pants and thongs. She must decide I'm telling the truth because she gestures that I follow her.

'We can't keep Commander Amundsen in his bed. He wants to discharge himself. I suppose it can't hurt for you to see him.'

Per is sitting on the edge of a chair at the nurses' station, slumped over a desk. One long arm is stretched out on the surface and there's a cannula in the back of his hand. His head is resting on his bicep. He's filling in a form.

I take a few deep breaths before I speak. 'Per?'

He stills, then he turns towards me. His skin is flushed and his eyes are heavy. His voice is a raspy wheeze. '*Trøbbel*.'

'Yeah, like you can talk.' I put my hand on his shoulder. He's burning hot. The nurse's eyes meet mine. She's hovering protectively, reaching for his wrist to take his pulse.

'His temperature was thirty-nine an hour ago,' she says. 'It was higher when he came in.'

When I ate my breakfast on the deck and watched Per swim laps of the beach, I'd hold my breath when he disappeared beneath the waves. Sometimes I got light-headed. That's how I feel now.

I clear my throat. 'What's his oxygen level?' I say.

The nurse frowns like I'm being a busybody. 'It was down to eighty-five at one point, but we've brought it up to ninety-three.' She shakes her head when she releases his hand. 'His pulse is over a hundred, his heart rate's erratic.'

He raises his head when I squat at his side. He blinks, and lifts his hand to rub his jaw. His stubble is dark—it's the first time I've ever seen him unshaven. His eyes are unfocused. How he thinks he's going to walk out of the hospital on his own is anybody's guess.

'Per,' I say, 'the nurse has filled me in. Discharging yourself is against your doctor's advice. The nursing staff are concerned about you too. They want to admit you to the respiratory ward.'

He shakes his head, struggling to breathe. 'Base.'

'I've spoken to the medical staff at Balmoral,' the nurse says. 'They don't want you there. They deal with coughs and colds, not pneumonia. You need intravenous antibiotics, rest and regular fluids. If your oxygen saturation levels drop again your blood pressure will fall, and then anything could happen.'

Per ignores her. His handwriting slips above and below the lines on the form, but he continues to fill it in.

The nurse sighs. Our eyes meet over Per's head. 'Even if he leaves the hospital,' she says, 'he'll have to come back morning and night for antibiotics.'

'Did you hear that, Per?' I say.

She puts her hand on his arm. 'You need full time nursing care, Commander, at least for the next few days.'

He puts both hands on the desk. Then he stands, sways, and steadies himself. His face is still flushed, but now that he's standing it's losing colour quickly. His T-shirt and black fatigue pants are rumpled. He's wearing socks but no shoes.

The nurse backs him into the chair again. He's too weak to resist. 'You'll have to go to the respiratory ward,' she says.

'No.' He swallows. 'Discharge.'

'I'll be annoyed when I have to readmit you.'

Per shakes his head.

'Very well, Commander. I'll get a dish for the cannula.'

I follow the nurse down the corridor. 'Can't you leave his cannula in?' I say.

'No. The risk of infection's too high. If he's silly enough to discharge himself he'll have to put up with being jabbed again, night and morning.'

'Not if I take him home and look after him.'

She stops. Raises her brows. 'Are you medically qualified, as well as all the other things you do?'

'No … but I'll get a private nurse from an agency to administer the antibiotics. That will save him travelling. I can do the rest, use the cannula for fluids if I can't get enough into him by mouth. I'll keep an eye on his oxygen sats as well. I guess I'd better get an oxygen cylinder as a backup. Will you give me his doctor's details? I'll need a copy of his discharge summary, and scripts for the medications he's on. A wheelchair too if you can spare one, so I can get him to my car, and out of it at the other end.'

The nurse is silent for a few seconds. Then her expression softens. 'Your father. He had paraplegia, didn't he, after his accident?'

'Quadriplegia—C4.' I give her a shaky smile. 'That reminds me. I'll need to get a blood pressure monitor. My housemate's a doctor. He's away, but I can hassle some of his friends for the things I need. Guess I'll need a decent thermometer as well.'

'Was you father intubated?'

'Only a couple of times a year, whenever he got a chest infection. Mostly his diaphragm was functional. Per is fit, with lungs like a whale, so it's unlikely he'll need tubing once the antibiotics kick in. But I'll know when to call for help if he does.'

She squeezes my arm. 'I have nothing to worry about then.'

★ ★ ★

I stroke Per's hair. 'You're the worst patient in the world.'

I'm sitting on my bed with pillows stacked behind me. Per is lying between my outstretched legs, with his head against my chest. In this position he's upright enough that he can sleep without coughing himself awake too often. And his feet don't dangle off the end of the bed. He clung onto the doorframe to my room when I brought him home, insisting he wanted my room in preference to Liam's. Having him in a single bed is easier for me anyway. He's always within reach, and it's easier to change the sheets. I sleep on a camping mat on the floor next to him.

He burrows closer. 'Stay with me.'

'I warned you not to get too comfortable. You're hot again so I have to cool you down, and do your observations. That bossy nurse will be back soon. She spends more time criticising me than she does looking after you.'

He moans when I wriggle out from under him, and prop him up. I go through my hourly routines. Temperature, pulse, blood pressure, oxygen level, medications. I listen to his chest, front and back, with a stethoscope.

'There are more gurgles now. That's positive. Helga made you another pot of soup. Vegetable or chicken?'

He crooks his finger and I perch on the bed. He strokes my arm and plays with my fingers. I do my best to harden my heart, remind myself that this isn't real, that needing me won't be long term. He's sick as a dog. Asleep twenty hours out of twenty-four. He's like Superman after a Kryptonite episode. He's my little boy with dark hair.

He watches me with sleepy eyes as I massage his upper body.

'You should have stayed at Royal North Shore,' I say. 'The nurses could have propped your bed up there, and you would have had physios. Kat said you had a thing about hospitals. Why?'

He points to his scar, and mumbles. 'Infected. Questions. Lots of questions.'

So hospital staff asked him questions? He mustn't have answered them because he told me only his brother knew the truth about his scar.

He was only ten years old. I kiss his forehead. Trail my fingers over his cheek until his lids finally close. His raspy breaths are shallow, but even.

'What did I say?' My voice catches. 'Worst patient *ever*.'

★   ★   ★

Like he's done a few times a day for the past five days, Per is sitting on the end of the bed, willing himself to stand on his own and walk to the bathroom.

'Why can't you behave like a normal sick person?' I say. 'Take a bed bath, pee in a jar, grow a beard.'

Per's lips are tight. 'Because I refuse to.'

I pull him to his feet. 'Come on then, lean on me.'

He puts his arm around my shoulders as we walk down the hall to the bathroom. It's dawn; dim light filters through the frosted glass panel in the front door. There are shadows on the rug. Perhaps that's why I catch my toe on the fringe and stumble.

'Shit!'

There's no way I can support Per's weight, so we go down together. I land on my knees, and then fall onto my side. He collapses on top of me. As soon as he pushes himself onto his hands and knees he starts coughing, huge wracking coughs. He gags and wheezes until he's breathless.

I wrap my arms around him and help him into a sitting position. He rips off his T-shirt and wipes his face, and spits out the mucus he can't keep in. I ignore him when he tries to shrug me off. I rub his back in big firm circles.

'Take your time, Per. You're always in such a rush.'

When he bunches the T-shirt into a ball, I try to take it out of his hands.

'No, I'll have a shower,' he says. 'Rinse it out.'

I push his hair back from his forehead. It's nowhere near his eyes, but he must have missed his fortnightly haircut because it's marginally longer than usual.

'You must be improving because you're getting to be a control freak again.'

He looks up at me with heavy eyes and shakes his head.

'It's true,' I say. 'And it's not fair. My vomiting was way more revolting than anything I've ever seen from you.'

Each breath he takes is an effort, but he laughs. Just for a second or two his teeth flash white and his eyes are bright. It flusters me. He barely ever smiles, and even when he does, all that happens is a twitch of the lips. His chest is right there in front of my eyes. It's more slender than it was when we made love, but perfectly proportioned. I ache sometimes with wanting to hold him close, skin to skin.

Later in the morning, when he's asleep, I sketch what he looked like when he was on the floor, just before he laughed. He opens his eyes when I'm only halfway through. He holds out his hand.

'Show me,' he croaks.

'No way. Go back to sleep.'

When he pats the bed I go to him and perch on the edge. I'm still wearing my pyjamas. Stripy cotton shorts with a pink drawstring, and a blue sleeveless top. He's propped up on his pillows. He lifts his hands and fastens two tiny buttons at my throat.

My breath catches. 'Why did you do that?'

He's staring at my breasts. 'Cold.'

I can't look at him. I didn't even realise my nipples were erect until he pointed it out. Does he know I'm not cold at all?

He touches my arm. 'Maybe your other pyjamas are better. The ones made out of winter sheets.'

I stand. Turn my back. Line up his medications. 'It's too warm to wear them,' I say. 'We're midway through spring.'

'What's the date?'

I'm doing my best to keep my voice even. I've been counting down the days until *The Adélie* leaves for Palau. There are only five to go.

'October 17.'

'Harriet. Come here.'

'What?' My hair is loose and it falls over one side of my face. He puts it behind my ear.

'*Beklager, lille venn.*'

I shrug, and stand. Get all businesslike again. 'There's no point saying sorry.'

A shadow crosses his face but I ignore it.

'You'd better go to the bathroom before the nurse comes. Don't forget your sample for the jar, or she'll collect it personally.' I take his hands. 'Come on. I'll organise your shaving things as well.'

He needs me for now. My feelings about Palau can wait.

CHAPTER

39

Per gasps for air. It takes me a second or two to get up from my bed on the floor and shove the puffer into his hand. He inhales, coughs, and inhales again. Then he leans over pillows and takes a series of shuddering breaths. When I open the window a breeze blows into the room. It ruffles his hair.

'Did you have a nightmare?' I pass him a glass of water, and rub his back. When I listen to his chest it crackles. 'Were you running in the dream? Or swimming? Slow your breaths, Per. Try to relax. Listen to the rustle of the leaves, and the sounds the waves make.'

He's only just got his breathing under control when he grabs my wrist. At first I think he's feverish again because his eyes are bright. But he's cool when I feel his forehead with my other hand. I take his temperature anyway, and do the rest of his checks. I stroke his cheek.

'You'll do.'

'You were lost in the snow.'

'In your dream?'

He nods.

'Well … If I really were lost you'd have found me. It's two in the morning, Per. Are you ready to go back to sleep? Or should I get you one of your boring iceberg books?'

He touches my hair. Runs his hand down my arm. 'Will you hold me? Like before?'

We've kept our distance since the day I stared at his chest and he did up the buttons of my pyjamas. I take a breath and blow it out in a rush. 'Just for a little while. You need to sleep without worrying about squashing me.'

I adjust the pillows and clamber onto the bed behind him. He waits until I'm comfortable, and then he rests against me. He's lying sideways, with his head on my chest. One of his legs covers one of mine. The weight of him feels so good it puts a lump in my throat. It's stupid to pretend I'm not in love with him.

'What does "*lille venn*" mean? You've called me that a few times since you've been sick. Is it nurse?'

I feel his smile against my breast. Then he coughs, and steadies his breath again. 'The direct translation is "little friend" but that's not what it really means.'

'But it's a nice thing to be called?'

He nods, and breathes deeply into my cleavage. 'Yes.'

It's easier to talk in the middle of the night, when we're not look-ing at each other.

'What's "*stakkars liten*"?'

He hesitates. 'Poor baby.'

'You called me that once, when I had a nightmare. What about "*det går bra*"? You said that as well.'

He smiles again. 'That means it's fine, it's okay.'

'I thought it was an endearment.'

'There aren't as many in the Norwegian language as there are in English. There's *min skatt*. That means … my treasure, my dear.'

'That sounds very old-fashioned.'

'It's not used much. Mostly by older people, who've been married for a long time.' He threads our fingers together, unthreads them and threads them again. He holds on tightly. 'Why didn't you want me to meet Drew at the fundraising dinner?'

I'm too surprised by the question to hide my response. My whole body stiffens. Drew and Per have spent hours together in the last few days, and I've thought nothing of it. Hardly anything Drew says makes sense anymore, and he's lost just about all of his memories from the past few years. Allan's been picking him up and dropping him here, so he can see more of me in the school holidays, like he usually does. He sits on a chair at the foot of my bed, or on the deck, and watches Per reading and sleeping. Per answers all of his questions, no matter how many times he's answered them before. I don't bother correcting Drew when he calls me Maggie anymore. We reminisce together about events that happened before I was born. In the afternoons Jonty or Helga walk with him along the beach.

'I wanted to protect him.'

Per knows Drew loves being around people, even if he can't remember who they are. But he mustn't want to pick a fight by calling me a liar. Instead, he says, '*Umulig.*'

'You're the one who's impossible,' I say. His scar is silvery in the moonlight. I trace it with my finger. 'Tell me about your scar.'

He hesitates. Presses his face into my hand. Closes his eyes for a moment. Then he opens them and holds my gaze. He guides my finger along another scar, just inside his hairline. It's about ten centimetres long.

'*Stakkars liten,*' I whisper.

'Afghanistan, four years ago, peacekeeping force, landmine. Or do you want to know about this?' He lifts his T-shirt and points to a ragged-edged scar on his hip. 'Shrapnel wound, Guinea.'

'You know I want to know about this.' I put my hand on his cheek again. 'You told me you fell through a roof, and you hid it from your father. Why would a ten-year-old do that?'

'My father was an alcoholic.'

'The other night you said something about people asking questions. I think you meant in a hospital. Didn't your father look after you properly?'

'It was worse than that. No more questions, Harriet.'

I could return to my bed on the floor to show him I'm not happy, that he should trust me more. I could walk out of the room and sleep in Liam's bed. Per's arm had been loosely draped around my hip. It tightens. It's too dark to read his expression but I'm pretty sure he's my little boy with dark hair again.

I adjust my position and pull him even closer. He relaxes, takes my hand and brushes my fingers with his lips. 'You looked after your father, didn't you?' he says. 'After the accident.'

'Most of the time. I travelled with Drew when Dad was in respite care or hospital. Dad didn't want me around then. He only needed me when we were at Newport.'

Per stills.

'I'm not going to explain that. I loved my father. He meant everything to me.'

'But you were what, fourteen, fifteen—'

'I wanted to be with him.' I close my eyes. 'We lived in a tiny apartment at Newport. It overlooked a strip of ocean, framed on either side by pine trees. I'd open the doors to the balcony and we'd sit for hours, gazing at the play of light on the water. Dad would spot whales, dolphins, all sorts of things.' I rest my cheek on top of Per's head and breathe into his hair. It smells of my shampoo. 'I must've sketched that view hundreds of times.'

'How long were you there?'

'About four years with Dad. It's where he died.'

'Yet you never went to school?'

'No.'

'Harriet?'

'Stop asking questions.'

'One more. Your father was wealthy. But he hardly left you anything. Why?'

'He set up the foundation.'

'You were eighteen.' He refuses to budge when I try to get off the bed. He kisses my throat, and settles his head between my breasts again. Then he takes my hand and matches our fingers up. 'I don't want to upset you. I want to understand.'

'You're such a snoop.' I relax against the pillows. 'Dad knew I'd be all right, that I was strong. That's why he set things up like he did. Thinking about what happened in Brazil, and afterwards, has made me remember that. He lost a lot in the accident—my mother, his health. But never his belief in me.'

Per pushes himself upright and frowns down at me. He opens his mouth as though he'd like to argue, but I put a finger over his lips. I try to make things clearer for him.

'One of my first memories of Dad was when he told me I could do *anything*. I made plenty of mistakes when he was alive, but he always trusted me to get things right in the end.' I stroke the crease between Per's brows. 'My mother would tease him sometimes, about the faith he had in me.'

Per is still frowning when he kisses my cheek. He breathes into my hair. 'Stay with me?' he says. 'All night.'

I lie on my side. He spoons behind me, putting one of his legs between mine. We're both propped up with pillows so he doesn't cough as much. But he's tense; his arm is like a steel band around my waist.

'Relax, Per. Aren't you tired?' I stroke the soft hairs on his forearm, and trace the vein on the back of his hand. The cannula came out a couple of days ago, but the bruise is still there. I yawn. 'I'm tired.'

'*Sov, lille venn.* Sleep.' His heart thumps against my back. Something is bothering him. It's the last thought I have before I close my eyes.

CHAPTER

40

The first thing I'm aware of is the sound of a car pulling up at the kerb outside my house. Then I realise that Per isn't hugging my back anymore.

I yawn and stretch. A car door slams. Morning light is peeping in under the blind but it's too early for Allan to be here with Drew. The click of the door latch jerks me upright and I'm out of bed in time to see Per in the front garden, gesturing to Kat to give him ten minutes. I almost bump into him in the hallway. He's dressed in trousers and a white cotton shirt with a collar. The clothes were in the suit carrier that was sent from Balmoral; they've been hanging on the door all week. He's shaved and showered. His hair is damp. He's focusing on the ribbon strap of my pyjama top that's fallen off my shoulder.

'Per?' I rub sleep from my eyes. 'What time is it? What's going on?'

When he smiles it's merely a movement of his lips. 'I've made coffee,' he says. 'C'mon.' He holds out his hand—but walks away before I have an opportunity to grasp his fingers. His stride is lengthening every day. It's not panther-like yet but it won't be long.

'What's Kat doing here?' I say.

Per takes our coffees out to the deck. I sit, and nurse my mug on my lap. He stands and rests his on the railing. His face is thinner, but other than that he looks much the same as he did. In a dissolute-pirate sort of way, he's even more handsome than he was before he was sick.

When the kookaburra appears he and Per scrutinise each other. The kookaburra looks away first.

'I asked Kat to come,' Per finally says. 'She's taking me back to Balmoral.'

The urge to burst into tears is as sudden and unexpected as his words are. My voice wobbles. 'Why?'

'I called Professor Tan, told him to let you on *The Adélie*. As you know, she sails tomorrow.'

'What?'

'Tom and the other members of crew can keep an eye on you while you're on board. Tan assures me you'll be safe with the film people for the two days you're on the islands.'

Within five minutes of waking I've been told he's leaving me, and that I'm going to Palau. I don't notice my hand is shaking until he takes my coffee and puts it on the railing next to his.

Finally I find my voice. 'Why did you change your mind?'

He looks out to sea. 'Tan altered the terms of our agreement. I shouldn't have gone along with it.'

It unsettles Per, not telling the whole truth.

'There was something else,' I say. 'What?'

'You'd better get organised if you're going.'

I can hear that his chest is tight. It's in the way that he's speaking, and in his short sharp breaths. His eyes are guarded, defensive.

Suddenly I'm angry. 'Why won't you tell me? Is letting me go to Palau the equivalent to a thankyou fuck? Because I looked after you?'

Thick heavy clouds hang in the sky but his eyes are much darker. 'I refuse to even respond to that,' he says.

'Well what am I supposed to think? How can I understand if you won't give me a reason? Why now? Why not yesterday, the day before?'

'We'll talk when you get back ...' A coughing fit takes the rest of his words away. When I push him into a chair he leans his elbows on his thighs and fights to get his breath back. I automatically put my hand on his shoulder but as soon as he can sit straight again he shrugs me off. It feels strange not running my fingers through the hair at the nape of his neck like I usually do after he coughs.

'I'll find your puffer.'

He wheezes. 'Kitchen.'

The puffer is on the kitchen bench, next to my sketchbook. Last time I saw the sketchbook it was on the floor under my bed. It's open now, and the image of Per in the hallway—just after we'd tumbled to the floor together and he'd taken off his shirt—is staring back at me. There's a mixture of desire and vulnerability on his face. If he's seen this sketch, I have to assume he's seen all the others. He was aware I'd been drawing him all week. Often he'd wake up as I was doing it, just like he did when I was sketching this one. His lips would twitch, and he'd hold out his hand. I'd take it, and smile, and pretend I didn't know what he wanted.

He's not an action hero in any of the sketches. Sometimes he's frightened. Sometimes he's breathless. Sometimes he's afraid I'm going to leave him. Sometimes he's my dark-haired little boy. As I sketched I highlighted the things that he was trying to hide. They're there in every line, every shadow, every smudge.

When I get back to the deck he's standing again. I hand him the puffer and throw the sketchbook onto a chair.

'You had no business snooping.'

'Bullshit. I'm the subject.'

'You want to get rid of me. That's why you're letting me go to Palau.'

He's with me in two strides, standing so close that I see he has tiny lines near his mouth, as well as at the outsides of his eyes. 'This isn't easy, Harriet. Stop provoking me.'

'Is that an order, Commander?'

He puts his hands either side of my face, and softly presses his forehead against mine. Then his fingers skirt over my shoulders, pulling my straps down to the tops of my arms. He's looking down, watching what he's doing. He sucks in a breath, and clenches and unclenches his fingers as they slide up and down my arms. His thumbs stroke the tops of my breasts through the soft white cotton of my top, and then they slip lower. A warm familiar ache builds between my thighs and I press my body closer to his, until his erection nestles against my stomach. Then I stand on tiptoes. Our lips almost touch before he turns his head away.

'I can't,' he says. 'Not when I'm like this.'

I run my hands over the familiar contours of his chest. He's not well, but there's only a tiny chance that he's infectious. Not that he'd ever take that chance. When I stroke his nipple through his shirt it puckers.

'Yes you can,' I say. 'But you won't.'

His voice isn't much more than a croak. 'Fuck, Harriet.' He kisses a path from the sensitive hollow beneath my jaw to my temple and then he rests his mouth against the pulse that's madly beating there. He touches it with the tip of his tongue. Pulls the hairband from my hair and undoes the plait. Bites my earlobe. Nuzzles along my jawline.

I pull his shirt out of his trousers and rest my hand on his abdominal muscles. His stomach is firm but his skin is soft and silky. Thinking about how we touched each other when we made love intensifies my longing to do it all over again. My fingers glide over his belt and slip lower until I'm stroking his erection through his trousers. I'm tentative at first, but then he clamps his hand over my fingers and I increase the pressure. My head rests on his chest. I'm trembling, and my breathing is shallow. I tug at his belt. My sentences run together when I speak.

'Please come back to bed. I'll tell Kat to go away. You'll get tired afterwards but then you can sleep. I'll prop you up if you cough. I don't care.'

He lifts his head, and strokes my bottom lip, back and forth, with his index finger. He must be as aroused as I am. His eyes are silver.

'Per?' I whisper.

We both start when the front door bangs open and Kat shouts out that she has to get to work. But it takes a little while to let each other go. He manages it first, taking me by the shoulders and nudging me away so we're standing close but apart, our breath mingling in the no-go zone between us.

'I'm going,' he says.

He walks away. I hear him collecting his things. By the time I step into the hall they're assembled along the wall, and he's leaning over his kit bag. When I put my hand on his arm his body snaps upright.

'Per?' We stare at each other, and then I grasp his wrist. I refuse to let it go when he turns away. He won't look at me. But maybe it will be easier to talk to him this way. My voice is quiet, but steady.

'Come to Palau with me. Let me take care of you on *The Adélie*. We'll stay for a day or two and then we'll fly home. I'll tell you what I've been hiding. You won't like it, but I'd better tell you anyway. And you can tell me about your scar, if you want to.'

He closes his eyes for a moment and takes a couple of breaths. He tips his face to the ceiling, and then, very deliberately, he opens my fingers one by one to release my grip on his wrist. My hand is still in midair when he gets to the door. When he turns to me I can barely see his face because I'm blinking back tears.

'Going with you would defeat the purpose of sending you away,' he says.

* * *

By the time I go outside he's pale and breathless, leaning against the car. The boot is open. I brush past him and shove my sketchbook into the top of his kitbag.

'As you pointed out,' I say, 'you're the subject, so you may as well keep the drawings. If you don't want them, throw them away.'

'Don't you dare do that, sir,' Kat says, taking the sketchbook out of the bag and opening it.

Per snatches it away. He scowls, first at Kat and then at me, as he puts the sketchbook back in the bag. 'I'll see you when you get back,' he says.

I refuse to look at him. And I hold back my tears until I shut the front door behind me.

He's stripped my bed bare. His reference books are gone from the side table. The sheets and pillowcases, and my pyjamas, are neatly folded and placed there instead. So are my pencils. They're lined up side by side, seven of them. Some are blunt and some are sharp.

I don't know what he'll do with the sketchbook. He should have looked at it more closely when he found it under my bed. Then he would have seen that only someone who loved him could have drawn him like that.

CHAPTER

41

Professor Tan has been leaning against the deck railing and giving me advice for over half an hour. He arrived a few hours after Per left. The kookaburra is perched on a branch of the spotted gum tree at the bottom of the garden. He hasn't been fed since Liam left for Byron Bay, but he's looking at me hopefully.

'We'll do everything possible to make this trip a successful one for you, and the foundation,' Tan says. 'I'm delighted that you're going.'

There's something in the tone of his voice that tells me he's less delighted than he's letting on.

'You were worried about me letting the foundation down. Why did you change your mind?'

He purses his lips. 'Let's just say the commander was persuasive.'

'So he wanted me to go on *The Adélie*?'

'Frankly, Harry, I think he has the same reservations I have. So don't let the foundation down. The ship, the documentaries, this is what you've been fighting for, after all.'

We were with Per's lawyer and the mediator when I thought up the campaign. I sketched a lion, a rhinoceros, and a bull elephant. Tears clog the back of my throat. I have to forget Per. He didn't like me seeing him weak, or vulnerable. Even though he's attracted to me, he made it plain that whatever we had, or might have had, is over.

'And don't worry about Drew,' Tan says. 'I'll keep an eye on him.'

Tan is a pragmatist. And a strategist. I'm about to tell him that since he's made his threat I don't trust him to have anything to do with Drew, when an idea takes shape in my mind. I race to the kitchen and grab a pad and pen. Then I sit at the table on the deck, and start a list.

The professor consults his watch. 'I'll leave you to it, then.'

'Wait!' I look up. 'I've just had a really good idea.'

He looks at me with suspicion. 'And that is?'

I take a breath. 'My school principal's been offering me compassionate leave for months because of Drew's diagnosis. My seniors have more or less finished for the year, and a temp can step in for my juniors.'

'Your point, Harry?'

'I'm going to take more time off work. I'm taking Drew to Palau with me.'

The professor blinks. 'Is he well enough?'

'He's not bad physically, it's just that he forgets everything. But we'll be together most of the time. We can stay on *The Adélie* until she heads back to Sydney to get ready for Antarctica, and after that we can live in villages on the islands. It'll just be the two of us, and maybe one of the film crew. Think of all the stories we can tell— fishing villages, plantations, markets and schools. We can look at Palau in the context of rising sea levels, sustainable fishing, all sorts of things.'

'How long would you be away?'

'Not too long. I'll have to be back mid-December to finish off the school year.'

'But that's over six weeks away.'

I take a deep breath. 'I'd better get organised then.'

The professor frowns. 'The commander said a week, Harry. He won't approve.'

This trip will be wonderful for Drew, and a good opportunity for the foundation to pursue its environmental agenda. And perhaps I'll miss Per less if I'm looking at the Pacific Ocean north of the equator, instead of south of it. I clear my throat. Even so, my voice wavers a little.

'One week or six weeks doesn't make a difference. The commander wants me to go away. That's what he said this morning.'

*　*　*

The Scott Foundation: Environment Adventure Education
Roald Amundsen once said, "Adventure is just bad planning."

Drew and I are enjoying our adventure in Palau. This morning, the Prime Minister of the tiny island nation and I went snorkelling, and in the afternoon I interviewed him. This was the culmination of weeks of talking to people about Palau's future. At the local level there are sustainability and land care challenges, and globally there are the implications of warmer oceans and polar melts. As usual, Drew spent most of his day on the wharves with the fishermen—we've got some wonderful footage of him exchanging tall tales with the other old salts around here. I can't wait to start working with the producer to put the first couple of episodes of the documentary series together.

And as for The Adélie's second voyage ... after weeks of preparation, the ship is now kitted out for Antarctica.

Commander Amundsen and his fellow scientists will work with Captain Tom Finlay and the other crewmembers to ensure that this year's voyage to the South Pole region will be rewarding both environmentally and scientifically. The foundation's film crew will go with the ship and report back regularly, while Professor Tan and I will continue to work on the Scott and Amundsen fundraising campaign at home.

Incidentally, I think that risking heartache by falling in love is far more dangerous than an unplanned adventure is ever likely to be …

Harriet

* * *

Liam grins. 'Risking heartache by falling in love is far more dangerous than an unplanned adventure—'

I push him in the chest with both hands. '*Shut up!*'

He laughs and kicks whitewash from the waves at me, until my board shorts and bikini top are dripping.

Drew and I flew in from Palau this morning, and it took most of the day to settle Drew back into his care home. The sun was going down by the time I got home but I was desperate to stretch my legs. I dragged Liam away from the television and over the dunes to the beach.

We sit on the sand facing the ocean. The last of the sun is on our backs.

'God only knows what was in Drew's drink,' I say. 'I only had a few sips but I could hardly string a sentence together afterwards.'

'Not necessarily the best time to publish something,' Liam says. '*Heartache?*'

'I was drunk! And if I change it now it'll look suspicious. I just have to hope Per doesn't understand it.'

Liam ruffles my hair and messes it up. 'Maybe Polarman won't read it.'

'It mentions Amundsen so he's bound to.'

'Well … he may think you were referring to *his* heartache.'

'I'd prefer not to talk about it.'

'That's a shame. Because I have a personal interest in your relationship with Polarman. My condoms have a personal interest. You didn't hear anything from him in the six weeks you were gone? Nothing today?'

'Nope. And he leaves tomorrow.'

Liam slowly shakes his head. 'Polarman works in mysterious ways.'

'Why couldn't I fall in love with a human, like you?'

He nudges my knee. 'Good point. Let's fall in love.'

'Idiot.' I take his hand and pull him upright. We brush the sand off our legs. 'You don't know what proper love is because you haven't experienced it yet.' I can't keep the wobble out of my voice. 'I thought I had it with Grant, but that was nothing compared to this.'

Liam shakes his head. His sun-bleached hair is stiff with salt. 'Don't tell *me* that, Harry. Tell Polarman.'

'I did tell him.'

'In a drunken postscript message? In doodles in a sketchbook? I'm not sure even Polarman's that smart.'

He's not smart all of the time. Just like he's not always in control. He hasn't learnt to trust me. And he thinks he doesn't need me. Going to Palau didn't make things easier like I'd hoped it would. I'd lie awake at night and think of everything we did together at the beach, and in my bed. And everything we talked about. Glaciers, and kookaburras, and cheese and tomato on toast. His eyes are the colour of the ocean. He's in the scent and taste of the sea. Storms and rain remind me of him. He's there in the sounds of the waves crashing on the shore. He's everywhere I go.

'I'll be glad to get back to school tomorrow,' I say, 'to keep my mind off things.'

'So you're not going to the fancy Antarctica send-off the professor's organised?'

'Nope. I've got a double period of Year 7 Geography to go to instead.'

It's evening, so the sand is warm rather than hot, but we race down the path to the house anyway. The kookaburra is waiting for us on the railing. He puffs out his feathers and preens.

Liam catches up while I'm hosing my feet. 'Do you know what Tan's going to do about Drew?' he says.

'I don't think he's changed his mind. I'll never forgive him if he goes to the maritime authorities or makes a public announcement.'

'Even though it'd enhance your reputation? You know my feelings. Drew's never going to know the difference, and he wouldn't have wanted you to do this.'

'I don't care. I want him to be respected for his years on *The Watch*. It'll make the Palau documentary even more special. Drew's connections to the ocean, marine life, the people, hasn't changed at all. The footage is amazing.'

Liam snatches the hose. He's grinning.

'What?' I say

'I've seen *some* footage of Palau,' he says. 'Climate change news, reef damage reports, other environmental stuff. Your shapely arse in Polarman's wetsuit has been featured quite a bit. Hasn't that helped the foundation's bottom line?'

I flick him with my towel. 'Yes, but not enough to permanently secure *The Adélie*. That's something else I have to see Tan about. But I'll put it off for as long as I can.'

'What about seeing Polarman?'

'I asked him to come to Palau and he refused. Anyway, he knows where I live.'

On the other side of the dunes, waves crash onto the shore. The sounds are carried on the breezes. *He's everywhere I go.*

Just like I told Liam yesterday, I'm happy to be back at school today. I watch my Year 7 class file into the classroom. I'm sure some of them are taller than they were when I left.

'How was *The Adélie*, Harry?' Jonty says.

'Would you like to rephrase that, Jonty?'

'How was the ship, Miss Scott?'

'She was great. So was Palau.'

'The commander's taking *The Adélie* to Antarctica today,' Lucy says.

'Yes,' I say.

'I don't get the commander,' Amber says. 'Why'd he bother rescuing you from *The Watch* if you don't get to go back to Antarctica? He's sexist.'

'No he's not!' Lucy says.

'My gender has nothing to do with it,' I say. 'I never intended to go on the Antarctica voyage.' One day I will go back to Antarctica.

I'll say farewell to *The Watch*, but I won't apologise to Mum and Dad for losing her. It's the last thing they would have wanted because I didn't fail them in Brazil, or afterwards. I've finally worked that out.

Jonty raises his hand.

'Yes, Jonty?'

'I reckon the commander would've taken you if you'd asked.'

I have to swallow the lump in my throat before I can reply. 'Not sure about that.'

He points to the screen at the front of the room. 'Can we watch the TV? *The Adélie*'s on the news channel.'

'Today we're looking at mangrove swamps, and I'll—'

There's a collective groan from the class.

'I'll tell you how Dad's canoe sank in the Serengeti, when a hippo—'

'Please, Miss,' Jonty says. 'It's *educational*.'

Even Alex, one of my quieter students, is linking his fingers together and pleading. Jonty's hand shoots up again.

'Yes, Jonty?'

He's looking at his laptop. 'The commander, Miss. He's on the ship. Lisa Toohey's there too.'

I've been telling the class about Scott and Amundsen and their treks to the Pole for months. This is the final school week of the year. It's unfair to deny them because I happen to be heartbroken. I open my laptop and connect it to the screen at the front of the room.

'Fifteen minutes, tops,' I say.

*   *   *

I know him, yet I don't. His jawline is more angular. The shadows beneath his cheekbones are pronounced. He's grim and unapproachable. He takes himself far too seriously. I watch him on the screen as a gust of wind lifts the dark straight hair off his forehead. For an instant I see his widow's peak before it's hidden again. He mustn't have had his fringe cut since he was sick. I've never seen his hair kink up at the collar. He's dressed from head to toe in black fatigues. There's a discreet Norwegian flag affixed to one arm. He looks like the man I sketched in March. He's Polarman.

He's standing to one side of the group assembled on the deck of *The Adélie*. If I were there I'd take his arm and introduce him to everyone so he'd feel more comfortable, and they'd feel less intimidated. Tan and the other foundation board members are chatting with the dignitaries. Tom is there too, with senior members of the crew. There are a few people I don't recognise, probably Per's scientific colleagues. They're dressed appropriately but their clothes appear new, and freshly pressed. Some members of the group fan their faces with their hands. A woman's hat blows off in the breeze and dances across the deck. Per picks it up and smiles when he returns it. It's a formal smile, a courteous one. It's not like the smile he has when he's trying *not* to smile and his mouth twitches. The expression in his eyes softens when he smiles like that.

Tan gestures that Per join him, and he walks gracefully to his side. He's got his panther stride back. Then the professor starts talking into a microphone, giving a run down of what's planned for the voyage and how delighted the foundation is to have its regular crew on board, together with a Norwegian naval officer and his scientific cohort. Per shakes Tan's hand, and then he takes his place at the microphone, standing at ease with his hands behind his back.

'*Miss Scott!*'

I wrench my attention away from the screen. I'd forgotten about the class. Most of them are staring at me. 'Yes, Lucy?'

'The commander's hair. It looks nice, doesn't it?'

'Shhh,' Jonty says. 'He's saying something.'

Per talks about being a scientist and a sailor, and describes the vital role research plays in working out the best ways to protect fragile environments like the North and South Pole. When he says that environmental policy should be based on scientific evidence and informed opinion, the Environment Minister nods in agreement. Per doesn't use notes, and he doesn't seem to be nervous. He seems no less stiff than when he talks to people one on one. Professor Tan, beaming, steps up to the microphone after Per has finished, and asks whether there are any questions for the commander.

Lisa Toohey raises her hand immediately. Her vibrant orange dress stands out among the dark colours that most of the others are wearing. She smiles brightly as she gazes at Per.

'Hello, again, Commander,' she says, reaching into her handbag for a small black notebook. 'I have some questions.'

'What's she going to ask him about?' Lucy says.

'Maybe Syria, or Africa,' Jonty says. 'The commander knows all about peacekeeping forces. And guerrilla warfare.'

The camera pans out over the audience. The documentary team, foundation volunteers and a few others are on a lower section of deck. Many turn their heads to look in Lisa's direction. She smiles at Per again.

'You've been working for almost a year with the Scott Foundation on the Scott and Amundsen campaign,' she says. 'And for the next two months you'll be living on the ship it's hoping to purchase. Is it safe to assume that you have a more favourable view of the foundation now than you did at the beginning of the year?'

Per nods. 'Professor Tan and his colleagues play an important role in the environmental movement in terms of research and public education.'

'You mention his colleagues? Does this include Harriet Scott? What is your opinion of her?'

Everyone in the class starts talking at once, and then they all yell at each other to be quiet. I was leaning my bottom on the desk with my legs stretched out in front of me but I jump to my feet. Per is looking through the heads of Sydney Harbour and out to sea. He *always* tells the truth. He could say anything.

'I'm not going to answer that question. This isn't the right place, or time.'

I didn't realise I was holding my breath until it whooshes out of my mouth.

'Isn't it?' Lisa says. 'When you wouldn't be on *The Adélie* if *The Watch* hadn't sunk?'

I don't think Lisa has anything in particular against the foundation or me, so it's unlikely she's angling for Per to be too critical. And I'm not sure why she's risking annoying him when he's made it clear he doesn't want to answer her question. Does she want him to defend me? Is she fishing for a romance angle? Should I phone her and tell her he's not interested in romance anymore?

'It's a simple enough question,' she says. 'What do you think of Harriet?'

Per narrows his eyes. 'I repeat, I won't answer—'

'Can we take a raincheck on that question, Lisa?' Tan says, stepping in front of the microphone. 'I can't say much at the moment, but I'm hopeful that the foundation will be making its own announcement about Harry quite shortly. It will throw a new light on—'

Per takes Tan's arm. 'I'll deal with this,' he says. Tan nods, but he's pursing his lips and rubbing his arm as he moves away from the microphone.

I back up until I feel the desk against the tops of my thighs again, and then sit. A few students are looking at me. I'm probably pale. I should have seen this coming. The departure for Antarctica is a small-scale event. A news channel is covering it already and they'd share their footage with any other media outlet that asked for it. So why would someone as well known as Lisa Toohey turn up? Tan must have told her something was going to happen. He's ready to *un*-tarnish my image. He wants to force me into confessing to the maritime authorities. After I do, assuming I'm not thrown into jail for perjury, he'll repackage my image as flawed, but competent. Then he'll bundle Per and me together and flog us off to *National Geographic*.

'Yes, Commander?' Lisa says.

Per tips his face up to the sky and takes a couple of breaths. The action is so typical of him that even though I feel sick with apprehension I smile. He can't avoid her question, and he has to tell the truth. Yet … he won't want to hurt me. I must be like one of the men or women under his command. Kat said he treated admirals and seamen the same. He may still want to know what I'm hiding, but he knows this isn't the right way to get the information out. He's fair, and just.

'The first time I saw Harriet she was on board *The Watch*,' he says. 'She was standing on the bridge in gale-force winds. The waves were breaking all around her ship.'

'Why does the commander call you Harriet?' Lucy says.

'Shut up!' Jonty says.

Per is looking directly into the camera. His eyes are dark grey under his straight black brows. 'I thought she was courageous,' he says. 'I also thought she was dangerous, and out of her depth.' He shrugs. 'First impressions.'

'That's character assassination,' Amber says. 'It's sexist.'

'No it's not!' Lucy says. 'He said she was courageous. That means brave *and* beautiful. Just like Joan of Arc. Cleopatra. And Boudicca!'

'*Jesus*,' Jonty says.

'And second impressions, surely?' Lisa Toohey says. 'In one of her speeches, Harriet said that she'd been accused of incompetence. Was that you?'

'Yes.'

'You flew to the mountains recently, to rescue her again?'

'Correct.'

'She didn't need rescuing!' Amber says.

The lump is back in my throat, but I can't take my eyes off the screen. Tan is itching to get back to the microphone. Per blocks him with his shoulder.

'Perhaps you can elaborate?' Lisa Toohey says.

The wind picks up. Per swipes his hair off his face. Then he addresses the crowd. They all have their eyes pinned to him. So does my class.

'Scott and his team were eleven miles from their supply base when they died. Although the weather was abysmal, there's an argument that it wasn't as bad as Scott recorded in his journals. Why the discrepancy? There's a theory that Scott's men lied to him about the conditions, knowing he was too unwell to travel imminently, if at all. They also knew that if he'd thought it was feasible for them to leave, Scott would have ordered them to do so. Scott earned the loyalty, admiration and affection of the people who followed him. Harriet has earned hers too.'

'Are you saying she has your support?'

'She doesn't need my support, or approval.'

A slight crease puckers Lisa's brow. 'Do you agree she's good for the foundation?'

'Her association with the foundation, and the environmental work she does—that's only a part of who she is.'

'I'll go back to my original question, Commander. What do you think of Harriet Scott?'

He peers into the distance again, out through the heads. Then his gaze returns to Lisa.

'I'll be back in Sydney in two months. That's when I'll see her, and answer that question.'

*   *   *

Two months! The image of Per disappears when I yank the cord out of the computer.

My black marker pen flies over the whiteboard. Polarman is on the bridge of *The Adélie*. A segment of fringe is across one eye, and his scar is a thin black line on his cheek. His hands are on his hips, and one leg is slightly in front of the other. He's looking over the bow at the wild seas that seethe around the ship. In the distance I draw the shoreline, dominated by a jagged glacial wall. I take a couple of steps back.

The Polarman I've sketched is an action hero. Per is *my* action hero. I know the difference between them now. Per is smart and shy. He's brave and afraid. He's strong and vulnerable. He's arrogant and kind. Does he need me to show him all that?

'Um. Miss Scott?'

I spin around. The students are looking from me to the drawing. We're supposed to be studying mangrove swamps today. And marshes, bogs and quicksand.

'Yes, Lucy.'

'Is that the commander?'

'Course it is,' Jonty says. 'Look at his muscles and his scar.'

'He said you were courageous,' Lucy says.

'He said you were like Scott,' Jonty says.

'You reckon?' Amber says.

If Per was sending me a message it wasn't very clear. Which confirms he's not only useless at communicating with me by email, phone and text, but in interviews as well.

CHAPTER
43

A week ago I told Liam I wanted to avoid Professor Tan. Not any-more. When I requested a meeting with him he said, 'Excellent. Let's put this business with *The Watch* behind us and start fresh for next year.' I asked Per's lawyer and Neil the mediator to join us. We're assembling in the conference room in James's building in Macquarie Street.

When the lift stops, I walk straight to the bathroom. I tidy my hair and tuck my shirt neatly into my jeans. Last time I was here I was dry retching into the toilet because Per had asked whether I'd been paddling in the ocean since *The Watch* had sunk. He waited for me outside and told me not to rush things, that I shouldn't swim if I wasn't ready. I elbowed him in the stomach for his trouble.

He's been gone for almost a week. I'm not sleeping well. I won-der whether he is.

Neil kisses my cheek when I walk into the meeting room. James shakes my hand.

'Thanks for doing this,' I say.

James smiles. 'It's a pleasure. You've piqued our curiosity.'

Professor Tan walks into the room shortly after I do.

'James and Neil,' he says, shaking their hands, 'delighted to see you both again.' He smiles at me. 'I was surprised when you said we should meet here, but perhaps it's for the best. I presume you want to ensure your interests are protected, in respect to the maritime inquiry?'

After we sit at the giant oak table, I open my pad and glance at the notes I wrote last night. Neil cranes his neck to have a look.

'Oh,' he says. 'I was hoping for a picture.'

'Can I start?' I say.

'As you were the one who called us together, certainly,' James says.

I clear my throat. 'First, I want to make sure everything I say is confidential. I can't get into trouble for telling you things I *might* have done wrong, can I?'

James shakes his head. 'Unless you've committed a heinous crime ... no.'

'I *might* have committed forgery. And I *might* have lied under oath.'

He grimaces. 'Off you go then.'

I give James and Neil a sanitised version of everything I lied about while covering for Drew. When Tan pulls a copy of my evidence to the inquiry from his bag I hold up my hand.

'What I said at the inquiry *might* have been true,' I say.

He purses his lips. 'But it wasn't.'

The mediator takes a deep breath. 'Harry,' he says, 'what do you want to achieve from this meeting?'

'I want the professor to agree that he'll say nothing about what I *might* have done wrong. Or talk about Drew's diagnosis. I don't want him to leak to the media and pretend he did it by mistake. That's why I want witnesses.'

'I'll agree to no such thing,' Tan says. 'In fact I'll do the opposite.' He opens a folder and shows me a press release, and a series of ideas he's formulated to publicise the fact that I shouldn't be held responsible for losing *The Watch*.

I try to stay calm. 'Have you seen the footage of Drew in Palau? People adore him, they always have. You should be promoting his reputation, not diminishing it. What people are going to remember, no matter how you pitch this in the media, is that he was to blame. That he lost *The Watch*.'

The professor raises his brows. 'That's what they say about you.'

'I can show people I've learnt from it, that I won't make the same mistakes again.'

'If you pursue this course, we won't get the funds to finance *The Adélie*,' Tan says. 'Are you willing to accept responsibility for that as well?'

On the day *The Adélie* left for Antarctica, Per said my association with the foundation and the environmental work I do is only a part of who I am. Tan heard what was said but he didn't listen. It's about time he heard it from me.

'The foundation is Mum and Dad's legacy. It represents the passion they had for the environment and the causes they believed in. Like them, I care about the environment, and I'll keep fighting to protect it. But that doesn't mean I'll continue to do whatever you want me to do. If you release information about Drew, I'll leave the foundation.'

Tan blinks. 'What did you say?'

'You know as well as I do that the foundation is an independent entity. Dad set it up like that for a reason. He wanted it to carry on whether a Scott was involved with it or not.'

Tan collects his papers and stacks them neatly on the table. He smiles stiffly as he gets to his feet.

'What are you going to do, Professor?' James says.

He looks at James and Neil, and then he looks at me. 'It wouldn't appear I have a choice,' he says. 'There's a slim chance the foundation will get *The Adélie* permanently if Harry continues to support the foundation. Without her support there's no chance at all.'

He's at the door when he turns and faces me again. He doesn't seem to be particularly angry or upset, even though he didn't get his way. Then again he's a pragmatist and a strategist. I'm valuable to the foundation, even with a tarnished image.

He raises his brows. 'You haven't posted anything on the website recently about the commander. Why is that?'

Because whenever I type his name all I can think about is how much I miss him. And that makes me cry.

'I'll write something, Professor. Later today. I promise.'

★ ★ ★

The Scott Foundation: Environment Adventure Education

The Adélie has been gone for a week. She's in the Ross Sea, in the Bay of Whales region. This was the starting point for Roald Amundsen's expedition to the South Pole (Robert Falcon Scott left from Ross Island—he followed Ernest Shackleton's route up the Beardmore Glacier, and onto the Polar Plateau).

Captain Tom Finlay and the film crew are shooting a documentary highlighting how Antarctica's pristine marine ecosystem could be threatened by commercial activities in the area. Meanwhile, the foundation continues to do everything it can to push for the protection of the Ross Sea under a UN sanctioned treaty (similar to the one that applies to Antarctica's land area).

Commander Amundsen will work with his colleagues and a band of international collaborators on Roosevelt Island (the Ross Sea Ice Shelf surrounds Roosevelt Island—it's impossible to identify it as an island at ground level because of the ice). The scientists are part of a project to drill an ice core over 700 metres deep that will be used to analyse past climatic and atmospheric conditions. Ice core research assists scientific understanding of ice shelf disintegration rates. This data is vitally important for predicting future sea level rises.

The weather in Antarctica has been mild. Zero degrees by day, with sunny skies. Winds have been moderate. This is unusual for Antarctica. It's the windiest place on Earth!

Harriet

*   *   *

Ten minutes after I've posted on the website, I receive an email.

Harriet. Your post was informative. Its content was factual. You made reference to environmental considerations, global concerns, and an important research project. There were no hidden messages or derogatory references to Amundsen. Are you all right? Per

*   *   *

It's been a warm Christmas day, well over 30 degrees. I made Drew wait until after five o'clock for our walk along the beach so the sun wasn't so high in the sky. Now we're sitting on the back deck, with our feet propped up on the railing. We're watching the tide go out.

Drew turns to me. He's still tanned from our trip to Palau. I couldn't get him off the bridge of *The Adélie* and later, when we were on the islands, he only went inside in the evenings. His brown face contrasts with his white hair, tousled from the wind on the beach.

'Where's Matthew, then?' he says. 'Where's our captain?'

I point to the horizon. The sea is dark blue; the sky is a lighter shade and cloudless.

'I guess he's out in the ocean,' I say. 'That's what he loved.'

'Well, you'd better get going then.'

'What?'

'He'll need you out there.'

I'm not sure whether Drew thinks I'm Mum or me. *He'll need you out there.*

I jump to my feet. Per tried to communicate *something* when Lisa Toohey asked him questions. And he asked if I was *all right* in his email. He's the one who needs me out there.

* * *

Liam is hosting a Boxing Day party. He's invited the Amazons, and other friends and neighbours we see at the beach. We're having a barbecue on the back deck. Liam knows what my plans are for the next two weeks. The others think I'm hiking in New Zealand.

'Well, lassie,' Allan says, 'we'll miss you terribly at the football.'

'But I'll be back before the season starts.'

'Don't get lost on the Milford Track,' Jonty says. 'The commander's too far away to rescue you.'

'Thanks for that, Jonty.'

Drew winks, and pats my leg. 'Don't you worry. I'll keep an eye out.'

'Have you packed warm clothes?' Helga says. 'You know how you feel the cold.'

'But it's summer in New Zealand. Just like it is here.'

'Condoms,' Liam whispers in an undertone. 'Don't forget those.'

The other passengers taking the cruise ship from New Zealand to Antarctica will be tourists. I'll pay my way by writing about the trip when I get back. During the six-day voyage I'll keep my head down, because only Liam and Tom Finlay are to know what I'm up to.

I want to surprise Per. I want to see the expression in his eyes when he sees me. Then I'll know whether he wants me there or not.

CHAPTER

44

The Scott Foundation: Environment, Adventure, Education
  For the next couple of weeks I'll be hiking in New Zealand.
Please contact Professor Tan and his team in my absence. I'll
be back in touch later in January!
  Harriet

★ ★ ★

Tom picked me up from the cruise ship two hours ago. Ever since
then I've been standing on the bridge of *The Adélie*, waiting for Per
to come back. It was stupid to think I could surprise him in his
cabin as he studied a reference book, or rested on his bunk.

He's in the ocean, gesturing to the pilot of an inflatable boat.
Even if I weren't watching him through binoculars I'd recognise
him. It's the way that he moves. When the inflatable gets close
enough he grasps a handhold and lifts himself out of the sea. He

rolls over the rounded side and gets to his feet. The Ross Ice Shelf, palest blue, soars vertically behind him.

The Adélie rocks on the swell. Tom reaches for my arm but I regain my balance on my own. Then I hold the handrail tightly. The air temperature is minus fifteen and the winds are gusty. Tom and I are both wearing hooded jackets and our faces are covered up to our eyes against the icy gusts of wind and snow and sleet.

I shout above the squall. 'What's Per doing?'

'Got back from Roosevelt Island last night. Wanted to get a dive in. Storm's coming through.'

The inflatable boat ploughs haphazardly through the waves, dodging the chunks of ice that flow into its path. Mists roll in. They blanket the ocean like low-hanging clouds.

There are three regular crewmembers on the inflatable with Per, and two women and a man from the documentary team. Per is sitting near the bow, wrapped in a grey waterproof blanket. The others in the boat are blanketed in white—the sleet and sea spray has frozen on their outer layers, and their hair and beards. When the inflatable pulls up alongside *The Adélie* Tom takes my arm and shouts into my ear.

'Don't hang around on the deck, Harry. You're frozen. And he'll have the film crew all over him when he gets on board. They've been waiting for him to get back from Roosevelt. Go to my cabin. It's bigger than yours. I'll send him down to you.'

My fingers are stiff with cold, and so is my face. My body is cold as well, but that's not the only reason I'm shivering. I feel sick with apprehension.

'I'm all right,' I say. 'I'd prefer to wait here.'

For the thousandth time I remind myself that Per feels something for me. Even on the day he sent me to Palau it was clear that he desired me. And it doesn't matter whether he admits to needing me as long as I'm certain that, deep down, he does. It's been almost a month since I saw him on television, and ten weeks since we've seen each other in person. I hope he's missed me as desperately as I've missed him.

★   ★   ★

When he strides up the ramp from the loading dock to the main deck, our eyes lock. He stops and stares. A gust of wind blows his fringe into his eyes. He brushes it away with an impatient sweep of his hand. His eyes travel downwards from my face to my feet, and up again. It's very unlike him, staring at me so obviously, in front of all these people. He still hasn't moved.

I walk towards him. When I pull back my hood my hair, damp with mist and cold, flies around my head. His eyes are dark, even darker than I remembered them. Is it the reflection of the leaden skies, or the grey of the sea? They're obsidian.

When he still doesn't move I put my hand on his arm.

'I guess you're surprised.'

His voice is raspy. 'I hate surprises.'

'I thought you might. You like to have time to think things through.'

He stares at my mouth. 'You're cold.'

The film crew is hanging around near the galley door, waiting for Per to go inside.

I touch his arm. 'We'd better get out of the wind.'

He nods jerkily, and follows me.

As I shrug out of my coat, the documentary producer and a cameraman corner Per in the galley. Just like Tom said, they're determined to pin him down while they have the opportunity.

Per takes off his dry suit. He's wearing tight black thermals underneath. I'm reminded of the wetsuit he wore in Avalon, the one that matches mine. The film crew ask him questions. Even though he rarely takes his eyes off my face, his responses are thoughtful, detailed and complex. He talks about his research, and communicates all the reasons why Antarctica needs to be protected. His dark hair is damp. I'm weak with wanting to hold him.

The film crew finally leave Per alone, but the producer still hovers in the background. The cook is here too, sorting out a problem with the coffee machine. A few other members of the crew are playing cards in a booth. One of Per's colleagues is lounging in his chair with a book on his lap. I'm not sure how Per would react if I launched myself into his arms so I walk slowly towards him.

When I take his hands he squeezes my fingers tightly. Then he raises them to his mouth and glides my knuckles across his lips. He warms them with his breath.

'So cold,' he says.

'You said that before.'

He brings my hands to rest against his chest. 'When we were in the mountains you said I shouldn't touch you in public.' He looks over my shoulder. I can't see who's there but I know we're being watched. 'This is in public.'

I take a step closer. Our hands are pinned firmly between us.

'I think I've made things public already, coming to claim you like this.'

His eyes flash silver. He dips his head and whispers against my lips. '*Jeg elsker deg.*'

I recognise the words. He said '*jeg elsker deg*' when he backed us up against the door and kissed me in the professor's office. And I'm pretty sure he said it at the pool. We were on step two because I couldn't stop throwing up on step three, and I was crying because we were going in the wrong direction. He brushed my hair off my face and rested his chin on the top of my head while I sniffed against his chest. 'Stop crying, Harriet,' he said. 'We have plenty of time. *Jeg elsker deg.*' I was too miserable to ask him what it meant.

I want to know what it means now. 'What did you say, Per?'

He breathes the words into my mouth. 'I love you.'

I wrap my arms around his neck and press my body against his and kiss his salty mouth.

CHAPTER
45

Per slams his cabin door shut with his foot, leans against it and pulls me into his arms.

'*Gift deg med meg.* Marry me.'

His body is rigid with tension. I put my hands on his shoulders and shake him, trying to loosen him up.

'I want to kiss you first.'

I explore his mouth slowly. I stroke his face and examine his jawline and his perfectly straight nose and his cheekbones. He's tolerant at first. But then his kisses demand more and the heat builds between us. His taste, the feel of his tongue stroking mine, the way he supports the back of my head. His touch is familiar yet new and it's all that I'm ever going to need to make me happy. He lifts his arms when I pull at the hem of his thermal top. He's wearing other layers underneath. I smooth my hands over his T-shirt, tracing the lines of his abdominal and pectoral muscles, his ribs and sternum. And then, even though I'm fully dressed, he runs his hands over me. My face and neck. My breasts. My waist and bottom. My arms. It's like he has to reassure himself I'm standing here in front of him. I thread my fingers through his dark straight hair. Then I kiss his mouth, hard and possessively, and hold his head between my hands. I step back, and scrutinise his face.

'What?' he says.

'You have to get your hair cut. Your bone structure is far too good to hide under a fringe.'

He kisses my nose. 'Whatever.'

I kneel, and try to pull his thermal pants down past his hips. He laughs as he hauls me to my feet again. And that's when I see Liam's kookaburra.

The cabin is tiny. All it accommodates is a long narrow bed and a built-in side table, cupboard and desk. And four sketches pinned to the wall at the foot of the bed. In the first sketch the kookaburra is a fledgling. He has creamy fluffy feathers on his chest. It's the drawing I did in March, the first time I saw him. Drew and I were sitting on the deck and a storm was brewing. In the next two sketches the kookaburra is a cocky adolescent, waiting for Liam to feed him, or for me to tell him how handsome he is. The last sketch is the picture I finished in October. Per was sitting next to me, convalescing on the deck. The kookaburra is almost fully-grown. He's puffing out his chest and preening, showing off the blue adult feathers on his wings.

When Per squeezes my shoulders I turn to him again.

'You told Tan you were donating your sketches to your school,' he says. 'I called Allan, asked him to bid for me.'

Tears fill my eyes as my gaze shifts from Per, to the sketches, and back to Per. He's standing stiffly as if he's in control, but his expression is wary, guarded.

'The blue,' he says, 'it's like your eyes.'

I put my hand on his arm. 'Liam only stopped bidding because Allan seemed to want them so much. Liam was furious when he discovered they'd been bought for someone else.'

Per points to the cupboard. 'The drawings you did when I was unwell. They're in there.'

I swallow. 'I thought you didn't like them. You sent me away.'

Within a heartbeat he's kissing me again, hungry rough kisses that leave me breathless. But then he pulls back, and I'm teetering on my feet.

'I'm salty,' he says. 'I'll shower.'

'I like salt.' I put my hand on his arm. 'Why did you send me away, Per? I told you how I felt in those sketches. You should have come to Palau with me.'

He reaches for me again, holding me tightly. Then he puts his forehead against mine.

'You said your father trusted you,' he says. 'Had faith in you. I had to let you go on your own.'

I step back and release the breath I've been holding. My words run together. 'I have to tell you what Tan knows. I don't want you to think I'm hiding things from you, or that I'm a liar. Even though I lied on oath. And worse.'

He stares into my eyes. 'Are you taking risks keeping this to yourself? The sort of risks I'd want to know about.'

I give him a shaky smile. 'I don't think so.'

'So don't tell me. If it comes out, we'll deal with it.'

I'm not sure that I deserve this sort of trust. But not telling Per protects him. He can't get into trouble for a cover up if he doesn't know the facts. When I rest my hands on his chest he puts his hands on my waist, drawing me closer again.

'Tan told me you'd given him an ultimatum,' he says. 'That he had to keep quiet or you'd leave the foundation.'

'It wasn't an ultimatum. I was cool and calm and I gave him a *choice*. You would've been proud of me.'

He rests his chin on my head. 'It's not official yet, but the foundation is getting *The Adélie*. It reached its funding targets just a couple of days ago. The support it was getting in Norway led to additional backing in Australia.'

I shut my eyes. *The Adélie*'s motors hum softly. She moves gently on the swell. When I open my eyes again Per is staring into them. He frowns.

'I'm still pissed with you for disappearing to Palau for so long.'

I wrap my arms around his neck. 'How do you say sorry again? Not *beklager*. The other kind of sorry. When you're *very* sorry?'

'Jeg er lei meg.'

'And how do you say "I missed you"?'

'Jeg har savnet deg.' He narrows his eyes. 'Stop making me say things. *Six fucking weeks*. And it wasn't like I could bring you back. Not after what happened when I came in the chopper.'

I smile. 'I guess not.'

He rubs his thumb along my lip. 'Your lips were bleeding on the *Torrens*. I wanted to touch them even then.'

I cup his cheek, the one with the scar. When I trace it with my thumb he turns his face into my hand for a moment. Then he pulls back. He looks at me with troubled eyes.

'You don't have to tell me,' I say.

He rests his chin on my head again. 'My father had told me not to go out. I disobeyed him. He was abusive. Often. That's why I hid. I was afraid.'

I stand on my toes and kiss his throat. I told him about the accident in Brazil but I didn't want to talk about it afterwards. He said there was no rush. There's no rush for him to talk either. Because even though he may never admit to being vulnerable like regular, non-action-hero people, he knows I've seen that side of him. And if he ever forgets it, he can get out my sketchbook. Wherever he goes, it will be kept safe and sound in his cupboard.

★ ★ ★

Per takes the hem of my jumper and eases it over my head. My long-sleeved T-shirt is next. He sits me on his bed to yank off my socks and boots. Then I'm pulled to my feet again while he removes my jeans and thermals and underwear. He's not kissing me, and he's only touching me in order to undress me, but I'm weak with lust by the time he's finished. He mutters and curses as he drags off his clothing. When we're facing each other again I rest my hand on his chest. His skin is burning hot and his heart is thumping. He puts his hand on the side of my face.

'D'you think you can love me, Harriet?'

My voice is shaky. 'I'm frightened of doing it. You have shrapnel wounds. And you swim lengths of the beach. What if I lose you?'

He slowly shakes his head. 'Like I'm the dangerous one? The risk taker? The one who dives in at the deep end?'

I'm so choked up I can't say anything.

He takes a breath, and studies my hair as he threads his fingers through it. 'You love the foundation, and all its members. Your school kids. The love you had for your parents, and the way you love Drew—a tenth of that would be enough for me.'

I cup his face and kiss him gently on the mouth. 'No, Per, you deserve much more than that. And you have it. I love you to death. That's why I'm frightened.'

He yanks me into his arms, wraps one of his legs around one of mine, and trips me. I lose my balance and we tumble onto the bed together. And before he has the chance to protest I wriggle under him, wrap my legs around him and position myself against his erection. I raise my hips.

'Please, Per. Now.'

He hesitates, but when I grasp his bottom with my calves he groans, and enters me a little. Then I tighten my legs around him even more, and in one long thrust he's deep inside me. Except for our pounding hearts and harsh breaths we're perfectly still. Until I smile against his neck. 'Per?'

He rises up on his elbows. His eyes are dark and sombre. 'Harriet?' He smooths my hair from my face. 'What are you doing?'

'I want a dark-haired little boy.'

His breathing is all over the place. I've never seen this expression in his eyes. The longing. The relief. It warms me. Just like the heat of his body.

'*Gyllen dusk*,' he finally says. 'Tassel.'

'Do you mean you want a fair-haired girl with a ponytail?'

He nods as he holds my hips and turns us on to our sides so we're facing each other. I run my hands over his back as his hand feathers over my breasts and stomach to the tops of my thighs where we're joined. He shudders when he feels the moisture there. He moans against my mouth, and then he starts to move.

'Can you teach her Norwegian?' I say.

'Yes.'

'It's important to do it early.'

'All right.'

'Even before she's born. As early as that.'

'*Lille venn?*'

'Yes.'

'Can't ... talk.'

We make love to the rhythm of the ocean. The skin of his throat is salty. Afterwards, our limbs tangled, he falls asleep. When he rescued me from *The Watch* I sensed he'd come up and get me if I refused to go down. Neither of us knew that I'd be rescuing him just as much as he'd be rescuing me.

When he stirs, I trail my fingers across his shoulders.

'Per? I've been thinking. We could have a Scott and Amundsen Polar family. Or an Amundsen and Scott one. Polarman, Polarwoman, Polarboy and Polargirl. With matching wetsuits and sashes. What do you think?'

He rises up on one elbow and kisses my mouth, and then he looks into my eyes. It never gets dark at the Pole in the summer months but it's late afternoon and stormy so the light is dim. His face is in shadow and his eyes are silver.

I'm trying not to smile as I trail a fingertip down his scar. 'Well?'

He dips his head and mumbles against my neck. '*Du er trøbbel,*' he says.

ACKNOWLEDGEMENTS

To Jo Mackay, Publisher at Harlequin Australia, thank you for your belief in this book. And thanks to Laurie Ormond, Julia Knapman and the rest of the Harlequin team for your support over the past few months. To my editor Dianne Blacklock, your suggestions were invaluable.

Steve, many thanks. Any mistakes relating to ships and nautical matters are mine—and creative license. Andreas Lamo, your assistance in respect to all words Norwegian was wonderful. Thanks to my lecturers and fellow students at UTS for accepting (sometimes even falling in love with) my romantic leads, and teaching me so much. Vani, Helga, Irina and Kelly, thank you for your feedback on messy early drafts. And eternal gratitude goes to my friends in the romance writing community—your wisdom and generosity amaze me.

A hug for my mum, who always said I should write a book, and for my dad, for being a dad. Thanks to my daughters—author Tamsin for 'getting it', Michaela and Gabriella for telling me everything's going to be fine, and Philippa for being my literary go-to girl. Finally, thanks to my sons Ben and Max who said (whenever they saw me typing at the kitchen bench), 'How's Harriet going, Mum?'

Turn over for a sneak peek.

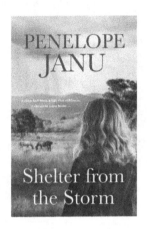

Shelter from
the Storm

by

PENELOPE
JANU

Available now!

CHAPTER

1

A grey gum towers over the windswept scrub that borders the path to the beach. The shadows are deep in the moonlight, but my watch lights up when I push back the cuff of my wetsuit: ten forty-five. An hour has passed since I ordered the recruits to join me at the tree. *Yes, lieutenant. Sure, lieutenant. We won't let you down, lieutenant.* They've probably gone back to sleep.

The breeze is light, whispering through the foliage and warming my skin. Dropping my backpack at my feet, I pluck a leaf, fold it in half and then in half again. Summers in the country, long sunny days, starry skies at night. The scent of eucalyptus, the sharp and the sweet, always takes me back.

Distant applause rings out from the parade ground. HMAS Creswell is hosting an environmental summit and the delegates, seated at tables in a marquee, are attending the opening night dinner. Amplified voices suggest the speeches have started. I check my watch again: ten fifty-two, and still no sign of the recruits.

It's a fifty-metre walk to the beach, where small but busy waves, like silver-edged ribbons, rush to the shore before dashing out again. A jetty, a solid timber structure where naval craft are moored, juts out from the wide strip of sand, and a breakwater, an artificial out-crop a hundred metres long, shelters the beach from the ocean. Four tall poles mark the end of the break, and two broad banners hang between them.

The recruits, drunk on shots and high on exam results, rowed to the breakwater at dusk, took down the official banners and strung up alternatives. In the first banner, a whale and calf float lifelessly in the water. In the second, a koala, her joey clinging desperately to her back, falls from a tree. The images are underlined with bold black text. *Our leaders have blood on their hands.*

How could the recruits have been so stupid?

Particularly as everyone on the base had been instructed to treat conference delegates—environmentalists, scientists, industry leaders and politicians—with discretion and respect. We're hosts. This is a demonstration of community engagement. *No controversy.* I couldn't *strictly* be blamed for something the recruits did off duty, but …

When I discovered they'd switched the banners, I should have reported them.

I didn't.

If I get caught, I'll be in trouble too. But …

The recruits shouldn't lose their careers over this. *Technically* they're adults, but they're barely out of school. Which was why they let themselves get talked into trouble. Was I ever so fun-loving and idealistic?

I doubt it.

I glance towards the marquee, just visible at the top of the rise. Can they see the banners from there? Kicking off my thongs, I store them in the backpack alongside the banners that should be on the poles. *HMAS Creswell. Welcome to Jervis Bay.* Single handed, I won't be able to rehang them, but I can take down the offending ones.

Leaving my backpack by a post of the jetty, I walk to the water and splash my face. I untie my ponytail, comb through my hair with my fingers, twist the curly lengths into a bun and secure it at my nape with the band. Whitewash gathers at my ankles as a blanket of lightning brightens the sky. Thunder follows, rumbling from the east. The waves on the jetty slap a beat. One two three. One two three.

There's another sound as well.

'Hey!' The voice is male and close—on the beach on the far side of the jetty.

I'm a sitting duck out here. And if I'm caught, I'll have to explain what I'm up to. My body pings with adrenaline as I run, ducking behind the post closest to the shoreline. I risk a glance at the man rounding the jetty twenty metres away. My view is obscured, but he's tall and well-built. He has a long stride.

He's walking directly towards me.

Is he another officer, or part of the summit's security contingent? Has he seen the banners? If he has, I won't want to answer the questions he'll have. I push back my shoulders and step out of the shadows.

'Identify yourself!' My voice is brisk and assured.

He stills for an instant. 'Imp?' And then he keeps on walking, stopping only metres away. Square jaw, straight nose, nice mouth. There's not an ounce of fat on him. *Confident, athletic, capable.*

'Hugo.' Tightness cramps my chest. 'What are you doing here?'

His dark blond hair is shorter than it was, the sun-tipped ends less marked. I can't see the colour of his eyes, but I know them so well I could never forget them.

Clear and bright. Sea-green like ocean.

'I'm a delegate at the climate summit.' When he folds his arms, his shirt pulls at his shoulders. 'How about you?'

'I work here.'

He indicates the banners. 'Who put them up?'

I lift my chin. *Push back the memories.* 'This is a restricted area. You'd better get back to the marquee.'

He looks me up and down. 'Small. Barefoot. Trouble. Are you involved?'

'I could have you removed.'

'Imp?' He scrapes a hand through his hair. 'What's going on?'

'Don't call me that.'

'Lieutenant Patience Cartwright.' His eyes narrow. 'Is that what you want?'

'I want to know why you're here.'

'I've already told you.'

'You weren't on the list of delegates.'

'A colleague roped me in.'

'What kind of work are you doing?'

'Biodiversity, habitat, amphibians.' He's wearing a collared white shirt. He rolls up the sleeves and loosens his tie. 'How about you?'

I focus on the cuff of my wetsuit, pulling it over my watch. 'I have a temporary posting on the base. I train the new recruits.'

'Last I heard, you were a maritime warfare officer, navigating ships at sea.'

'I'll be back on my ship after Christmas. And I really need to—'

'That's ten months away.' He smiles stiffly. 'Where's your uniform?'

'I'm off duty.'

'And swimming in the dark.'

'There's nothing new in that.'

When he was still at school, Hugo's mother drove hundreds of kilometres from Horseshoe Hill so he could swim with other squad members at the Olympic pool in Dubbo. Almost three years older than me, popular, tousle-haired and easy-going, he was the swim club captain. Anti-social, argumentative and small for my age, I was a town kid swimmer, one of the many who looked up to him.

'The banners.' His brows lift. 'Who put them up?'

'I'm going to take them down.' Before I can block him, he swoops, grabbing my backpack and yanking it out of reach. 'Give that back!'

'Tell me what you're up to.'

I grasp a strap of the backpack, but he holds fast. Our fingers touch. 'Oh!'

When we let go of the backpack, it falls to the ground between us. His eyes stay on mine as he bends at the knees to pick it up. Immediately he stands, I grab the strap and yank the bag free, dropping it behind me.

'Leave, Hugo.'

When he holds out his hand, I take a hurried step back. Frowning, his hand drops to his side. He opens his mouth and shuts it again. And then,

'There are environmentalists and scientists here, but also economists, mining representatives, lobbyists, politicians. Anything controversial or overtly political,' he indicates the banners, 'we lose the collaboration.'

'I get it.' A bolt of lightning highlights his features, the planes of his face, the shades in his hair. 'That's why I'm taking them down.'

Now. Right now. Without delay. Immediately. Yet my feet stay firmly on the sand. My lips open. No words come out.

'How are your sisters?' he asks.

'They're well, thank you. How is Greta? And Derek? Your brothers?'

'It's been a year since you were in Horseshoe. They ask about you.'

I'm a hundred and fifty-two centimetres to his one eighty-six. I lift my chin. 'I was back for Phoebe and Sinn's wedding last month.'

'Two days in Warrandale.' He squares his shoulders, stands even straighter. 'This naval base. Is it your home?'

'It's where I belong.'

'It wasn't always.' He jerks his head towards the sea. 'Out there on your ship. Is that home too?'

'It's like the song.' I smile sweetly. 'Home is where I lay my hat.'

Hugo is glaring when I see Commander Ruddock, the executive officer at the base, standing at the end of the track. Middle-aged but fit and dressed in naval whites, he holds out his torch, throwing an arc of light onto the sand. Scooping up my backpack, I dart around Hugo and into the shadows.

'Hugo!' I hiss. 'I don't want him to see me.'

He crosses his arms. 'I noticed.'

'Come over here. Stay till he's gone.'

'Tell me what you're hiding.'

'Shhh.'

'Imp!'

Ruddock turns off the torch as he crosses the soft sand to the harder sand at the shoreline. He's at least thirty metres away. He's increasingly short-sighted, but hates wearing glasses. Does he know that Hugo is here? That he's with someone? Has he seen the banners?

I glance longingly at the scrub that borders the beach. If Ruddock saw me running towards it, he could recognise my height, my build. Even if he didn't, I'm not dressed for a formal dinner—Ruddock would want to know what business I have being here. And if he gets close enough to ask ...

He's been looking for an excuse to get rid of me since I arrived.

I grab Hugo's arm, tugging until he faces me. 'Stop looking at him!'

Hugo speaks through his teeth. 'I have nothing to hide.'

'I don't want Ruddock to identify me. You're ...' I consider his build, the breadth of his shoulders. His tawny hair isn't quite short enough for the military. 'He'll know you're not navy. A few of the delegates have partners here. If Ruddock thinks I'm one of them,' I drop my backpack at my feet, 'there's a chance he'll go back to the marquee.' Ruddock walks along the sand in the opposite direction. He peers towards the cliff on the far side of the beach.

Hugo swears under his breath. 'What are you afraid of?'

'Please, Hugo.' I focus on his tie and the unfastened button at his neck. 'Pretend we're together.'

'I don't pretend.' Immoveable. Unwavering. He could be a statue. A tall bronze statue on a stormy summer's night.

I glance around him. 'If Ruddock sees us, he'll leave. You're thirty. I'm twenty-eight. Why can't we pretend?'

'You're twenty-seven.'

'Almost twenty-eight. And I'm trying to put things right. Please, Hugo.'

'Tell me what you're up to.'

'After Ruddock has gone, and if you swear not to tell anyone, I'll brief you about the banners.'

Another frown. 'You're dictating terms?'

'I said I'd explain.'

'You never do.'

I put my hand over his mouth. 'Shhh.'

His breath is warm on the palm of my hand. And then, all of a sudden, I'm warm all over. The nape of my neck, my face and my breasts. There's heat in the air that blows on my skin and in the waves that sweep on the sand. When I draw in a breath, he does the same. My breasts so close to his chest; the touch of my hand on his face.

I pull away, take a backwards step, and hold out my hands. 'Take them. That's all you have to do.'

When he finally does as I ask, holding my hands in a cool firm grip, our eyes lock. Do I imagine the deep green of his? I must. Because there's not enough light for—

He pulls me closer. 'Oh!'

For a heartbeat, he stills. 'Do you want this or not?'

I look past him to Ruddock, still staring out to sea. 'Yes.'

Head lowered, he threads our fingers together. His thumb slides over the back of my hand. 'There's salt on your skin.'

My breath hitches. My heart tumbles.

Breathing and tumbling.

When we swam together, Hugo taught me how to breathe to the side, and helped me with tumble turns at the end of each lap. He didn't laugh or turn away when I sucked in water or coughed until my nose bled. He'd pull me out of the pool, wrap a towel around my shoulders and tell me to stop trying to do everything at once. *Don't be so impatient.* Then he'd hand me over to one of the swimming mums and dive back into the pool. He was tanned, tall and mature for his age. He had a face that people looked at twice—as if the first time around they might have imagined how attractive he was.

They hadn't.

Nothing has changed.

Ruddock's phone rings and he answers, walking towards the treeline before turning and facing the ocean again. He's closer than he was, but still twenty metres away.

When I pull Hugo further into the shadows, the sand is wet under my feet. He's looking at me, but I look out to sea, the sparkles of light on the ocean.

Hugo swam like a fish. *A merboy.* We often argued, but I looked up to him. He'd grin and praise my tenacity. And when I stood back at the social events at his family's farm, he'd encourage me to join in with the others. Greta, his mother, was kind, paying me to help in the kitchen when Derek employed itinerant workers to labour on the farm. Hugo scrubbed the roasting trays and saucepans. He treated me the same way he treated the other kids, but I imagined I meant more to him than they did. In any case, I'd made up my mind. I wanted to be with him.

I was nineteen the first time we kissed.

The last time we kissed.

Now?

Breathing.

Tumbling.

The waves on the beach whisper to the shore. An owl calls two shrill hoots. 'Is Ruddock still there? Is he looking this way?'

'Yes.' He squeezes my hands. 'And no.'

Need and sadness all mixed up. I swallow, focus. 'Do you think he knows we're here?'

When he looks into my face, what does he see? Parted lips, wide eyes. Does he recall the blue in the way I recall the green? His breathing is deeper than it was, but his body is rigid. He lowers his head, my stomach flips.

'He's unlikely to leave,' he says quietly. 'I should have warned you.'

Real sounds come back. Cicadas. The slosh of water on the posts of the jetty, the rush of the waves on the shore. Distant thunder.

The jangle of the keys on Ruddock's belt.

talk about it

Let's talk about books.

Join the conversation:

 facebook.com/harlequinaustralia

 @harlequinaus

 @harlequinaus

harpercollins.com.au/hq

If you love reading and want to know about our
authors and titles, then let's talk about it.